SOLARFLARE AND THE SAPPHIRE RING

MATT HENSELL

I hope this is as fun to read as it was to write!

— Matt

Copyright © 2023 by Matt Hensell

ISBN: 978-1-62429-489-1

All rights reserved. No part of this book may be used or reproduced in any manner whatsoever without written permission except in the case of brief quotations contained in critical articles or reviews.

Published through Opus Self-Publishing Services
Located at:
Politics and Prose Bookstore
5015 Connecticut Ave. NW
Washington, D.C. 20008
www.politics-prose.com / / (202) 364-1919

To Mom, Dad, Stephen, and Lauren,
in no particular order

ONE
The Fisherman

Edmund Price was a simple fisherman. His scrawny body was covered with the wiry muscles of a fisherman, one accustomed to hard physical work. A thick, coarse, jet-black beard covered his chin and extended downward. He didn't shave very often; he didn't see much point in it. He owned a modest boat that he took out on the water once every two weeks. He never brought in any fish large enough to afford a larger boat or a crew, but he got by. He knew the sea, he knew his boat, and he knew what he could handle on his own.

He took his unnamed boat out to sea off the coast of North Carolina one early summer morning, expecting a modest but worthwhile haul. Conventional wisdom says an unnamed boat is bad luck, but Edmund figured bad luck was his lot in life regardless, so he never bothered. The forecast had called for storms later in the day, but he expected he'd be back in harbor by then. He was not a particularly daring fisherman. He had no one to rely on other than himself. He had been raised by his grandfather since he was six years old, and his parents had died in that fire. That fire took everything from me, he thought bitterly as he secured his fishing supplies for the day's trip. It was a regularly occurring thought. He tried to brush the thought from his head. It did him no good out on the water to think of how things might have been.

But it was true. That fire had taken away his chance at a life of privilege, one of ease.

Edmund was only six when his father made a terrible, stupid decision that led to his demise, along with the demise of his wife, leaving their young son all alone in the world. All alone, save for a bitter grandfather who took every opportunity to spout superstitions about mystical fires and legendary magic weapons and how that weapon and that fire had killed his son and daughter-in-law. All that talk did nothing to soothe the heartache of a child who had lost his parents. And so it was that Edmund would have been better off alone.

Edmund spent the next twelve years of his life living with his grandfather on his meager fishing boat. He listened to the inane ramblings of his clearly disturbed grandfather. When his grandfather passed, Edmund was already legally an adult.

He accepted the simple inheritance of his grandfather's fishing boat and moved to put all thoughts of magic and fire and superstition out of his mind.

That is, until one day.

The rough sea came earlier than expected. Edmund had a modest number of fish, enough that he could turn for shore and not make a loss of the whole day. But for some reason, he stayed out. He was confident that he could still fish.

And that is where our story begins.

The sky opened up and rain began to fall in sheets upon the deck of this simple fishing boat. Edmund stood firm, holding his line in his hand, expecting another fish to come along. Maybe he wouldn't even need to go back out for another month, he thought.

He grinned as he imagined a world in which he could take a breath and relax for more than a day without worrying about his finances.

As he tended the line, he felt a presence behind him. He brushed it off. He was miles and miles away from shore, out on the open ocean. No one could be out here.

He was wrong.

A sopping wet figure, his eyes filled with malice, glowered at Edmund.

Edmund's common sense only held out for so long. He had to see what had made him feel so uneasy.

He turned and saw a man standing mere feet away. His face was masked in the shadow of the oncoming storm, but Edmund could feel the rage in his shrouded countenance.

He attempted to turn back to his fishing, hoping that the man had simply been a mirage, an illusion of his solitude.

No such luck.

Edmund felt the spool of his reel unravel beneath his hand. As he desperately tried to grip it, he realized that the only thing capable of exerting such rapid, powerful force on a line would be a blue whale.

In his heart, he knew that it was the stranger aboard his boat.

As the line ran out and flew out into the ocean, Edmund turned to the shadowy figure with a sad resignation. Maybe his grandfather's madness, the same madness he saw in his father, was genetic. Or maybe the warnings weren't the ramblings of a madman.

The figure's eyes glowed blue for a moment, and the figure rushed along the deck, suddenly mere inches from Edmund. Edmund stared into the otherworldly, glowing blue eyes. He felt a fear greater than he'd felt when his father lit their house aflame, and a chill ran up his spine.

"The ring." The figure declared in a calm, authoritative voice.

Edmund nodded and walked below deck, into his quarters. He knew what the figure was referring to.

A simple bed sat within his cabin with a crude excuse for a desk resting across from it. Within the single drawer of that desk was a leather-bound journal. A journal Edmund's grandfather had left to him, detailing the legend that had taken Edmund's parents' lives in that great fire. The legend of a simple ring shrouded in superstition. A ring Edmund had never even seen.

The figure rummaged through the desk furiously, pausing only once he found the journal. He flipped through a few pages and, deciding he finally had what he needed, pocketed the book. He turned towards the simple fisherman.

The figure nodded and marched above deck. Edmund followed obediently.

"This is what I needed," the figure said calmly.

"So, you'll leave?" Edmund asked, hoping for nothing more than to simply return to his fishing.

"I'll leave," the figure replied. "But I do not want to have to worry about any others attempting to secure the ring."

"What do you mean?" Edmund whimpered, fearful of the implication of the figure's words.

"I mean that I cannot simply let you return to shore."

The figure avoided Edmund's gaze. He did not enjoy what would come next.

The figure leapt off the boat, into the rough, stormy seas. Edmund saw a shape move rapidly through the water, faster than any fish.

As he marveled at the movement of the ominous figure beneath the waves, the sea began to tear at his boat. Lashes of angry water roped across the unnamed vessel, tearing apart the deck and smashing the hull.

Edmund looked about desperately. A simple life jacket hung along the boat's railing. He pulled it on just as the hull cracked and seawater flooded in.

In an instant, the mediocre, unnamed fishing vessel was sucked beneath the waves. Edmund was left floating in his life jacket, miles from shore. The few possessions he had that morning when he set out, a pitiable amount by any standard, were now gone.

What the fire failed to take from him was now claimed by the water. Everything except for the fisherman's life.

Any other man might take the recent events as a sign to avoid the water from here on out — an omen that neither land nor sea was safe for him — and thus resign himself to a cursed existence. But Edmund arrived at a different conclusion.

He now knew that his father died for something. He knew that his grandfather had not been overtaken by madness in his grief. The legend of the ring, of the flame, was real. And he would do whatever he needed to do in order to achieve that power himself.

He literally had nothing to lose.

TWO
Origin Story

Many years later, the Advanced Placement Chemistry students of North Delfield High School, a decent but unremarkable public high school in northern Virginia, took a field trip. This may not immediately seem related to the unfortunate fisherman, but it is.

Mr. Cranston's AP Chemistry class numbered 14 students. A much smaller class size than the other ones he taught during the day, but that was no surprise. Mr. Cranston was a great teacher, but his class was tough and the vast majority of students at North Delfield High didn't want to take it. The coursework was exhausting, the readings were long and dry and filled with technical language, and his tests were unforgiving. But that's to be expected in AP courses, he would reply when confronted by parents over their child's workload and grades. The AP classes are offered by the school so that high school students could, at the end of the school year, take an exam on the subject matter that could be exchanged for college credit, provided that they passed the test. And, out of all the AP teachers at North Delfield High, he was the most successful in getting students those college credits.

Mr. Cranston's class was almost always exclusively Senior students who used his class to strengthen their college applications before leaving in the fall, but this year he had two ambitious Juniors. Mr. Cranston admired their hard work and noted that the two had exceeded his expectations. They both planned to ask Mr. Cranston for letters of recommendation when they applied to colleges next year.

One of those Juniors was Mark Michaels. Mark was exactly six feet tall, a fact he was proud of in the way that teenagers are often proud of things of little consequence, with a lanky build. He was boyishly handsome, though he spent much of adolescence being told that he looked more like his mother than his father. It made sense, though. He definitely looked more Asian than white. His mom was Chinese-American and his dad was white, and pretty much the only feature he got from his dad was his nose, which was relatively round and wide. His shaggy black hair was parted off to the right, swooping along his forehead and frequently falling into his face. He wore a bright red t-shirt and a pair of clean, yet broken-in, jeans. It was his favorite shirt and, had he known how the day would proceed, he likely would have opted to put on something else that morning.

Chuck Currant, Mark's best friend, was the other Junior in the class and the brightest student Mr. Cranston had ever taught, though he never said this aloud. But everyone knew. He was the same height as Mark, but with a very different build. While Mark was effortlessly thin, even athletically so, Chuck was a bit stouter. He had a round face, with a long, thin nose and a pair of stylish, black-rimmed glasses sitting upon it. Beneath the glasses, his eyes were a deep shade of blue. His blond hair was neatly cropped and parted much like Mark's, though copious amounts of product kept it from falling in his face. Finally, a luxury watch hung from his left wrist.

Chuck was a young man of taste. He dressed sharp, not in the overbearing sense of a kid who wears a blazer to public school, but like he had purchased every casual ensemble from a high-end catalogue. And as a result, the watch he wore, worth somewhere in the ballpark of a used car, did not seem quite so out of place. On this day, he wore a crisp blue polo and khaki shorts, as if he were planning for a day on the boat after school. Actually, that wasn't particularly unrealistic, Chuck's father did own a very nice boat.

Speaking of, Mr. Currant was also in attendance. George Currant, Chuck's father, was a statuesque, sophisticated man and the principal of North Delfield High School. Most high school principals could not afford the high-end clothing and accessories sported by the Currants, but Mr. Currant came from money. He said little about it and, though there was much private speculation, most of the community respected his privacy on the matter.

Mr. Currant's presence was not an imposition. He and his son were respectful of boundaries to the point that most staff and students would hardly have realized that the two were father and son if it were not for their similar appearance. Additionally, Mr. Cranston did not mind Mr. Currant being there since Mr. Currant was the one who secured the field trip in the first place. Mr. Cranston had never expected to receive permission for this field trip from one of the hottest scientific firms in the country, but here he was with his students in tow.

It was late May and the AP test had already concluded a week prior. The outside air was hot and humid, but it was a sunny, cloudless day. It was perfect for the day's purposes.

The bus rolled to a stop in front of the facility and the name of the company shone in clean white marble on the face of the building: **Oracular Technologies.**

Oracular was a company that worked in just about everything. They built exciting new types of body armor for the military, alternative energies, renewable resources, you name it. "Anything that could be made with chemicals, we can work with," the CEO had once said in an interview with a gentle chuckle a few years back. The joke being that everything is made of chemicals. So, yeah, they had their hands in almost everything. And technically, it was their previous CEO who had said that. The new CEO was a far more reclusive man about whom little was known. Or maybe it was a woman. Either way, the current CEO did not participate in fun little puff-piece interviews.

While the students craned their necks to look at the slick modern façade of the building and chatted amongst themselves, Mr. Currant whispered something to Mr. Cranston. Mr. Cranston nodded his head in enthusiastic agreement.

Mr. Currant stood up and subtly adjusted his fine linen suit. With a slight glance, the bus went quiet with respect.

"Good morning, everyone," Mr. Currant began, a slight, almost-English accent in his voice. Mark had pressed Chuck on the matter once before. It wasn't quite British and it wasn't American. It turned out to be Bermudan. Not something Mark would've ever guessed. "We have secured access to this facility thanks to a personal favor from an acquaintance of mine. With that in mind, I trust that you will all be on your best behavior. Today we will be granted exclusive access to Oracular's latest alternative energy project. Please, enjoy yourselves and learn something new." He concluded with a subtle nod to his son, sitting near the back.

Chuck responded in kind. This was the most affection Mark had ever seen between the two of them.

Mr. Cranston stood up and enthusiastically clapped his hands. "And we would all like to thank you, Principal Currant, for securing this trip for us. Let's all give him a round of applause."

The class broke into a half-enthused round of applause.

Amid the clapping, Mark whispered to Chuck, "Is your dad ever not just business all the time?"

"What do you mean?" Chuck asked as the clapping died down and the class began to make their way off the bus, murmuring amongst each other.

"I mean the, you know," Mark said, imitating Mr. Currant's nod. "Like the two of you are business partners or amicable politicians from opposite sides of the aisle."

"Yep, that's us," Chuck said. "I'm secretly a Senator."

"The only reason I know that isn't true is that you're too young," Mark said with a laugh as the two of them hopped off the bus and onto the curb. "That said, you literally look like the most stereotypical politically-minded teenager."

"You're too kind," Chuck muttered. "I don't know, maybe my father just didn't want to make a public spectacle of it all. It's not like he's some unfeeling robot."

"Dude, he's kind of a robot," Mark pushed as the two joined the rest of the group in walking towards the entrance.

Before Chuck could protest, Mr. Cranston glared at the two of them, signaling that they needed to cut off their conversation. Chuck just shrugged and let Mark have the final word.

The whole class entered the building silently, walking into a great, open lobby with polished black and white and grey surfaces.

The place had an air that it was ahead of its time. What was once silence as a point of obedience was now silence in awe.

Mark glanced around the lobby, hoping to find some hint of the other projects that were worked on at Oracular. In the days leading up to the trip, he had done his research. He knew all about their high-tech military armor and their sophisticated, next-gen aircraft. But no, this field trip was only about the alternative energy sources and the chemistry that went into that. In summary: their most boring projects. Everything else was strictly off-limits and largely hidden from public view.

As Mr. Cranston's class solidified before their tour guide, Mark and Chuck made their way to the front of the crowd and Mr. Currant hung towards the back.

Mark was a little disappointed that they wouldn't see any of the cool stuff on this trip, but if he had known what would come from it, he wouldn't have complained internally so much.

"Welcome everyone," the tour guide began with more enthusiasm than could possibly be necessary. Mark surmised he must be paid on some sort of sliding scale tied directly to the enthusiasm of his presentation. The tour guide then entered some sort of monologue about the significance of Oracular's new facility, but it was all white noise to Mark as he craned his neck to spy anything of interest or anyone that even looked like they were working on something cool.

"Does anyone know how Oracular first entered the boutique chemistry space?" the tour guide asked eagerly, drawing Mark from his exploration. "You, sir, in the smart suit, do you know the answer?"

All eyes turned towards Mr. Currant. He was the only person there wearing a suit.

He chuckled modestly before answering, "I believe that Oracular originally patented a process to produce aluminum from raw materials before expanding into other ventures, though I do not believe it was known as Oracular at the time."

The tour guide stood dumbfounded. This was the correct answer. No tour group had ever been correct.

While the tour guide stood stunned, Mr. Cranston's class was unsurprised. Mr. Currant's encyclopedic knowledge was almost as legendary as his mysterious wealth.

"That is absolutely correct, sir. Well done. Let's move on, then," the tour guide tried to recover as he led them off towards the day's exhibit. "The project we will be visiting is currently in development. We have developed an alloy which is able to conduct heat incredibly efficiently. If we are able to prolong its heat-retention, solar power would not just be limited to modern solar cells."

The tour guide tried to make the project seem exciting to a group of over a dozen high school students, the vast majority of whom were busy counting down the minutes to graduation. Out of the group, there were maybe five who were paying any attention to what was said. Mark wasn't exactly one of them. They had been walking along for what felt like hours, listening to the tour guide describe the development of various energy resources and all the faults and issues inherent in them. Mark stifled a yawn and struggled to stay awake as he kept pace with the rest of the group.

This field trip may have been boring, but it wasn't a day at school. This was the general consensus with field trips. No matter how boring a trip might be, no one was going to collect homework or give tests that day. And that makes it a good day.

"Isn't this cool?" Chuck whispered to Mark.

Mark rolled his eyes. If anyone could actually find this lecture engrossing, it was Chuck. Chuck was more concerned with his grades than anyone Mark knew. Chuck was the type of friend who couldn't hang out because he was studying for a test that was a week away. He was always that friend. There were more than a few instances where Mark's mother used Chuck as an example of how much effort a student should put into his studies. Chuck's study habits were working well for him, though; he was on track to become the school's valedictorian when they graduated next year. He already had an early draft of his speech, though he'd sworn Mark to secrecy on that.

Mark looked over at his friend. The look on his face said it all. Chuck was genuinely excited about this trip. Behind his simple, black-rimmed glasses, Chuck's eyes were wide with anticipation to learn more about the project.

"Chuck, it's just a piece of metal that gets really hot," Mark deadpanned, his derision largely accurate, based on what he had picked up in half-paying attention to the guide. He almost wished he was still in school. Almost.

"This might revolutionize energy across the entire world," Chuck defended, flustered by Mark's comment. He brushed his hair out of his face and continued. "Clean energy, solve climate change, all that jazz. Who knows exactly how far this project could go or what it might one day lead to?"

"You are aware that solar power already exists, right?" Mark jabbed. Every once in a while, Chuck would get a little too excited over something trivial and Mark was always there to keep him somewhat grounded.

"And you are aware that producing solar cells actually causes pollution? Or, that there's a finite amount of the minerals used to produce them? This is a far cleaner process. Or haven't you been listening?" Chuck shot back. He didn't think he was necessarily being overeager. While Mark thought that the presentation sounded like a recitation of the thesis behind the concept, Chuck thought quite the opposite. Why hadn't they explained what the alloy was exactly? He had his own theories, but he didn't want to reveal exactly what he knew.

The tour stopped midway along a corridor. Their guide led them through a set of double doors and into several curved rows of seats surrounding an impressive display. Massive computer monitors hung from the walls and various mechanical arms protruded from the floor. Now they had the whole class's attention, especially Mark.

"If everyone will please sit down," the guide began, "we have a special surprise for you. Right now, we are about to begin a test with the alloy. The alloy is placed at the focal point of a parabolic mirror, where we will allow it to collect immense quantities of solar radiation."

The class took their seats. Mr. Currant and Mr. Cranston sat near the back, while the students congregated towards the front.

As the tour guide finished speaking, a massive metal bowl emerged from the center of the stage and a small, golf ball-sized, golden ball of metal was placed above it by one of the mechanical arms. When the arm released the ball, it simply floated above the bowl. The metal was difficult to see from the seats, but half of the monitors switched to various camera feeds to show the audience the ball. Everyone could see it now.

"As you can see, the alloy floats just above our parabolic bowl thanks to magnets built into the structures in the walls and ceiling.

Here, the alloy is at the focal point of the bowl and will absorb the most energy."

Chuck raised his hand. Of course, he had a question or comment. He almost always had something to add. It was never useless, but it got tiresome after a while.

"Yes, you have a question?" the guide asked, gesturing to Chuck.

"Yes, thank you," Chuck began, standing up from his seat. "You said that the alloy is held in place with magnets —"

"Yes, I did."

"And this demonstration will heat the alloy?"

"Yes." The tour guide's tone was polite yet felt slightly condescending.

"Get to the point, please," Mark groaned quietly so that only Chuck could hear him.

The Seniors sitting in the row in front of Mark and Chuck snickered quietly. Jason Sherman turned around in his seat and shot the two a dismissive look. Mark glared back and clenched his jaw, defensive of his friend, even if he personally agreed that Chuck was wasting everyone's time.

"If metals lose their magnetic properties when heated, what will happen when the alloy ceases to be magnetized? Will it just drop into the bowl?" Chuck asked. He wouldn't have asked if it seemed obvious. "Wouldn't that damage it, or at least waste some of its heat potential?"

"Very good question," the guide mused. He was not expecting a high school student to be thinking of something so important to the actual logistics of the demonstration.

Chuck sat down and smirked at Mark. Mark shrugged. Chuck did normally know what questions were worth asking. Even the students in front of them shrugged in a silent admission that Chuck's question was worth the time. There was a reason Chuck was top of the class.

"Once the alloy heats up enough to lose most of its magnetic properties," the tour guide explained to the class, "it will be heated enough to partially ride on a cushion of hot air within the bowl. This, in turn, will keep it locked in its position at the focal point and allow for continued conduction of heat and solar radiation."

"Nerd," Jason muttered, just loud enough for everyone to hear it.

Chuck shrugged; he didn't care. Mark, however, stared daggers at Jason. Only he could make fun of his friend for being a nerd.

"Now, fans of science," the guide began with a dramatic flourish as a scientist entered the room and flipped a series of switches on a nearby control panel, "it's time for us to begin our little demonstration."

With a loud whirring, the ceiling began to open up above them. The sun was bright in the middle of the sky. Ideal conditions for the demonstration.

Within just a few seconds, displays on many of the monitors began to show readings on the heat of the alloy. The temperature was climbing exponentially. The late-May sun shone directly upon the metal ball. The ball was beginning to glow and gently spin from all of the heat energy being applied to it. Everyone in the class was paying attention now. It was amazing. This was why they came here.

Suddenly, a warning flashed across the monitors. There was something wrong. The ball began to wobble within its fixed location.

"Don't worry," the guide called out to the class, "this is nothing out of the ordinary."

The scientist tried to hide her concern, but everyone could tell that the guide was lying. Something was wrong. Half the class ducked down in their seats; the other half craned forward to get a better look. Chuck crouched down, but Mark leaned up, as did most of the students in front of them.

More warning signals on the monitors. The guide wasn't even trying to put on a brave face anymore. The scientist was trying to think of what to do if she couldn't stabilize it. The alloy needed to be allowed to cool on its own, slowly while remaining suspended, or they would destroy the product by contaminating it. It had cost them too much to make for them to afford going back to step one. A rapid cool-down to room temperature was out of the question. They had never needed a failsafe before. She input a series of commands into the control panel to scan the alloy and see if it could be salvaged.

FOREIGN CONTAMINANT DETECTED!

The words flashed across the monitor in large, white, unmistakable letters. That was why this was happening. The alloy wasn't being heated evenly. It was being thrown off balance. It was already ruined.

But knowing why didn't bring any Ocular employees any comfort. It only confirmed what they already knew: this would not end well.

"Everyone get down!" Mr. Cranston instructed. He was also terrified. Mark bent down slightly, but curiosity would not let him avert his gaze. Most of the class acted similarly. They were afraid, but they also wanted to see what would happen.

"Get down!" Mr. Currant commanded, and the entire class crouched below the seats. Everyone except for Mark and Jason.

Their curiosity was seemingly greater than their self-preservation instincts.

The ball rapidly shook and spun over the top of the bowl, trying to free itself from its fixed point. Sparks flew from the equipment as energy reflected off the alloy fried their circuits. And finally, with a mighty jerk, the alloy pulled itself out from above the bowl and came crashing down on the bowl's edge.

The molten metal ball exploded as it met the edge of the relatively cool bowl. Hundreds of tiny fragments flew out in all directions, like a hail of bullets. The students now scrambled for even greater cover.

In an instant, Mark saw what was coming. Acting faster than he could consciously think, he climbed over his seat and pushed Jason to the floor. But it was too late for him to save himself.

A shard of white-hot metal tore through the left side of his chest and exited through his shoulder blade, coming to rest buried somewhere in the auditorium's rear wall.

He fell to the ground with a scream of agony. It was like he had been shot, not that he would have known the feeling. He reflected on the pain for half a second before he passed out. The wound would have been fatal to anyone else.

Mark woke up several hours later in a bed in the Emergency Room of St. Erasmus Hospital, a mid-sized facility in Delfield that did well enough on its own but was close enough to hospitals in DC, that more complicated cases could easily be shuttled off there. Mark's case was routine.

The beeping of his heart monitor had roused him from his sleep. He glanced around. He didn't appear to be hooked up to anything else. It took a moment for him to remember why he might be in the hospital.

He bolted to an upright seated position and began clutching at his shoulder. For some reason, it didn't hurt. He pulled out the collar of his gown and checked. There was no scar, no stitching, nothing on him to indicate that he had essentially just been shot with an experimental superheated metal. Did it even happen?

A nurse entered the room. She seemed awfully calm. Mark tried to appear as calm as he could. He wasn't doing a great job.

"Mark," she greeted him cheerfully, "you're awake."

"Yeah," Mark answered, still confused and still anxiously looking at his chest, "What happened? Why am I here?"

"Well, there was an accident on your field trip. It looks like you fainted from the excitement. Your parents are in the waiting room, I'll send them in."

"Fainted?" Mark muttered under his breath.

The nurse made her way for the door.

"Wait," Mark called out, losing any illusion that he was somewhat calm.

She stopped and turned around, her face full of genuine concern.

"What is it, Mark?"

"I was hit," Mark tried to explain. He was appearing more and more on edge with each passing second. "I nearly died. Didn't I?"

"Mark," she answered, shaking her head gently, "from what we heard, it must've been a very scary experience. And you did come very close to being hit. Your shirt was ripped and you hit your nose when you fell. But we checked, and you don't have a scratch on you. No one did. Everyone is fine."

Mark touched his nose gingerly. It was sore. He did hit it on the way down.

Mark took some comfort in the last thing she said. He smiled weakly. At least everyone else was fine. But how could he not have been hit? He remembered the pain. It couldn't have just been in his imagination. It felt so real. So intense.

"Will you be okay while I get your parents?" she asked after a moment. She could tell that Mark was still freaking out.

"Yeah," Mark lied. He didn't want her to leave, but he really wanted to see his parents.

"Okay. I'll be right back."

Mark lay back down in his bed and closed his eyes. What if it was all in his head? He wasn't looking forward to the next day at school. He would be *that guy* who passed out during the field trip over nothing. He groaned audibly.

"Mark?"

Mark opened his eyes. His parents and younger brother stood in the doorway, looking in. Seeing them, Mark suddenly felt much better. He rubbed his eyes and put on his best face.

"Are you okay, buddy?" his dad asked as he approached the bed. John Michaels may not have looked exactly like his son, but there was a resemblance. They had the same nose, the same smile. He was in his late forties and barrel-chested, his once jet-black hair now graying. He liked it though, said it made him look distinguished.

"Yeah, I'm fine," Mark lied once again, smiling awkwardly, "just embarrassed."

Mark's mom stood by the door, trying to hold back tears. She was clearly upset but was working very hard not to show it. She didn't want to upset Mark any more than he already was. Lucy Michaels did share a considerable resemblance to her sons. Hair color, eye color, face shape, lean build, the list could go on and on.

Mark knew that he couldn't tell them about what he thought really happened. That would freak them out. He needed to just play it off as basically an exaggerated panic attack.

"So, what happened?" Mark's younger brother, Sean, asked. Sean was almost an exact copy of Mark, just two years younger and with a nose more reminiscent of their mother. He was curious and, if Mark wasn't dying, there wasn't any reason for him not to ask.

"Sean!" Mrs. Michaels hissed. She didn't want Mark to have to think about the incident any more than he needed to.

"No, it's okay," Mark pressed on. He needed them to believe that he wasn't too shaken up from the experience. "They were showing us some demonstration with a superheated metal or something and it got too hot and sort of exploded."

Mark's parents gasped and Sean's eyes widened. Mark regretted using the word *exploded*. He had their attention, at least.

"Yeah," Mark continued. "The metal shot off in a bunch of fragments that went everywhere, and I thought that one of them hit me."

"They didn't have any way to protect you all?" Mr. Michaels fumed. He was furious that the scientists could've left his son, and all the other students, exposed to such a dangerous experiment.

"No, that's not it," Mark explained, "there was a barrier, but the metal was so hot that it sort of easily passed through it."

Mark neglected to mention to them that he hadn't taken cover when he could have. He didn't like thinking that he might be the one at fault for their distress.

There was a long silence as everyone wondered what there still was left to say. Mark broke the silence.

"It was just something they didn't see coming, I guess."

Mark's parents murmured in agreement.

"We're glad you're okay, sweetie," Mrs. Michaels said as she kissed his forehead.

"Thanks, me too," Mark reciprocated. Then, after a slight pause, continued, "So should I just get dressed and we can head out?"

Mark's family exchanged nervous glances among one another. Mark wasn't going home tonight. The doctors had told them that they wanted to keep Mark for observation, just in case. They knew he wouldn't be thrilled about that.

"The doctors want to keep you here for a night, just to make sure everything is okay with you," Mr. Michaels finally explained once he felt that Mark was getting suspicious.

"But your father will be right here with you tonight, and you can come home in the morning," Mrs. Michaels quickly added.

Mark groaned. He just wanted to sleep in his own bed and pretend today never happened. Was that too much to ask for?

"Hey," Sean jumped in, "Mom and Dad said they'd let you skip school. I still have to go. Unless you want to switch places."

"Go right ahead," Mark countered. He was annoyed at the prospect of sleeping next to a beeping heart monitor all night while his father slept uncomfortably in a chair.

Mark's brother and mother left soon after. He had tried to convince his father to go home too, but Mr. Michaels was quite stubborn.

"Your mom will be back in the morning to pick us up," Mr. Michaels explained cheerfully as he got as comfortable as his chair would allow, "She'll bring a change of clothes for you, and you can have tomorrow to just relax. Don't worry about school right now. It'll be fine."

"Sure," Mark lied. He pulled up the blankets and turned over onto his side. He closed his eyes and tried to tune out the incessant beeping just inches away from his face.

This field trip was awful. Mark wanted, more than anything, to have gone to class that day instead. He wanted it to be someone else who humiliated themselves during the trip and gone to the hospital.

He didn't know that the experience would change his entire life. In fact, that day set in motion events that would change the world. But how could he have possibly known at that point?

"Good night, son."

"Night, Dad."

When Mark finally did return to school the next week, people didn't mention, or ask about, what had happened. At all. People asked if he was okay, but no one asked for any more details. They all seemed to think that what had happened to Mark must have been so traumatic that he couldn't possibly put the ordeal behind him.

Mark thought this was annoying. After a few days of dealing with everyone walking on eggshells around him, he confided in Chuck about how he felt.

"I'm just saying," Mark stated one day, seemingly out of the blue, "people are acting like someone died."

"You screamed like you had been shot," Chuck whispered. "A lot of people think maybe you actually did get seriously hurt. Or that it was psychologically scarring. Or something. I don't know. Isn't this better than being mocked?"

"Not really."

"Do you want me to start calling you a crybaby in public? See where it goes from there?"

"No," Mark confessed with a hint of anger. His eyes flashed red for a split second.

"There's no 'good' outcome here. You screamed and fainted during something that was genuinely frightening. You'll get a little bit more of people being delicate around you before it fades. There will be a time when it's funny to joke about this. And when that day comes, just go with it. It will go away a lot quicker if you embrace the jokes. You just need to wait until everyone gets to that point."

"Any way we can speed it up?" Mark hoped.

"Probably not," Chuck answered as soon as the words left Mark's mouth. "If I start it now, then I seem like an insensitive jerk. If you start it, you would seem to be trying too hard to prove that everything is okay when it clearly isn't."

"Makes sense," Mark conceded.

"You can be a massive crybaby sometimes."

"You're a good friend," Mark said sarcastically.

"Just trying to help," Chuck offered with an unapologetic smile.

It did help, even if Mark didn't necessarily want to admit it.

A few weeks later, Mark and Chuck were officially finished with their Junior year of high school. They were looking forward to a nice relaxing summer before their Senior year. Senior year was going to be hectic for both of them. College and scholarship applications were already on Chuck's mind. He had a few half-finished drafts saved on his computer. Mark wasn't quite as prepared.

"Finished!" Mark announced as he walked out of his English exam and strolled casually towards his locker. He was ready for his two months of freedom.

Chuck was already at his locker, checking for anything he might have missed.

"Took you long enough," Chuck joked as Mark came into view.

"Bite me," Mark snapped as he began to fiddle with the combination to his locker. "I like to double-check my work. Besides, you didn't get out much earlier than me. You're still cleaning your locker."

"Yeah," Chuck admitted, before adding, "But I also grabbed my summer assignments before I came here. And I triple-check my work."

Mark audibly groaned. He had been putting off collecting his summer homework from next year's teachers. It was not something he looked forward to.

Mark looked at the clock. Did he still have time to go to his teachers? He tried to remember the times for exam periods. Would his teachers even still be in their rooms anymore?

"I got you a copy too," Chuck tossed in, off-handedly, waving a stack of papers in front of Mark's face. "For most classes, anyway. We have basically the same schedule."

"Thanks, man."

"Don't mention it. So," Chuck began, intending to change the topic back towards their exam, "how do you think you did?"

"On English? Fine. I don't think I set any new precedents for literary analysis, but I think I'll be happy. Especially considering I barely got any sleep last night," Mark confessed.

"Late-night cramming?"

"No. Well, not entirely," Mark admitted. "I was still set to get a solid six hours."

"And?"

"I kept waking up with headaches and sweating."

"You take anything for it?"

"Yeah. I took something for the headache and turned on my desk fan, but I woke up again less than half an hour later. I don't feel sick. Everything just feels hot all the time."

"That sounds like you're sick."

Mark chuckled weakly. Maybe Chuck was right. As much as Mark didn't want to spend part of his summer in a doctor's office, maybe a quick checkup would help.

"Maybe you're ri—" Mark began before a sharp pain in his temple cut him off. He winced visibly and was starting to sweat.

"Mark, are you okay?"

Mark swallowed hard and looked at his friend. His eyes were definitely glowing red this time, Chuck was sure of it. Still, Chuck kept calm as they faded to normal.

"Yeah, fine. I'll probably go see a doctor soon."

"Good idea. You want to get something to eat? I'm thinking of heading to the mall, might get wings to end the school year."

"Sounds good to me. I'll meet you there. I either need to give Sean a ride home or he can come with."

"Cool."

Chuck left as Mark returned to emptying his locker of its contents. He pulled tests and homework assignments out that were from months ago. The deeper he went, the farther back the dates. Amid the boredom of the task, Mark found something fun in the nostalgia of looking back at his past year. He would only do this one more time before going off to college. He smiled as he caught himself thinking about how quickly this year had gone by.

"Are you seriously just now emptying your locker?" a girl's voice asked from just a few feet behind Mark.

Mark laughed. He knew who that voice belonged to.

"I didn't want to have to part with these precious memories," Mark explained, brandishing a wad of old math tests as he turned to face the speaker.

The speaker was a girl with long, braided hair and deep, dark eyes. Her smile was warm and pleasant.

"Please," the girl countered with a laugh, "I've been ready to dump this stuff since the beginning of March."

"Well, Lauren," Mark began in a matter-of-fact tone, "that's because you're an emotionless robot who can't understand the bond between a young man and his math tests. Some of these tests were flawless. They could not find one flaw."

"I'm so impressed," Lauren stated sarcastically.

"Thank you. So, are you finished with finals?" Mark asked as casually as he could.

"As a matter of fact, I am. I just grabbed my last few books out of my locker."

"Cool. Once I finish here, I was going to head to the mall. You're welcome to come too."

"Thanks. I can't today, though. I'm actually going to meet with Derrick," Lauren sincerely explained. "But I'm sure that I'll see you over the summer at some point."

Derrick was Lauren's boyfriend. He was nice, even if Mark did need to consciously tell himself to like Derrick. Mark had a little crush on Lauren, and as genuinely nice as Derrick was, Mark was a bit jealous and predisposed not to like him. So long as it was never spoken aloud, he felt he was good.

"Yeah, that's fine," Mark said, his pride a bit more stung than he would ever admit.

"Are you kidding me?" an exasperated Sean asked as he approached his older brother and his messy locker with half of its contents sprawled across the floor.

"Good to see you too," Mark said as he returned to his locker.

"You were supposed to clean out your locker weeks ago," Sean groaned before he noticed Lauren, "Hi, Lauren."

"Hi."

"I was supposed to," Mark shrugged as he continued digging through old papers, "Doesn't mean that I did."

"Well, I've got to get going. Bye," Lauren excused herself before the two brothers began to truly tear into one another.

"Okay, see ya," they accidentally answered in unison.

Sean waited until he was sure she was out of earshot before he spoke up again.

"So, are you going to make a move anytime soon?" Sean asked.

"What do you mean?" Mark wondered aloud without looking up from his task.

"You know what I mean. Are you ever going to ask Lauren out or are you just going to obsess over her quietly?"

"I'm not obsessed with her," Mark explained, still continuing to work. *Obsessed* was too strong a word, but he was acutely aware of her favorite musicians, movies, and TV shows. But that's just so they'd have things to talk about. And, in his defense, there was a considerable natural overlap between her interests and his. "I liked her a few years ago, but it didn't work out. We're just friends. And she has a boyfriend anyway."

"A boyfriend who's going to college soon," Sean pointed out as his brother picked up the last of his papers and tossed them into a nearby garbage can before picking up his backpack.

Mark stood up and slung his backpack over his shoulder. His brother might have had a point, but Mark wasn't about to admit it. He felt that he was better off not focusing on what might happen in the future. In the past, Mark's plans had never really worked out how he expected them to. Still, Sean pressed.

"Come on. You don't think they'll break up over the summer? Long-distance doesn't work."

"Right, and you're such an expert." Mark muttered. "You're what? Twelve?"

"You know I'm right," Sean persisted, ignoring his brother's hyperbolic dig at his age.

"I think that if it happens, I'll see how I feel then. Right now, she's my friend and I don't care that much about her relationship status. So," Mark began, changing the subject, "I'm meeting Chuck at the mall, probably going to get something to eat. Do you want to come with, or do you want me to drop you off at home?"

"Will you pay for me?"

"No."

"Fine. I'll still go, I just thought I'd ask."

"Are you sure you don't want to pay for me?" Sean asked one last time as he exited the car in the mall's garage. He had asked this question several more times during the car ride over.

"Positive," Mark answered.

Sean slammed the passenger-side car door shut in response. Mark winced again and clutched at his temple.

"Are you okay?" Sean asked with concern.

"I'm fine," Mark lied before adding, "I told you to not slam the doors."

Sean rolled his eyes as the two of them made their way for the food court. If Mark was lecturing about not slamming the car door, he must be fine.

"There you guys are," Chuck announced when he saw the two brothers. "Took you long enough," Chuck countered, "I've been sitting here by myself like some friendless loser for the better part of half an hour."

"Maybe you should make more friends," Mark offered.

"Or maybe you should have spent less time flirting with Lauren and more time cleaning your locker," Sean jumped in.

"Oh," Chuck exclaimed with a smirk, "So we're back to this again?"

"We're back to nothing," Mark declared. "She saw me cleaning my locker, she said hello, and I paused to have a short, friendly conversation. That's it. Sorry that I'm polite and talked to a friend."

"At any point in this friendly conversation, did you tell her you love her?" Chuck joked.

"Shut up," Mark declared, trying to end the conversation or at least shift it somewhere else. "Did you order anything yet?"

"Nope. I was waiting for the two of you to get here. It would've been rude otherwise."

"You're so polite. Well, I'm going to use the bathroom," Mark explained, "Can one of you just get me a dozen 'hot' wings?"

"Will do, Romeo," Chuck responded with a thumbs-up.

Mark groaned and made his way for the bathroom as Chuck and Sean laughed. It's not even that funny, thought Mark.

Mark turned to the sink and activated the motion-sensor. A small trickle of water began to flow. Mark hated these sinks. They never worked right. Another pang of a headache and heat washed over him. He steadied himself with the sink. He washed his hands and glanced in the mirror. He was sweating profusely. He was definitely sick. He hoped no one else would catch it because of him. He felt miserable. Mark splashed some of the cool water into his face. It felt amazing. He grabbed a pair of paper towels and dried off his hands. He pulled out a last one to dry off his face.

Another wave of heat hit him. Again, he clutched the sink for support, crumpled paper towel in his right hand. He strained to open his eyes this time. For the first time, he saw what Chuck had seen. Staring back at him from the mirror was a pair of bright, glowing red eyes. He fell back in shock and landed hard on his backside. He supported himself against the opposite wall. The paper towel he had been clutching just a minute ago was now ashes in his hand. Mark simply stared in disbelief. He had no idea what was happening, what this was the start of.

Mark took a moment to compose himself before exiting the bathroom. He couldn't tell Sean and Chuck. Or could he? He decided against it for now. At least until he knew more about what just happened, it would stay his secret.

"We didn't know what you wanted to drink, so we just got you a water," Chuck announced when he saw his friend exiting the bathroom.

"We should go," Mark told Sean as he walked up to the table, not even waiting until he had reached his brother.

"We just ordered," Sean protested.

"I need to get home," Mark muttered weakly. He was definitely shaken by what had just happened. He tried to hide it in his voice.

"Well, can't I stay?" Sean asked. At that point, Mark thought about how he was lucky his brother wasn't great at picking up subtle clues.

"Chuck, do you mind giving him a ride back after?"

"No problem," Chuck answered before taking a big drink from his own glass of ice water. "If you aren't feeling well, you should rest."

Mark nodded at his friend's suggestion. He glanced down at the water. He picked up the cup and chugged the contents all at once. He felt the cool water prevent another blast of heat from inside him.

"Water probably helps too," Chuck added, seeing his friend down the beverage so quickly and eagerly. "Just, you know, not too much at once."

"You okay?" Sean asked. He wasn't exactly concerned at this point. Rather, he was more confused. Why was Mark acting so weird?

"Yeah, that definitely helped," Mark replied. It really had. He felt much better now. He exhaled in relief, producing a small, unnoticed steam cloud that once again set Mark slightly on edge. "I better get going."

"Okay, see you at home," Sean called out as his brother left.

When Mark arrived home, he climbed up to his room, closed the door, and passed out on his bed for ten hours. His parents tried to wake him up for dinner when they got home but had no luck. They decided to let him sleep.

What was happening to him was draining him. If he didn't get a handle on it soon, whether he knew it or not, it would destroy him.

The Michaels lived in a modest three-bedroom house in the part of Delfield where you can see the landscape shift from urban to suburban in the span of a few blocks. The house had been built in the mid-1930s and was the same house Mr. Michaels grew up in. Mark's grandfather had also grown up there. The elder Mr. Michaels left it to his son when he passed, a few years before Mark was born. Mark's dad did not like to talk about him. In fact, Mark hadn't heard his grandfather's actual name since he was a little kid.

The house was brick and, by all accounts, a lovely home, smartly furnished and without any major issues. But its real value was the land it sat on. A bare lot of the exact same size a block away would be quickly snatched up at almost any cost and turned into a row of townhouses. In fact, Mr. and Mrs. Michaels had often discussed selling the house, buying an identical place an hour south, and just retiring off the profits. But all their friends lived in the area and it was an easy commute to work for both of them, so they kept the house. Maybe once the boys were out of school, they thought.

About a week into the summer, Mark was still fighting off his 'symptoms' as best he could. He had gone with his mother to see the doctor, but they told him it must have just been exam stress. They couldn't find anything medically wrong with him. He was advised to relax during his summer and come back if things still didn't feel right. Mark took this advice to heart. For the first couple days after, he was a typical high school student on vacation if there ever was one. He had been unable to find a summer job, so he committed himself to sleeping and drinking plenty of water. He knew that those two things seemed to help. Still, even if he slept in until noon, he still felt exhausted by dinnertime. He hardly ever hung out with Chuck in the evenings because he simply couldn't stay awake.

Soon, Mark began trying to fight the lethargy away. He thought that perhaps his exhaustion was a self-fulfilling cycle. He was tired because he slept too much, and he slept too much because he was always tired. He began to go on runs and exercise in different ways. He tested out every old piece of workout equipment in the basement and looked up body-weight exercises online. He soon found that his "heat attacks" provided him with energy in some strange way. He would be running and he'd suddenly feel a surge of energy and strength. Maybe that was why he had felt terrible when he got them before, he thought. He wasn't using them for anything. He was just letting all that energy build up inside of him without doing anything with it. He still didn't have an explanation for the paper towels, though. He figured that he must've imagined it, or it was some sort of one-off event. He decided one day that he needed to tell Chuck. Chuck loved studying this kind of stuff, even in his free time. Maybe he could explain some of it.

"How're you feeling?" Chuck asked as he and Mark sat down on the Currant's living room couch one summer afternoon. While Mark's family home was pleasant and warm, Chuck and his father lived in what can only be described as a mansion, atop acres of Virginia's most expensive real estate, complete with a backyard that extended north to the Potomac River and a private dock. Maybe it could be called a castle, it did have a sophisticated stone façade, but to call it a house would've been an insult. The interior was sleek and modern, with each room perpetually kept so neat that Mark often wondered if Chuck and his father actually lived there or just maintained it for appearances. After a decade of friendship between the two, Mark still felt uncomfortable doing anything more than sitting on the couch. It felt like being in a museum: very beautiful, very cold.

It was one of the first times they'd really hung out all summer. Mark had his own stuff to work out, including the five-figure settlement with Oracular Technologies that was immediately put aside for Mark's college fund. Meanwhile, Chuck's dad had managed to get him some type of internship. All Mark knew about it was that it was apparently very boring and definitely very secret. He was jealous, though. At least Chuck was getting paid for being bored over the summer and he actually had a say in how the money would be spent, unlike the settlement.

"Still a little weird after all this time. Better, but weird," Mark confessed. He had kept Chuck updated via text but hadn't gone too in-depth. That's just not what texts are for. He was planning on easing into the big reveal about the strange bursts of energy and then, once Chuck had been appropriately primed for bigger news, the glowing red eyes.

"Did you see a doctor about it?" Chuck asked, pulling a large bottle of water to his lips. Chuck always drank water. There was a genuine interest Mark could sense, but he didn't feel that Chuck was too concerned.

"Yeah, saw one a few weeks ago," Mark replied.

"What'd he say?" Chuck continued. He must've found something fascinating about all this. Mark was now sure Chuck would know something.

"He said the headaches were probably from stress and just told me to rest more," Mark explained as Chuck took another long drink of water.

"How'd that work?"

"It helped with the headache a little bit, but I just felt tired all the time and would sometimes wake up randomly sweating."

Chuck just nodded. Mark stared at him inquisitively for a moment.

"Anything else?" Chuck asked in a knowing voice.

Mark shifted uncomfortably in his seat. Chuck had been his best friend for so many years, yet now he seemed so different. He seemed to know exactly what was happening to Mark and seemed content to let Mark twist in the wind and suffer whatever this was in silence. Mark wasn't sure if he wanted to trust Chuck now.

"Yeah, there's something else," Mark finally revealed after a pause. He couldn't keep this a secret from everyone around him. He needed to tell someone. And if Chuck somehow had answers, Mark was determined to get them.

Chuck leaned forward and tried to hide a slight smile. He was excited. He knew what was coming and he was happy his friend was going to share it. He'd seen the glowing eyes already.

"So, the sweating usually comes when I feel, like, this wave of heat hit me from nowhere. And sometimes, there's…" Mark paused; he didn't know exactly how to phrase the last part.

Chuck remained silent. He couldn't push his friend along. This needed to come from Mark by himself.

Mark took in a deep breath and closed his eyes. He concentrated and tried to summon a wave of heat. He had done it once or twice before in the last few days, just standing alone in front of his mirror, trying to get a glimpse of his glowing red eyes like he had seen after his last exam. As terrifying as the changes were, he still thought the eye change was cool. He thought it made him look intimidating.

As Mark tensed his muscles, he felt it. He felt the strange tingle in his irises. He opened his eyes to show Chuck.

Even though Chuck had seemed to know exactly what was going on a moment ago, he still seemed quite surprised by this. His friend's irises were both glowing a bright shade of crimson, like red-hot steel.

"Huh…" Chuck finally muttered after Mark's eyes dimmed and returned to their normal brown color. "How often has this happened?"

"Not sure. I don't always see it happen. There's a feeling to it, but it's usually pretty faint," Mark explained as he closed his eyes and massaged his eyelids. How was Chuck not freaking out more about this?

"Has anyone else seen it?" Chuck continued before taking another drink.

"Doubtful. I think someone would've mentioned it before. So," Mark began to ask, choosing his words carefully. "Why were you so calm seeing it?"

"I saw it before," Chuck answered without hesitation, setting his water bottle down on the nearby coffee table.

"And you didn't think to mention it?" Mark asked, trying to remain calm. "Where could you possibly have seen this before?"

"It was on the last day of school. After exams, by your locker," Chuck revealed. "And a few days after the field trip accident, but I didn't get a great look that first time."

"Why didn't you say something to me?" Mark demanded. It was ironic: Mark had wanted to ease his friend into the conversation so that Chuck wouldn't freak out, but he was the one failing to keep calm.

"I wasn't sure what I had seen. I needed to look into it."

"I've been freaking out about this for weeks and you could've helped?" Mark was livid. He stood up from his seat and felt his eyes glow with heat once again.

"I wasn't sure," Chuck repeated, not acknowledging his friend's unintended transformation.

Mark took a few deep breaths and sat down again as his eyes returned to normal. He wasn't happy that Chuck kept it from him, but he was eager to hear what Chuck had found.

"Are you sure now?" Mark asked as he adjusted himself in his seat.

"Very," Chuck declared, pulling his laptop out from his bag near the couch. "There's a fairly wide range of things that your eye… *thing* could be related to, but they're almost all supernatural in origin."

"What, like ghosts?" Mark was skeptic.

"More mythological, like Greco-Roman or Hellenistic. You know, ancient gods and goddesses," Chuck continued, despite his friend's lack of faith. "There's frequent mention of eye color and a sort of radiance in all of their myths."

"Quit messing with me, did you find anything or not?"

"I'm not messing with you. I'm serious. When the metal at the lab hit you, it must have triggered some sort of reaction that awakened this supernatural ability, or abilities, within you."

"I didn't get hit with the metal, though," Mark protested. "It just came close, and I blacked out."

"Fainted," Chuck corrected.

"Fine," Mark conceded. "Fainted. But it never hit me."

"That was what I thought too, but I remember what I saw. That thing passed right through your shoulder. It should've killed you. And when you emerged without a scratch, I figured I must've been wrong about it too. I accepted that it barely missed you, that my eyes had played a trick on me. And that somehow your shirt got ripped some other way in that exact spot. But then I saw your eyes change that one day. That's when I knew I had to look into this."

"But wait," Mark pressed, "If I did actually get hit with the metal, wouldn't it make more sense that it's the cause of all this instead? It's a far jump to go from mythical deities to me without anything in-between to back all of this up."

"That metal isn't magic or radioactive or cosmic or any sort of comic-book gimmick that might explain this. The answer for all of this weirdness is inherently you." Chuck declared firmly.

"What weirdness? My eyes glow. That's it." Mark replied, getting a little angry.

"No, that's not it." Chuck threw back at him, raising his voice, "You forgot to mention the paper towel you burned to ashes in the bathroom and the cloud of steam you exhaled after drinking a glass of water."

"You noticed that?" Mark asked quietly, shocked that something he thought was so minor had been noticed. And that Chuck had apparently taken the initiative to sort through the bathroom trash for ashes.

"Yes, I noticed it," Chuck answered, calming down, though still annoyed. "I noticed you winced before taking the drink, and I figured something must've happened in the bathroom right before you left. I connected the dots. I just thought you were actually planning on telling me something yourself."

"I'm sorry," Mark muttered, staring at his shoes. "It freaks me out. I have all this weird energy and it feels like I'm literally on fire inside sometimes. And it doesn't help that your only answer is over two-thousand years removed from any sort of evidence."

"That wasn't my only evidence."

"What do you mean?"

"That wasn't my only evidence." Chuck stated again, matter-of-factly. "There's other stuff than just mythology."

"Then why would you lead with mythology? Why wouldn't you mention the other stuff sooner?" Mark asked incredulously.

"Because you made me work for all the information. Eye-glowing is the center of my theory here, Mark."

"Fine," Mark sighed, "What's the rest of your theory?"

"Blackbeard."

"Blackbeard the pirate?"

"What other Blackbeard is there?"

"Fair point, what does he have to do with anything?"

"He also fits this mold," Chuck explained.

"How so?"

"There are stories about how he would tie cannon fuses into his beard and light them to terrify people or how his eyes glowed with hellfire. But what if they weren't fuses? What if he actually lit his beard on fire himself?"

"Seems a little shaky."

"I'm not done, though," Chuck continued, "The day Blackbeard died, he was shot five times and stabbed twenty before he died. What if there was more? What if he could heal really quickly, and that's why it took so long for him to die? Maybe that's what gave him the strength to fight so many men for so long. You can heal too. I saw that thing pass through you, and you don't have a single scratch there. The blood on your shirt wasn't from hitting your nose. That's just the only way they could explain it to themselves."

Mark pulled the neck of his shirt aside and glanced at his own chest. No hint of the wound that he and Chuck both knew should be there. Healing was a solid argument. But Chuck had glossed over the most likely evidence for their connection.

"And there's something else you forgot, Chuck," Mark began to add, "I'm descended from him on my dad's side." This was true. Mr. Michaels would recite that fact at least once a year. It was easily the most interesting thing about his family. Rather, at least it was, prior to the events of this story.

"Why do you think I thought to research him?" Chuck smirked. "I had to let you get one of these on your own."

"So, Blackbeard was whatever I am, apparently," Mark pondered aloud.

"I guess so. And there are probably a lot of other examples out there in history that we just don't know about. Maybe there are even more answers about what exactly you can do."

Mark looked down at his hands with a slight curiosity. So, this was all real? He slowly turned them over and stared at his palms. He concentrated for a moment and, with a thought, summoned twin flames as his eyes glowed red.

"So," Mark asked with a grin, "What next? Superheroism?"

"It's almost like you read my mind."

THREE
First Flight

"Happy birthday, Mark!"

Every year, during the last week of August, the Michaels family would travel to a small beach house. Mr. Michaels' parents had rented that same beach house when he went to the beach as a kid, and the tiny shack held a lot of memories, the best ones from a complicated childhood, and when it went on sale, he had to have it.

The beach that they made the pilgrimage to, year after year, was located in the Outer Banks. The Outer Banks are a stretch of small, connected islands along the coastline of North Carolina. A short enough distance away from home that the Michaels could drive there in a day from Virginia, but far enough away that they felt separated from the stresses of work and school.

Every year, Mr. Michaels made a point of reminding Mark and Sean that their ancestor, the infamous pirate Blackbeard, Edward Teach, was killed not too far away from where they stayed. And every year, an unenthusiastic murmur would be the response from the backseat. This year, however, Mark didn't answer. After learning that his connection to Blackbeard might explain his newfound abilities, he could only sit in thoughtful silence at the mention of the name.

The beach house was a tiny, one-story house with three cramped bedrooms and a single bathroom. Even when it was brand-new, the house would've been less than ideal, and the years had not been kind, despite Mr. Michael's best efforts at restoration. The roof would leak every time it rained and the carpet carried over two decades' worth of sand in its shag. The yard was a mess of sand and weeds, and the road into the neighborhood did no favors to their car's suspension. Though *neighborhood* may be putting it gently, as the house's only neighbors on all sides were the ever-shifting sand dunes. It was as isolated as could be, unintentionally. But it was a family tradition, so they went every year.

Mark smiled and blew out the candles on his cake. His family stood around the table as he was sitting. And Chuck was there too. He had been a part of the Michaels family vacation for the last six years, ever since Mark's parents learned that the Currants never took a vacation. Mr. Currant insisted that his role as principal of one of the top high schools in the country allowed no opportunities for time away. And so, the backseat became a bit more cramped, but Chuck's presence was generally welcomed by the whole family.

Mark shared a knowing look with Chuck, as they'd spent the better part of the afternoon debating whether or not fire-breathing could be part of Mark's skill set. In nearly three hours of trying, all Mark managed to do was cover the practice candle with spit and give himself indigestion.

Mr. Michaels cut the cake while Mrs. Michaels went to get Mark's presents. Mark didn't know where she'd hidden them, and neither did Mr. Michaels. If it were up to Mr. Michaels, Mark would just get them when they got back home a few days later. They had tried that once, on Mark's seventh birthday. It led to Mark sulking for the rest of the trip, and Mrs. Michaels declaring that Mark wouldn't have to wait until his actual birthday to open presents. And sure enough, she had kept her word for the last ten years.

"Here you go, buddy," Mr. Michaels said, putting down a larger-than-average piece of cake in front of Mark.

"Thanks, Dad."

"So, seventeen. One more year and you'll be out of the house," Mr. Michaels joked thoughtfully as he continued cutting the cake.

"That's assuming I go to college," Mark shot back sarcastically. "I could just room with you guys forever." He would absolutely not be willing to live with his parents forever, but it could not be understated just how little he wanted to work on college applications.

"Count me in too," Chuck laughed. Chuck was probably sincere. Mr. and Mrs. Michaels treated Chuck like family. Actually, better than family, Mark would say if he thought about it. His parents showed Chuck more affection than he'd ever seen Mr. Currant give him, and Mrs. Michaels was a lot less shy of singing Chuck's praises than she was of her own sons. Not that Mark was bitter, it was just a fact.

"No way," Mrs. Michaels declared with a smile, walking back into the room and balancing a stack of nearly a dozen boxes in her arms. "You boys are going to college whether you like it or not. Here, these are from us."

Mrs. Michaels set down the gifts on the table and Mark carefully examined the pile.

Most of the boxes were small, with the larger ones certainly containing clothes.

"If you insist."

"While we're on the subject," Mrs. Michaels continued, "How are the personal statement essays coming along?"

Mark rolled his eyes as he tore into the first present; a large one. He had barely started on his college application essays, even though he'd told his mom they were practically done. In reality, he had an introductory paragraph. And about 30 hours' worth of other summer assignments left to do in the next few days. He did not look forward to it.

"It's going fine," Mark lied, hands full of wrapping paper. It was a nice, light blue collared shirt. "Thanks."

"What's 'fine'? Like you're finished with the first draft?" Mrs. Michaels persisted.

Mark rolled his eyes and exhaled. "Yep, pretty much."

"Chuck," Mrs. Michaels began.

"Yes ma'am?"

"Have you seen Mark's essay?"

Mark took a big bite of cake to try and hide his expression as he waited for Chuck to answer on his behalf.

"Not exactly," Chuck said timidly, as he accepted his piece of cake, not yet daring to take a bite. "But we did talk about the topic a lot a while ago, so it's probably pretty fleshed out by now."

Mrs. Michaels shrugged. She could trust that Chuck was telling her the truth. He was always quick to own up to any wrongdoing on his or Mark's part.

"Okay." She then turned to Mark, "But it better be ready by admission deadlines."

"I know," Mark sighed, mouth full of chocolate cake. He took a swig of milk and added, "Besides, I've still got a lot of time. It'll be finished by next weekend. Promise."

It wouldn't be finished by next weekend. But it was far from the biggest promise Mark would break.

"Did you know there's going to be a solar eclipse visible from here near the end of October?" Chuck asked the room, steering the conversation away from Mark's many neglected academic commitments. Mark was grateful for it.

Later that night, Chuck lay awake in his bed, ignoring the sleep-inducing rhythm of the ocean's waves hitting the shore not too far outside.

"Hey," Chuck whispered, breaking the silence, "Are you still awake?"

"Yeah."

Suddenly the room was full of light, as Chuck had hopped out of his bed and flicked the light switch. The two of them had shared this room for beach trips for as long as they could remember. The window that they kept ajar was notorious for letting bugs in, despite the screen, but they both agreed that hearing the sounds of the shore was worth the price.

"That doesn't mean turn on the lights," Mark hissed, pulling the pillow over his head.

"Sorry. But I got you another present," Chuck happily announced as he closed their window fully shut. Lights on, window closed. It kept the bug problem from getting too bad. That was the deal they had worked out with Mr. Michaels several years ago.

Chuck pulled a box out from under his bed. Mark slowly pulled himself up to a sitting position with a smile, eager to open another gift.

"Why didn't you give it to me with everything else?" Mark asked.

"This isn't exactly a normal gift."

"This isn't something weird or anything, is it?"

"Just open the box."

Mark's hands trembled slightly as he opened up the box.

"Rainboots?" Mark asked incredulously.

"Nope," Chuck replied with a laugh. "These are for the supersuit."

Mark grinned from ear to ear. They had been working on the project off and on for several weeks now, but he still beamed whenever it was mentioned. Soon he'd actually be able to put on the suit and have some fun with it.

"These are great, but how are they different from the ones on the suit now?"

"The soles," Chuck explained.

Mark turned the boots over and took a look at the bottoms. The soles of the boots were some sort of metal mesh, colored somewhere between gold and copper.

"What metal is this?" he wondered aloud.

"It's called conductium," Chuck quietly blurted out in excitement. "It has the property of conducting heat more efficiently than any other metal available."

"And with it on the bottom of these boots…" Mark began in confusion.

"You can fly!" Chuck nearly shouted.

He quickly covered his mouth with his hands, realizing the volume of his outburst. He sprung from the bed and turned off the light, and sprinted back into bed, hoping that it wouldn't look suspicious if Mr. Michaels came down to check.

They both held their collective breath for a moment. No sounds came from outside of their room except for the soft snoring of Mark's dad.

Chuck slowly crossed back to the light and flicked the switch. Mark was still holding the boots as he was before, examining them closely.

"Where'd you get them?" Mark whispered, with an air of suspicion.

"Online." Chuck answered, attempting to brush away Mark's concern.

"It's just that that description sounds a lot like the stuff they had at the solar reactor. You know, where I got these powers."

"I bought it online from a normal website. They sell to school chemistry labs and stuff. This is all totally fine."

Mark nodded, not completely sure if he believed Chuck's words. He felt around the inside of the boot, wondering how it would feel on his feet. He pressed his hand up against the bottom and looked at the sole. The soles seemed thin to him.

"So, if I shoot fire out of my feet, the metal on the soles will let me fly?"

"Yeah. Cushion of superheated air," Chuck answered with a yawn. "Alright, now that I've shown you them, let's get some sleep. I figure we can try them out tomorrow."

For the last time that night, Chuck tiptoed to the light switch and darkened the room. He crossed over to the windowsill and creaked open the window so that he could feel the breeze. As he smelled the salt air, a peaceful smile stretched across his face. Chuck closed his eyes and got into his bed.

Mark, meanwhile, still sat with his new boots. He couldn't see them anymore, now that the lights were off, but he held them as he had been. The one boot still sat on his right hand, as the left pinched and felt all along the outside.

As he realized he'd never be able to wait until tomorrow morning, Mark's eyes began to softly glow. Not the red-hot glow that he had seen all those times, but a much more gentle, curious glow. Without thinking, his hand began to heat up.

A blast of heat shot out from the end of the boot, pulling Mark out of bed and to the ground with a loud thud. Chuck shot up from his sleep, his eyes darting around the darkened room. As Mark pulled off the boot and stuffed it back into the box and under the bed, his eyes dimmed to their usual color.

On the other side of the house could be heard the stomps of Mr. Michaels as he made his way to the boys' room, upset over being awakened. He flung open the door and stood in the doorway. In the darkness, Mark thought he could see his own father's eyes glowing.

"Go to sleep," Mr. Michaels commanded. There was a note of anger in his voice. It was not threatening, but it was not one to be taken lightly.

"Sorry, Dad," Mark muttered sheepishly as he climbed back into his bed.

Mr. Michaels stood in the doorway a moment longer. Mark could hear his angry breaths and closed his eyes tight, as if to bring sleep faster and escape from this position. Chuck had done likewise.

The door closed and Mark exhaled greatly. He turned over in his bed and began to drift off to a peaceful sleep, assisted by the sound of the waves. Before sleep took him, he heard one last word from Chuck's bed.

"Smooth."

"Up."

Mark buried his face into his pillow and groaned.

"Come on, you want to try these things on now or what?" Chuck asked quietly as he stood over the bed with a water bottle in hand.

Mark rolled over and peered through his eyelids.

"The sun's not even up yet," Mark muttered angrily.

"I'm aware," Chuck said, taking a sip. "We don't exactly want spectators for this. Test run, remember?"

Mark rolled up wordlessly, pausing as he sat upright in his bed.

"You coming?"

"Give me a minute," Mark exhaled with a glare. Chuck rolled his eyes.

"I've got your suit, mask, and the boots in here," Chuck gestured to a small athletic bag resting on his back. "Just put on some jogging stuff and we can get going."

Chuck left the room and Mark considered lying back down and falling asleep again.

"Put on some jogging stuff," Mark muttered sarcastically as he pulled on an athletic shirt and shorts and joined Chuck in the kitchen.

"What're you guys doing up this early?" Mrs. Michaels whispered as she peaked out of her room, rubbing her eyes.

"Going for a run," Chuck answered without hesitation but with an unusual amount of energy for so early in the morning. "I have to get ready for cross-country in the fall."

"Right," Mrs. Michaels nodded. "But why is Mark up too?"

"Because I'm a very supportive friend," Mark yawned. "We going or what?"

"Sorry to wake you, Mrs. Michaels, I planned on leaving a note," Chuck apologized, holding up the note in his hand, as if to prove the validity of his statement.

"It's fine, just be safe and don't go too far out."

"Will do."

"No problem, Mom," Mark assured, as he dragged himself to the kitchen sink and splashed some water in his face.

The master bedroom door closed behind him. The sun's first rays began to stream through the blinds of the window, gently warming Mark's face. His eyes flashed and he turned to Chuck.

"Let's fly."

"So, what happens if we get caught?"

"Shut up, I'm making sure we're clear."

"You didn't do that before I started changing?" Mark asked as he emerged from behind a large clump of dune grass, pulling the pants of his suit up. "Hand me the mask, will you?"

"I never said you were clear to change," Chuck shot back, tossing Mark his mask. "And that grass wasn't as concealing as you thought," he added with a grimace.

"Mch," Mark conceded with a smirk from behind his mask.

The two of them stood atop a large sand dune in a park, as far out from the main streets as they could get. Just out of view were the same dunes where the Wright brothers had their famous first flight. The sun was still just above the horizon, but every minute they wasted brought them closer to early park-goers discovering them.

"Alright. It looks like we're good," Chuck declared.

Mark bent down and adjusted the boots. He wiggled his toes and noticed just how flexible the soles actually were. He started to feel a little nervous.

"So, can we go over this one more time?"

"Light a fire in your hands," Chuck instructed.

Mark's eyes flashed beneath the visor of his suit and twin flames appeared in his palms.

"Okay, now you just do that with your feet, and then the special metal on the soles will take care of the rest."

The small flames in Mark's hands faded.

"Trust me."

Mark nodded.

Mark felt the warmth fill his body and focused on sending it down to his feet. The sand beneath him began to shift wildly. With a mighty jerk, his feet shot up into the air behind him, flinging Mark onto his face.

"Are you okay?" Chuck asked as he helped Mark to his feet.

"Yeah," Mark muttered, shaking his head.

"You were leaning too far forward," Chuck explained. "The heat from your heels pushed you forward, and it just escalated from there. Are you good for round two?"

"How else will I learn?" Mark answered, brushing sand off his front.

Mark tried over two dozen times to just get off the ground for a moment, but each one saw him landing in the sand. Some face-first, some on his back, and a few on each side. One time Mark even did a complete flip, with his feet shooting out from under him and still landing flat on his face.

"What're we at now?" Mark asked, still face-down in the sand.

"You really want to know?"

"Hit me."

"Twenty-seven unsuccessful attempts."

"Maybe a jetpack-type thingy or wings or something would work better."

"You think it'd be easier to accurately control fire out of your back than your feet? Besides, I couldn't find that much of the stuff."

"Bummer," Mark sighed, pulling himself up. "Alright, twenty-eight it is."

"Make it quick," Chuck whispered. "Sun's starting to get up there. It's almost seven. We should call it after this, so we don't get discovered."

"Right," Mark muttered in a disappointed voice as he rubbed his hands on the back of his neck. It was starting to get sore after so many attempts, even if he had special healing abilities. He paused and pulled away his hands. He took a glance at them and smiled beneath his mask. That's it.

Mark crouched down and his eyes lit up. He took a few strides and leapt into the air. As he came down, he pushed the flame down to his feet. As he began to tumble forward, he put his hands in front of him and unleashed a burst of fire for balance. As he started to fall back, he twisted and did the same. With a few twists and pivots, he managed to get a sort of balance, just floating in the air. It felt like he was standing on top of a beach ball that was just about to burst. But he was doing it. He was flying.

Chuck, who had been somewhat reserved throughout everything they'd been through recently, let out a single long obscenity with a laugh.

Mark laughed at the top of his lungs and caught himself before falling once more.

"Okay," Chuck laughed, "We really should get going. There are other runners out now. Let's jog back to the house, call it a day."

"Nah, I'm good," Mark announced. "I think we're just starting."

Mark clenched his hands tight and his eyes flared. Heat flooded the boots and he shot straight up another fifty feet instantly with a cheer. At the top of the arc, his joy was immediately replaced with exhaustion. He used way more energy than he meant to with that burst. In a panic, Mark lost balance, and he kicked his feet out from under him, shooting himself forward. Rapidly losing altitude, Mark turned and tried to return to his starting point. He twisted and strained in the air, managing largely by luck to point himself back in the intended direction. He shot right past Chuck and landed face-first in the sand with a mighty thud.

"Are you okay?" Chuck asked as he rushed over to his friend.

Mark flopped over onto his back with a groan. He was completely drained, but still shaking from the adrenaline. He had never felt so tired before. Nothing felt broken. He'd be sore, he figured, but he could probably make it back to the house.

"Water."

"Yeah, sure buddy," Chuck responded, enthusiastically handing Mark his water bottle. "Drink up. Yeah, water's a good idea."

Mark pulled off his mask and poured over half of the remaining water into his mouth, with the other half landing on his chin or splashing on the sand. He gargled briefly and spit it out onto the sand, much to Chuck's dismay.

"You were supposed to drink it."

"I needed to rinse out my mouth, be glad I didn't actually puke into the mask."

Chuck rolled his eyes and took back the empty water bottle.

"Sorry," Mark apologized, genuinely sorry for wasting so much water.

"It's cool," Chuck muttered. "So, how was it?"

Mark, still lying on the sand, shot his friend a look.

"You're not dead. You're fine. And it's not like I can ask you back at the house with your family around."

"It was…" Mark paused, trying to find the words to describe it. He propped himself up on his elbows so that he was sitting, rather than lying down.

Chuck waited silently, ready to mentally note Mark's words. He needed to document everything once they got back to the house. He needed it to be recorded, even if they would be the only two to ever see it.

"This is where this became real. This was one of the most important moments of my life — of our lives." Mark concluded with a solemnity that he seldom used. But he truly meant it. This meant that their ridiculous little plan for Mark to be a hero would actually come true. Mark knew the significance. Now that he could fly, it was all really going to happen. He turned to Chuck and added, "Thank you for that."

Chuck smiled and offered a hand. He helped Mark stand up, who dusted himself off and went back behind his less-than-opaque clump of dune grass and changed back into his athletic shorts and t-shirt. As he changed, he kept muttering to himself with a soft smile and a deep reverence. "I flew."

Every morning for the rest of the trip, Mark and Chuck would return to that same spot and work on Mark's flight. It was the only vacation where Mark wanted to get up early. They'd start with balancing attempts, helping Mark developing the skill to hang in the air when necessary, before moving on to forward flight. Mark preferred forward flight. It was a lot easier, and the speed was unreal. He begged Chuck to buy some sort of speedometer, so they'd have an actual number. Well, Mark liked forward flight in the moment, but the crash-landings and post-crash exhaustion were less than ideal.

Then, once they finished twenty-eight flight runs, which Chuck had declared the magic number after the first day, they'd return to the beach house, sleep for an hour or so, and then join the family for the rest of the day. It was hard work, trying to act like it was a normal trip, when really they were making history.

During the days, after flight lessons, Mark and Chuck would laze about on the beach and read; Mark reading for school, Chuck reading for pleasure, since he'd completed his summer assignments back in June.

"Hey," Mark began one day after he mentally noted his page number, closed his book, and set it down on the sand. "Can I talk to you about your college applications?"

"Yeah, what's up?" Chuck asked, wedging in a bookmark to save his place.

Mark looked up and down the beach; there weren't a ton of beach-goers at this point in the summer. Mr. and Mrs. Michaels had gone for a walk along the shore and Sean was back at the house. They had this part of the beach to themselves. "This stays between us. Don't go and report back to my parents, but I'm worried that with all this superhero stuff we've been talking about, it'll be a lot harder for me to stay on top of my grades and wrap up college applications on time."

"Are you suggesting we bail? I mean, it's been a fun idea to kick around, but it's not like Delfield, or even DC, is currently in much need of a superhero," Chuck offered, trying to keep his voice neutral and not betray the fact that he'd hate for all his hard work to go to waste.

"Like, with the college essays, it's been hard getting traction. It feels like schoolwork. And, all things considered, I'd rather actually enjoy the summer," Mark answered, frustrated by the time-crunch he himself was responsible for. "I've still got summer assignments I need to finish, so those take priority."

"Alright, I get that," Chuck conceded. "Which classes do you still have stuff for?"

"Which ones do I *not* still have assignments for?" Mark laughed bitterly before rattling off nearly his entire class schedule. "AP U.S. Government and Politics, AP Comparative Government, AP Statistics, AP Latin, and Honors English." He picked up the book he had just set aside for dramatic flourish. He was about halfway through, and luckily, it was the last book he needed to read. "Drama and Sports Marketing are the only two that didn't have summer assignments."

"Which is exactly why you chose them," Chuck asserted, more playful than accusatory, but it still landed poorly.

"I like sports," Mark shot back.

"I'm sure the admissions staff will buy it," Chuck mumbled.

"Sorry I didn't stack my entire schedule with only AP classes, like you. You sound like my mom." Mark's eyes flashed red. Chuck was getting on his nerves. What part of a vacation did he not understand?

The two of them were quiet. Only the sound of the waves broke the silence.

"I don't get why you went with Honors English." Chuck pried.

"It's half the work of AP English —" Mark started.

"And half as impressive on a college application." Chuck interrupted.

"You're going to be valedictorian. You can try and act coy and modest about it, but we both know it. And my parents know it and, eventually, you're going to get into schools that I won't, and my parents will be disappointed that I didn't work as hard as you. I just want to be able to get into *most* of the same schools." Mark finished his rant with a sigh. He'd never explicitly stated it to anyone, but he hated being compared to Chuck.

"Our applications won't be that different," Chuck offered. He saw Mark still looked unsure. He held up his right hand, thumb holding down the pinky finger, while the other three were pointed up. "Scout's honor." He was right, Mark wasn't valedictorian, but his grades had comfortably landed him near the top of the North Delfield student body. "Keep up your grades and maybe put in more work in extracurriculars. You're taking Drama, use that to get a small part in one of the plays or something. It would make more sense to be taking the class if that's the case, and it's not too much of a time commitment. Then Eagle Scout on top of that. Maybe you could volunteer at the kung-fu studio you went to as a kid."

Mark grinned. Maybe Chuck had a point. There wasn't that big of a gap between them. The biggest difference between their schedules this year was that Chuck had AP Physics and AP English, and he could keep them. They'd both been involved in Boy Scouts when they were younger, with Mark reaching the rank of Eagle Scout before Chuck primarily because he wanted to prove he could.

On the last day of the trip, Chuck was surprised to see Mark awake and ready to go first. It had always been the other way around. Mark still looked tired as he had every other morning, but this was still an impressive accomplishment.

"I've got a challenge," Chuck announced, looking away as Mark changed into his suit.

"Go for it," Mark replied, pulling on his boots.

"No crashing."

"No crashing?" Mark repeated, considering the challenge carefully as he stood up and walked over to the same spot as every morning before.

"No crashing on forward flight, and no hard landings coming down from balancing," Chuck clarified.

Mark paused and thought. This was hard. He hadn't done either of those things yet. Every balancing act ended with a heavy thud and his feet plummeted into the soft sand. But he didn't want to turn it down. He knew he wouldn't always be able to count on a soft landing.

Chuck turned around and faced his friend, waiting for a reply.

"Sure," Mark finally replied with a shrug and a nod before he pulled on his mask. "Why not?" After a pause he added, "What's in it if I win?"

"Fifty bucks."

"Done," Mark accepted instantly, slapping Chuck's hand in agreement before his feet lifted him off the ground again.

"And you need to be in the air for at least ten seconds each time," Chuck added, making sure that Mark wouldn't just jump and try to count it.

Mark rolled his eyes beneath the mask, as if Chuck knew exactly what he was planning on doing. As he counted to ten in his head, he gently lowered himself down to the ground, sand flying out in all directions beneath the boots' heat. "One."

"Twenty-seven more," Chuck pointed out.

Mark took to the air again, this time giving himself a very quick count before landing just as smoothly as he did before. He repeated the next ten or so at a similarly rapid pace before he realized just how tired he was. The energy he was using to come down carefully was tiring him out, he never realized how much he had been saving by just dropping down. Mark paused and tried to catch his breath.

"No breaks," Chuck declared.

Mark shot a tiny blast of fire at Chuck's feet to shut him up.

"You have energy to waste on fireballs?" Chuck pressed on.

"Not wasted if I enjoyed wasting it," Mark replied, standing himself straight up, hands resting on his head as he took a few deep breaths. He was starting to get a cramp in his side like he had just sprinted a mile.

Chuck stood there and let Mark catch his breath without further protest.

With a big sigh, Mark went back to work. He performed each one even faster than before, trying to get it over with as soon as possible. Each time he landed he clutched at his side, trying to work out the ever-growing cramp. Finally, Chuck relieved him.

"Alright, by my count that's twenty-five. Now just three distance flights."

Mark grinned from ear to ear under his mask, which was becoming wet from all the sweat. Three more and I'm done, he thought. Three more for fifty dollars.

"How far?" Mark asked, trying his best to hide how winded he was.

Chuck scanned the landscape for a suitable landmark. He spotted it.

"That rock out there," Chuck answered, pointing in its general direction.

Mark looked for himself. He didn't see it at first. He squinted and tried to get a better look, positioning himself right behind

Chuck's finger to make sure he was looking exactly where he needed to. The lens had fogged up only a tiny bit, which was admittedly impressive considering how much Mark had been sweating. He spotted it, a good hundred yards away, sticking out of the sand. It was the only rock Chuck could be pointing to.

"That's a football field away," Mark declared, half-frustrated, half-exhausted.

Chuck didn't say anything, but simply shrugged, suggesting that if Mark didn't like it, he could quit. No way, there was money on the line.

Mark took off and shot through the air to the rock and swung around so quickly it nearly gave him whiplash. He nearly crashed feet-first into his starting point but slowed his approach just in time.

"Two more."

Heat from Mark's soles propelled him forward rapidly. When he reached the rock, he swung the lower half of his body around and blasted forward like a shot. This time the landing was less gentle, sending sand all over Chuck's shoes. Chuck glared at Mark to give a warning.

Mark breathed deeply and his eyes glowed brighter before he flew off again. But this time he didn't fly off at breakneck speed along the ground. This time, Mark flew high above the sand, taking in the sights around him as Chuck yelled for him to come down before he blew their cover. Mark ignored him. There wasn't anyone around that was looking for him. The only people out now were joggers, and they were all focused on the path in front of them.

Mark moved swiftly towards the rock and, when he was above it, flipped and twisted to turn himself around. He liked the feeling of weightlessness, and performed a few more acrobatic feats in midair, seemingly getting his second wind. Chuck stood powerless at the other end, unwilling to shout at Mark out of fear of discovery. Instead, he just fumed and made angry faces and considered telling Mark this violated the spirit of the bet, and he wouldn't pay.

Soon enough, Mark began his trip back to the starting point, traveling even higher into the sky. He had been so caught up in hovering just above the surface that he seldom actually explored all the space now available above him. In a passing thought, he told himself it was out of respect to Chuck standing there earth-bound. But that was a lie. He just had been too narrow-sighted to go for it. Well, no more.

Mark arched his body and began an even steeper upward ascent. As he climbed higher and higher, he focused not on the ground below him as it grew smaller and smaller, but on the approaching clouds as they grew larger and larger. Mark flew into the midst of a giant puffy cumulus cloud and hung there. He moved his hands through the cloud curiously. He knew that it was just water vapor, just gas. But to be inside of one and to experience how it truly felt like nothing was something else entirely.

Mark felt the wind blow against his back and swam against it as he would a wave, as it pushed the cloud away from him, his body instinctively distributing heat to keep him balanced. The sun shone bright into his eyes, despite Chuck's use of a UV-blocking lens in the mask. Mark looked down and saw just how tiny everything looked from where he was. He couldn't even see the rock anymore, and Chuck was barely noticeable. It made him a bit dizzy. Mark took a slow, deep breath to calm himself and started back down, feet-first. As he descended, he thought he noticed a jogger briefly glance up at him and upped his pace before the jogger had the opportunity to look closer.

The jogger had, in fact, seen Mark flying that day and quickly snapped a single, blurry photo taken on his camera phone. It wasn't until a month later, after Mark's official debut as a hero, that the jogger was taken seriously.

Mark landed a few feet in front of Chuck, this landing barely displacing any sand on impact. Mark ripped off his mask and slicked back his hair, now soaking with sweat.

"That's fifty you owe me," Mark declared, louder than Chuck would've liked.

FOUR
Enter Solarflare

"It's got to be today," Mark muttered to himself as he stood in front of the TV, watching the news with an excitement that seemed more appropriate for a child on Christmas morning than a high school Senior on the last day of his summer vacation. Yet, here he was, grinning from ear to ear and frantically trying to reach his best friend.

Mark had just turned seventeen a few days prior, but this news broadcast was putting every birthday and Christmas that he could remember to shame.

"No," Chuck answered on the other end of the phone. He knew why Mark was calling and did not share Mark's enthusiasm on this breaking news story.

"Trust me, this is a good idea," Mark pleaded into his cell phone. He needed Chuck's help to pull this off.

"This is an awful idea," Chuck said, once again acting as the voice of reason. "I know for a fact that you're only at home right now because you still have summer assignments you need to finish. Do those instead. No superheroism until you've finished your homework."

While Mark wanted to put his long-developing plan into action, Chuck wanted Mark to finish the last of his summer assignments. Normal summer stuff. He wished Mark shared the same summer priorities as him.

Mark held the phone away from his face and angled it towards the television, so Chuck could hear the news alert.

"Yeah, I'm aware of what's happening," Chuck said, his voice devoid of excitement at the prospect.

"It's a great idea. There's a supervillain robbing a bank downtown and I'm going to go fight him." Mark explained as he sprinted up the stairs to his room. "Summer assignments can wait."

"I'm not doing it. I'm not helping you with this. This is crazy."

"We've been talking about me doing this for months. Now a supervillain finally shows up and you want me to sit out?"

"I never thought we would actually be following through with this. Who would've thought supervillains would be real, too? And again, you still have homework."

"Please. You knew I was serious since day one. Okay, I'll check back with you in a few minutes. Bye." Mark didn't give Chuck's comment about summer assignments the dignity of a response a second time.

"I'm not going —" Chuck began, but there was no one on the other side at this point.

Chucked stared at his phone in angry disbelief before resigning himself to go get ready. Mark was going to need his help on this one.

Mark thought about how Chuck wouldn't be happy that he had hung up on him. He quickly justified it as a problem for later.

Mark sprinted into his room, slammed the door, and tore open his closet. Behind all of the dress shirts he never wore, Mark had hidden something: his superhero costume.

Mark pulled out the supersuit that he and Chuck had spent much of the summer working on. He had been waiting for months to have a reason to use this. Now it was finally that time.

Mark had put on the suit countless times before. He had done dozens of speed-runs so that he'd be able to put it on and take it off as quickly as possible. Yet, even with all that preparation, he was still fumbling to put it on. He tripped twice just trying to get his legs into the holes, the second time convincing him to just figure it out on the ground and go from there. Once his pants were on, he pulled on his boots. He hopped to his feet and threw on the top of his suit and his gloves. Those gave him much less trouble.

Mark glanced into the mirror before he put on the mask. He had always taken time to admire the costume every time he put it on. This was no exception. He had always felt more confident wearing it, even if it was just in his room for a few minutes before going to bed. Mark had been a comic book nerd for as long as he could remember, but he always tried to hide it. This costume was his way of coming to terms with that. He wouldn't just be another fan. He would get to live it. This was his chance.

Mark gripped the mask tightly before putting it on. The mask was made to cover his whole face. Mark wasn't exactly thrilled about that. Honestly, a small part of him wanted to show off his teeth. Why else spend so many years in braces if you can't show them off? Then Chuck had mentioned that they'd be more likely to be knocked out in a fight if they were uncovered. The whole mask issue was one of Mark and Chuck's biggest design arguments.

"I'm just saying, why would it be such a bad thing for me to show part of my face? Plenty of superheroes do it," Mark had asserted weeks ago, two days before the beach trip. He held up his hand halfway along his face, indicating where he felt the mask could cut off.

"It's an awful idea. Most superheroes prefer to stick to the shadows. You like attention too much. And also, as I keep bringing up, other superheroes aren't real," Chuck explained. "There is no way you'll be able to stay away from the spotlight. And that spotlight will catch anything and everything we leave exposed. Think about how many people on the internet will try to figure out who you are. Think of the time and resources that some people have. We have to hide everything."

Mark sat quietly for a minute, examining the mask that Chuck had made. The mask was orange with a pair of stylish snowboarding goggles incorporated. That was Mark's idea; he thought they'd look cool. He was right, it did look cool.

Mark liked it. It was simple, yet clear. They had been arguing about costume design for weeks now. The mask was the first concrete piece of this exercise in absurdity.

"The more general and vague they are in their assumptions about you, the better off we'll be at keeping this a secret. Eyes, mouth, nose, anything could give you away. If we let them make the standard assumptions, like that you're white, we'll both be better off since they'll be wrong."

"It might lead them to you, though. You're white," Mark suggested as he pulled the mask on over his face for the first time.

"True. I am white. But I'm covered. Why do think I joined the cross-country team?"

Chuck was too focused on his computer to notice Mark fiddling with the mask. They still needed a design for the full costume. They had decided on the general color scheme a few weeks ago: mostly yellow, some orange, and a little red. Warm colors but in ratios that hadn't been done too excessively in fiction. Even if other heroes weren't real, it was still important that Mark's look be distinct. They just needed to wrap it all up.

"Oh yeah, you did mention that. I assumed it was just you being awful at decision-making. Why not football or something people actually care about?"

"I chose cross-country because people don't care about it, but it gives me plenty of alibis," Chuck explained as he turned away from the computer. He didn't even react to Mark wearing the mask. "They practice every weekday, either morning or afternoon, and have meets almost every Saturday. If I chose football, it would've been too easy for me to lead a secret life on the side. I'd have my entire weekends free."

"But you are leading a secret life," Mark pointed out as he pulled the mask off. "You're mission control. You deal with the non-superhero aspects of me being a superhero."

"I know. But most people would assume that keeping up grades, college applications, and cross-country wouldn't leave any time for this kind of vigilante nonsense. They'll be wrong, of course, but they're going to assume it."

"You really think you can handle all of this without it seeming suspicious?"

"I like a challenge."

"Fair enough," Mark conceded as he continued to fidget thoughtfully with the mask. "The mask fits well. I can see out of the goggles okay, but it does take me a second to adjust them after I put it on."

"You'll probably get used to it the more you wear it. Right now, I think the goggles are the best option. They cover the eyes well, protect against glare —"

"And they look cool. So, there's that. Yeah, I'm sure it'll get more natural."

"Ok," Chuck began as he grabbed his laptop and wheeled around to show Mark. "How do you like this for the design?"

Mark leaned forward and carefully examined the proposed suit. The suit was mostly yellow with orange along the sides and the ribs, as well as just below the neck. Gloves and boots were also orange, with a flame design connecting them to the rest of the suit. Mark really liked it, except for one flaw.

"It's too empty."

"What?"

"Too empty. I need a logo, or something."

"Ok. What if we use a red triangle?"

"Why?"

"It's the alchemical symbol for fire," Chuck said as he added the logo to the suit on his computer, "That's why we drew triangles to represent energy when we did equations in AP Chem. How's this?"

Mark looked at the screen and shook his head.

"No. It's too simple."

"Simple is good. It's iconic, recognizable."

"It's not mine. It's something people have been using for hundreds of years. And it's boring. We need something more substantial."

"Ok. What do you suggest then?"

"Maybe the Chinese character for fire? It's simple and iconic, and it's a lot more interesting than a triangle."

"That one's also not our idea, either. And it has also been used for hundreds of years, if not thousands." Chuck lectured, getting more and more frustrated with each word. "And what were we just talking about? You cannot give people any hint that you're Chinese. Especially not one as big and obvious as that."

"Well, I'm not just going with a triangle. I'm not Triangleman," Mark muttered in a barely audible voice.

"We don't even have a name yet?" Chuck practically shouted, shocked at this somehow sudden revelation. Mark tried to read if this was a bit or not. "How have we done this much work without a name? We are idiots."

"Relax, I got a name: Fireman." Mark said, confident that they had already had this conversation. It was settled.

"No."

"It's simple, it's elegant."

"It's confusing. People still call firefighters 'firemen.' It needs to be more original."

"Okay. Then what are you thinking?"

"Well, you got your powers when that solar-energy reactor flared up back in May, why not go from there?"

Mark grinned from ear to ear. "Oh. I've got it."

Back on the day of the robbery and northern Virginia's first supervillain appearance, Mark was all suited up. He turned to his open laptop, pulled up his music library and set the playlist to "shuffle" with the volume down low. If anyone tried to get him, it would sound like he was just working on his homework and listening to music. A decent enough cover for now, at least until he and Chuck worked out the kinks. He climbed out of his bedroom window and swung himself up onto the roof. His mother would kill him if she knew he was up there. He kept himself crouched down so no one would notice him and scanned the street. Plenty of people were outside on this, one of the last days of summer, but they were all preoccupied. No one was going to look up. He was good to go.

Mark jumped into the air as hard as he could and, at the top of his arc, let his boots do their thing. Chuck had, repeatedly and very pedantically, pointed out that Mark should avoid making direct contact between his superheated boots and anything that he did not want to catch ablaze. The roof was such a thing. With minimal effort directed to the soles of his feet, Mark was flying up to the treetops. As Mark cleared the trees, he paused for a moment to enjoy this moment of peace. It would be the last one in his life for a long time.

In just a few short minutes, Mark was in downtown Delfield, near the bank robbery. Mark had landed on a nearby building and looked down to scope out the situation. As he approached the scene, he grinned so hard that he was sure it could be seen through the mask. This was the real deal.

A large, tawny figure pushed through the wrecked entranceway, dragging behind him a large sack, presumably filled with stolen cash. The only thing missing from this picture was a dollar sign on the man's bag.

The robber, or supervillain, depending on who was describing him, was at least 8 feet tall with an incredibly disproportionate body shape. His torso was massive. It took up at least 75 percent of him. His arms and chest looked like overinflated balloons covered in spikes, and his legs and head looked comically small. If bystanders weren't so afraid of him, they probably would've been laughing.

"This is the police," an amplified voice announced, "We have you surrounded. Drop the bag and place your hands over your head."

Mark's stomach sank. He didn't come all this way to have the guy just turn himself in, did he? Why did he waste so much time?

"You could have another hundred officers here and it wouldn't even be close to enough," the criminal replied, his voice booming.

Yes, Mark thought almost selfishly. Time for some heroics.

The figure grabbed a nearby parking meter and flung it at the nearest police car. The meter barely missed an officer and embedded itself halfway through the door. He was serious. And strong. He was very, very strong.

One officer started firing at the villain. The bullets bounced off his armor. If the villain felt it at all, it didn't show. He wasn't going to be stopped that easily. He ripped another parking meter out of the ground and advanced.

Other officers opened fire against the villain, but to no avail. The targeted officer backed up, still firing, until he ran out of ammo. The figure raised the meter in his hand and prepared to strike.

"Hey!" Mark yelled out as he leapt from his building, flying straight towards the attacker.

Mark flew down from his vantage point and tackled the enemy, knocking him away from the officer and causing him to drop his weapon.

Mark got to his feet, rubbing his head and wishing that he had said something more clever or iconic than *"Hey!"* He could've made a joke about how no one likes to pay for parking, but the moment had passed.

The nearby crowd of onlookers began taking pictures and recording on their cell phones. The villain was one thing, but this challenger had flown right out of the sky to stop him. He must be a superhero, many of them exclaimed.

Mark's costume looked incredible, many other passersby mentioned. Mark's ears couldn't help but pick up on the conversations. They liked the yellow and orange color scheme with the red belt and logo. They loved the logo. Mark and Chuck had finally found something they agreed on.

The logo was a red sun. A red circle surrounded by eight stylized red triangles. Mark knew that this was the kind of image that would stick with people.

"Who do you think you are, punk?" The figure asked as he picked himself up, muscles quaking with anger. The villain's entire body, from head to toe, appeared to be covered in a synthetic skin that had caused his *unique* shape. Even the man's face was completely covered. His eyes, ears, nose, and mouth were all present and visible, but they were fully enmeshed with his suit. If ever there was a real-world application for the uncanny valley, this was it.

Mark's answer came out like a reflex, with a confidence that had never been there when he rehearsed it by himself.

"I'm the guy who's going to stop you."

The villain laughed until Mark continued.

"And who are you?"

The laughing ceased. A look of sheer annoyance immediately fell over the criminal's face. This job was more trouble than it was worth, he thought. Still, the least he could do before he killed this poor kid was tell him his name.

"Name's 'Pufferfish.'"

Mark giggled. Then he tried to affect a deeper laugh, just in case any of the amateur videographers caught the audio of this encounter.

"Makes sense," Mark offered between laughs. It was a terrible name. "Can I make a suggestion?"

"I'm not going to let you live, if that's what you're going to suggest," he asserted as he cracked his massive hands, getting ready for what he knew would be a merciless beating.

"Wasn't going to ask for that," Mark countered, holding his ground. "Don't think I'll need to. What I was going to say is that if you drop the 'fish,' it might sound a little better. Shorter, maybe more intimidating."

"I think I'm intimidating enough," Puffer replied with a scowl.

"Not really," Mark chuckled as he warmed up his own hands. "To me, you look like a big marshmallow. With a few toothpicks sticking out."

"Really?" Puffer was getting really annoyed now. He was ready to end this.

"Yeah. And I'm gonna roast you," Mark answered as he unleashed a fireball from his fist, knocking Puffer off his feet and hard onto the sidewalk. The crowd gasped. Did they really just see this man shoot fire?

Mark laughed. He knew he shouldn't get cocky, but it was hard not to. This guy had been asking for it. He was a jerk. And he had tried to hurt and kill people; that was much worse. And now Mark was going to be the one to send him to jail.

"Don't like fire? Fish normally don't."

Puffer climbed up just to his knees and let out a primal roar. Beneath his suit, something was happening to his muscles. Puffer's torso nearly doubled in size and the needles sticking from his suit became even more pronounced. Smaller needles also appeared on the ridges of his knuckles. Built-in brass knuckles. Cool, Mark thought with almost a nervous admiration.

Mark gulped. Sweat on the bridge of his nose started to fog up his goggles. The air beneath his mask became stale from too many nervous breaths. Was it too late to back out now?

He looked around. All the people nearby were fixated on him. They wanted to see how this turned out. They were more excited by Mark than they were afraid of Puffer. That was enough for him right now. He could do this. He was ready for this.

"Scared?" Puffer asked in-between heavy breaths.

"No. You can't see it under this mask, but I've been making funny faces at you for the last few minutes," Mark answered as he gestured to his face. He kept mocking the criminal. That was the plan. "You know, like people do when trying to console a baby having a tantrum."

"Save it."

"It might be better for you to save it," Mark pointed out. "You getting a little winded there, Stay Puft?" Mark mocked his adversary's heavy breathing. It seemed to strike a nerve.

Puffer lunged at Mark and put all his might into a single, devastating punch. If it had made contact, the fight surely would've been over. Instead, Mark was able to quickly dodge the blow with a small blast of fire from his feet. The boots propelled Mark back several feet from the crater made in the sidewalk by Puffer's fist.

"Swing and a miss," Mark chimed as Puffer pulled his fist from the concrete.

Puffer stood. His breathing was even heavier now. Whatever was in the suit that allowed him to increase size and strength was clearly taking a toll on him. Mark could basically just play the waiting game if he could manage to avoid getting hit. But where was the fun in that?

"Is it my turn now?" Mark called. "You go, then I go, right?"

Puffer let loose another roar and leapt for Mark. Another fireball caught him in the air and brought him down onto his backside.

"It was my turn," Mark protested. "First, I go, then you go, then you go again, and so on. Come on, man, it's basic playground rules."

The crowd was loving this. Mark was in heaven. This was almost too easy.

A right hook took Mark out of his daydream. He flew from the sidewalk into the side of a police car. The impact left a massive dent in the door and Mark crumpled on the street. This guy was faster than he looked.

Mark's head was spinning. He got cocky. And it hurt. He wasn't about to make that mistake again. He wasn't sure he could afford to.

"How's that?" Puffer jeered. He was certainly cocky for a guy who seemed like he was on the ropes a few seconds ago.

Mark pulled himself up using the car for support. His head was pounding. He looked in the car's rearview mirror. Luckily, Puffer's punch hadn't torn through the mask. Whatever material Chuck used to make it was working perfectly.

"Barely felt it," Mark lied. "I didn't expect you to hit me. You're pretty quick for a guy who clearly skips leg-day at the gym."

"Let's just end this," Puffer declared.

Mark's fists tightened and his eyes glowed red-hot beneath his mask. He braced himself against the car for what was about to come. "I agree."

Puffer once again let out a primal scream as he launched himself at Mark with his right arm once again cocked back. This would be his finishing move.

Mark screamed back as he unleashed a blast of flame from both his fists. Even with all his momentum, Puffer was easily thrown back against the building, knocking him unconscious. He fell, for the last time on this day, to the sidewalk below as onlookers continued to photograph and record the event.

The crowd erupted into cheers.

Mark slowly approached Puffer, his first supervillain. He was proud, if not more than a little sore. As he neared his unconscious enemy, Mark heard the whirling and popping noises of broken electronics squeaking from Puffer's suit. The suit slowly began to deflate to the size of an average man. Mark knelt down to get a closer look.

"Stop right there!" a voice commanded.

One of the police officers stood just a few feet behind Mark, his gun drawn. Mark placed his hands in the air and slowly turned around, complying with the officer's demands.

"Who are you and what do you want?" the officer demanded.

"I just came to help," Mark answered coolly as he slowly began to hover off the ground. He added, to appear more polite, "sir."

Before he took off, he needed to make sure that everyone knew one thing. He raised his voice and announced just who he was.

"And since you asked, I'm Solarflare."

FIVE

Immediate Aftermath

"Did you see that?" Mark shouted into his cellphone as he landed atop a building several blocks down from the bank. Eight blocks south, four blocks west. Chuck had figured that would be far enough away from the excitement for Mark to change back into street clothes to avoid any suspicion.

Three months ago, Mark was just the kid who passed out during the field trip. He never could have imagined he'd one day be dressed in a bright yellow and orange suit, shooting fireballs at a man covered in spikes with bulletproof skin. But he had just done exactly that. Life is funny like that sometimes.

"Yeah," Chuck replied, seemingly distracted by something other than his friend's superhero debut. "You let him punch you in the face. That wasn't part of the plan. What if the mask was compromised? Or, you know, if that punch killed you? He was a big guy."

Mark sighed audibly into the phone. "Seriously?"

"Yeah," Chuck shot back, annoyed but still sounding very much distracted. "We talked about the importance of a full face-mask in keeping your identity secret."

"Well then, I guess it's a good thing that your hypersilk, or whatever you called this stuff, held up. Am I bothering you right now?"

"Little bit, yeah."

Mark unleashed a slew of expletives into the microphone. "Are you serious? I follow all your rules and you can't even congratulate me on a job well done? Fine then, I guess this can just be a one-off kind of deal, then."

"Just hang on," Chuck murmured.

Mark looked at the skyline around him. There was a lot of excitement in the distance, but luckily, it didn't appear anyone was looking for him where he was currently. The sun was about to set pretty soon. Mark glanced at the clock on his phone. It was already almost 6 o'clock. He groaned as he thought of the summer assignments he still had to do.

"Done." Chuck declared proudly.

"Done with what?"

"Done with building you an online presence and substantial buzz. You're welcome."

"What are you talking about?"

"As soon as the fight started, I began to post links to the live news coverage on different websites, using different usernames, emails, IP addresses, all that stuff. Untraceable. Then, just before you announced your name, I trademarked it and launched multiple, mediocre fansites. Basically, I prevented any massive corporation from declaring your name or suit or anything else to be their intellectual property which would leave us dead in the water."

Mark was momentarily stunned. He didn't know much about computers or intellectual property law, but it sounded like Chuck knew what he was doing. There was a lot of logistical stuff that Mark hadn't even thought about.

"Uh, thanks."

"No problem. So, are you back at your place already?"

"No," Mark nearly shouted in disbelief. The fight had barely been over for 5 minutes at this point. "I'm on top of some building, catching my breath, waiting for you to pick me up."

"That wasn't part of the plan," Chuck chimed in off-handedly as he continued to type away on his computer.

"That was always part of the plan. I do hero-things, you deal with the nuts and bolts."

"Yeah, like intellectual property rights of your persona and an online presence and supplying you with a costume."

"I felt like extraction would've been covered by that umbrella of responsibilities."

"Can't you fly?" Chuck quipped. "I'm pretty sure when I made you the costume, I found a way for you to use your powers for flight."

"Yeah, well, I'm tired and there are police helicopters, and I could be seen," Mark pathetically countered.

"Okay, but the alternative is me waiting over an hour in traffic to go just a few miles with the streets filled with police and pick you up, before sitting in even worse traffic on the way back home. And am I supposed to supply you with a change of clothes? Maybe a juice box?"

"Traffic isn't that bad."

"Traffic here is always that bad. Even when people aren't flocking to see the aftermath of a superpowered showdown on Main Street. I've got traffic on my phone right now. Trust me, it's that bad."

"It was on Jefferson Avenue," Mark corrected sheepishly.

"Whatever. The point is, I can't pick you up. We should've discussed this more before you went out. My bad. I'll send out a false alert on police radios that you're half a mile north of your location. That should throw off the helicopters and most squad cars."

"That'll work. Thanks," Mark agreed as he adjusted his mask back into proper position and headed for the edge of the roof.

"Don't mention it. And Mark," Chuck added, "You did a good job. You'll be a real superhero in no time."

Mark smiled as he hung up the phone and secured it in the pocket of his suit's pants. He realized that next time he should probably leave the cellphone at home. Mark climbed up onto the barrier along the edge of the roof and stood proudly for a moment. He took in a deep breath and felt the setting sun renew his energy before he took to the skies once more. A single thought occupied his brain.

"I am Solarflare."

"Mark," a voice called out, banging loudly on the other side of the door, "Get up, you and your brother are going to be late."

Mark groaned and rolled over in his bed, dragging the entirety of his sheets and comforter along with him. Several thoughts flooded his mind. Why did he have to make his hero debut on the last day of summer? Why did he have to stay up until 3 a.m. finishing up summer assignments? He knew the answer to that one. He was a habitual procrastinator, but he just hated to admit it. How could his mom's voice be so loud so early in the morning?

Mark managed to open his eyes, ever so slightly. He glanced at the clock on his phone. It was almost 7 a.m. He needed to be at school by 7:30.

"Twenty-five more minutes," Mark muttered through his pillow.

The knocking persisted. He knew how this worked. She was just going to stand outside his door until he got up and opened it. He knew it would never work to try and sleep through it.

With an angry groan, Mark dragged his body out of bed and stumbled to the door.

"I'm up," he weakly announced as he cracked open the door.

"Good morning to you too," Mrs. Michaels replied, "Happy first day of school. Sean's already downstairs, ready to go soon."

"Okay then," Mark murmured as he shuffled to the bathroom, "I'll be down in like 10 minutes, and we can go."

"Please hurry. I don't want you two to be late."

Mark nodded weakly before shutting the bathroom door. He took a glance in the bathroom mirror to gauge how tired he looked. Not too bad. He checked to make sure the door was locked and looked again. He focused and his eyes flashed a bright crimson. Mark smiled. He was already feeling more awake now. It was amazing having this kind of energy whenever he wanted it. And yesterday, the whole world saw him make his debut. This was going to be an exciting day.

Eleven minutes later, Mark casually strolled down the stairs, ready for his Senior year of high school.

"Finally," Sean called out when he saw his brother. He was not particularly patient. The first day of school was important to him; more so than it was to Mark. Every aspect of Sean's appearance on this day — from his stylized hair to his preppy clothes — looked like it had been lifted from a catalog. "We're going to be late."

"You look like a member of a Korean boy band," Mark replied as he made a beeline for the kitchen pantry. They weren't going to be late. They weren't going to be particularly early, but they were fine on time. He grabbed a Pop-Tart from the box and began unwrapping it with his teeth.

"We need to get going," Sean pressed on.

Mark said nothing as he moved around the house collecting his various books and homework assignments from the summer. He stuffed them into his backpack and counted on his fingers to make sure he had everything he needed. He paused.

"I'll be right back," Mark announced through a mouthful of toaster pastry as he made his way back up the stairs. He ignored his brother's muttered grievances as he headed for the stairs.

Back in his bedroom, Mark grabbed the last of his assignments and books off his desk. There. That was everything he needed. Or, at least, everything he could think of right now. He zipped up his backpack and started for the door. As he crossed his room, his eyes were drawn to his closet where his Solarflare suit was.

"I should probably make sure I hid it well," Mark murmured.

There it was, just like it had been before yesterday evening: safely tucked away behind a row of dress shirts he never wore. He held the suit's sleeve and lingered for a moment. Maybe he should take it with him. What if he needed it during the day? What if Puffer came back? Or what if some new villain showed up before school was out? His mind raced with all of the reasons he might need the suit.

"Mark!" Sean shouted, interrupting Mark's contemplation, "Get down here! We need to leave now!"

"I cannot believe you," Sean snapped as he slammed the passenger-side car door shut as they arrived at the school parking lot.

"I said I was sorry," Mark groaned before snapping back, "And don't slam my door."

"I told you I wanted to get here early."

"And I wanted to sleep in a few minutes. I had a lot more summer assignments than you did. I was up late finishing them. If you hate waiting for me, take the bus or walk. We still have plenty of time —" Mark began to say, but was cut off by the first warning bell.

"Yeah, plenty of time. I've got all of five minutes to get to my first class on the opposite side of the building," Sean hissed sarcastically as he stomped towards the school.

Mark rolled his eyes as he reached into the car and grabbed his bag. Five minutes was more than enough time. Not that it really mattered today. The first day of school always allowed a short grace period for people who were late. There was still a line of cars waiting to enter the parking lot.

Mark lingered by the car for a moment. He wasn't wearing the suit right now. He had managed to sneak it undetected into the trunk of his car, partially in case of emergency, partially because he liked seeing it.

"Maybe I'll need it today." His thumb gently caressed the trunk-open button on his key-fob. He looked around and saw that there were still a lot of students in the parking lot. Too risky. He couldn't chance that someone would see the suit and make the connection.

Mark headed for the school's entrance. Another year, he thought, a final chance at a truly great high school experience. His previous years weren't bad or anything. They just weren't great. He was a Senior now. Top of the high school food chain. And also, a superhero. This was his year.

Mark casually strolled up to the large double doors to the school's side entrance. There was a line to get in. He craned his neck to see what was going on. Inside of the school, students were being waved down with security wands and undergoing bag checks.

Good call on leaving the suit in the car, Mark thought.

Mark overheard a snippet of a nearby conversation. "You know that supervillain they caught yesterday? Turns out they can't remove his suit or whatever, it's like fused to his body."

"Hey Mark," Chuck called out from alongside the doors as Mark neared the front of the line. Mark shot him a confused glance. Chuck held up his large, now half-empty water bottle and gestured with it before taking a giant swig. Mark was still confused.

"No outside liquids in unsealed containers," Chuck explained in-between gulps.

"They can't be serious," Mark replied incredulously. "What is this, the airport?"

"Oh, they are very serious," Chuck sighed as he finished the bottle and tossed it into the nearby recycling can and rejoined the line. "Apparently, the appearance of a supervillain and superhero last night is cause for increased security at every school within the city."

"Yeah, they've this going on at Colonial too," a voice beside the two spoke up as he was being patted down by a security officer.

"Hey Robbie," Mark and Chuck answered in unison. They glared at one another. Answering in unison was weird. Robbie chuckled and the security guard waved him through.

"I thought you guys were going for the football team this year?" Robbie asked as Mark offered up his backpack to be checked. "Seniors usually make the varsity team, pretty much by default. No offense."

Mark shrugged. "None taken."

Robbie wasn't worried about not making the varsity team himself, though. He had been in starting positions since his Freshman year. At around 5'10", Robbie Perez wasn't quite as tall as Mark or Chuck, but he was more physically imposing. The high school coaches usually shuffled him to wherever they needed him most. Basically, any skill-position on the team, he could do, and he could do it better than anyone else at the school. He had been getting recruitment letters from top football schools for so long that his mother was pretty much on a first-name basis with several athletic program directors.

"Nah, I'm going out for cross-country this year," Chuck answered, craning his head around Mark's bag check.

"Cross-country?" Robbie repeated with a laugh, "Running for no reason? Why would you want to do that?"

Chuck poked his stomach and shrugged.

Robbie laughed. "What about you, Mark? You were a solid kicker Freshman year."

Mark had indeed been a decent kicker. Nowhere near good enough for varsity at the time, but he knew the technique. His dad had been a kicker in high school himself. Maybe the skill was genetic. Or maybe his dad was a better coach than Mark had ever given him credit for.

Mark thought for a moment before he came up with the perfect response.

"My mom doesn't want me playing," he explained as the security guard's wand waved up his torso, internally breathing a sigh of relief for leaving the suit in the car.

"Really?" Rob asked incredulously. "Not even kicker?"

"Yeah, not even kicker," Mark continued, "She saw some college kicker get absolutely wrecked during a game last year and she forbade me from even thinking of trying out this year. If she found out I played football, even as a kicker, I'd be a dead man."

Robbie took a moment and nodded thoughtfully.

"Yeah," he noted after a pause, "My mom's a little too protective. I told her that it was what my dad taught me and she backed off."

This was a touchy subject.

Robbie's father had died years ago. Mark and Chuck had gone to school with Robbie since elementary school. They knew the story, but never dared bring it up. Mark had met him a few times. He was a youth soccer coach, he was involved at school, and he and Mr. Michaels were pretty good friends. To be honest, the sudden death of Mr. Perez probably hit Mr. Michaels harder than it hit Mark.

"He'd be proud of you, man," Chuck said calmly, breaking the silence as he too stepped into the security sweep.

"Thanks, man," Robbie laughed, as he moved his hand to scratch his chin, possibly to hide any excess emotion.

"Seriously," Mark added, "So, what position are you in this year?"

"I'm QB," Robbie confessed after a moment. Quarterback was the heart and soul of any football team. No team was great without a great quarterback. And Robbie was ready to place that pressure on his shoulders. "I know coach wanted me in a receiving position, but this is what I want. I know I can get the job done," he finished slowly. "It's what my dad played."

Mark and Chuck shared a knowing glance. The quarterback was easily the most important position. Robbie had always been there to help cover up a quarterback's mistakes. He was that good. What if Robbie made a mistake? Who would cover for him?

"If that's what you want to do, do it," Mark declared. "It's yours for the taking."

The warning bell sounded.

"Alright guys," Robbie announced as he slung his backpack over his shoulder, "I'll catch up with you two later. I'm disappointed in you both for not going out for this school's real sport, though," he added with a laugh as he turned and walked off to class.

"Yeah, I'll see you too —" Mark began, but Robbie was gone.

"On the topic of football," Chuck quietly began as he approached Mark after his screening wrapped up and he was waved through, "We should go over your game tape from last night: what worked, what didn't work, what can be improved upon."

"Don't you have pointless running practice after school?" Mark asked.

"Cross-country had morning practice today," Chuck answered as they made their way down the hall, "It's something I'm able to wake up and do because I was able to go to sleep last night before 3 a.m." Did Chuck know Mark was up until 3 or was it just a lucky guess? "Because I, like some people, have decent time management skills and didn't put off an entire summer's worth of homework until the very last night of break."

Mark yawned angrily. "I will burn your backpack and all of your assignments to ashes."

"Oh, by the way, your girlfriend is also on the pointless-running team," Chuck casually mentioned as he stopped at the nearby water fountain. "And I heard she is officially single."

Mark rolled his eyes. Fighting the joke just made it worse.

"She looks good in shorts," Chuck said offhandedly between sips of water.

Mark's ears perked up and he blushed slightly.

"Whatever," Mark muttered, trying not to giggle as he said it, before addressing what Chuck said. "What do you mean 'can be improved upon'? I got the guy. That's the job."

Chuck finished drinking and stood up with a stern look in his eye.

"Yeah," Chuck replied curtly. "You stopped one guy, once. You have no idea if that was just a fluke. What if next time you face him, he doesn't go down so easily? What if there are others like him? What if they're stronger than he is?"

"There aren't going to be others like him," Mark shot back in a whisper, careful not to talk too loudly, "He was dressed in a balloon suit with spikes coming out of it. That's a once in a lifetime kind of deal."

"Yeah. And we found him within three months of you developing your powers. We agreed to wait for a daring daytime robbery for your debut because it would give you the introduction you wanted, and it would allow me greater control on releasing specific information. It would be a big step, a big adjustment for the world, but people would be able to handle it.

"But I wasn't expecting this. Instead of two big, separate steps away from normal, the world's suddenly thrown into the deep end of some comic-world. I was expecting something normal. Superhero versus criminals, and then maybe, eventually, several weeks or months down the line, a supervillain arrives. This is a game-changer. That guy was not the last. He was just the first. We need to make sure that you'll be ready when other guys like him turn up; otherwise, I'm on the hook for maintaining half a dozen Solarflare memorial websites."

Chuck grabbed his bag off the ground and flung it over his shoulder before walking away without another word.

Mark stood there for a moment. The weight of Chuck's words hit him hard. He had always pictured Solarflare going after supervillains at some point, but Chuck was right. His first fight ever should've been a bit more normal. The world had completely changed in the last twelve hours. First a supervillain, then a superhero. Things were far from normal now, and Mark was the last one to get the message.

This realization stayed with Mark all day.

SIX
Atlantis

"I have to tell you something," Chuck began, speaking slowly, nervously.

It was Friday afternoon and Mark had just arrived at Chuck's house. They were going to celebrate the conclusion of their final first week of high school the way they celebrated most things: with video games and junk food.

Mark stood where he was, nervously clutching his backpack, suddenly very uncomfortable with Chuck's tone.

"Could you sit down?" Chuck asked, avoiding eye contact with his friend.

Mark slowly sat on the couch. He shifted himself once and looked back at Chuck. Chuck's eyes were darting around the room, not wanting to stay fixed. Mark had known Chuck long enough to know that this was the equivalent of pacing in circles. Chuck did not get nervous like this.

Had they been found out? Did someone know Mark was Solarflare? He'd gone out in the suit one time. Yeah, getting caught was a risk, but he figured they had at least three or four months before anyone came close to finding out.

"You are not as special as you think," Chuck awkwardly blurted out after a several tense seconds.

"What?"

"You're not the only one who can do what you can do," he elaborated, much more calmly this time, but with a deep, sorrowful tone of voice. He turned away from Mark in what looked like shame and rubbed his temples deeply with one hand.

"You found other people?" Mark asked excitedly, ignoring Chuck's tone in light of this news. "Chuck, that's great! We can learn more about my powers. This is a good thing."

"No. No, it's not."

"Yeah, it is. We'll be able to learn so much —"

"I already know." Chuck said before repeating quietly, "I already know everything."

"Already know what?" Mark pressed, slowly and carefully, now fully appreciating the mood of the room.

"About what you are. I know everything about your powers. I've known since the beginning," Chuck finally continued, as if reciting a passage memorized a long time ago. "You are a man who cannot be harmed by flame, one who wields fire as an extension of himself. Hundreds of years ago, you would have been called a dragon, demon, or djinn. But the most recent name for what you are is 'pyrate.'"

Mark sat there with a bewildered look on his face for a moment.

"Demon... Dragon... Djinn... Pirate?" Mark muttered quietly as the words sank in.

Chuck nodded slowly. Suddenly it dawned on Mark.

"Pirate? Like Blackbeard?" Mark asked, realizing that Chuck had truly known everything since the beginning.

"Sort of. It comes from the Greek root, 'pyro' meaning 'fire.'" Chuck continued, as he appeared to have rehearsed. "Pyrates are a group of people — a race, I guess — that are able to control fire. The reason the word exists in English is that the term spread by word of mouth. Throughout history, pyrates used their skill to attack vessels on sea routes, more or less up until Blackbeard's era, and people believed that it described a thief. People had no idea what it really meant."

"Uh huh," Mark uttered as he gazed into the carpet, trying to take in all that he was hearing. "So how did you figure all this out?"

Chuck sat silently for a moment. He looked around the room and sighed deeply.

"If you don't want to tell me about how you came to this theory, I can leave. I can't do this," Mark muttered, and stood up to leave. But he wouldn't leave. He knew this was more than a theory. Chuck knew what was going on.

Chuck struggled to find the words.

"Tell me how you know all this," Mark demanded as he grabbed Chuck's arm, his eyes glowing a deep red.

Chuck said nothing but allowed his own eyes to flash a deep blue light in return.

Mark let go of his friend's arm in disbelief. He had seen his own eyes turn dozens of times. Honestly, he liked seeing it and would do it just to amuse himself. But this was entirely different. Mark's eyes returned to their normal brown.

"So, you're one too?" Mark asked as calmly as he could.

"No," Chuck replied softly as his own eyes faded. "It's more complicated than that."

"I've got time, if you want to explain."

Chuck smiled weakly and sat back down.

"I am not a pyrate," he began, "I am an Atlantean."

"What?"

"A merman, if that makes more sense. I was born in the city of Atlantis."

Mark glared at his friend. The last couple months, and last weekend especially, had strained his understanding of what was and was not real. If anyone else had said what Chuck just said, he would've called them a liar. But he believed his friend. "Atlantis is real too?"

"Yes. Anyway, I've had powers of my own for as long as I can remember."

"Like what?" Mark interrupted.

"I'm getting to it. Quit interrupting," Chuck laughed softly, attempting to ease the tension. It did not work. Mark was as tense as he'd ever been. "I can control water with my mind. If I'm underwater for an extended period of time, I can grow gills that allow me to breathe."

Mark remained seated, now glued to the couch, nodding as he processed all the new information. It could have been earth-shattering news, it should've been, but it made sense. If he could control fire, it would make sense that there would also be people out there that could control water. But he wondered why it took Chuck so long to tell him. What did he mean when he said that he knew *since the beginning*?

"You're not telling me something," Mark said cautiously. He was sure that Chuck still had something left to tell. Mark's eyes flared a bright red, almost reflexively.

Chuck reacted faster than Mark had ever thought possible. He sprung from behind the couch and pulled a narrow thread of water out of his water bottle and held it aloft in the air, poised and ready to strike like a whip.

"Calm down," he said slowly, taking a defensive stance, yet still holding his whip at the ready. "I told you it was complicated. It's going to take me a while to explain everything, but I promise I will tell you everything."

"Start talking," Mark muttered as his eyes returned to normal and he plopped back down into his seat.

Chuck slowly placed his whip back into the water bottle. He had expected a reaction like that from Mark. He hoped that the reaction meant it was already out of the way, but he knew Mark well enough to fear that this oncoming conversation and all the secrets it would reveal could inspire a few more, similar outbursts.

"Atlantis is real," Chuck began, starting with the basic facts that Mark would need to know in order to follow. "It's located in the Atlantic, somewhere in the Bermuda Triangle. The city is a little over a mile below the surface, and there's a big dome protecting it. I don't know where the dome came from or how it works, but it's about 300 years old."

Chuck paused for a moment, waiting for any objection from Mark. He continued.

"Atlanteans mastered sea travel before any other ancient society. They could swim and breathe underwater, but boats were as much a necessity for them as carts were for everyone on land. So, Atlantis used this to easily travel across the world, trading Atlantean tools and weapons for gold and other precious metals. Eventually, many Atlanteans began to live within these societies. Their knowledge and wealth gave them a position of power over the common people. The Romans were the first major example of this, though a few Atlanteans did live among the Greeks first. Under the rule of Atlantean-born consuls, Rome became the greatest empire the ancient world ever knew.

After the fall of Rome, people of Atlantean-descent retreated back to Atlantis. Rome's might had made them targets, hated for their position over others. The removal of Atlanteans from society led to the Dark Ages. Those who successfully made it back to the city were welcomed and protected. Atlantis isolated itself, becoming self-sufficient for hundreds of years. Atlantis became a myth, and its citizens were happy that way."

"And where exactly do the 'pyrates' fit in?" Mark asked, his face unreadable.

"Pyrates," Chuck further explained, "also built great empires in the ancient world. Command of fire led to forges, tools and weapons made of metal, rather than stone. Carthage was one, Egypt another. Egyptian pyrates traded skills and knowledge with Atlanteans and became familiar with boats and ships, as well. Carthage, on the other hand, was a pyrate empire that saw Rome as its enemy. And Rome saw Carthage as a threat to be dealt with. They fought for generations. Eventually, Carthage was defeated. Rome offered to spare many noble-born Carthaginian pyrates in exchange for knowledge and service. But they refused and were executed.

"This placed Egypt in an unfortunate position. Egypt had an understanding of and respect for the Roman people and Atlantis. But now many pyrate refugees who escaped Carthage were clamoring for revenge. They demanded that Egypt strike back, to avenge a fallen pyrate empire. But Egypt did not, and for around one hundred years, Egypt and Rome remained peaceful, and even shared their cultures with one another."

"So why did it go bad?"

"Unfortunately, the cries for revenge never truly faded away. When Cleopatra took the throne, she carried with her a desire to see Rome burn. She joined with Marc Antony and tried to help him win power."

"After Julius Caesar died, right?" Mark finished, remembering just enough of that era from world history classes.

"Exactly. She knew that if Antony won, she could command both empires. If Antony had any Atlantean lineage, it was heavily diluted. All of their children were born pyrates and developed powers early on. Once the civil war was over, if she needed to, she could remove Antony without much difficulty. Then, she could weaken Rome's strength from the inside and then lead her people in an assault to destroy Rome once and for all. Atlantis saw this coming and began to heavily isolate itself. But after Antony lost the naval battle of Actium, she knew that she had been defeated. She allowed a snake to bite her, and she died from the poison.

"When Augustus Caesar took power, he did so with full knowledge of exactly what Cleopatra had intended. He found the letters she and Marc Antony had exchanged and was so enraged that he had their children paraded through the city in shame before killing their oldest son. He expanded the Roman Empire so that there would be no nearby force of pyrates that could stand against him or Rome. Every emperor that followed him shared an equal, if not greater, hatred and distrust of pyrates. The gladiatorial games were designed to keep Roman pyrates distracted. They enjoyed fame and fortune, and if they seemed to be a threat to the peace of the empire, they could easily be put to death. And this went on for almost another five hundred years before the fall."

Mark had listened carefully. He had made a conscious effort to distance himself emotionally from these events while he listened. He sat in silence for a moment, waiting for Chuck to continue.

"Is that it?" Mark asked in a voice so calm that it seemed unnatural.

"More or less," Chuck confessed. "When Rome fell, neither pyrates nor Atlanteans had an empire to call their own. Their legacies still existed, but they became folded into ancient mythologies or religions. Occasionally, a pyrate or an Atlantean would rise to power in some nation or empire, but their desire to avenge an ancient loss always proved to be their undoing. They'd alienate their own citizens or attack another nation without cause. Western history is full of examples.

"The last major incident was Blackbeard. Going off of what I've read in Atlantean records, it is believed that he was either raised with knowledge of his powers, or that they awoke in him very early. By the end of the 17th century, he was working on ships as a privateer for the British Empire, but took a special pleasure in the looting and destruction of ships manned by anyone of Atlantean descent. His enthusiasm helped him become a captain and earn a loyal crew. Soon, he began to exclusively attack ships that he believed were sympathetic to Atlantis."

"How could he tell?"

"It was the way that they sailed," Chuck explained. "People are not made for the ocean. Sea travel in those days was exhausting and difficult. Food and water were always scarce, disease was rampant, and the weather would crush any normal man's spirit in a matter of weeks. Any time he saw a captain who did not already seem defeated by the sea, he figured they had to be Atlantean.

"So, he became the most notorious pyrate in the New World. He recruited dozens of other pyrates to his cause. His ship was the strongest in the world. He made a fortune and made many powerful enemies. But he also made some friends and admirers. The governor of North Carolina at the time —"

"Governor Charles Eden," Mark interrupted. He knew the normal parts of the story well enough. It was his ancestor that Chuck was talking about, after all. The familiarity of the subject made their conversation easier to stomach. Chuck was hitting him with a lot of info.

"Right," Chuck continued, "So Governor Charles Eden, somehow, had gotten his hands on a ring that he thought Blackbeard would be interested in. Eden isn't believed to have been a pyrate or an Atlantean, but he had somehow learned about their world, our world, and knew that the ring was a part of it. He offered Blackbeard a pardon and the ring if he would meet with him just once, in person.

Their meeting occurred sometime in June 1718. Eden presented the ring — a simple silver ring with a flawless sapphire — to Blackbeard. Blackbeard took the Sapphire Ring, set Eden's dining room table on fire with his hand, and left without a word. Eden took the demonstration as enough. Blackbeard took the ring with him into retirement —"

"Which gave him time to marry my great-great-grandmother."

"Right. It was less than three months before he went back to piracy. And when he returned, it was ugly. The ring made him stronger, more ferocious. At this point, he was often attacking ships just to watch them sink, regardless of who was onboard."

"The ring made him stronger?" Mark asked, glancing at his shoes as he thought of the soles of his boots.

"No, the ring wasn't like your boots," Chuck answered, sensing Mark's apprehension. "That's just a metal that works with your powers. According to the stories, the ring had a mind of its own, and drove Blackbeard absolutely mad. I don't know how it worked, but I'm sure that it was nothing like what I've got you using."

Mark nodded. That helped a little. "And then he died. Right? That's pretty much the end of it. The Governor of Virginia sent a British lieutenant named Robert Maynard after him. The two fought on Maynard's ship, where Blackbeard died only after being stabbed twenty times and shot five. That's the end of the story," he finished matter-of-factly.

"He didn't have the ring on him. And they never found it."

"So?"

"That governor, Alexander Spotswood, and Maynard were allies of Atlantis. They were supposed to get the ring so it could be kept away from the surface. But they failed. Atlantis completely isolated itself after that, maintaining zero contact with the outside world and sinking any ship that strayed too close to our waters. The people of Atlantis were scared of what the ring could do. Isolation was better than death. It was at that point that they fully dragged the city below the surface.

"Until that ring is found and kept from our enemies, my father and I will never be safe."

Chuck took another drink of water and set the bottle back on the nearby coffee table. They both sat in silence for a moment. Chuck, as if to signify that the story was over, and Mark, waiting for something else.

"What happened to Atlantis? So why are you here?" Mark asked, realizing that he would not get an answer he was going to like.

"It fell too," Chuck answered in a voice that was barely a whisper. It held a reverence that Mark had never heard before. The room fell silent for a moment under the weight of his words.

"When?" Mark continued.

No response.

"Chuck," Mark persisted, as gently as he could manage. "You said you were going to tell me everything. When did Atlantis fall?"

"Nearly thirteen years ago."

He was there when it happened, Mark realized.

"And no," Chuck continued, as if he knew Mark's next question. His voice was steadier, closer to normal now. "I don't remember it at all. I don't remember what the city was like, I just know how my dad described it: a classical paradise like Athens, but times a thousand. The whole city was contained within a single sophisticated, miles-long bubble under the sea. It was arranged in a series of concentric circles, alternating between housing and farmland and markets. Within the city, it was just like any other city on land. We breathed air and walked on land. Only warriors and fishermen left the safety of the dome.

"But then one morning there were flames everywhere within the city's protective dome. A shield that had not failed in over a millennium had been beaten. I don't remember the attack, and my dad refuses to talk about it. All I know is that pyrates found it and it burned to the ground. I don't know how they found it or how they got in. I only know life here."

Mark nodded solemnly, recognizing how tragic that event was, though his mind was largely occupied with how it would even be possible.

Chuck took a deep breath and continued on his own, "And the guy you fought the other day is from Atlantis, too."

"What?" Mark shouted in shock, pulled from silent reverence.

"The suit is a form of Atlantean armor. Obviously, it was based on a pufferfish. The suit expands with the addition of air or water, which then functions as additional muscle mass and activates a number of venomous spines. Oh, and the whole thing is bulletproof."

"Yeah, because why not?" Mark muttered sarcastically, trying to laugh.

"And there will be others," Chuck added, timidly.

Mark's eyes flashed red-hot, and he stood over Chuck, breathing slowly and deeply to try and calm himself. Chuck could feel the heat radiating from his friend, and a small part of him worried that the carpet would catch fire.

"You didn't think to tell me this?" Mark asked in a calm, but angry, tone.

"How was I supposed to tell you? I didn't know they even made it to the surface. I didn't know anyone else had survived the attack. It was over a decade ago! I thought it was just us!" Chuck cried out in a rare show of emotion.

A wave of pity washed over Mark, and he felt his body instantly cooling to its normal temperature and his eyes returned to their normal shade. His friend believed he was alone in the world a few weeks ago, but what should have been a happy revelation was now a sign of worse things yet to come.

"A week ago, I thought it was just an illustration in one of my dad's books," Chuck finished as he hastily wiped tears from his eyes.

"So why rob a bank?" Mark asked, still standing over Chuck, his hands slightly clenched.

"I don't know," Chuck answered calmly. "I honestly have no idea. But I think he's just the beginning. If he showed up, I think that means that those suits have fallen into the wrong hands. There are dozens of different suits with different abilities, all of which we should assume are out there. And there are going to be people using them."

"So, what does that mean for me?" Mark asked, once again sitting as comfortably as one could, given the preceding flood of information.

"They now know that there's a pyrate living around here. They're going to keep coming and hoping you show up. They want vengeance for Atlantis.

"And they probably think you know where the ring is, or that you could lead them to it. Like I said, it's a weapon. That means we're going to need to start training so you can stand a chance against them. And we should be looking for the ring ourselves."

"Now's as good a time as any to start." Mark smirked and his eyes flashed red.

"Mark?" Mr. Currant's voice asked from behind.

Mark turned around suddenly and his eyes reflexively cooled to their normal color. "Mr. Currant, good to see you." Mark greeted him nervously.

Now that Chuck had mentioned it, Mark could see how Mr. Currant was royalty. He had a regal air about him and his every word seemed to carry a certain weight.

"So, Charles, I take it that you have told him everything? He knows of Atlantis and the war?" Mr. Currant asked gently, looking past Mark and to his son.

Chuck nodded solemnly.

"Very well. Mark, I may need to ask your assistance in the coming months. I hope to resolve things myself and make matters right for my people," Mr. Currant said. Then, noticing Mark's discomfort, he continued. "Mark, I hold no ill-will against you. I have seen the worst that war may offer, but it has not hardened my heart. I do not seek revenge, only the safety of those who fled Atlantis and the chance to rebuild our home."

Chuck shot his father a look. How did his father know that others survived the siege, and how could he have allowed Chuck to believe that they were the only two survivors for so long? Mr. Currant noticed the look and replied with a subtle nod. Now was not the time to discuss this. Chuck understood. They would talk about it later.

"Do you understand?"

"Yes, sir," Mark muttered shyly in a strained voice. His throat was incredibly dry and his discomfort made each word difficult to speak. Mr. Currant's words helped a little, but after everything Chuck had just told him about what happened to Atlantis, Mark felt incredible guilt. He hadn't committed any wrongs against Atlantis himself, but it was enough that he felt a deep unease in Mr. Currant's presence.

"And if I should need your assistance to achieve this in the coming months, would you be willing to help, if possible?" Mr. Currant continued. "We have reason to believe that an upcoming solar eclipse in late October of this year will offer a limited window for us to secure the ring."

Mark nodded, not wishing to speak again anytime soon.

"Excellent. Thank you, Mark. I am sorry if my presence is discomforting to you now. I shall leave you and Charles to it."

Mark shook his head and waved his hands in vain opposition. Mr. Currant was making Mark feel very uncomfortable, but Mark couldn't tell him that.

"Mr. Currant?" Mark asked, shocked that he could even speak considering how uncomfortable he felt right now.

"Yes, Mark?"

Now Mark's throat failed to produce a noise. His mouth hung open awkwardly as he tried to say something, anything. But he wasn't even sure what he wanted to say.

"What happened to Atlantis?" Chuck asked, giving voice to Mark's question.

"That," Mark said, in an inaudible whisper. He wasn't proud of it, but he wanted to know the answer, too.

"I never believed they would be able to attack us," Mr. Currant said carefully. "We were protected by a mile of ocean above us and a dome that had never failed in hundreds of years. But they found us and they found a way for their weapons to penetrate our defenses. I awoke to explosions within my city. I sounded the alarm and ordered my people to evacuate, but generations of life within the city had led to an unfortunate evolutionary divergence in which many Atlanteans did not develop sufficient gills. There was nowhere for most of them to run. I escaped with my son and made a life up here. And then we found you, Mark."

The room was silent for a few seconds, neither friend willing to speak first. Mr. Currant's words had finally caused the gravity of their situation to truly set in.

Mr. Currant broke the silence. "I must be going. I am relieved that you now know, Mark, but I have a prior obligation."

Mark muttered a goodbye as Mr. Currant left. He and Chuck still sat in silence for a moment.

"So," Chuck finally began. "You ready?"

Mark took a gulp and nodded. "Yeah, I'm ready."

SEVEN
Montage

"I still think we might want to start training a bit harder," Chuck mentioned quietly one afternoon as he and Mark passed the school's security checkpoint.

"How so?" Mark asked, pulling his keys from his pocket as the two of them stepped out of the school building into the student parking lot.

"Work on general things that it might be good to know. Like blocking, deflection, and grappling, for instance," he continued, lowering his voice to a whisper. "You need to be a bit more well-rounded."

"Really?" Mark groaned, "This again?"

"Yeah, really. This again." Chuck hissed. He glanced in every direction before continuing. "You almost got your teeth knocked in last time because you took a punch right to the face."

"I didn't, though," Mark shot back, gesturing at his own teeth with a fake, showy smile. "And you keep saying there will be a next time, but it's been a week since your big reveal and I'm still waiting for a next time. I've stopped two muggings since then, but neither of them had an Atlantean suit, just a knife, which might have been intimidating to anyone who can't shoot fire. I think maybe it was a one-off kinda deal."

Chuck opened his mouth as if to respond but stopped himself as he felt his cell phone go off. Mark's did as well. They both pulled their phones out and glanced at the text message they both received. It was from the city's new safety alert message system, yet another safety feature that had been deemed necessary following the appearance of a supervillain.

ALERT: POLICE CONFRONTATION. AVOID ADAMS PARK AREA.

Chuck gave a smug grin. "Speak of the devil."

"You don't know that yet," Mark began before he conceded with a shrug, "Fine. This might be similar. I'll head out."

"So do you have a plan?"

"Not really. Probably wing it. Shoot some fire, throw some punches. The text message doesn't really outline what's going on, but it's probably super-shenanigans."

Chuck stared at Mark and raised an eyebrow, waiting for Mark to realize that he couldn't just "wing it" when this sort of stuff happened in the future.

"What? You're not my boss." Mark defended.

"How are you going to get there? Where do you plan on changing into the suit? What are you going to do with your car? How's your brother going to get home?"

Mark muttered an expletive under his breath.

"Alright," Mark said, eyes closed as he listed off his plan point by point. "I'm driving to your place. I park my car in the driveway, get changed into the suit, and then I fly to Adams Park from there, which should only take about five minutes. You give Sean a ride back to my place and make up some reason I had to go to your house. Then you head back to your house, get online and do whatever media-monitoring and police redirecting you did last time, and then I'll meet you back there once I'm done."

"Not bad."

Mark arrived at Adams Park a few minutes later. Well, eleven minutes to be exact, but given the drive, changing, and flying to downtown, it was actually a pretty impressive time for Mark. And technically he was hovering in the space just over Adams Park as he looked for whatever caused the text alert. He just hoped that whatever was going on wasn't over yet.

A strange feeling passed over Mark, similar to déjà vu. Without thinking, he shifted his position in the air. Just as he did, a bolt of lightning split the sky, narrowly missing Mark by inches.

He glanced up. There wasn't a cloud in the sky right now. He looked down and saw it. That's where the lightning came from. A single figure backed up against a storefront, surrounded by police cars.

"I see you!" he shouted at Mark and launched another blast or electricity.

Mark dodged this one as well and flew down within the barricade to meet this new foe.

"I was wondering if you'd even show up," the criminal remarked.

"I have a life outside of you people," Mark deadpanned as he took everything in. This guy was clearly different from the last one, but he seemed to go to the same tailor. His suit was a dark green color and stretched across his entire body, fusing with his facial features and twisting his mouth to an animalistic extreme with rows of pointy teeth. He towered over Mark, with his torso three times the length of a normal person's. And from every inch, he seemed to be dripping with a sort of slime.

"Well, I'm glad you made it," he admitted, his stance shifting back and forth, as though he could strike at any moment. "I spent a lot of time watching your last fight."

"Yeah, I can't blame you. It was good TV," Mark joked before turning serious. "But was he a friend of yours? Two bad guys with special suits in just a few weeks, I imagine you two know each other."

"Maybe," he answered coyly.

"Listen, I'll give you a chance to turn yourself in. Just power down the suit, take it off and get on the ground. Otherwise, it's not going to end well for you."

No response.

"Silent treatment? I guess I'll take that as a 'no' then," Mark sighed, secretly a little glad he was going to get to fight. "At least give me your name first."

"My name," he began, "is Eel!" As he declared his name, Eel shot another blast of electricity from his hand. Once again, that feeling passed over Mark, giving him the chance to dodge the attack. But there were people behind him. He made the split-second decision to take the hit, rather than risk it hitting someone in the crowd. The blast knocked him back five feet and sent him crumpled to the ground.

Eel leapt over to Mark, who was still twitching on the ground. The electricity surging through his body felt very different from the energy he could control. It wasn't warm or constant like his flame, but rather cold and random.

Eel laughed over him. "I can't believe YOU managed to beat the Pufferfish."

Mark gritted his teeth and his eyes flared red. His own energy washed away the electricity. A ring of flame expanded out around his body. Eel jumped back.

"So, you do know him." Mark picked himself up off the ground. "And he goes by 'Puffer' now."

Eel tried to fire a bolt of electricity, but Mark's hand was already around his wrist. With a smile, Mark heated his hand and fried the circuits. No more electricity.

"I think we're done here," Mark declared.

"That's not all I can do," Eel announced as he effortlessly slid his wrist out of Mark's tight grip and delivered a powerful jab against the side of Mark's head.

Mark staggered. Punched in the face again. He thought maybe Chuck did have a point about training more.

As Mark fired a blast of flame, Eel dodged and wrapped himself around Mark's body in a complex submission hold. This suit definitely had enhanced strength, Mark thought.

"I'm better at close range fighting," Eel whispered over the mask into Mark's ear as he tightened his grip.

Mark could feel the hold already. He couldn't breathe. He struggled, but that only allowed Eel to grip tighter. He couldn't slide out of it either. He felt himself starting to get dizzy.

"Just let go," Eel insisted, his face now in front of Mark's.

Mark glared at him beneath the lens of his mask. No, he thought, no way was he going down like this. Mark gathered as much of his breath as he could manage and exhaled a ball of fire from his mouth and through the mask.

The fire wasn't particularly large, but the sight of flames shooting out from the mask surprised Eel enough that he loosened his grip. Mark took in a desperate breath and engulfed his entire body in flames.

Eel let go completely. The flames had shorted out much of his suit. No more enhanced strength. His suit broken, Eel wordlessly assumed the position, lying on the ground, face-down with his hands on his head.

Mark stepped back and rubbed his throat gingerly. The fight was over. His opponent had surrendered. He wanted to get in another shot at Eel but decided against it. That wouldn't be fair. Police officers cautiously approached.

"Nice to see you again," an officer said to Solarflare as other officers secured Eel.

Mark looked. She was one of the officers from when Puffer tried to rob that bank. She seemed to mean it.

"I'm glad I could help," Mark replied graciously. "Do you have everything under control?"

"We do. I'd like you to come with us for questioning, though," she stated matter-of-factly.

"Sorry, can't do that," Mark replied, as he took to the air again.

"Just tell me," She persisted before Solarflare flew off, "Do you know anything about these guys? I don't think he and the other guy are isolated incidents."

"I don't," Mark lied. He didn't want to explain the existence of Atlantis and all that right now. He just wanted to go home. He gestured to Eel as officers placed him in the back of a squad car. "Maybe you can ask him."

"I'll tell you something, Solarflare: The Abyss is deeper than you could ever imagine," Eel cackled before the car door slammed shut in his face.

"I'm guessing that means he has more friends," the officer said.

"We'll be ready," Mark replied confidently.

The officer gave a subtle grin of agreement before Mark flew away.

"'The Abyss is deeper than you could ever imagine,'" Mark repeated to Chuck for a third time later that afternoon, standing in Mr. Currant's home office. Chuck had once again managed to throw police and news crews off Mark's trail so he could get away undetected. Mark was still wearing his Solarflare suit, though the mask had been casually tossed aside. Chuck and Mr. Currant both already knew his identity, so it's not like he needed it.

"The Abyss?" Chuck questioned yet again, sitting behind his father's desk and a dual-monitor computer display.

"Yes. How many times do I need to say it?" Mark asked. "I get it. There are a lot of things in the ocean, so he's just saying that others like him are coming. We'll be ready."

"That's mostly right," Chuck explained. He pulled something up on the computer. "Except, he wasn't just referring to an abyss in a general sense, he was referring to The Abyss, a former Atlantean terror group."

"Oh, so like a proper noun. What were they about?" Mark asked, leaning in closer to the screen to read the information Chuck had pulled up.

"They existed during my great-grandfather's era. They were armed with suits that were high-tech even by Atlantean standards, hardware *and* software."

"Because Atlantis invented computers," Mark added facetiously.

"I mean, we did," Chuck replied without breaking away from the screen.

"Wait, really?"

"Anyway," Chuck continued. "The records on here are incomplete, but it lists at least a dozen different suits based on different sea creatures."

"But there could be more?"

Mark's mind flashed back to the oceanography class he took last year for an easy A. Over half of the coursework covered the various species living in the ocean and the myriad evolutionary traits adopted for survival. That meant a lot of dangerous possibilities for evil villains in high-tech suits.

"Yeah," Chuck replied solemnly.

"So, what do we do? How do I train?" Mark asked.

"I think I've figured that out," Chuck answered with a grin. "Follow me."

Chuck led Mark down the steps into his basement. Mark wondered why he was acting like this was some big revelation. Mark had been in this basement a hundred times before. It was a normal basement. Not big enough, or fireproof enough, for them to get any real training done. It might be good for sparring though, he thought, provided he kept the fire out of it.

But Chuck didn't stop once they were in the basement. He kept walking, over to a small closet in one corner. He reached in and pressed against the back wall. The back swung inward and revealed a second descending staircase.

"Where do those go?" Mark asked, pointing at the revealed stairwell, amazed that Chuck's house had a secret passageway. He was probably more excited about this than he was about finding out Chuck was an Atlantean. Though, in his defense, he couldn't have known to expect Atlantis to be a thing at all, and he had always wanted to use a secret passageway.

"Down," Chuck answered, not wanting to give anything away.

"You have another basement beneath this one?"

"Yep," Chuck replied without looking back as he descended this staircase as well.

Chuck's footsteps echoed as he went down the steps. Mark hung back for a moment and carefully examined the stairs before taking the first step. They were made of metal. Probably iron or something, he thought. He grabbed the railing and took the first step. The handrail was wet. Not soaking wet, but damp.

Mark looked down and his eyes strained to adjust. He couldn't even see the bottom of the steps. But he could clearly smell the faint odor of slightly rusted metal and water. Mark carefully made his way down, his eyes gradually adjusting to the darkness as much as they could, though it wasn't much.

"Chuck?" Mark called out, standing at the bottom of the steps, still holding onto the railing since he couldn't see anything more than a foot away on any side of him. There was no light down here. That is, aside from the light beaming out the open door to Chuck's regular basement. It seemed so far away. The staircase must've been at least two stories long, a straight shot up and down. The area before him stretched out in inky blackness.

No answer from Chuck.

Mark considered heading back up the steps. He was feeling really uneasy down here. He looked for any sign of Chuck.

"Chuck?" Mark repeated.

"What's your superpower again?" Chuck asked in the distance, his echoed voice sounding slightly annoyed.

Mark sheepishly ignited his right hand. Immediately, it felt less intimidating. He grew the flame larger and held it in his upturned palm. The glow radiated out around him and allowed him to see what exactly was in this subbasement.

It was a cave. The walls and floor were a slick, clean white rock. Limestone, to be exact, but Mark could hardly be expected to know that himself. The ceiling was as well, but at this depth, the light of Mark's flame didn't reach that high.

Mark figured that Mr. Currant must've intentionally built his house on top of the cave and dug down into it. There was a large, open area next to the stairs. By Mark's best guess, it was probably about the size of a football field, though it might have extended even further into the darkness.

Mark walked into the cave, into the open space, holding his enflamed hand in the air to better illuminate the area. Still no sign of Chuck.

A light flicked on in front of Mark. He had no idea how big it was or how far away it might be, but that's probably where Chuck went. Mark trudged across the damp cave floor towards it. It grew bigger with each step but was still too far for him to make out what it was.

Suddenly, lights flickered on above Mark's head. They lined the entire length of the cave. Bright, long rows of sterile light humming with electricity. He winced from the abrupt change. When he opened his eyes again, he saw that he was less than a third of the way to Chuck, who was standing in front of what Mark could now see was a massive computer display.

"On your left," Chuck called out.

Mark looked to his left side. Less than a foot away was a deep pool of water. He eased away from it nervously. He had no idea how deep it was, but the light shining through it told him it was deep enough for him to be unnerved. He looked back. This cave pool ran all along the side, all the way back to the stairs.

"Get up here," Chuck shouted, pulling Mark back from his thoughts on the pool.

Mark broke into a careful, hurried jog towards Chuck and the computer display. As he got closer, he could see that it was set up on a sort of elevated platform. Made sense, he thought; this cave floor wasn't exactly the best surface. He could just picture himself slipping on a patch of water and falling on his face.

When Mark reached the platform, he climbed up the few steps and found himself right in front of Chuck. The platform was roughly the size of Mark's bedroom, and it held a staggeringly impressive computer display of six massive, interlocked screens. He looked back at the stairs and the doorway to Chuck's house. It was the faintest dot of light in the distance. When Mark looked back at Chuck, he noticed his friend was soaking wet.

Before he could ask why, Chuck gestured towards the water nearby. "I'm better at swimming," he explained. He stepped back and shook himself dry, not unlike a dog. The water droplets hung in the air, and, with a casual wave of his hand, Chuck sent them back into the pool.

"Makes sense," Mark accepted before continuing. "So, when were you planning on telling me about this place?"

Chuck sighed deeply before answering. "This computer houses all my father's files on Atlantis. Our history, our culture, our people. This may be all that remains of them."

Mark nodded solemnly. Of course, Chuck would keep this place close to the vest.

"But," Chuck continued. "This is a good open space. We can train here without risk of being seen or burning anything down. And you need the training."

"I didn't do that badly," Mark protested.

Chuck pressed a button on the computer and the computer's screens played silent clips from Mark's fight where Eel had the upper hand and the fight with Puffer when he got punched in the face.

"You won," Chuck said as Mark watched the fights replay on-screen. "You're now undefeated in two fights. But that doesn't mean you're guaranteed to win the next one, or the one after that. Here, we'll review your mistakes, correct them, and build you into the best Solarflare you can be. Does that work for you?"

Mark's eyes were focused on a screen that showed Eel's hold on him in a loop. He remembered the sensation of losing his breath. If Eel had held on any longer, he would've won. Chuck was right. Training was necessary.

"Right here," Mark said, pointing to the upper-right screen. "He had me in some kind of hold. I didn't like it. I don't know anything about submission fighting. I don't want this to happen again."

Chuck smiled. "So, let's get to work."

Chuck took a step back and his eyes flashed a deep blue, and water from the pool nearby swirled, rose up and splashed onto the platform. The water shifted and turned, and Mark was staring at a human-sized figure made entirely of water.

"How long have you been able to do this?" Mark asked, before adding, "This is awesome!"

Chuck smiled for a second and returned his focus to the figure. He needed to concentrate to keep it like this. He stuck out his hands and, like a puppet master manipulating a marionette, the figure began to move.

The water-dummy took on a fighting stance and swayed back and forth.

"I'm supposed to fight this thing?" Mark asked.

Chuck nodded to confirm. The dummy nodded as well.

"But I just fought —" Mark began, but he was interrupted when the dummy struck him across the face.

Mark's eyes flashed a bright crimson, and his hands became covered in flames. He lunged toward the dummy.

The dummy ducked beneath him and wrapped itself around Mark in a hold identical to the one he had faced earlier. Mark struggled and felt the grip tighten. He felt himself unable to breathe.

Mark's eyes locked with Chuck's. Their eyes were both glowing with their respective colors. Mark felt a sense of anger and shame that Chuck was beating him without even lifting a finger. Why wasn't he the superhero then? Why did Mark have to take on all the risk? Why was Chuck even training him?

Mark's eyes glowed brighter with his frustration. His body began to heat up, and steam began to flow from the water-dummy. The grip on his neck lessened. He could breathe again.

Mark centered his footing and flung the dummy over top of him. When it crashed to the ground, he struck it in the center with a flaming punch. The sudden evaporation of the dummy's center seemed to give Chuck a slight shock, as his eyes dimmed for a second and the rest of the dummy splashed into a puddle on the platform. Chuck was dazed and had to balance himself on the computer.

Both Mark and Chuck stood there wordlessly for a moment, breathing heavily. Chuck was nursing his head. Mark was the first to speak.

"You okay?" he asked.

"Yeah," Chuck replied. "Making one of these —"

"Water-dummies," Mark offered, as Chuck seemed to search for a word.

"Yes," Chuck accepted. "A 'water-dummy' takes a lot of concentration."

"Sorry I smashed it, then," Mark apologized.

"It's alright. You got out of the hold without just relying on the shock of a sudden burst of flames. That was the goal. Are you alright?"

"Yeah, I'm good."

"So, I'm thinking that maybe we do a water-dummy session every day or so," Chuck suggested.

"Sure," Mark agreed, gingerly rubbing his neck.

"And you'll get more out of it if you don't use fire," Chuck added.

"Are you serious?" Mark asked, incredulously.

"Yeah," Chuck said, standing firm. "You don't want fire to become your crutch. This'll make you a better fighter."

Mark was silent for a moment. He knew Chuck was right, but it didn't sound appealing to him at all.

"Fine," Mark eventually conceded, his eyes still faintly glowing.

"Alright, so let's try another round without the fire."

"Fine." Mark tersely repeated. With a deep exhale, his eyes fully cooled to their normal brown color.

"You think you can handle me?!" a gruff voice asked with a scream.

"I've handled worse," Mark answered, as he shot a burst of flame at his latest superpowered enemy. It'd been a couple of days, and Mark had almost gotten worried that no one else was coming for him.

This guy was part of The Abyss, Mark thought. Bright red and cream-colored suit, armor, and giant claw-like gauntlets suggested this one was based on a crab. Maybe a lobster, but that was way less likely considering how stout the man was. His shoulders and chest were nearly wider than he was tall.

Mark doubled around and shot another burst of fire. The villain responded by grabbing a streetlight out of the ground with his hands and swatting away the flames. Yep, that settled it. This guy was one of them, and not just some cosplayer. Maybe he'd be able to get some info out of him.

"So, you're friends with the other two guys, right?" Mark asked, trying to get a secondary confirmation.

The villain answered by flinging the streetlight at Mark. The large, unwieldy streetlight twisted in the wind and caught Mark's foot, throwing him off balance. Mark crashed to the ground hard.

"You're crabby," Mark pointed out, pulling himself off the ground. "Hey! That's a perfect name for you."

'Crabby' lunged at Mark with his hands open, trying to grab at him. Mark sidestepped this attack and launched himself back with his boots to gain some distance.

"Don't like it?" Mark asked in mock-sincerity across the gulf between the two of them.

Crabby violently shut his hands, which rang with a deep metallic clang.

"Guess not."

Crabby and Mark charged at one another. Mark swung his right leg up and tried to kick Crabby in the head. Crabby caught his leg in mid-air and clamped down on it. It felt like he was about to snap Mark's ankle in half.

"Sonuva—!" Mark shouted in pain.

Crabby laughed a sinister cackle.

"You think that's funny, you bright red —?" Mark asked in genuine frustration before Crabby squeezed tighter and the pain cut him off. Mark grunted in rage.

Mark twisted his other leg and fired a blast of heat from the boot, pulling him up against Crabby. He grabbed him by the collar with his left hand and began punching Crabby in the face with his flaming right. After about three hits, Crabby let go and fell to the ground.

When Crabby's grip released, Mark caught himself on his one good leg and balanced there for a moment. He gingerly held his nearly crushed leg and tried to rub the feeling back into it. He tried to wiggle his toes. There was still some feeling there. He wasn't sure if he'd even be able to fly home. That would be a problem. It's not like he could just call a cab.

Crabby groaned and began to pull himself up.

"Not happening," Mark declared, as he fell forward and punched Crabby in the face once again. He was out.

Mark awkwardly rolled off Crabby and put weight back onto his right foot. It seemed alright, but really sore. He crouched down and grabbed Crabby's wrists.

"Yeah, that's where I'd put the important stuff," Mark muttered.

Mark's hands heated up and he heard popping and whirring noises within the wrist gauntlets that were connected to Crabby's oversized gloves.

"That should do it," Mark declared when he stood up.

The nearby police officers that had been maintaining a perimeter rushed in and surrounded Crabby.

"You should come in with us," an officer stated.

"Nah," Mark said quietly, testing how much weight he could put on his right leg. Yeah, he'd be able to fly back alright. He finished his statement as he took to the air. "I really don't see that happening today."

"When I was leaving, I overheard one of the cops call the guy 'Pincer.' Apparently, they get to name my enemies, not me," Mark declared bitterly as he marched down the stairs to Solarflare's new underground base, while Chuck sat at his command center deep in the cavern.

Speaking of names, he realized that their base needed a name too. He made a note to start jotting down ideas and mention it to Chuck after he had a couple good ones ready. It might have been a bit petty, but he wanted to name their base. After all, he was the superhero. It barely mattered that it was in Chuck's basement.

"It's a better name than Crabby," Chuck responded without looking up from the screens. Today, they were already replaying a half-dozen different angles of the fight.

"Says you."

"Alright," Chuck said, changing the subject. He paused and pointed at one of the screens behind him, in the upper left-hand corner. It was frozen on an image of Mark with his ankle locked in Pincer's grip. "Looks like we need to go over grabs today."

"Let me guess," Mark sighed. "'Break the wrist and walk away'? I'm not five; I know how to get out of a grab." Mark was half-right. He was not five, but it had been a while since he had any sort of experience getting out of a grab. Or being in any sort of fight, for that matter. A few years of kung-fu lessons as a kid and a fondness for the movies of Bruce Lee, Jet Li, and Jackie Chan didn't prepare him as much as he liked to claim.

Admittedly, Chuck should have noticed this sooner. But learning to fly and discussing suit designs took priority in Mark's mind as well. At least he was addressing this now, before they got any further.

"You punched him in the head, and he let go. Doesn't exactly illustrate a mastery of the skill," Chuck countered.

Once again, Chuck pulled up a water-dummy and took a fighting stance. His eyes glowed brighter, and the dummy's limbs took on a more defined hand-shape.

Mark cracked his neck and rolled his shoulders before his eyes blazed to life.

The dummy grabbed Mark's left wrist with its watery tendril. Mark yanked his arm back, but it held tight. Mark grabbed the dummy's "hand" with his right hand and tried to break the seal, but the water shifted and wrapped itself around his other hand.

"Chuck!" Mark shouted in frustration.

"What?" Chuck shouted back. "You don't think someone might grab both your hands, or you don't think anyone else has my powers?"

Mark struggled and cursed under his breath against the dummy, but he knew Chuck was right. He couldn't just count on standard fighting. Things might get weird out there, so it was a good idea to practice against weird in here.

Mark's eyes flashed a deep red.

"Mark!" Chuck interjected before Mark turned the dummy's arm to steam. "You're trying this without fire."

Mark exhaled loudly and angrily. He twisted his wrists in separate directions, causing the water between them to weaken. He pulled them apart quickly and they were free!

Mark turned and swung at the water-dummy's head with his right. It ducked beneath his hand with unbelievable speed. When

Mark realized this, he tried to bash it with his right elbow. Again, the dummy ducked right beneath it.

A tendril reached up and grabbed Mark's wrist, dragging him off the ground. His feet dangling in mid-air, he considered using fire. But that was a last resort, he thought. If he could get out of this without fire, he should do it that way. Chuck's words rang in his ears, that was how he'd become a better fighter.

Mark kicked at the center of the water dummy with his left. His foot became lodged in the dummy's chest. The water collected around the foot and pulled it out, creating another limb.

The dummy held Mark suspended in the air, his right arm trapped in one watery limb, and his left leg trapped in the other.

Mark struggled and twisted against the dummy, but with no luck. Last resort, Mark thought. A burst of heat erupted from his right boot. With opposite limbs being held at different heights, this caused Mark to spin within the dummy's grip. The spinning caused the grip to loosen enough that he was able to yank his hand out.

With his hand free, Mark shot away from the dummy, ripping his left leg from its clutches, and sending him across the platform. Mark crashed at the edge of the platform, half his body dangling over.

"Ow," he muttered. He stood up and dusted himself off.

"What are we learning?" Chuck asked, the water-dummy still standing. The lesson wasn't over. It wouldn't be over until Mark learned what Chuck wanted him to learn.

"I don't like being grabbed," Mark answered sarcastically.

"So, what should you do?"

It dawned on him. "Not let them grab me."

"Exactly," Chuck replied proudly. "If you get better at dodging hits and grabs, this will get a lot easier for you."

Mark ran from the edge of the platform towards the water-dummy. The dummy took a swipe at Mark's head, which he barely dodged by leaning backwards. The dummy shot out a tendril to grab Mark's left hand. He leaned right, causing it to shoot right past him. The tendril hooked around and tried to grab Mark around the center. Mark leapt up in the air and flipped over it. He was starting to get the hang of it.

Chuck smiled, and the dummy became more ferocious. They spent another half hour with Mark just dodging the dummy's attacks. It was exhausting, but it meant Mark probably wouldn't get hit so much.

Three days later, there was a new one. This one was a woman. She, like the last three villains, had a colorful supersuit and outrageous body proportions. Her suit was an amber mottled pattern with tan highlights. Her arms stretched twice as long as a normal woman's arms would. And she, or her suit at least, had a tail.

She was robbing a jewelry store or something. It didn't matter all that much, just that she was a supervillain, and she was stealing and Chuck gave the word. Their motivations were all starting to seem the same to Mark, hardly seeming like a terrorist group from deep in the ocean. Still, it was fun to fight them and be featured in the news.

"I don't want to hit a lady," Mark declared when he landed on the scene as Solarflare.

"Oh, you won't," she replied, as she hurled a bolt of electricity at Mark, sending him to the ground. As Mark twitched on the ground, she lifted her arms into the air, revealing a fabric that stretched from her forearms to her torso. With a heave, she flew into the air.

Mark picked himself up and saw her flying off. He smiled widely beneath his mask and his eyes burned an intense red. He crouched down and fired blasts of intense heat out from the soles of his feet and shot into the air in pursuit.

"We've got a flier!" Mark declared into the new communication system built into the mask. Chuck had set up a secure line for the two of them when Mark was on patrols. And he had woven it into the mask so that it couldn't get knocked loose during a fight. He added as an afterthought, "I mean, glad it's not *just* another electric-type because that'd just be lame."

"Just focus on pursuit," Chuck commanded authoritatively.

"Yeah, yeah, fine." Mark answered as he put even more heat behind him and rocketed forward. In mere moments, he was easily able to catch up.

"So, what's your name?" Mark shouted over the sound of rushing wind as he flew directly over top of the villain.

She flipped in the air and faced him. She seemed startled that he caught up so quickly.

"Manta," she answered as she reached up and grabbed Mark's suit, releasing a massive charge of electricity.

Mark screamed in pain as the electricity surged through his body. Manta pulled her feet up and kicked off Mark's chest and flew straight down before leveling off and ducking into an alley. As Manta flew off, Mark flew uncontrollably through the air until he crashed through an upper-floor window of an office building.

Mark groaned loudly on the floor, broken glass all around him.

He had crashed into the middle of a conference room, in the middle of a meeting. He noticed a couple of flashes from the cell phones nearby.

"Sorry," Mark said as got to his feet. He dusted himself off and made his way to the window he had just crashed through. He stood at the edge for a moment and inspected himself for any rips or tears in the suit. It held, that was a good sign.

Mark scanned the area, looking for Manta. No sign of her. He figured he'd be more likely to find her if he got above the skyline.

"You may want to mark off this area. Broken glass and all that," Mark added before he flew out the window.

"So," someone at the table began, trying to return to work. "About our numbers from last quarter…"

Mark flew up and above the Delfield skyline. His eyes scanned in between the buildings for some sign of Manta. He looked in every direction. Nothing.

He returned to where the chase began. The crowd had mostly dispersed. It wasn't like there was much for them to watch this time.

Mark landed and looked around. He looked to the police officers that had responded to the scene. The one nearest him shrugged and shook his head.

Mark hung his head sadly. This was the first time a supervillain got away from him.

"Where is she?" a voice from the remaining crowd called out. There were murmurs of agreement. How did Solarflare let her get away?

Mark took to the air wordlessly and flew off. This was a loss. It didn't feel good.

Mark debated just going straight home, doing homework and going to sleep. But he decided against it. His first loss meant he needed training more than ever. He dutifully returned to Chuck's house and made his way downstairs.

"Hey," Chuck said when he saw Mark making his way down the steps.

Mark didn't say anything. He walked down the steps and towards the platform.

"So," Chuck continued, trying to sound sympathetic. "This wasn't a great day. But we can work on it. And the next time you see her, you'll be prepared."

Mark muttered something that sounded like agreement as he stepped onto the platform.

"We've never dealt with a flier before. She got out of your sight for a second and that's all it took. But we can work on that."

"How?" Mark asked, annoyed. "It's not like we can go out into the streets and practice. As big as this cave might be, it's nothing like being in the middle of the city with buildings everywhere."

"I know," Chuck said, cutting Mark off before he got too upset. "But I thought of something similar we can do down here." He pulled a nickel out of his pocket and held it up. "I want you to catch this."

"How's that going to help?"

"It'll be more difficult than it sounds," Chuck added. His eyes glowed blue and a great amount of water lifted itself out of the nearby pool and hung in the air beside the platform. Chuck extended his arms in front of him and spread his fingers apart, causing the mass of water to break into countless droplets, each about the size of the nickel. The droplets spread farther and farther apart from one another, quickly covering the platform all the way up to the cave's roof.

Chuck held the droplets in place with his left hand extended, as his right hand drew a single one towards him. It enveloped the nickel and lifted it out of his hand, then rejoined the other droplets, floating high towards the ceiling. Mark could just barely make it out.

"Interesting," Mark noted. "I think I've got it."

Chuck gave Mark a nod and he was off. Mark rose into the air and flew after the coin. Just as he was about to grab it, the droplets shifted and swirled around him, the nickel-droplet flying across the cavern.

Mark kicked his feet out from under him and started after it. Again, as he got near, the droplets spun and twirled across the air, and the nickel was lost.

He hung in midair, trying to scope it out.

There. It was now down towards the bottom, just above the cavern's pool.

Mark leaned forward and dropped his body through the air towards the nickel at a frightening speed. He was blasting straight towards the ground and it was coming fast. He reached out his hand.

And the nickel shot back up and behind him.

Mark tucked his knees to his chest and, with less than an inch between his feet and the hard stone floor, rocketed back into the air.

After just over fifteen minutes, Mark finally caught the nickel. The second round, it only took him eleven. Round three took seventeen, which Chuck took to mean that they should probably call it a night. Still, it was a fun new training exercise.

This was new. There were two of them, one large man and a petite woman, and it seemed like they were a couple. Their costumes seemed to be coordinated with one another: one dark blue, the other light blue, and they both had dorsal fins on their backs. Mark spotted the two of them as they sprinted down Fairfax Boulevard, weaving between cars and up on the sidewalk, jewelry draped over their arms and clutched in their hands.

Wasn't Manta stealing jewelry? Mark tried to remember as he flew down and narrowed his pursuit. Was it some sort of Atlantean thing? He made a mental note to ask Chuck about it later; right now, he had supervillains to catch and couldn't get distracted. He was determined to not let them escape like Manta did.

"You know," he said, announcing his presence from behind, "The two of you are dropping a lot of jewelry on the road. I mean, you're definitely going to jail regardless of efficiency, but it's still poor form."

The small one stopped, planted her feet, dropped the jewelry, and turned to face Mark. Before Mark had even reached the two of them, she inhaled deeply and hit him with a high-pitched sonic scream.

Mark clutched his ears and violently tumbled to the ground just ahead of them as nearby storefront windows shattered.

"Sonic scream?" Mark asked across the distance as he picked himself up.

"Yep," the woman replied with a smug grin.

"Sonic scream?" Mark shouted.

"I said —" the woman began.

"Sonic scream?" Mark asked again.

"Yes!" the woman shouted.

"Sonic scream?" Mark asked, laughing at his own joke by this point. "I'm just kidding, I can hear you. It's not a very impressive sonic scream." He concentrated for a moment and his hands erupted in flames.

The big guy chuckled a bit, but the woman seemed livid. Mark liked the big guy more at this point. The woman shot her partner a glare and he shut up immediately.

She turned her attention back to Mark. "Not very impressive?" she asked. Mark winced. It wasn't deafening, but it did hurt. He wasn't a fan of what he knew was coming.

A second shriek split the air. Mark stood firm as the sound waves washed over him, but when he looked down, he noticed something. His hands had gone out.

"Oh yeah." Mark muttered, mostly to himself. "Sound waves can extinguish fire." Over the last few weeks, Chuck had insisted on sending Mark fun facts about how fires can be extinguished. It was intended to make Mark a better hero, but it felt vaguely threatening at times. But now he had some real-world experience. Fires can be put out with sound.

The woman was charging at Mark, rapidly closing the gap.

"Guess I need a lot more fire then," Mark said, as he threw his hands together and a large burst of flames erupted from them. He was aiming for a lot of low-heat fire. Quantity, not quality.

It worked. She didn't even have the opportunity to try and put them out with another scream. The flames washed over her and she crumpled to the ground in a heap, muttering weakly.

"Dolphin!" the big guy shouted with concern.

"I mean, maybe, just maybe," Mark declared. "If all of you are weak against fire, then maybe The Abyss should leave my town. I'm just saying."

The large man stood off, radiating pure rage. His hands were fists that could crush bricks. And Mark worried that his head looked like a brick right now.

"So, her name's Dolphin?" Mark asked with sincerity, trying to defuse the tension. "So, what's your name, my man?"

"Whale," the man said as he cracked his neck. Then he cracked his knuckles.

"I get it," Mark said, nodding, as he prepared another large wave of flames. If it worked once, why not twice?

But Whale realized what Mark was up to. Before Mark could fire off his shot, Whale offered his own superpowered shout, only much deeper. The shout knocked Mark right onto his back.

"Nicely done. That one hurt more," Mark groaned from his position. "Any chance you want to help me up? You know, call it a draw?"

"Nah," Whale answered as he charged at Mark. Based on size, Mark figured Whale was also equipped with a bit of superstrength. He wasn't about to see exactly how much superstrength, though.

With a groan, Mark kicked his legs into the air and rolled up onto his shoulders before popping himself up and launching backwards. He dodged the blow by inches. He righted himself in midair and put heat to the soles of his feet, hovering above Whale's head.

"Too bad you can't fly, tiny," Mark taunted, just out of Whale's reach. Mark noticed Dolphin starting to pick herself up. He was not trying to face the two of them at the same time. He needed an idea.

Mark rocketed upwards and hooked back at an angle. He needed Dolphin to be directly behind Whale. He saw Whale draw a deep breath, as if getting ready for another shout. Now or never. Mark put everything he had into his feet and collided with Whale at top speed, sending him back onto Dolphin with a loud thud. Mark then climbed on top of Whale and, using his hands and feet, blanketed the two of them in heat as he flipped to safety.

Mark landed a few feet away and checked out his handiwork. They were both down. Mark saw police gathering on the scene. That was his cue to head out.

"For the record, everyone, I just took down two supervillains at the same time. That's right, two," Mark gloated to any and all passers-by on the street as he took to the sky once more. He was shouting a lot louder than he realized. Sound-based villains were the equivalent of a rock concert. "Greatest hero ever!" Mark flew off, confident that even Chuck had to admit he handled this one really well. When was the last time Chuck fought any supervillains, much less two at the same time? Never, that's when.

EIGHT
The Girl in Green

"We have a traffic collision on Layhill Road, near Bellwood," Chuck called out.

"Got it," Mark answered, already miles away from base. He had been out flying before he got the call, trying to test his speed and altitude. He paused and floated in the air. He had found a speedometer app for his phone and, according to it, he had been going just under 60 miles per hour. Not bad, he thought.

Mark glanced at the map on his phone. He wasn't far. He put his phone back into the special pocket Chuck had added and, with a burst of heat in his boots, he swung in the air and headed towards the crash.

He reached the street and flew closer to ground level than Chuck would've wanted. Mark weaved in and out of traffic as his eyes scanned for signs of the crash.

"You're going the wrong way," Chuck scolded.

Mark muttered an obscenity and made a sudden U-turn, flying up and over the oncoming traffic.

Mark saw the accident in the distance. It was pretty bad. Around four or five cars, all smashed into each other. He hoped no one was too badly hurt. "Chuck, how far out are emergency services?"

"Maybe five minutes or so," Chuck answered, pulling the information from a display on the massive computer in his basement lair.

"That's not too bad," Mark hoped out loud.

"Just get people out if you can," Chuck advised. "What I'm seeing from bystander reactions online is that the cars are all sort of jammed together and the passengers are trapped inside."

"Got it," Mark replied as he came in for a landing.

Chuck was right, the five cars involved in this were all tightly packed against one another. One was flipped on its side, and another was completely upside-down. There didn't seem to be any blood though, which was a pretty good sign.

"Help us!" a muffled voice shouted from inside one of the cars.

"It's alright," Mark declared, trying to calm everyone down. He spoke slowly and loudly, just like Chuck had told him to do in an emergency like this. Authoritative and soothing, Mark remembered. "I will get you all out of here. Just be calm."

He went for the car that was upside-down first. It seemed to merit the priority. Mark assessed the situation. Just two passengers and they were both conscious, but they weren't freaking out. Might be shock, he thought. He should probably learn that.

The driver's side door was smashed in. Mark struggled with the door handle, but it wouldn't budge. His eyes glowed red and he felt the door move. But he also felt that his hands had warped the doorframe with their heat. He didn't know how badly the passengers were hurt, but the extra heat couldn't help.

He exhaled deeply and his eyes cooled. He had practiced and trained without fire enough. He was confident he could muscle this car open. He pulled on the door handle as hard as he could with both hands.

It snapped off. The door was still shut.

Mark looked around frantically for a moment. He stepped back and tried to collect his thoughts. He heard the crunch of broken glass beneath his foot. That's when it hit him.

"Supersuit," Mark muttered, disappointed it took him this long to think of it.

The suit couldn't be cut by glass. He punched through the car door window with his left arm and placed his hand against the side, while his right hand rested on the outside of the car. Mark took a deep breath and gave the door another mighty pull. Nothing.

Mark swore loudly. His eyes involuntarily flashed a deep red beneath his mask. He took another deep breath and set his feet. He jerked the car door with all his might.

The door was yanked clean off its hinges. He reached inside, unbuckled seatbelts, and pulled out the passengers carefully, setting them down on the sidewalk away from the scene. But he didn't immediately notice the now-flaming car door he had just thrown into the middle of the accident scene. Fire powers weren't always obvious.

Not worrying about the broken glass was a definite relief, though he knew the people being rescued didn't quite have that luxury.

He rushed over to the next car, the one on its side. Mark climbed up onto the side not pinned to the ground. Just one guy in this car, Mark saw. And he was definitely okay. He was freaking out and violently trying to open the door, but he was fine.

Mark held up a hand as a sign for him to calm down. The man stopped yelling, but he was shaking uncontrollably. Mark held up his other hand and slowly lowered them both. No real change, that was as calm as the man was going to get right now.

He straddled the driver's side door uncomfortably and reached down. Mark gripped the handle tightly and prepared to pull another door off its hinges, but it opened normally.

Mark laughed as he swung his leg over the door and reached into the car. He pulled the man out of the car, and they stood on the upturned side together.

"Yeah, yeah, you're fine now," Mark said in his most comforting tone as he tried to steady the man.

He debated internally over whether or not the man could make the jump down. It wasn't too high, only about four feet or so, but he didn't want the guy twisting an ankle or anything. So, Mark scooped the man into a fireman's carry and flew him to the same spot as the others.

It didn't look particularly dignified, but the man had no objections to it.

Mark turned back to the scene and saw a figure in a green hoodie carrying two people from one of the other cars. Their car door was also ripped clean off.

"Did you do that?" Mark asked when the figure placed the passengers down, pointing to the car door. The figure turned to look at Mark, they were wearing a mask that covered the bottom half of their face. The two locked eyes for a moment, and Mark could swear he saw a flash of green.

The figure wordlessly pointed across the accident scene, alerting Mark to the growing fire. The car door he had tossed aside earlier had caught on a nearby spill of oil and gasoline, and the fire was spreading.

Mark winced. Darn. That was a big mistake.

No time to focus on it now, though. Two cars left. Both of them still upright and not in too bad a condition.

"Alright, you take that car, I'll take the other," Mark commanded, gesturing to the accident.

The figure nodded in agreement, and the two of them were off. Mark and the new hero sprinted to their assigned cars, Mark running as fast as he could. He told himself he needed to save the people in his car, but the truth was that he mostly wanted to prove that his mistakes so far today weren't the norm. But, if pride got those people to safety quicker, what's the harm?

Mark arrived at the car and assessed the situation. Everyone inside was conscious, but apparently in shock. As much as he wanted to place a premium on time, he recognized that he needed to be careful. Okay, there was a family of four, they didn't show any visible signs of injury, but obviously they hadn't expected their day to go like this. And this car was absolutely wrecked; the front of the car was crumpled like a stepped-on soda can.

"Hi everyone," Mark declared in a loud, calm voice as he walked up to the car. "Is anyone hurt? I'll get you all out of here."

The driver nodded meekly and pointed to the backseat, as if to indicate that Mark needed to take care of the kids in the backseat first. Mark nodded an agreement and went to work. He quickly and carefully evacuated the kids from the backseat, they were maybe around 7 and 10, if Mark had to guess. He led them to safety and then went back for the parents. The driver was a bit shaken and needed some encouragement to get out of the car, but ultimately, he left on his own.

With the family safely delivered away from the accident scene, Mark turned to survey. All of the cars had been evacuated, people were maintaining a distance, and he could see lights from police cars, ambulances, and firetrucks not far off. He could take off and call it a success, minus a few points for the still-ongoing fire. The firetruck would get there in time, right? He looked at the truck's lights. They seemed too far off to leave this to chance. He looked at the fire. He noticed that the new person had suddenly bailed without a trace. But it was fine, he could just leave. Except he couldn't just leave.

"Alright! Fine!" Mark declared to no one in particular.

He sprinted towards the flames, driven by instinct and a vague idea of what he might do. He skidded to a stop right at the edge of the flames and braced himself. He reached out towards the fire and pulled it towards himself. I hope this works, he thought. His eyes flashed red, and he kept moving his hands in circles, pulling at the flames. Weak flames flickered in his hands as he tried to catch the blaze in front of him.

And then, finally, it worked. The blaze fluttered towards him, pulled by his hands and towards his core. He dragged the flames towards himself as if pulling a massive rope. He felt the heat filling his gut, up to his chest, into his throat. He struggled to continue pulling in the flames. He glanced at the scene and saw just a little more.

"Come on, almost there, almost there, almost —" Mark said to himself, feeling as if he would burst. He knew that if he let up, the blaze was likely to spring back to its full size. He didn't even dare take a breath for fear of losing his concentration.

He couldn't do much more. With a wild flurry of his hands and his eyes clenched tight, he desperately pulled at the flames, seeking to end it with a final exertion. He glimpsed through one eye and saw the last flickers of a flame pulled into him. He stopped moving and tried to figure out what to do next. He had all this fire inside him now, fire he'd pulled from elsewhere. This was a new feeling. Every muscle burned and twitched with the extra energy, but he was frozen to the spot. He felt like he was made of lead. He needed to just let it out.

He looked around desperately, seeing no options on his left or right, or in front or behind. He needed somewhere.

And then he looked up. Yeah, that'd work. He pulled up the bottom of his mask and roared into the air, sending a column of flames over fifteen feet up in the air. He was lucky there weren't any birds immediately overhead at the time.

When the flames had finally finished flowing from his mouth, he yanked the mask back down. He was going to get an earful from Chuck about that later, he thought. He could already hear Chuck's lecture on the importance of a full-face mask. Mark instantly felt better, though.

"Drive safe, everyone," Mark declared to the crowd breathlessly, figuring he needed to say something before he left.

With a wave, he took to the air and made his way home. That was enough superhero work for the day, he reasoned. As he flew off, he noticed the figure that had helped him was perched on a nearby rooftop and gave him a nod. Mark grinned. Nice to meet someone else in the business, he thought.

The next day, when Mark returned to school, he saw that the first decorations for the Homecoming Dance had already been put up. He checked the date: October 25th. Not too soon, he thought. That still gave him just under a month to get a date and everything.

He wanted this Homecoming Dance to be good, which meant he needed to find a Homecoming date. He already had someone in mind, but he didn't want to be overeager. He was so wrapped up in his Homecoming preparations that he didn't hear Chuck come up behind him.

"Homecoming decorations are up," Chuck said, revealing his presence as he popped open his giant water bottle and began his usual, unending task of hydrating.

Mark turned around and smirked. "Yeah, I can see that."

"Just making small talk," Chuck muttered. "But fine, we can stick to business. So, you caused a fire in the middle of an accident scene."

"Yep. And, as I've already pointed out, I fixed it," Mark answered, nodding and wishing he'd just let Chuck stick to pointing out obvious decorations.

"Fair point. But you've got to be more careful. Just because you're fireproof doesn't mean everyone else is. Fire tends to make accident scenes a lot worse."

"Yeah. I think I got it," Mark said, annoyed that Chuck felt the need to spell it out for him. He'd like to see him do better.

"And you had help."

"Yeah!" Mark answered, a lot louder than Chuck would have liked. He dropped his voice low. "Tell me you know something about this."

"I know that someone else showed up. And that this person wore green," Chuck responded, deadpan. "That's all I've got so far. I'll keep an eye out moving forward, but this is totally unrelated to what I've been doing for you the last couple months."

"Darn," Mark muttered. He was genuinely disappointed his friend didn't have any worthwhile leads.

"Sorry, man," Chuck said, reading his friend's frustration. He opted to change the subject. "So, Homecoming. Any ideas on who you want to go with?"

"I might," Mark revealed coyly. "I'll keep you posted."

"Alright, well, just make sure you're free the next day."

"Why? What's the next day?" Mark asked.

Chuck pointed to his right ring finger before he turned and walked off without another word.

It took Mark a beat before it hit him: the Sapphire Ring. Why did it have to be the day after Homecoming, though? He quickly brushed it off. Securing a date was the more pressing thought.

As much as Mark hated to appear overeager, he knew that the sooner he got to work on finding a Homecoming date, the better. Once the poster went up with the date, it officially became Homecoming Season. Mark had learned in his three years at North Delfield High School that there is an art, almost an etiquette, to asking a girl to a dance. It even had an unofficial set of rules.

The first rule was that it was a good idea to preempt the ask. Knowing ahead of time if a girl would say yes was a great way to avoid an outright rejection and the associated embarrassment. Mark didn't have a great track record when it came to asking someone out of nowhere. His Freshman year came to mind. He'd asked Celine Andersen to go to the dance with him and, although she had been very polite in declining Mark's offer, it still crushed him. He didn't ask anyone else and wound up leaving the dance early, feeling the hurt of the rejection all over again when he noticed her across the dance floor. Three years later, he still felt awkward around her. Luckily, the only class they had together was Drama, so their interactions weren't particularly frequent.

So, for this year's dance, he decided he'd check with Ana Kekoa, Lauren's best friend. And how fortuitous it was for Mark that Ana happened to sit one row over from him in AP Statistics. Mark made sure to arrive to class with as much time to spare before the bell, hoping that he'd have a chance to talk to Ana. For Mark, that was the most important thing going on in Statistics that day.

Mark took his seat and tried his best to look casual as he waited for Ana to arrive. Of course, she arrived right before the bell, same as always. How dare she not take into account that on this particular day Mark had important questions to ask her about her best friend's availability for the Homecoming Dance. Selfish.

There wasn't time to say anything before class started, so he opted to play it cool. Act like he wasn't stressed out about the conversation he was about to have. Wow, he thought, if I'm this stressed about just asking Ana about asking Lauren, actually asking Lauren will be way tougher.

Mrs. Cobb took her place at the front of the classroom, flicked on the antiquated overhead projector, and started her lecture. Something about standard deviation in a normal distribution; Mark could not have been paying less attention. His hand mechanically copied every word, but not a single line of the content was retained in conscious thought during that process.

Eventually Mark had his opening. Mrs. Cobb turned off the projector, passed off a thick stack of worksheets to Achal Chopra, and returned to her desk before typing away at her computer. The general consensus among her classes was that her furious typing during class worksheet time was not related to statistics at all, but actually an attempt at a novel. According to a rumor, a kid in one of her classes last year saw her internet history filled with searches like "how to write a novel," "first time writer," and "mythology of vampires." An even less likely rumor said another kid found a rough draft. In that rumor, she was indeed writing a vampire-themed romance novel. There was no mention of the quality of her prose in that rumor, though, so maybe she'd find a market for it one day.

Regardless of Mrs. Cobb's writing ability, Mark recognized a narrow window while Achal passed out the worksheets by the class's unspoken rule: one person at a time. It was a clever move to eat up time and get them closer to the end of class. The trick was to be a good student and not be too slow in how you passed out the papers.

"Ana," Mark whispered after he graciously accepted his worksheet from Achal.

"Yeah?"

"I have a question about Homecoming I wanted to ask."

"Well, I'll probably be going with Ben since we've been dating for over a year. But shoot your shot, I guess," Ana said in a low voice. Achal overheard as he gave her the worksheet and snickered but kept on moving.

Mark took the joke in stride. "Please, you should be so lucky." He dropped his voice lower. It didn't quite make sense why, but it felt embarrassing to be asking. Maybe because this indirect ask could still receive an indirect rejection. "No, I was actually wondering if you think it might be a good idea for me to ask Lauren to the Homecoming Dance."

Ana took a moment, as if she was thinking about how to respond. Her face was stone, completely unreadable. What was only a second or two felt like an eternity to Mark. He resisted the urge to anxiously drum his fingers or tap his feet.

She looked over to Mark, gave him a once-over as if this was the first time seeing him, and gave a shrug that suggested the affirmative.

Still, this was not exactly a situation in which Mark was prepared to accept much ambiguity. "So, you think she'd say yes if I asked her?" Mark asked, trying to keep his voice sounding cool and neutral.

"Yes." Ana whispered before she turned back to her worksheet.

But it wasn't over just yet. Mark glanced over to Mrs. Cobbs, still pounding away at her keyboard, some unknown length into her vampire romance novel of unknown quality.

The second rule that Mark had learned was to scope out any other potential suitors. Just because Ana had said that Lauren would probably be interested in going with him wasn't enough. Last year, he had heard rumors that Ana would've gone to the dance with Chuck if he had asked her. But before Chuck worked up the nerve to ask her, or really even talk to her at all, Ben Daniels had made her a playlist, bought her flowers, and asked. She said yes, and the two of them were still together almost a year later.

Mark never found out if Ana would've said yes if Chuck had asked first. He realized it was a bit of an awkward question, so it remained unasked.

Mark pressed on about the dance, though, still in a low whisper. "But do you know anyone else that might want to ask Lauren to the dance?"

Ana kept her eyes down but shook her head from side to side. Nope. Ana was not aware of any other potential suitors.

All signs were good. He just needed to make the ask. That brings up the third rule.

The third rule was to ask in an interesting way. That was going to be a bit trickier, Mark realized. He halfheartedly started his stats worksheet as the bulk of his subconscious brainpower turned towards finding a good way to ask.

"The girl in green —" Mark began, a few nights later, when he and Chuck were down in Chuck's cavernous subbasement for training.

"Girl?" Chuck interrupted. "How can you tell?"

"I ran into her last night. I'm pretty sure I heard a woman's voice, or a girl's voice, beneath the mask," Mark confessed. Chuck wanted Mark to stick to mostly superpowered crime or daytime incidents, operating only when he was available for support work. Mark disagreed; he'd been going out as Solarflare every night, with or without Chuck.

The girl in green shared Mark's work ethic. She'd been stopping street-level crime every night since the multi-car accident. She stopped a few muggings and carjackings, incidents that Solarflare heard about second-hand. Mark often wondered how she was beating him to these scenes. He could fly, after all. Word was that she'd broken a couple of would-be assailants' arms in the process. Nothing too gruesome, but if they were going to take a swing at her, she had every right to counter.

Last night, he went out and ran into the girl in green. She wasn't much for conversation, but she did thank Mark for rescuing people from the car accident before she got there to help. She ran off before Mark had a chance to ask her anything, but there was something else he noticed.

Chuck glared at Mark.

"She got to a mugging before me, I can't be everywhere at once," Mark said, before adding earnestly, "She kicks butt. I think she's another legitimate superhero."

"She's wearing a hoodie and trying to hide in the shadows. She might as well be wearing a paper bag on her head," Chuck pointed out, as he pulled apart a nearby newspaper to show Mark the security camera photos. "She's not even in the same league as us."

"Because of her costume?" Mark asked incredulously. He wouldn't even be in his own league if it wasn't for Chuck supplying the suit. Maybe once this new crime-fighter got a custom suit, she'd be ready for the big time. "She's not some weird vigilante in over her head. She's taken on a lot of tough guys and hasn't been beaten."

"Sure, she's knocked around a few punks, but that doesn't mean she'd have any chance against members of The Abyss. If she got hurt because we let her in over her head, that's on us," Chuck pointed out. "You've been training almost every day to face them. How's she training? Can she even get better than where she is now?"

"Yeah, but you haven't seen her in action. But what if she's like us?" Mark asked, finally getting to the point he was trying to make. "Not in terms of costumes, or web presence, or ability to keep a secret identity, but the other thing." Mark's eyes glowed a deep crimson to punctuate his sentence.

Chuck's eyes glowed blue in response. "I don't think that's the case."

"I saw her eyes flash green," Mark revealed.

Chuck was speechless for a moment. The two sat in silence.

"You're sure?" Chuck asked.

"Positive."

"She have a name?" Chuck asked, resigned to accepting that Mark had judged her abilities correctly. She might very well be in their league, and he was now thinking about the work he might need to do to manage her superhero profile, as well. Even if she was a competent hero like Mark thought, Chuck still saw her as a liability. He'd prefer it if she was affiliated with the two of them, even if only tangentially.

"I got nothing," Mark replied with a shrug.

"That's not too helpful."

"Green Lantern?" Mark joked. "Green Arrow?"

"Green Hornet."

"Yeah, I doubt it's any of those," Mark said. "I'll ask her next time I see her."

"Please do. It might make things a lot easier if we build a relationship. I'm not in love with the idea of someone else out there doing what we do, but if she's out there, it may be easier for all involved if we bring her in."

"What I do," Mark corrected. "Unless you're itching to put on a suit of your own. Need I remind you that you're also packing superpowers?"

Chuck offered Mark a rude gesture and turned back to his computer.

"So, thinking about Homecoming?" Chuck asked as he typed away, shifting away from the subject.

"Yeah, actually," Mark answered, blushing slightly. "I'm going to ask Lauren."

Chuck turned back around in his chair, nodding in approval. "I think you two would be good together."

"Thanks, man," Mark muttered, blushing even deeper now and trying to hide it. He was not hiding it well. "Yeah, I have my sources, and it seems like she isn't going with anyone yet."

"So how are you going to ask her?"

"I have an idea, but it does kind of involve Solarflare," Mark said as carefully as he could. It was not careful enough for Chuck.

"You want to bring your superhero persona to ask the girl you like to Homecoming?" Chuck asked, his voice not any louder but much angrier. If he was trying to control his temper at this moment, he was not doing a good job. He continued laying into Mark for the suggestion. "You don't see how that could backfire? How it could put us in danger? How it could put her in danger? Why not paint the largest possible target in the world on her back?"

Mark had expected Chuck to dislike the idea in general but did not expect him to get so condescending. "Are you done?" Mark asked, his tone perfectly flat.

Mark took Chuck's silence as a yes.

"Obviously, I can't have Solarflare ask Lauren to go to Homecoming with me. That would be stupid and even if it didn't immediately out me as Solarflare, it'd absolutely indicate that I have some sort of relationship with him and that is also very dangerous. Solarflare is not doing the asking, he's doing recon."

Chuck shrugged. "I'm sorry I overreacted. That does sound a lot less likely to blow up in our faces. What do you mean by 'recon' though?"

"Okay, here's what I'm thinking," Mark began as he took to the air on a cushion of heat. He climbed high above Chuck's head and pointed at one end of the platform as he outlined his plan. "Lauren lives a couple blocks away from school. When the weather is decent, she walks to school early for cross-country practice." Mark traced an imaginary walking path towards the opposite end of the platform. "I can suit up, take to the sky, and see what route she takes. Then, at night, I can set up a series of signs asking her to the dance, so she'll see them on her walk to school."

Mark landed gently and looked for any sign of approval from Chuck. It wasn't creepy, was it? He worried it might be a little creepy. Maybe if he was regularly watching Lauren walk to school it'd be creepy, he tried to rationalize it, but this was just a one-time thing. Chuck wasn't saying anything. Maybe he should try to think of another idea.

"Why do you need to do anything as Solarflare for it to work?" Chuck asked after a moment. "I mean, isn't it a pretty straight shot from her house to the school?"

"Fair." Mark conceded. "But I want to double-check. I don't want to set up a sign somewhere she won't see it. Each sign will be one word."

"What if you had a sign at the end that recapped them? That way, it looks like you didn't know her route perfectly ahead of time. You know, so she won't think you're a stalker."

Mark winced at being called a "stalker," but he realized that Chuck made a good point. If it seemed like he expected to make a mistake, she'd never know about the prep work he was about to do. Chuck was the smartest guy he knew.

The next morning was a Tuesday, the weather was cooperating, and Mark actually managed to wake up to his early alarm: the one at 5:30 in the morning. Mark groaned as he silently rubbed sleep from his eyes.

It was just like flight training, he thought. That was Chuck's fault, too.

Chuck, also being a member of the cross-country team, told Mark that if he wanted to be sure to follow Lauren's route from the air, he should be in position no later than 5:45.

Mark pulled on the suit, climbed out his window, and took to the sky as he felt himself tapping into his deep reserve of literal firepower. He immediately felt more awake and pushed more heat to his soles, climbing straight up as quickly as he could so he wouldn't be spotted. The suit's design was not very conducive to covert work. He made a mental note that he and Chuck should really consider an alternate suit coloring if stealth missions were ever necessary.

Mark headed vaguely towards the school and tried to make out Lauren's street and house from the air. He'd been over there before as a kid, but it was harder than he expected. He'd gotten relatively good at spotting major streets from above while doing Solarflare-work, but suburbs came up a good deal less often. He had to pull out his phone and check. He was six blocks off target.

As Mark pulled over the familiar side street, he was just in time to see Lauren leaving her house. Well, he was pretty confident it was her. He was too high to be completely sure, but that was a necessity so that she wouldn't look up and see Solarflare watching her walk to school. But it had to be Lauren. She was wearing a backpack and she was walking towards the school and school wasn't going to start for almost another two hours. At the very least, Mark had found a member of the cross-country team.

It's not like the cross-country team was all that big, Mark thought. In fact, North Delfield High was one of the larger high schools in the country and had a proportionally large cross-country team. Roughly 40 students ran for the school between the varsity and JV programs. Luckily for Mark, though, it was Lauren.

In that moment, watching Lauren walk to school from his invisible vantage point in the air, Mark realized that this was way creepier than it had seemed when he first thought of it. He wished Chuck had talked him out of involving Solarflare for recon. The sign idea was fine on its own. Especially since, so far, she was taking the exact route he would've assumed.

Mark rose higher in the air until the clouds were beneath him and Lauren faded from view. He then made his way back home, ready to pretend he hadn't just done that. He needed to swear

Chuck to secrecy. If Chuck ever mentions this, Mark thought, I'll tell everyone he's a merman. Yeah, the nuclear option seemed appropriate right about now.

Later that same day, the suit was completed for the girl in green. Chuck worked fast. Various tones of green and black, all made of Chuck's Atlantean hypersilk. Since they didn't know the new hero's powers, they made it as basic as possible: head-to-toe coverage, sturdy, and as form-fitting as they could tell from grainy ATM security camera footage which was currently displayed across the six-monitor setup in Chuck's subbasement. And she seemed to work almost exclusively at night, so dark colors were the move.

"Looks good," Mark said as he examined the suit and tested its flexibility. It felt basically the same as his suit and he didn't have any complaints.

"Glad you approve. Hopefully she feels the same," Chuck said. "By the way, how did your recon mission go?"

Mark couldn't detect judgement in Chuck's voice. It sounded like a sincere question. "It went okay, then I realized it was way creepier than I expected, so I bailed and I'm just going to do the plan like I don't perfectly know her walk to school. And I'd kind of prefer that we never speak of this again."

"Okay," Chuck said, taking in everything Mark had said. He recognized that Mark was indeed embarrassed, but he needed to twist the knife a tiny bit. "I mean, I told you so."

Mark's eyes flashed crimson.

"Just saying," Chuck continued, not even phased by Mark's fiery reaction. "And that's the last time I'll mention it."

That night Mark ran into the girl in green again. In all, it had been a busy day for him. He was on a nightly patrol as Solarflare and happened to be soaring above an alley where three guys had apparently tried to rob an old man. Mark saw the man thank her before leaving as she secured the criminals.

"Hey," Mark announced cheerfully, as he descended into the alley. He landed gently and extended his hand.

The girl in green cautiously approached Mark. He smiled beneath his mask, one hand still extended to offer her a handshake for a job well done, the other holding the package with her costume.

"I was hoping I'd run into you again," Mark said in a cheerful whisper. It was late and he was half-listening for any approaching police sirens.

She nodded, as if in agreement, and paused for a second.

Suddenly, she broke off into a sprint towards Mark. She leapt over top of him and grabbed the bottom rung of a fire escape ladder. She climbed and flipped up the escape ladder faster than Mark could even process.

Mark stood stunned for a moment before going after her. His eyes flashed red and he flew to the roof. She had already reached it before he got there. She was making her way across rooftops. Mark was barely able to make out her silhouette against the night sky as she sprinted along and jumped between roofs. She was heading towards Adams Park. Once she got there, there was no way Mark would be able to find her.

Mark put as much power to his boots as was safe and flew as quickly as he could to cut her off. He hung in the air blocking her way. She stopped.

"I just wanted to give you something," Mark said slowly, in the friendliest voice he could manage. Tone was really all he could convey with his face totally covered. He gently put down the bundle containing the suit he and Chuck had made.

She remained in her spot eying the package.

"It's a suit," Mark explained. "I mean, I'm sorry if I ruined the surprise, but I feel like you'd leave it otherwise."

She cautiously approached the package and unwrapped it. She held the suit in her hands, feeling and testing the material.

"It's strong," Mark continued, pulling at his own suit to illustrate his words. "It's like mine. It'll stop a knife or bullet, but they can still hurt. A lot."

The night air was silent except for the very faint sounds of police sirens arriving to the scene they had just left, several blocks over.

"You've been doing good things and I think this could help."

"Thank you," she said with a grateful nod.

Her voice was kind, and somehow familiar. Mark chalked that up to their last conversation, as if she had said more than three words to him last time. Her eyes flashed green again as she spoke. He smiled. He wasn't alone in this league anymore.

"You're welcome," Mark replied, flying off into the night. It was getting late, and he had school the next day. He didn't realize at the time that he had forgotten to get her name. Chuck wasn't going to be happy about that at all.

While I'm out, Mark thought, I may as well take care of other business. His eyes flashed crimson beneath his mask and he jetted back home to pick up his supplies. He grabbed the posterboards, the markers, and the tape he needed, and hauled his supplies to the roof so he could get to work. He knew himself well enough that if he went into his room, there was the very real chance that he'd climb in bed and fall asleep until his alarm went off in the morning. And then he'd be dealing with the risk of his mom coming into his room, seeing him in the suit, and blowing up his superhero career no more than a month and a half after it started.

As Mark sat on the roof and looked out at the skyline of downtown Delfield against the dark sky, he thought about how strange everything was after only a couple months. How strange everything had been since that field trip. He was the biggest superhero in the world. And, prior to a week or so ago, he was the only superhero in the world. To his knowledge, there were now two of them. And he still didn't have a name to go with the other one…

Anyway, he wondered about what would've happened if he'd crouched down like he'd been told to during that field trip. That shard of molten metal would've passed harmlessly over his head. But if that had happened, it'd mean no superpowers, no superhero identity, no reason for Chuck to tell him about Atlantis. Wow. Would Chuck have even told him about Atlantis if Mark had listened back then? Without powers or Solarflare, how much of his friend's life would he have been privy to?

Mark paused for a moment before ultimately shrugging it off. There was no sense in driving himself crazy over what could've been. He had signs to make for his Homecoming proposal and that seemed like the greater priority. After all, existential questions on his life wouldn't help him get a girlfriend.

He pulled out his phone and drafted up the actual text to put on the signs. He had bought ten pieces of posterboard. It seemed like a reasonable amount at the time he bought it, but he hadn't yet figured out exactly what to write.

Mark ran through a couple drafts. It would look best if he broke it up into one word per sign. Any more than one word per sign would look amateurish, he thought. It made sense.

The posterboards were held down beneath his thigh against the roof. If they blew away, he didn't really have an alternative. The night air was also starting to feel a bit chilly, but he knew better than to use his powers to warm himself. He wasn't sure he could confidently ride the line between warming himself and burning up his posterboard. What temperature did posterboard burn at? He made a note to check that out later.

As his conscious thoughts drifted towards a new subject, the back of his mind figured it out. It landed on the perfect text. Nine boards were needed.

The text: *Hi. Lauren. Would. You. Go. To. Homecoming. With. Me.* And then, on the last board, Mark would sign his name. The final board's *Me* wouldn't work without any additional context. Anyone could take credit for Mark's inventive Homecoming proposal.

Yep. That was it, Mark thought as he pulled his mask up and uncapped the marker in his teeth. He wrote out his words in the neatest script he could manage, which was honestly very good, especially for a high schooler.

Once he was done, he took the posterboards in hand and admired his handiwork. Phrasing was good, penmanship was good. Those were the main criteria. He clutched the boards in one hand and the markers and tape in the other. This next part had to be done carefully, he realized. He needed to fly in order to get the signs up, but he needed to keep the flames limited to just his feet. The tape and the posters absolutely needed to be kept safe from heat and fire. That said, he did still have one spare posterboard. No harm in wasting that one piece of posterboard that wasn't needed, Mark thought. He placed a foot over the top of that last piece of posterboard and, when his eyes flashed red, heat blasted from his boots and ignited the unnecessary paper.

"Alright," Mark said aloud, breaking the silence of 3 o'clock in the morning atop his roof in the Delfield suburbs as the ashes from his superfluous posterboard swirled about the air. "Time to ask a girl to Homecoming." His eyes glowed a gentle red before the heat built up exclusively in the soles of his feet and lifted him into the air as he set to his task.

Mark awoke the next morning to a text notification.

Mark, I'd love to go to Homecoming with you. See you in class.

It was well worth the sleep he'd lost.

NINE
The Inferno

"She's wearing the suit," Mark pointed out to Chuck, as the two of them scoured local news for anything relating to Solarflare or the girl in green. Mark had found an online article about the girl in green with a photo taken from a security camera two nights ago. He had given her the suit Chuck made about a week ago, but he hadn't run into her since. Mark handed Chuck his phone with the article's photo pulled up.

It was a cool, mid-October afternoon. The leaves had all turned shades of yellow and orange and red, but they still stubbornly held to the trees. Mark liked the change this year more than usual. Largely due to his new autumn-colored persona. He and Chuck were spending their Saturday walking around downtown. Chuck had learned that the city was installing new security cameras at the street level in order to crack down on Mark's vigilante efforts, and he wanted to scout out their locations so Mark could take advantage of their blind spots.

"It's bulletproof," Chuck muttered as he gave Mark's phone screen a cursory glance. "Of course she's wearing it. It's a lot sturdier than a hoodie. Also, I'm still mad at you for putting up the signs in your suit. What if someone saw?"

Mark rolled his eyes. No one had seen Mark putting up the signs. It was 3 in the morning when he had done it and he made a point to be discrete. This was not an argument worth having again.

"She have a name yet?" Chuck asked. "Because everyone's still just calling her the 'girl in green.' She's been on the radar for about a month now, it's a little annoying that she hasn't chosen a name."

"What, are you trying to launch a toy deal for us? Can't sell action figures without a name?" Mark asked. "Why does it matter?"

"A legitimate costume and name make it harder for anyone to impersonate you," Chuck explained in a hushed tone as they continued walking along the busy sidewalk. "You, Mark, have a clear modus operandi when you're in costume. The costume is meticulously detailed, you have a distinct personality and voice, and, finally, fire-based superpowers. You are hard to imitate. She was just running around in a green hoodie breaking guys' arms last month. It wouldn't be hard for someone to find a similar hoodie and start breaking into stores and houses and pin it on her. The more developed you are as a hero, the less likely people are to believe it if someone tries to ruin your good name."

"That makes sense," Mark conceded.

"I've put a lot of thought into all this stuff. I think we've established a good balance for you, but I can't speak for her. Our ties to her could bring all three of us down if we're not careful. Forty-eight."

"What?"

"Forty-eight cameras along the last ten blocks, on both sides of Gardner Street; more along side streets. I can probably figure out their distribution throughout the rest of downtown and make you a map of good blind spots. Alleys still seem like they're fair game for changing."

"Alright, so should —"

Sirens drowned out the rest of Mark's question as a firetruck barreled past the two and disappeared down a turn.

Mark looked over the row of buildings in the direction the firetruck was headed. Black smoke was billowing from somewhere just a few streets over.

"There's a fire," Mark said.

"Yeah. Very observant. And firefighters are heading there now. I don't know how much help you'll be," Chuck pointed out. "You generally make fire; I don't know how much help you'll be when it comes to putting one out."

"I'm fireproof, I can help get people out," Mark declared after a moment.

"Are you sure you're actually fireproof? Being able to make fire may not mean it can't hurt you at a certain temperature. And even if you are, the people you'd be rescuing aren't. The firefighters are better trained for this."

"I have to do something," Mark announced as he turned down an alley and pulled off his backpack. "And besides, alleys still seem like they're fair game for changing."

Solarflare landed in front of the flaming building a few moments later, ahead of the barricade the firefighters and paramedics had constructed to keep the public safe. Firefighters were spraying along the edges of the building, trying to keep the flames from spreading. It was an apartment building, Mark realized. That meant a lot of people might be trapped inside.

"Hey, get back," a voice behind Mark shouted.

"I'm here to help," Mark said calmly as he turned around.

"Oh no," the man protested, "I've seen you on the news. I know all about you. If you think I'm sending another match into this fire, you're an idiot."

"I'm fireproof. Which is more than I can say for you and your team. Let me take the harder to reach floors. Those people might die if we keep arguing."

The man paused for a moment. He took a hard look at the fire and exhaled deeply.

"Fine."

"Thank you, uh, —" Mark began, searching for how to address the man.

"Captain," the man explained. "Captain Simmons."

"Right," Mark said, "Captain. Thank you. Do you know what we're dealing with?"

"Yeah," Captain Simmons replied. "The building is residential, seven stories, fire appears to have started on the fifth floor or so. We believe that there are individuals on floors five, six, and seven. We've begun getting people out of the first few floors, but the stairway is blocked after the fourth floor. You can fly, right?"

"Yes sir," Mark nodded, standing almost at attention in respect.

"Then we want you to fly up and rescue those people, one at a time, starting with the seventh floor and working down, from top to bottom. Do you understand?"

"Yes, sir. You may want to take a few steps back."

Mark's eyes burned a deep red and the soles of his boots heated rapidly, launching him towards the top of the apartment complex. He eased up and hung for a moment just below the roof. The heat radiating from the fire threw him off balance. Maybe Chuck had a point. He had never really been around this much fire. But he couldn't think of that now, he had a job to do.

Mark's eyes strained as he peered through the windows, looking for the people on the top floor. He heard them before he saw them. Someone was shouting and coughing out of a bedroom window. Mark flew over and noticed that the person shouting looked like he was younger than Mark. For a second, Mark wondered if they went to the same school.

"Is there anyone with you?" Mark asked, trying to maintain focus.

"Yes," the teenager responded, "My grandfather. This is his apartment, but I don't think he can breathe. Please help him."

"Ok," Mark said, in his most serious voice, "I'm going to come in, get your grandfather and fly him down. Then I'll come back for you. Do you understand?"

The teenager hesitated. The thought of being left in the building terrified him.

"Do you understand?" Mark asked again, this time in a more commanding tone.

"Yes," the teenager answered, with resolve.

Mark carefully climbed through the window and walked over to the bed where the old man lay. He was still breathing, but just barely. Mark picked him up awkwardly and carried him to the window. Mark swung his legs out of the window, sitting on the windowsill. He had never flown with a passenger before. Why was he just realizing this now?

"Are you alright?" the teenager asked.

"Yeah," Mark answered, his eyes flashing beneath the mask. He pulled the old man into his arms and hopped out the window. His boots took control as he descended. He had to twist and adjust to keep hold of the old man and keep his balance, but they made it to the ground safely, if not a bit harder than Mark preferred. He handed the old man off to the paramedics and went back up.

As Mark neared the top floor, he saw the teenager standing on the windowsill. The flames had spread even further. He wouldn't be able to stay there much longer.

"Hold on," Mark shouted, but it was too late. The teenager had leapt away from the fire, passing Mark in midair. Mark turned sharply and gave chase. He grabbed the kid's leg and the two of them twisted and spun in the air, barely better than a free fall. Just before they hit the ground, Mark managed to gain control and fired one last blast of heat from his soles. The heated air cushioned the landing as Mark landed on his back, the teenager right on top of him.

"You good?" Captain Simmons asked as he pulled the two of them up to their feet.

The teenager nodded slowly, shaking from his fall.

"And you?" Captain Simmons asked Mark.

Mark pulled his mask up to just above his mouth and took a few deep breaths as he leaned on the hood of an ambulance.

Without a word Mark pulled his mask back down over his face and flew back into the flames. He crashed through the nearest window on the sixth floor. There were still four people that needed to be saved, by the captain's count.

Mark stood in the middle of a family's living room. The walls and furniture were on fire, heat radiating all around him. He had never experienced heat like this before. He could tell that any normal person would be burned right here.

"Hello?" Mark shouted. "Is there anyone there?"

Muffled cries answered from an adjacent room. Mark grabbed the doorknob to the room and felt the heat through his glove. Even with his powers, it still stung a bit. He carefully opened the door, not wanting to hit anyone on the other side with the flaming door.

The room was a bathroom, and the woman was in the bathtub with two little girls, most likely her daughters. The three of them were covered in damp towels, to try and protect themselves from the heat.

"Are you all okay?" Mark asked.

The woman nodded, tears streaming down her face. She cried silently, while the two girls sobbed and screamed.

Mark looked around. There was no window. And the only way to get them out was the way he had come in. And that way was on fire. He could handle it, but there was no way that woman could make it out safely, much less the little girls.

A small fireball formed in Mark's hand, almost instinctively, and he looked at it with a mixture of disappointment and resentment. What good did this power do him here? Was he just good at starting fires?

"What are we going to do?" The woman asked as calmly as she could muster.

The flame in Mark's hand faded.

Mark reached outside of the bathroom and focused on a narrow area, a small flame on the floor. He held out his hand and took a deep breath in and held it. As he inhaled, the flame flickered and faltered. He gently exhaled and then took in another deep breath. This time the small flame went out. Mark smiled.

"Wait here," Mark instructed the woman, as if there was anywhere else she could go.

He stepped out into the room and stood in the center of the open space. His eyes glowed and he took in a deep breath. All around the room, the fire flickered, but did not go out. He inhaled again, deeper this time, and the flames grew weaker still, but did not extinguish. He tried a third time, inhaling so deeply that he nearly passed out, and the flames finally went out. The room cooled noticeably, but there was still fire on all sides of them.

The woman stood up in awe and her daughters' sobs quieted.

"Okay," Mark explained, when he went back into the bathroom. "I can't take all of you at once. I can take your girls down together, but I'll need to come back for you."

"Alright," the woman answered without hesitation. She gently laid her hand on Mark's arm. "Thank you."

Mark smiled beneath the mask and picked up the girls. The open window across the living room beckoned them. He could sense the room beginning to heat again and that the floors were becoming weaker. He ran through the room, one girl in each arm, and jumped through the window before flames cracked through the floor.

He flew them down to the ground and handed them off to the same paramedics as before. The old man was now conscious and coughing violently, though Mark didn't notice. He was already back on the sixth floor, climbing through the window.

"Great," Mark muttered as he looked at the living room, or rather, the giant flaming hole in the apartment where a living room once stood. Mark carefully flew through the area, heat greatly affecting his flight stability, and crash-landed in the bathroom. The floor seemed to still be pretty sturdy here, Mark thought.

"I can't take you out that way," Mark said. "It's too hot and I can't keep my balance when I'm flying."

"Can't you absorb the fire again?" she asked.

Mark stuck his hands out the doorway and concentrated. He took in a deep breath and tried to extinguish the flames, but he couldn't feel much of a difference. There wouldn't be enough time to put out the fire that way, if it was even possible.

"Please," the woman pleaded, crying even harder now than when Mark first saw her.

Mark clenched his fists and focused on the heat. He exhaled and felt the flames rise a little. He inhaled and felt them shrink slightly. He exhaled again and the flames stayed the same. He inhaled and the flames rushed into him. The fire that had consumed the woman's apartment now filled Mark. He held his breath and tried to get it under control. He felt so incredibly hot. Sweat flowed out of every pore and his goggles steamed up from the inside.

"Are you—" the woman began, reaching out to Mark.

"Don't." Mark said, his voice strained. The woman pulled her hand back, she could feel the heat radiating from Mark through the suit.

Mark carefully exhaled, still keeping the heat within him. He took several shallow breaths to prevent the fire from rising again. He glanced about the bathroom desperately and spotted the toilet.

Mark gestured for the woman to get out of the way and he made a beeline for the toilet. He flung open the lid and, seeing that the bowl was still filled with water, pulled up his mask and unleashed a torrent of flames. The bathroom filled with steam, but Mark could breathe normally again.

Feeling much better, Mark turned to face the woman, now standing just outside of the bathroom. The floor suddenly gave out from under her, sending her down toward the flames below.

"No!" Mark shouted, blasting himself through the apartment to catch her. He caught her right before she reached the flames, and the two flew out through the window.

The crowd of onlookers cheered from beyond the barricade, but Mark wasn't so sure.

He set the woman on the ground carefully.

"Are you alright?" Mark asked, looking her up and down for burns.

Wordlessly, the woman wrapped her arms around Mark in a hug.

"You're welcome," Mark said softly, tears welling up in his eyes. He led her over to the nearest ambulance and gave the paramedics a nod. The firefighters had saved another half dozen people from the lower floors who were now receiving care.

"There's still one more," Captain Simmons said from nearby. "We got everyone out from the lower levels, but we couldn't get the one man on the fifth floor."

Mark looked back at the building. The fire was raging all over. There was very little chance the man on the fifth floor was still alive. But he had to check.

Mark launched himself through the air and flew through the open window on the sixth floor and dropped down a level. The flames were all around him, and the heat poured into his suit. Mark feared the worst, yet he kept moving. He searched through the apartment he was in and made his way to the next unit. There was no one in that apartment either. The next one was empty as well, and the one after that, too.

Mark reached the final unchecked apartment, located just next to the emergency stairwell. The flames seemed hottest here, but Mark couldn't be too sure. The intense heat was affecting him. Solarflare or not, the heat was making it hard for him to focus. He tried to shake it off and concentrate. He opened the door and it splintered and crumbled to ash as he opened it, with the red-hot doorknob falling to the ground with a loud clang and hissing from the heat. He kicked the doorknob aside and made his way into the apartment, preparing for what he might find.

The apartment was sparsely decorated. The living room was completely empty, except for a single chair and a small coffee table. Mark wondered if the occupant had just moved in.

"Hello?" Mark called out, straining his voice so that it could carry over the noise of the fire. "Is there anyone in here?"

His question was answered with a blast of flames through a nearby wall. Mark fell to his feet and the floor began to crack beneath him. A small burst of heat to his boots kept him from falling to the next floor, but the surrounding heat of the fire caused Mark to crash against a nearby wall and slide down onto the single chair, breaking it.

Mark groaned and picked himself up. Had something exploded on the other side of the wall? Its timing was impeccable. No. That was a response.

Mark strained his eyes to see who it was that had attacked him through the flames. The fire was nearly opaque at this point. Mark was barely able to make out a man's figure, not much taller than him. And then Mark saw it. The man's eyes glowed the same red as his. This was another pyrate!

"Wait!" Mark called out as the figure sprinted through the doorway and down the emergency stairwell, also unhurt by the flames. It was too late; he was gone.

A million questions swirled in Mark's mind. But there was one thing he was confident of: that man set this fire. And Mark was going to see if he could find anything that might explain why.

Mark pulled himself to his feet and carefully made his way through the apartment, into the bedroom where the man had been. Mark's eyes scanned the room. It was just as sparse as the living room, with only a bed sitting in the middle of the room on a simple frame and a desk that held a sophisticated-looking computer. Mark looked closer at the computer. It wasn't nearly as damaged as it should've been. Mark was no expert on what heat did to electronics, but he was sure that this computer was more durable than most.

A flaming hunk of drywall fell from the ceiling, just barely missing Mark's head. The building was about to come down. He ran to the computer and began feeling around the desktop. He didn't know much, but he knew the hard drive had to be around there somewhere, and the hard drive must have something valuable on it. He clumsily clawed at the machine, his hands warping the computer's heated frame as he touched it. The frame was made entirely of metal, but the surrounding temperature had risen to a point where the metal flexed and gave like a soft plastic. Mark muttered profanities aloud as he worried that his search would destroy what he was looking for.

Mark finally felt a cube noticeably tougher than the rest of the desktop. This must be it, he thought. He yanked the hard drive out violently as the ceiling above him gave way. Mark dodged falling debris as he sprinted towards the bedroom window, each step leaving behind holes in the floor.

Mark leapt through the window, glass shards falling with him, just as the building shook violently, and the top two floors collapsed onto the fifth, sending the whole thing to the ground, showering the surrounding area in a thick cloud of dust.

Defenestration, Mark thought, his mind flashing to his SAT vocabulary prep. His boots caught him mid-air with a burst of heat. Wait, he realized, continuing the train of thought, defenestration means being *thrown* out of a window. Jumping through one doesn't count.

Mark landed gently on the ground, the force from his boots blowing the dust in all directions. He brushed off his chest, clearing his symbol, and looked around. Everyone he got out of the building seemed to be okay, just incredibly dirty now.

After a pause, the dust-and-soot-covered crowd erupted into cheers and shouts of praise for Solarflare. Mark smiled.

He scanned the crowd for the man he saw, the man with red eyes, but no such luck. Mark had no idea what the guy looked like, other than the eyes. He didn't know the man's face, or skin color, or hair. Just the eyes, glowing a deep red. And that wouldn't even help much. If this guy was anything like Mark, his eyes were normally brown, which wouldn't exactly eliminate a lot of suspects. He was gone, Mark realized. But maybe the hard drive contained a clue.

"You did good," a gruff voice behind Mark said.

"Thank you, Captain." Mark answered.

"I was wrong, you were a great help. I'm sorry I doubted you," he continued, extending his hand out to Mark.

Mark took his hand firmly and shook it.

"Thanks."

"Damn shame about the guy on the fifth," Captain Simmons said. "I don't blame you, though," he added, not wanting to undermine the compliment.

"Captain," Mark began in a hushed tone, "The guy on the fifth didn't die. He's like me. The fire didn't hurt him. He got out, but I didn't get a good look at him. I think he started this fire." He felt he needed to tell Captain Simmons what happened.

Captain Simmons was silent for a moment. One man with the ability to create fire was bad enough, now he had no idea how many of them there were.

"What's that in your hand?" he asked, his tone much more serious now.

Mark clenched the warped hard drive in his hand. "It's nothing."

"If that's evidence, the police will need it."

Mark shook his head in protest. "I'm on your side. I'm gonna look into this. I'm better equipped to handle it."

"Give me that evidence, son," Captain Simmons ordered, his tone now devoid of any of the respect for Solarflare he had held just a few minutes ago. Firefighters surrounded the two of them, ready to support their captain.

Wordlessly, Mark took to the air and flew off, Captain Simmons cursing below.

Minutes later Mark had changed back into his street clothes and emerged from the alley where he had left his stuff before the fire.

Mark did his best to casually blend into the crowded sidewalk, but there was no sign of Chuck. He pulled his phone out of his pocket and called his friend.

"Where are you?" Mark asked when Chuck picked up.

"I kept walking," Chuck explained. "I couldn't just stand there waiting for you."

"Where are you?"

"Coffee shop at the corner of Nelson and Venice. I've been working on a map. You know, like we planned on doing today."

Mark rolled his eyes and hung up before making his way to the coffee shop.

Mark found Chuck sitting at a table near the back, typing away on his laptop. Mark plopped down into the seat across from him with a heavy thud. He was exhausted.

"You smell like a campfire," Chuck observed, still focused on whatever task he had onscreen.

"It's a new cologne," Mark deadpanned, a little annoyed that Chuck hadn't even bothered to make eye contact. In the back of his mind, he worried his mom would notice it too.

"Sure. Women do love that smoky scent. Did you take your phone with you into the fire?" Chuck asked, only looking up from his computer for a second.

"What? No, I left it with my normal clothes," Mark exclaimed loudly before switching to a hushed tone. "And I'm fine, just saved five people from dying, but whatever."

"I mean that it would've been a good time to test the heat-durability of the phone pocket I put on the suit. Obviously, you did a good job."

"Oh," Mark mumbled, his face now becoming slightly flushed.

"Anything interesting? You know what caused it?" Chuck continued as he went back to work on mapping the street cameras.

Mark's mind immediately went to the hard drive in his backpack. He was sure he didn't want to tell Chuck. He wanted to find this out on his own.

But what about the guy who caused it? There was another pyrate out there. Maybe Chuck would have an idea who he was. Maybe he and his dad kept a database of people like them. Mark weighed this option carefully.

"Mark? Did you see what might have caused it?" Chuck repeated.

"Nope," Mark answered, deciding that he was going to keep this one to himself. If he wanted to tell Chuck, he could always do that later.

Chuck shrugged. "I guess it's just one of those things that happens. Good thing you were there, though. You made the right call."

Mark smiled. He appreciated Chuck's support but still felt a small twinge of guilt over his decision to keep a secret from him. He brushed it off. This was a good day. He didn't need to focus on something negative like keeping secrets from Chuck or the police.

Before they left the coffee shop, Mark handed over the super-suit to Chuck for cleaning, as had become routine. Mark did superhero-work, Chuck cleaned the suit, and Mark picked it up the next day. Made a lot more sense for Chuck to wash it since he actually knew what the suit was made out of and he wasn't at risk of exposing a secret by using his washer and dryer. After all, Mr. Currant was in on the whole thing.

TEN
The Abyss

Later that night, Mark took out the hard drive and readied himself to review the contents. He fumbled with the charred remains of the hard drive, looking for any part that he might be able to connect to his own laptop. This would go a lot easier if I just told Chuck, Mark thought. But he had made his decision. He would look into this on his own. Something told him that this needed to be played close to the vest. Maybe it was because this was the first time he had seen someone else like him. Chuck could help him deal with Atlantis stuff, but this was different.

He sat at his desk, laptop open. Mark had been trying to access the hard drive for almost an hour by this point. This was his third attempt at it. If he didn't find something in the next ten minutes, he'd call Chuck. Finding out anything would be worth the loss of secrecy. It might cause an argument about secrets, but Mark knew he could easily win one of those. Compared to all Chuck had kept hidden for years, this was nothing.

Finally, Mark found something that looked like a port, covered with ash and scorch marks. It was narrower than any cables he thought he had though. But Chuck might have them. He made a mental note to ask tomorrow.

"You ready for the comparative government test next period?" Chuck asked as he approached Mark's locker the next morning after their first class.

Mark groaned as he pulled out the books for his next class and plopped them into his bag with a heavy thud. He was not ready.

"You go on patrol last night?" Chuck whispered to Mark, noticing the dark bags under his eyes. "You look really tired."

"I'm fine. I was trying to catch up with the girl in green again, see if I could get some more information about her. Maybe see what her powers actually are," Mark lied.

"Not a terrible idea on a normal night, but this test is important. It's like thirty percent of our grade this quarter."

Mark groaned.

"How much does it cover again?" Mark asked, half-stressing the word '*again*' so it would seem like he had studied some. He hadn't, though. He was going into class almost completely blind.

"It's pretty much all the South American governments. Brazil, Argentina, Chile…"

"I'm familiar with the countries in South America," Mark interrupted. He racked his mind for what he might be able to remember on those countries. He remembered learning about them in class in that he had heard their names, but he couldn't think of anything specific right now. All his mind had been thinking about the last twelve hours was accessing the info in that stupid, useless, burned-up hard drive. It was even in his backpack right now, for some reason he wouldn't have been able to fully explain if he had to. He just needed to have it with him. It seemed too important to leave alone all day.

"Mr. Gottfried might give us some time to review," Chuck offered, sensing Mark's dread.

Mark shrugged a defeatist shrug and the two of them went to class. Mark sat down in his seat and desperately pulled out his comparative government textbook, hoping to refresh everything in the two minutes he had before the bell rang. Chuck approached their teacher's desk, saying something to him too quietly for anyone else to make out. Mark barely noticed; he was putting forth all his efforts to his rapid review session. He flipped through the pages so quickly that he tore one slightly and gave himself a nasty papercut with another. The bell rang. Too late, Mark thought with a sense of doom.

Mr. Gottfried stood at the front of the classroom as his students took their seats. Chuck calmly walked to his seat a few rows over from Mark. Mark and several other students in his same situation placed their books back in their bags or under their desks. Mr. Gottfried waited a moment for the room to settle before he began speaking.

"I know that we were planning on having our test today," Mr. Gottfried began, his voice a bit stilted. Mark raised his head slightly in optimism. "But, I gave this careful thought, and I think today would be better served reviewing the subject matter. There's some material on the test that I don't believe we sufficiently covered yet. We'll take the test next class."

Mark breathed a sigh of relief and looked over to Chuck. Chuck gave an incredulous look and shook his head with a slight grin. What a lucky break.

Mark spent the rest of class doing his best not to fall asleep in front of Mr. Gottfried, knowing that if he did so, the test would be back on. He didn't need everyone else hating him for that. He scrawled a few notes on the subject in his notebook. They were surely illegible, but so long as his hand moved, he was productive enough to ward off sleep.

The rest of the day went well enough, Mark had managed to hastily complete any homework that morning before school, and he didn't have any more surprise quizzes or tests. When the final bell rang, Mark breathed a sigh of relief, got his things from his locker, and made his way to the car.

"Where are you heading?" Mark asked, as he saw Chuck walking in the hall away from the parking lot exit.

"There's a meet today," Chuck explained, not stopping his stride.

"Alright, good luck," Mark said, just as Chuck got out of earshot. He often forgot about Chuck's cross-country meets. They really did not hinder his ability to support Solarflare in any noticeable way. Maybe Mark should show up to one to support his friend before the season was over.

Mark had a sudden thought. If Chuck wasn't expecting him to leave the school at the same time as him, then Chuck wouldn't know if Mark stayed behind for a little bit. Maybe the school's computer lab had something he could use.

Mark made sure that Chuck was out of sight before he made his way there. He took an indirect route, just in case Chuck turned around a corner and happened to see him. Mark opened the door to the computer lab and glanced inside. There wasn't anyone there. He looked at the sign on the outside of the door.

According to the sign, it's still open to students, Mark thought. He made his way inside and closed the door before he opened up his backpack and pulled out the hard drive. He moved back to the door stealthily and considered locking it as an extra precaution but decided against it. If someone did try to get in, it would look very suspicious for the door to be locked. If the door was just closed, however, that'd much easier for him to explain. He looked at the hard drive carefully and once again found the port. He examined the shape of the hole carefully before setting off to find a cable with that end that might fit one of the computers.

Mark's cellphone began to ring, and he nearly dropped the hard drive. After everything it had been through, Mark didn't want to do any more damage to it.

"Hello?" Mark asked in a slightly annoyed voice, not even looking at who was calling.

"Where are you?" an even more annoyed voice asked from the other side. It was Sean, obviously wondering what his driver was doing right now.

"Dealing with something important," Mark answered truthfully, before changing to a lie, "I've got to meet up with one of my teachers about an upcoming test. I'll be out in like five minutes."

Mark hung up without waiting for a response from his brother and went back to looking. After three minutes, the phone rang again. Mark simply ignored it. At the eight-minute mark, it rang again. Mark still hadn't found it after rifling through the connecting wires surrounding nearly half a dozen computers. The phone kept ringing. Mark answered and immediately hung up. One more minute, he thought. He couldn't ask Chuck about it now.

Then he noticed it, the stand-alone supply closet in the back corner of the room. That had to have a cable that would work. Mark fumbled around the closet knocking down several other cables as he searched for an elusive adapter. As they piled up on the floor around him, he found it. He held up the hard drive, scratched and mangled, and gently connected it to the cable.

"Yes," Mark muttered.

"What are you doing?" a voice asked from behind Mark.

He turned around suddenly, still holding the cable and his hard drive in his hands with a blank expression on his face. It was the librarian in charge of the computer lab. She stood in the doorway looking in on Mark and the pool of wires at his feet. She looked less than thrilled to find a student in there, much less the mess he had made.

"Uh," Mark began. Good start, he thought.

"What's your name?" She asked.

"Mark Michaels," he answered obediently.

"Mark," she started. "What are you doing here?" Her voice was on the gentler side of accusatory, but Mark still recognized need for caution.

"I needed an adapter," Mark explained, choosing to keep his lie partially grounded in reality. "My hard drive is really beaten up and I was hoping to find something in here that I could use to connect it to my home computer and transfer everything. I was hoping to find it and ask someone if I could borrow it."

The librarian looked at Mark for a second, trying to determine if he was lying.

Mark held up the hard drive carefully, intending to show her just enough to make the excuse believable but not reveal that it had been through a massive fire.

"Let me get a closer look at that," she requested.

Mark hesitated and slowly began to bring the hard drive closer to her gaze. She peered at it over her thick glasses, looking at every dent and scorch on the device.

"There you are," a familiar voice announced from just behind the librarian. It was Sean. When she turned to see who it was, Mark took the opportunity and stuffed the hard drive hastily into his backpack.

"Sorry," Sean apologized to the authority figure before turning to his brother. "What are you doing?"

"I needed to get something," Mark explained, "and I was just asking, Ms...."

"Briggs," she finished for him.

"Right, Ms. Briggs. I was asking Ms. Briggs if I could use a cable from the computer lab because my hard drive is messed up," Mark continued as he hurriedly put back on his backpack and then stuffed the wires back into the standing closet.

"Can we get going? I've been looking for you for twenty minutes."

"Sorry. So, can I please borrow this? I'll bring it back tomorrow morning, first thing," Mark promised as he walked out the door.

"I guess," Ms. Briggs conceded to no one in particular.

Sean spent the car ride back home complaining about being forced to wait, but Mark wasn't paying attention. He was too busy thinking about getting home and checking the hard drive. Unless someone else in an Atlantean supersuit started attacking people this afternoon, the hard drive was all that mattered.

When they arrived at the house, Mark wordlessly went straight to his room, leaving Sean without an outlet for further abuse.

"Finally," Mark declared as he turned on his computer. He nervously took the borrowed adapter cord and hard drive out from his backpack and placed them carefully on the desk beside his laptop, though he didn't plug them in immediately. He stood up, checked that his door was locked again, and took a deep breath.

Mark connected the cord to the hard drive. It fit. He paused and plugged the hard drive into the laptop. Nothing.

Mark leaned back in his chair and placed his hands on his head in disappointment. All that work for nothing. All that stressing out for nothing. Maybe I should just start studying for the comparative politics test tomorrow, Mark thought.

Suddenly the screen lit up. There was something on it after all. A tiny window opened on the screen. Mark examined it. There was a single folder.

"ABYSS"

Marks eyes widened in excitement. He glanced at the door again. Still locked.

He clicked on the folder. It opened to reveal over a dozen folders within. He glanced at the names but couldn't make them out. It was written in some foreign language. He clicked on one at random.

A complex data sheet filled Mark's screen. There were numbers and equations and symbols he didn't understand. He scrolled down and saw what the info was for: a supersuit. This one, coincidentally, was for the pufferfish suit. Mark grabbed a pen and paper and tried to jot down some of the equations he saw. They seemed to explain how the suit worked. Maybe Chuck could figure it out.

Mark groaned. If he had involved Chuck in this from the beginning, maybe they could've gotten it open sooner. And Chuck probably understood some of this information about how the suits worked. Mark held his phone in his hand, feeling incredibly guilty. Can't call him now, Mark realized. Chuck was at the cross-country meet, and even if the race was over, this wasn't something that could be talked about over the phone.

"Need to talk to you about something," Mark typed into a message before sending it to Chuck. "Might be important."

Mark nodded as he looked it over. This worked. It conveyed urgency and wasn't specific. He turned back to his laptop.

Mark went back to the previous page, with the other folders. Each one possibly containing designs for a different suit, he realized. He looked at his watch. He still needed to study for that test, but he needed to catalogue these, so he could be prepared.

He opened up one and wrote down the animal it appeared to be based on. He made a list of what he had seen before, and what was still to come.

Pufferfish? Check.

Eel? Check.

Crab? Check.

Manta ray? Check.

Marlin? Nope.

Seahorse? Not yet, but he couldn't imagine how that could possibly be intimidating.

Squid?

There was a knock at Mark's door.

"Mark?" called a voice on the other side of the door.

Mark turned around so quickly it nearly gave him whiplash. He minimized the display and pulled up his email. Nothing weird about checking my email, he thought.

"Yeah?" Mark asked as he barely cracked open the door and tried to put on an innocent face for his mom.

"Dinner's ready. Are you coming down? I tried calling you."

Mark made an involuntary glance at his watch. How was it already time for dinner?

"Oh, ok. Yeah, I'll be right down."

Mrs. Michaels eyed her son carefully. Something was off.

"Are you okay?"

"Yeah," Mark lied, "I just need to study for a big test tomorrow."

"Alright," she replied, seemingly accepting Mark's excuse. "Well, take a break and eat dinner, then get back to studying."

Mark smiled in relief and nodded before slamming the door shut for privacy once again. He made his way back over to his laptop and pulled back up the Atlantean suit display.

Something was wrong. The screen was blank. He clicked on it. Nothing. He tried clicking again. The computer whizzed and whirled before suddenly going silent and black. Mark tried to hide his panic. It was the stupid hard drive, he thought. It had to be. How could he have been so stupid? Of course, it would have some sort of protection or virus. Dang, he really should've brought this to Chuck first.

Mark stood there for a moment, just short of pulling out his hair. His breathing was short and shallow. He thought of all the things he had on this laptop: half-finished papers, study guides, and college applications. He gritted his teeth and groaned loudly.

"Mark!" Mr. Michaels shouted from downstairs.

"I'm coming!" Mark shouted back, his voice breaking from the stress of what had just happened.

Mark marched downstairs for dinner, heart heavy from losing everything he had on that laptop. He didn't talk much at dinner, and barely listened to his family's conversation. Something about Sean wanting to take a different elective class next year or something. It didn't really matter to Mark. He racked his brain. How could he get everything back? Why didn't he ask Chuck to look into it?

That was it. Chuck.

Chuck was good with computers. He might be able to save everything. He probably knew something about what the hard drive did to the laptop. It would be a little difficult to explain why he kept it a secret the last few days, but it was better than the alternative. Mark made up his mind, he needed to get the laptop to Chuck right away.

"Can I be excused?" Mark asked, interrupting Sean's conversation. Sean offered a stern glance towards his older brother.

Mrs. Michaels looked down at her son's plate. He hadn't eaten much. He was probably too nervous to eat, she thought. She was right, just not about the test Mark told her about.

"I guess," she began, to which Mark immediately got up and took his plate to the sink.

"I'm actually going to go over to Chuck's to study," Mark explained as he cleaned his plate. He was more giving them a heads-up than asking permission. "I'll be back in about two hours or so. Okay?"

Before a response was given, Mark ran up the stairs and grabbed his laptop and backpack. He checked again. Still nothing. Mark cursed at the computer before removing the hard drive and stuffing it in the bag. Mrs. Michaels said something about driving safely as Mark walked out the door, and he muttered something in agreement, but his mind was elsewhere.

"Laptop shut down on me. Need help," Mark explained as Chuck opened his front door.

"You could've called," Chuck said in weak protest before inviting Mark in.

The two of them made their way to the living room's coffee table and set the laptop down. Chuck fiddled with the laptop for a moment with no success before he ran off to get something. Mark looked down at his backpack with the hard drive in it. He felt several pangs of guilt over not telling Chuck immediately, but if he could get the laptop back, that could wait.

Chuck came back triumphantly with a mess of cables and wires in his arms a few excruciatingly long minutes later. He placed them onto the table, burying Mark's laptop before heading off again. In a few, much more bearable seconds, he returned with his own laptop, a top-of-the-line model that Mark suspected was Atlantean-made. Chuck plugged some cables into Mark's laptop, some into his, some connected the two, and some went off in weird directions into other devices or even other rooms. Mark didn't question it.

"Come on, come on," Chuck muttered under his breath, as Mark mouthed the words in unison with his friend.

A gentle ding went off on Chuck's computer as Mark's sprung back to life. Mark's laptop looked just as he left it, with a browser opened to his email.

"Awesome, thanks," Mark hurriedly offered as he tried to unhook his computer from the web of cables.

"Not so fast," Chuck said, stopping his friend in his tracks. "What is this?"

"What's what?" Mark asked, feigning ignorance, though he knew it wouldn't work.

Chuck sat in silence, not breaking eye contact. Mark met Chuck's gaze as best he could.

"There's Atlantean malware on here," Chuck explained. "How did you get it?"

Mark sighed and reached into his bag. He pulled out the charred hard drive and displayed it to Chuck.

"What's this?"

"I found it," Mark explained, as calmly as he could manage.

"Where?"

"That fire."

"The fire from Saturday?" Chuck asked.

Mark nodded slightly in agreement.

"And you didn't tell me?"

Silence.

"How long were you planning on keeping this a secret?"

Mark shrugged. He honestly didn't know when he would've told Chuck if it hadn't come to this. He was pretty sure he would've said something eventually.

"Why didn't you tell me?" Chuck asked. His voice was calm, but stern.

"I don't know," Mark answered quietly.

Chuck's eyes shone a deep blue, signaling his intensity.

"Because of that," Mark blurted out in frustration.

Chuck's eyes returned to their normal hue.

"Because," Mark began, finally being honest with his friend, "Because I didn't know if I should trust you with this right away. You hid so much of your life from me for over a decade, but when I found out about all this," with a snap of his fingers, a brief flame sprang to life and quickly dissipated. "I told you within a month. I've trusted you far more than you've trusted me. I needed to look into this on my own."

Chuck was silent for a moment. He grabbed the hard drive, plugged it into his own laptop and typed away. After a few seconds he disconnected it, looking somewhat accomplished despite his attempts to hide his emotions. He handed the hard drive back to Mark who stood for a second, completely dumbstruck.

"Here."

"What?"

"You're right," Chuck admitted. "I've lied to you a lot more than you've lied to me. It's not fair for me to be upset about this. I removed anything that might harm your laptop. The info on here is totally accessible for you. You can choose what to do with it. Whether you share it with me or not is your choice."

Mark held the hard drive in his hands for a moment. The scorched, twisted metal feeling uncomfortable in his hands, still feeling like it could fall apart at any minute. He thought carefully about his next move. Chuck appeared to be reviewing for the test tomorrow, completely uninterested in Mark's next move. Mark bent down and placed the hard drive into his bag.

"You want to study?" Chuck asked, not looking up from his laptop.

"Yeah," Mark answered with a laugh. He really needed to. There was no way they'd get another review day. "But I should probably do it at home. Last thing I need is for you to turn this into some additional superhero training." The joke fell flat, though Chuck offered up a meager laugh, and Mark left without another word.

Once Chuck heard Mark drive off, he went downstairs, down past the basement and into the cave. Mark had been pitching names for the cave for weeks now. If they were using the cave for Solarflare work, it should have a name to reflect that, he claimed. Chuck had argued that since the cave was under his house, he had final say over the name. And they absolutely were not naming it after Solarflare.

Chuck set his phone and his wallet down on the bottom step of the iron staircase and walked over to the water's edge. Water lapped up against the stone. Chuck peered into the water. It was black as pitch, save for the pinprick of one faint blue glow deep beneath the surface.

Chuck exhaled deeply and crouched down. He dipped his hands into the water and wet them before rubbing the water across the sides of his neck, the moisture revealing a set of gills. With one final, brief exhale, Chuck launched himself down into the water, swimming past the darkness. As he dove deeper, he felt his ears pop from the pressure change and saw the spot of blue light grow larger and the lights from above fade away.

Chuck came to a stop at the source of the blue light. It shone eerily through the water. Mr. Currant floated in between his son and the light's source. He turned to face his son and a chill ran down Chuck's spine. His father cut an imposing silhouette.

Chuck pointed to the surface and nodded.

Mr. Currant placed a hand on his son's shoulder, assuring him that he had done the right thing. His eyes shone, even as the rest of his face was covered in shadow. After a moment, he waved his son away and Chuck returned to the world of the surface. He was grateful not to remain down there any longer than necessary.

That night, after an earnest effort at studying for the next day's test, Mark copied all of the information from the hard drive onto his computer. Chuck was right. It didn't do anything. All of Mark's assignments and college essays were safe. The next morning before class, he returned the cable to the computer lab without issue. As he walked down to his locker, Mark thought about when he'd share everything with Chuck. Chuck's gesture had restored a lot of trust between the two of them, but Mark still wanted to keep this close for a while. At least until he had time to look through everything. He was confident he'd get through the suit breakdowns by this weekend.

ELEVEN
Football Game

"Mark, over here!" Lauren called out as Mark made his way to the football field for the Homecoming game. Her curly hair was up in a simple ponytail, and she had a streak of face paint on each cheek, green on her left, navy on the right. She wore her letterman's jacket, adorned with patches for gymnastics, cross-country, and that one season she did cheerleading. Mark was impressed and wondered for a moment why she didn't wear it more often.

"Hey," Mark replied with a wave as he walked towards her along the chain link fence surrounding the field. He wore his class hoodie and jeans. Mark was a little embarrassed he didn't have a letterman's jacket of his own.

He had driven Sean to the game with him, but almost immediately after shutting the car door, his younger brother was gone. Sean wasn't great at showing appreciation.

"Do you still need a ticket?" Lauren asked, with a sideways nod to the nearby ticket booth. The line was at least thirty-people long and was growing longer with each passing second.

"I'm good," he answered, offering up the ticket in his hand as proof.

"Smart." Lauren conceded before sheepishly adding, "I should go get mine before the line gets any longer."

"Actually," Mark began, revealing a second ticket in his other hand.

Lauren smiled and graciously took the ticket.

"I mean, I asked you to Homecoming. I feel like that includes the game and the dance, since I never specified which one. But you're paying for dinner tomorrow."

"Deal," Lauren said with a laugh.

"I'm going to get three steaks, then," Mark said.

"Then I'll duck out before the check comes," Lauren offered as she took Mark's hand.

Mark blushed a little and smiled, trying his best to look unaffected. If tomorrow goes well, he thought, this could be a regular thing. He followed Lauren through the gate and into the stands. His mind raced through pleasant thoughts of their potential relationship as they passed other students. Between this and the noise of the nearby band, it took Lauren three tries to get his attention.

"Mark!" She near-shouted.

"Yeah. Sorry," Mark replied, half-instinctively, pulling himself back to reality.

The two of them were standing near the top of the stands, where all of Lauren's friends were sitting. They took a seat on the bleachers together, right next to the stairs, and Mark blushed slightly again.

He scanned the group they were sitting with. There were seven of them sitting there, including Mark and Lauren. Conveniently enough, this was largely the group Mark and Lauren were going to the dance with tomorrow, save for the two football players currently on the field and the one cheerleader on the sidelines. It felt like a test for Mark, that he could remember everyone. He nodded politely towards the group as a catch-all greeting.

There was Nick Johnson and Sarah Hawke. Nick was Student Council President. North Delfield's golden boy. He was a nice guy; Mark liked him, but he was a politician-in-training if ever there was one. His relationship with Sarah made sense. They were both pleasant and well-off, but there was a hint of insincerity to them, as if they were putting on public personae. Worth noting, as comfortable as their families were, they were far eclipsed by the rumored wealth of Mr. Currant.

There was Caroline Harrison and her boyfriend. Mark was pretty sure his name was Ryan. He knew Ryan went to a different school. Somewhere in Arlington or Falls Church, maybe? Anyway, Ryan and Caroline had been dating for a couple of months. Mark didn't know Caroline very well. Her curly hair was bunched up on both sides of her head with streamers attached, and she wore slight streaks of paint on her face, as well. She was smart; she was in a lot of the same AP courses as him. Actually, she may have been in more. He was pretty sure she was in AP Art, a course that was so demanding it had less than a dozen students. And this was on top of more standard AP coursework. He knew she liked to speak up in class, probably more than anyone. Ryan was quiet. He seemed to like listening to her and often agreed with her points. Mark searched his mind. Had he even met Ryan before? He hoped it'd remain a non-issue.

Finally, of the group sitting in the bleachers, was Ana Kekoa. Mark grinned when he saw her. *You knew she'd say yes, didn't you?* She had to have known since before Mark even mentioned it in class. She was Lauren's best friend, after all.

Of tomorrow's Homecoming group, the missing three were Robbie Perez, Ben Davidson, and Lexi Brandon. Robbie was the North Delfield football team's starting quarterback, as mentioned before, Ben was a fairly talented wide receiver, and Lexi was on the cheer squad. Robbie and Lexi were dating, and Ben was dating Ana. Ben was a bit of a jerk and Ana could do better, Mark thought inadvertently. The thought was gone as soon as it entered his mind.

"Your spirit is terrible," Lauren criticized gently once they were seated, drawing Mark from his self-imposed pop quiz.

"My what?" Mark asked.

"Your spirit. Seriously, do you even care about this school?" she playfully jabbed, referring to the fact that he was merely wearing a North Delfield hoodie, "Ana, do you have any more face paint?"

"Yeah, of course," Ana replied, reaching into her purse and digging around.

"Hey, Michaels," Nick said, offering his hand. Nick was on the lacrosse team, and probably would've started for football if his lacrosse coach hadn't forbidden it out of fear of an off-season injury. His entire face was painted. One side was dark green, the other navy blue, and there was a large silver stripe down the middle.

"Nick, what's up?" Mark asked with a grin, as he awkwardly shook the hand that Nick offered for a high five. He nervously laughed to try and brush the issue aside. The moment passed quickly enough.

Mark suddenly realized just how rarely he hung out with people other than Chuck. It probably wasn't the healthiest friendship. Did Chuck even really have any other friends? He had pretty much only been Mark's friend since he moved here. Did he even have any friends in Atlantis? Would he even remember them?

"Got it," Ana proudly announced as she placed two gently used tubes of face paint into Lauren's hand.

"Hold still," Lauren instructed as she applied the face paint directly to Mark's forehead.

"Forehead, really?" Mark asked quietly.

"You lost your right to decide where it goes when you showed up without any on," Lauren countered without breaking her concentration from her work as she began to shape the glob of green paint she had just applied into the vague shape of an eagle. After a moment, she closed the tube and opened the next. She squeezed the blue paint onto her fingers and wiped them across Mark's cheeks, leaving aggressively large stripes. She then carefully adjusted them to make sure they were even before looking proudly at her handiwork. "Done."

"I'll take your word for it," Mark conceded.

"It looks good," Ana reassured him.

Mark smiled and continued greeting all of Lauren's other friends. Most of them he already knew and had taken classes with. And even though they all knew him well enough and were friendly, none of them mentioned Chuck. Mark tried not to focus much on it, but he now had a nagging feeling that he might be Chuck's only real friend.

Mark wondered what exactly Chuck was doing. Chuck hadn't been at school the last few days. When Mark tried to call him, he had said that it was something important, that it had to do with finding the Sapphire Ring. Mr. Currant told Mark not to worry, that they would give him a heads up when they found what they were looking for. He felt weird being given a night off like that, while Chuck and his father worked to finish their long search. On top of that, the last time they really talked much was when Chuck helped him salvage his laptop, which was not a conversation that went particularly well.

The marching band's music swelled; the game was about to start. A booming voice came from over the speakers.

"Ladies and gentlemen, welcome to tonight's game. Tonight, your North Delfield Eagles take on the Colonial Valley Wolverines."

The band played the school fight song and cheerleaders flipped and twirled along the edge of the field.

"And here they are, the Eagles!" the announcer shouted as the football team ran through a paper banner at the end of the field. The stands erupted into cheers and shouts. Mark saw Robbie leading the way and felt a small tinge of envy at not being on the field. Granted, it wasn't as nice as the reception he often got as Solarflare, but the idea of being able to show his own face was appealing.

The team gathered along the sideline near Coach Kekoa and Mr. Currant. Coach Kekoa was Ana's father. He was big and bald and the most physically imposing man in a hundred-mile radius. Mark had to give Ben some credit for asking out the coach's daughter.

It was surprising to see Mr. Currant down there. He must be down there because it's a big game, Mark thought. The Principal probably should show up for these things. Alongside Coach Kekoa, Mr. Currant didn't look much smaller. Honestly, though Mr. Currant was nowhere near as large as Coach Kekoa, they seemed equal. It was hard to explain. Mark searched his mind to see if there was any other instance where the two of them had stood side-by-side.

The crowd roared as the ball was kicked off and the game began. It was a good game. Colonial Valley was their toughest opponent in the district; they had nearly made it to the state championship the year before.

The Eagles scored a touchdown.

The Wolverines answered with one of their own.

The Eagles made a field goal.

The Wolverines faked a field goal attempt to score another touchdown.

Eagles touchdown.

Wolverine fumble.

Eagles punt the ball away.

Wolverine touchdown.

Eagles field goal.

Wolverines four-and-out.

The level of play on both sides of the ball, for each team, was far greater than the norm for high schoolers. Some of these kids would play for top colleges, one or two might even play professionally one day. Robbie was one of the guys who had a shot at playing professionally.

Robbie set himself and looked up at the scoreboard. They were still down by 1 point. He was frustrated at the missed passes he had thrown and the times when he wasn't fast enough to escape the Wolverines' defense, but he wasn't mad. Getting mad meant playing sloppy. He knew they could win this. They weren't about to lose the Homecoming game.

Robbie took the ball and stepped back as he waited for his teammates to get into position. He counted in his head. If no one was open after five seconds, he was going to go for it. His eyes scanned downfield. Nothing.

As the defense broke through, Robbie tucked the ball and ran. He ducked and spun and ran down the field, easily reaching open space. No one could touch him now. Touchdown!

Robbie tossed the football to the referee as his teammates ran up and congratulated him. In all the excitement, no one noticed the figures that had broken through the chain link fence on the other end of the field.

Mark was the first to notice them. He immediately knew something was up.

"You hungry?" Mark asked Lauren hurriedly, "I'll be right back."

"No, I'm good," Lauren said as the Eagles kicked the ball for their extra point, but Mark was already quickly making his way down the stands.

The fans were still cheering and the band still playing when one of the figures lifted his hand and unleashed a bolt of lightning which cut across the sky. The entire stadium went silent.

Mark sprinted towards the concession area and restrooms. He needed to get changed quickly.

There were five of them. They walked slowly towards the center of the field, with the players moving aside to let them through.

"Ladies and gentlemen, it appears —" the announcer's words were lost in static before the speakers went silent.

Mark flung open the men's room door and ducked inside. There was no one inside. How incredibly lucky, he thought. He entered a stall and locked it behind him. He didn't see any cameras near the entrance, and he was sure there weren't any inside, so he should be good. He pulled his hoodie off and revealed the suit underneath. He smiled, normally he would've just left it at home or in his car. As he pulled the mask out of his pocket, he noticed the paint smears on his hoodie. Mark swore. Now the paint was messed up and he got it on his hoodie. It was trivial, he knew, but he didn't look forward to trying to wash it out later. Mark kicked off his shoes and took off his jeans and put on the mask.

Now, he was Solarflare. And he was standing in a stall in a dirty bathroom.

"Attention, sports fans," one of the figures on the field announced, apparently having taken control of the stadium speaker system. It was Eel, his bright green costume now fully illuminated by the lights for the spectators. "We are looking for Solarflare. We believe that he goes to this school. And if he doesn't, he has fifteen minutes to get here before we electrify the stands."

Another one of the figures on the field laughed and lightning crackled all around her. This one was Manta, many of the spectators realized. She took to the sky and circled above the crowds, reminding those who needed a refresher.

"You see," Eel continued. "My friend and I possess powers of electricity. These stands are constructed of metal. Should either of us desire, we could kill you all where you sit."

At hearing this, someone panicked and tried to escape. But Manta hit him with a mild blast, like a taser, and he was floored. Lauren looked in horror and worried about where Mark could be. What if they came after him for not being in the stands?

Mark grabbed his clothes and stuffed them up into the tile ceiling. He mentally noted the stall. As Mark stepped outside, he heard the last of Eel's threat and the sound of Manta's electricity painfully stunning the man in the crowd. Mark took to the air and flew straight towards the field, unconcerned with any sort of planning.

Mark made a hard landing right in front of Eel, shooting flames out along all sides on impact. He stood tall and unflinching, hands now engulfed in flames and eyes burning a red-hot crimson. Some members of the crowd cheered, in spite of the threat from above.

Now in the middle of it, Mark realized the situation he was in. There were five of them he could see. Four on the ground, one in the air. And the sun had set almost an hour ago. These odds weren't great even when he got a boost from sunlight. He did his best to shake it off. He had beaten the Abyss before, he thought, just not all at once, and not at night.

"Prison lets you guys come to football games?" Mark asked, trying to raise his voice loud enough that everyone could here. He had to play up the humor, keep these people calm.

Eel chuckled a crazy, menacing laugh like Mark had heard the first time they met. It echoed through the speakers and across the field. He already knew that laugh, but it still made him uneasy. Mark shuddered. "You're a fool, Solarflare. We're going to destroy you, and all these people will see it."

Mark shook his head. "No, you won't." He paused and grinned beneath his mask. "Liar, liar, pants on fire." Mark unleashed a blast of flames at Eel's legs, knocking them back and sending him to the ground face-first.

Manta yelled and swooped down from the sky, her own arcs of electricity making their way to Mark. Mark shot flames at the bolts and directed them towards the ground. He had learned a little bit about how to use his powers against electricity by this point. He had already fought both of them.

Mark's boots heated up and he took to the skies in pursuit. But then he was jerked to a stop in mid-air. Pincer had grabbed onto his ankle, holding him down and ready to crush the bone. Mark saw Pincer smile with sadistic glee, but right before he had the chance to break it, Mark swung his other leg around and directed a burst of heat from the other boot towards Pincer's chest. Pincer let go of the leg in shock and pain and fell back.

Mark hung in the air for only a second before Puffer charged at him, taking him down to the ground. Puffer's suit inflated, and the pressure keeping Mark pinned to the ground increased with it.

"Hey, long time, no see," Mark strained, as the pressure Puffer was putting on his chest made it difficult to breathe.

Puffer laughed and breathed in again, and the spikes covering his suit extended further. He kept one hand on Mark and pulled the other back for a punch. Spikes covered the knuckles, and Mark wasn't so sure that they couldn't puncture the suit.

"He's mine!" a voice announced, as Puffer was kicked off of Mark. His large frame skidded along the field a good couple feet before falling over.

The figure kicked at Mark on the ground, with Mark barely managing to roll away from it. It left a small crater in the field. Mark rolled back onto his shoulders and popped up backwards, away from this opponent. He looked. This one was new.

"Sorry, have we met?" Mark asked.

This one wore a pale-orange suit. His chest jutted out in front of him awkwardly and his face was unnaturally long and small fin-like appendages stuck out along the sides. His legs looked like tree trunks, but his arms were scrawny.

"We've never met before," he replied, in a soft, unsettling voice. "I'm Seahorse."

"I was wondering when I'd meet you," Mark laughed. He was completely sincere. He had seen it in the files he got from the fire. But Seahorse probably didn't know he knew about him already. That may not have been the smartest move.

Seahorse lunged at Mark with a mighty kick which Mark barely sidestepped. Then he unleashed a volley of fast sidekicks, which Mark tried to block with his arm.

"I see you like kicking," Mark noticed, as he ducked to dodge a roundhouse kick aimed at his head.

Seahorse didn't reply but kept kicking. Mark's eyes flashed red and he smiled. About time he faced another martial artist. Even if this guy's skill just came from the suit, it was a better fight than he'd seen yet.

Mark tried a few kicks of his own, catching Seahorse once in the ribs, and taking a few shots of his own. The two traded kicks for a few seconds before Puffer rejoined.

Puffer swung at Seahorse, angry over having his spotlight stolen, but missed and swung wildly at Mark, managing to catch him in the shoulder.

Mark stumbled back but didn't fall. He briefly looked down at the suit. There was a hole right where Puffer had made contact. Puffer had poisoned him.

The toxin went to work quickly. The field faded into darkness and nausea swept through his body. He felt like he needed to pull up the mask to vomit, but he wasn't supposed to remove the mask. His thoughts felt slow.

Do I keep the mask on? Do I take it off? His stomach turned and he doubled over. He swayed on his feet.

The Abyss were frozen for a moment. Puffer took it all in. He'd been waiting a long time for that.

Mark felt chills and a warmth against the back of his teeth. His whole body tingled, and he thought he might shake apart if he didn't concentrate.

Mark, use your fire.

Mark righted himself and glanced around. Who said that?

Use your fire. Use it to burn away the poison.

Right. The poison. He needed to, he needed to burn something. His mind was swimming. He tried to fight through the fog and turn on the flames. He felt himself getting weaker, he felt the flames receding.

Mark!

The voice shouted, deep and harsh. Mark felt consciousness slipping. He staggered and fell to the ground, catching himself on his hands. His body spasmed.

And then he wasn't in control.

He felt something in his mind push right past him and take over. He felt the flames turn on, but it was like someone else was flicking the switch.

His body erupted and was engulfed in flames. He felt the heat rise. As it grew hotter, he grew stronger and more lucid. The Abyss was no longer holding back out of amusement of their fallen foe; now they were standing back because they couldn't take the heat.

His breathing returned to normal, the nausea faded. He felt fine. No, he felt great. He roared as he pulled the flames back into his body and leapt to his feet.

"Good hit," Mark called out to Puffer. "The first guy I fought and a new guy. Sunrise, sunset, huh?"

They weren't listening. And the crowd couldn't hear him. This was just to keep Mark from getting paralyzed with fear. As long as he could say anything, he could fight. The two of them attacked together. Mark stepped back and played defense. He avoided what he could, blocked what he could, and only took one or two hits in the process. Luckily, he only took hits from Seahorse. No more poison, but it still hurt.

Manta swung back around. She thought Mark had been pursuing her and wanted to lose him in the clouds. She saw him on the field, with Puffer and Seahorse bearing down on him. Her hands sparked and she unleashed twin bolts of lightning at Mark. Mark heard the electricity cackle and was able to roll out of the way, leaving Puffer to take the hit.

The electricity hit Puffer hard, and he was flung backwards off his feet. He landed on his back with a thud and, once again, gave off a sound like a deflating balloon as he returned to his normal size.

As Manta flew through the air, Mark launched a fireball at her left side. The fireball hit its target dead-on, knocking Manta off-balance and sending her crashing and tumbling to the ground with a noise not unlike the one Puffer had just made.

Alright, Mark thought, Puffer should be out. The sound of a balloon deflating had signaled the end of the last fight; he hoped it was true for this one, too. And a fall like that would've been the end of Puffer's day, so he figured Manta was done as well. Good, now the flier wasn't a problem. So, he just had Seahorse. And Eel. And Pincer.

As Mark remembered Pincer, he was struck from behind with Pincer's large, metal fist. Mark stumbled a few steps and clutched at his head in pain. Pincer took another swing, and Mark easily deflected the strike.

Mark was tired. Burning off the poison and the blast to Manta took a lot out of him. And with the sun already set, it wasn't exactly easy for him to get that energy back. Still, he had to press on.

"Hey," Mark pointed out in a mocking voice, addressing Seahorse and Pincer, respectively "You kick, and you hit. The two of you together might make a decent fighter."

The two of them looked at each other and nodded in agreement. How had they never thought of that before?

Mark muttered an expletive.

The two of them attacked Mark together, Pincer with his fists and Seahorse with his legs. Mark struggled to block their attacks and return some of his own, but two against one isn't particularly easy. He got a few weak shots in but took some hard hits. He stumbled for a second, dazed by a nasty kick to the head. Pincer took aim and jabbed at Mark's head.

Mark caught the fist in midair.

"That's enough," he said, his voice suddenly serious. His eyes glowed and his hand was engulfed in flame. Pincer struggled to pull his hand away. Mark yanked the hand towards him and kneed Pincer right in the stomach. Pincer fell to the ground gasping for breath.

Seahorse tried to kick Mark in the head, but he leaned backwards, and the foot hit nothing but air. As Seahorse tried to pull it back, Mark grabbed the ankle and dragged it further out, pulling Seahorse off balance. With a flaming hand, Mark struck Seahorse right in the center of his chest. Going off his experience, that seemed to be where the key components of the suit were housed.

Sure enough, once Mark pulled his hand away, Seahorse fell to the ground. He groaned in pain, but it wasn't anything too bad. The suit made whining and popping noises, as whatever powered it failed.

Mark gave a strained smile. This was taking a lot out of him. Maybe if he had actually grabbed some food before changing, he'd be less tired.

That just leaves...

"Solarflare!" Eel screamed, reverb nearly deafening the stadium.

He had been out this whole time, Mark realized. He had fallen face first and missed this whole fight. Mark would've laughed if he wasn't still worried about Eel hitting the stands with a lethal amount of electricity.

"You good, man?" Mark asked. "You were sound asleep for the last couple minutes. Thought maybe you called it a night early."

Eel shot at Mark with a blast of electricity, which Mark easily dodged. As Mark's hands grew hot for his counterattack, he was blindsided by another opponent. Mark flew across the field before tumbling to an unpleasant stop.

Mark picked himself up and saw who it was that had hit him. It was Whale, the only one of these jokers that could hit harder than Puffer. He wasn't poisonous though, so that was good, Mark thought. And Dolphin was with him, of course.

"Hey, big guy," Mark muttered, "gang's all here."

The two of them laughed. Their laughs were the worst. Whale had a slow, dopey laugh, befitting of someone his size and shape. And Dolphin's laugh was almost as high-pitched and nasally as her sonic-screech. Mark almost preferred her glass-shattering screech to her laugh.

They all stood in front of Mark, just at different angles. The odd couple on his left, and Eel to his right. Mark had to admit, staggering the attack was a pretty good plan.

"I have to admit," Mark began once the obnoxious laughter stopped, taking a defensive stance. "Staggering your attack was a pretty good plan." He needed to buy time, catch his breath. If he could get one of them to explain how they were the genius who planned to attack in stages or get them to argue about who it was that would actually get to kill him, then that could help him.

He thought about trying to get in touch with Chuck and asking for help. Surely Chuck would be able to handle one of them with his powers. Mark realized just how annoyed he was that Chuck didn't use his powers the same way. But there was no way to ask for help. He left his phone in his pants. Even if Chuck wasn't busy looking for the ring, Mark had gone into battle without his "phone-a-friend" option.

They didn't say anything and began advancing slowly on Mark. Sparks encircled Eel's hands as electricity surged through the suit. Whale and Dolphin both inhaled deeply, preparing their sonic attacks. Alright, if they weren't going to make it any easier for him, he needed to decide who to go after first. Mark's eyes darted desperately back-and-forth between the two.

"Ah, screw it," Mark shouted, as he launched a fireball at the ground just in front of Whale and Dolphin. The two of them jumped back in surprise as he made a beeline for Eel.

Eel launched a blast of electricity at him, but Mark leapt over it and flipped over Eel. Eel spun around to try and catch his opponent and Mark hit him in the gut. Eel doubled over in pain. Mark's hand heated up as he prepared to strike the chest and hopefully disable the suit.

An ear-splitting noise shook the air before Mark could strike. Dolphin was using her sonic ability. Mark immediately clutched at his ears in pain.

He launched a weak fireball in Dolphin's direction, but it dissipated quickly in the sound waves. He frowned. He was way too far away to do anything else. He probably should've gone after them first.

Eel regained his composure and tried to blast Solarflare. As the electricity flowed out of his glove, Mark grabbed it and aimed it away from him. One hand clutched his ear in pain, the other controlled Eel. It happened so fast that he seemed to be operating purely on reflexes. He twisted Eel's wrist so that the blast was put to good use.

The electricity flew and struck Dolphin downfield. Her shriek stopped immediately. That was unbelievably lucky, Mark thought. It was unbelievable. It was unbelievable, never-in-a-million-years, stupid-luck. He was getting every possible break this fight.

Whale screamed and checked on his partner.

"Thanks," Mark said, still holding Eel's wrist, painfully twisted, in his hand. He heated the hand that held the wrist and began gloating as sparks began to fly from Eel's gauntlet. "If you all weren't so incompetent, this would've been dangerous. I'm glad you're all such —"

Mark's insult was cut short as he was once again blindsided. He should've known better. Whale wasn't out. He knew that. But he was just getting so annoyed by this. He wanted to rub Eel's nose in it while he could. Maybe if he was properly humiliated, he'd think twice before taking on Mark again.

Mark picked himself up from where he landed. Whale probably broke something, he realized. He figured that it was only fair for Mark to break something of Whale's in return.

"You hurt her!" Whale screamed, his own vocal powers causing Mark pain.

He brushed it off. "No, *he* hurt her." Mark replied, pointing to Eel. "I don't shoot electricity."

Whale wasn't listening. He charged at Mark. Mark leapt out of the way, but fell on the landing. Whale hadn't hit him or anything, he was just that exhausted. His entire body ached, as if he'd run a marathon on zero preparation.

Mark was lucky Whale was as big and slow as he was strong.

I'm not going to be able to tire him out, Mark realized.

Mark lunged at him and put as much of his strength as he could into a right hook. His fist connected square with the side of Whale's face. Nothing.

"I don't suppose you just want to give up," Mark asked sheepishly.

Whale wordlessly wrapped Mark up in a bearhug. His arms crushing Mark and forcing all the air out of his lungs. Mark struggled for breath and flailed his feet.

"Hold him," Eel ordered.

"I'm not going to let you hit me," Whale roared.

"I can end him," Eel persisted, continuing to advance. He wasn't paying any attention to the crowd at all anymore, but they were all too paralyzed from fear to try and run. "I won't hit you. Let me just fry him. I won't hit you." Eel repeated himself, trying to calm Whale down.

It seemed to work. Whale lessened his grip slightly and swung Mark around so he could face his executioner.

"Whale," Mark pleaded, using the little air he had. "He's the one who hurt Dolphin. He doesn't care about her. He doesn't care if he hurts you too."

"I don't care if he hurts me," Whale said, his normally dopey, non-threatening voice now cold and frightening. "I want him to hurt you."

"Please," Mark pleaded quietly as Eel made his final approach. He was so close now that he heard Eel's remaining gauntlet hum with electricity. He gritted his teeth. He had no idea what would happen if Eel shocked him when he was out of energy. Maybe it really would kill him.

Eel held his hand up right in front of Mark's face. "Shame you don't have any friends of your own, Solarflare." Eel laughed maniacally as Whale stood silently.

"He does have friends," one of the football players announced, as he threw his helmet at Eel.

The helmet struck Eel right in the middle of his face, breaking his nose. The football player tackled Eel to the ground and took a few swings at the enemy pinned beneath him.

Mark was stunned for a second before he took advantage of the chaos. He swung his foot back, catching Whale between the legs. No matter how much blubber or padding the rest of the suit had, Mark was sure that area was vulnerable. Whale released Mark without thinking. Mark landed on the ground, adrenaline surging, and hit Whale with a blast of flame large enough to knock him into the air before he landed, unconscious.

He turned to Eel. The football player who had saved him was Robbie. Mark was filled with gratitude, but only for a second as Eel had now turned his weapon on Robbie.

Before Mark could warn him, electricity had erupted from Eel's gauntlet and struck Robbie in the chest. Robbie screamed for about half a second before he was out. The blast knocked him into the air, and he fell with a hard thud.

Mark felt sick to his stomach. He turned and looked at Robbie's body which twitched slightly from the electrical shock.

He saw Robbie's chest move up and down. Good, that meant he was still breathing.

Mark turned back and saw that Eel was standing once again. Not just standing, but smiling. Blood from his broken nose stained his teeth red.

Mark's eyes burned with a rage that he'd never experienced before. Mark ran and struck Eel across the side of the face. He grabbed him and pulled him close as he punched him in the throat. He kicked his knee out away from him. Mark wasn't fighting to win. He was fighting to hurt.

Mark grabbed Eel's suit, holding him up because his enemy no longer had the strength to stand on his own anymore. He felt his hands burning through the suit and heard the sounds as its functions failed.

He shook with anger. His mind raced. They hurt someone. They hurt his friend because he was trying to help. They could've killed him. They could've killed Lauren.

Lauren still sat in the stands watching this unfold. Everyone in the stands was watching this. Most had turned away or covered their eyes at some point. But Lauren didn't. She stayed watching the whole time.

Mark took a few deep breaths as he held the unconscious Eel. As angry as he was, he couldn't kill Eel. He couldn't let people think he was capable of that. He closed his eyes and let go of his foe. Eel crumpled to the ground in a heap.

Mark turned around slowly and saw the carnage from this fight. The various members of The Abyss unconscious across the field, Robbie lying a few feet away from him, scorch marks and divots and craters everywhere.

As the reality of what had just happened set in, Mark tried to calm himself. He tried to focus on breathing, but it was too much. His whole body shook, his nerves were shot, and he was on the verge of tears.

Coach Kekoa was the first to approach the scene. He knelt beside Robbie and gently touched him, afraid of a residual shock, before holding his hand. Robbie gently squeezed back. The entire team and medical staff swarmed Robbie, almost completely ignoring Mark.

He'll be okay, Mark assured himself. They've got him. He smiled slightly as tears filled his eyes. Robbie had saved him. He was immeasurably grateful for that and, at the same time, felt similarly guilty for allowing it to happen.

When the first of the football players looked back for Solarflare, Mark was already gone.

There was no applause for Mark this time. No celebrating. The crowd sat in near-complete silence until they could hear the sirens of police cars and the ambulance that took Robbie away. It was a rough night for everyone, but some more than others.

TWELVE
Charges Dropped

Mark hid in the woods just beside the school. He passed out from exhaustion and slept for at least an hour, sleeping through the noises of the police sirens. He was lucky no one found him. When he woke up, everyone had left. He didn't hear or see anyone around. Now it was safe to change and go home.

Mark flew back over to the stadium bathroom to retrieve his clothes. He tried to open the door, but it was locked. They actually went back and locked the bathroom after everything that had just happened, Mark realized, somewhat incredulously. Mark pulled it again to check and shouted an obscenity when it remained locked. He needed his clothes back. He needed his cell phone. He yanked on it violently several more times in frustration. He couldn't just fly home in his Solarflare suit and get everything tomorrow. His car keys and phone were in there. And even if that was an option, tomorrow was Homecoming, the school would be busy all day.

Mark took a step back and slammed his shoulder into the door. No luck. He rubbed his shoulder and eyed the door cautiously. He remembered something online about how it was preferable to kick in a door, rather than try to ram it in with your shoulder. He wished he had remembered it before his first attempt. He took a deep breath and kicked the door as hard as he could. Nothing. He tried again. Still nothing. After the third try, he realized that all he was doing was putting dents into the sturdy metal door. Brute force wasn't going to work.

Mark's eyes flashed red, and a small flame erupted in his right hand. He focused and the flame grew smaller, but more intense. He held his hand up to the lock on the door and blasted straight through. The lock and bolt fell to the floor inside with a heavy clang. Looking at the twisted, red-hot metal that had once held the lock, Mark realized that this probably wasn't a cheap door. He brushed it aside. Maybe they shouldn't have locked it.

He stepped inside and pulled off this mask and the rest of the suit and tossed it onto the dirty floor. He stood in the middle of the bathroom in just his underwear. The suit and mask were wet with sweat, which was impressive considering Chuck said that the material was supposed to be sweat-proof. It was also supposed to not tear or rip, so maybe Chuck was just overselling it. Mark smelled terrible. He leaned over the closest sink and splashed his face with water from the motion-activated faucet. Sweat had left his face streaked with the paint Lauren had applied earlier. He groaned. She was probably worried about him. He waved his hand in front of the sink's sensor again. Nothing. He tried again. Still nothing. On the third try, it turned on for about three seconds. He hastily splashed that water onto his armpits.

Mark climbed up on the sides of the stall and lifted the tile to get his clothes. They were still there, just caked in a thick layer of dust from inside the ceiling. So far, so good, Mark thought. He quickly pulled the hoodie over his head and yanked up his jeans. He slipped on his sneakers over his bare feet after failing to find his socks. They were probably disgustingly dirty now anyway, he thought. He pulled his phone out of his jeans pocket and checked the display.

He had a dozen missed calls from his mom, each one with their own voicemail. Obviously, she had heard about this. He felt a sinking feeling in the pit of his stomach for letting her worry so much and he felt even worse when he imagined how she'd feel if she knew he was Solarflare. Tonight had been his most dangerous night, by far. It was almost enough to make him rethink his super-hero-hobby. Almost.

There were messages and missed calls from Lauren as well. She had to have been worried, and at least a little suspicious. She obviously connected that Mark had run because he saw the Atlanteans before she did. The question was whether she suspected Mark was Solarflare or if she just thought he was a coward. Mark wasn't sure which he preferred.

Mark held the phone in his hand and wondered which one he should call first. Neither conversation would be pleasant. But he knew the conversation with his mom would last at least half an hour. He elected to call Lauren first. If it went badly, at least it would be over quickly.

He scooped up his suit into his arms and stuffed it into a small athletic bag that Chuck had convinced him to carry in his pocket. He said it would be good for when Mark didn't feel like wearing the suit underneath his street clothes. He was right.

"Hey," Mark said nervously when Lauren answered her phone with silence. He continued, "I'm sorry I left." This was as good an apology as he felt he could make without giving away why he left. He stood leaning against the outside wall of the bathroom, just by the door he had ruined.

"I was scared," Lauren said carefully, her voice full of emotion — half angry, half in tears.

Mark stood in silence as he thought about how terrifying the experience must've been for the people in the stands.

"And I was worried they might hurt you for not being in the stands with everyone," she continued.

Mark smiled a little. She cared about him. Obviously, she was incredibly upset with him right now, and him smiling wouldn't help that, but it was pretty obvious she cared.

"I was trying to get to the security officer," Mark lied, after he had composed himself a bit, in a false confession. "I saw those guys as they were coming through the fence and I thought he'd know what to do or he'd be able to call the police or something. I didn't want to cause a panic. I should've told you, though." He spoke carefully, pausing in just the right places so the words hit hardest.

Lauren contemplated her response for a moment. She understood Mark's excuse, and believed it, but she was still upset that he put her through all that.

"Why'd it take you so long to respond? Where've you been?" She asked.

"I lost my phone," Mark lied. It was a good, believable lie. "It must've fallen when I was running down the steps. I stayed back to try and find it. It was under someone's seat."

"The cops let you look for your phone?" Lauren asked incredulously.

"They may not know I'm here," Mark replied in a sly tone. This answer actually was true. "And I had initially been trying to find you, but I didn't see you in the crowd when everyone was leaving," he further explained, in a return to lying.

"Are you serious?" She countered, in complete disbelief. "They were taking statements from everyone for over an hour before they let us go. How did you not see me?"

Mark winced. He hadn't thought about the fact that the police would want statements from everyone after the first ever attack by a group of supervillains. He saw how crazy things got after the first attack by Puffer; he should've realized that this would be a big deal. It confirmed to the police what he already knew: that everyone he had faced so far was working together.

"I'm sorry," Mark said, sounding defeated. "I just didn't."

Lauren was silent for a moment, and when she spoke again, her voice was trembling. "Robbie's in the hospital."

Mark pulled the phone away from his ear. This was my fault, he thought. Robbie got hit trying to help him. He slowly sank to a sitting position and held his head in his hands. No one had ever really gotten hurt since he started being Solarflare. Had Mark not been consumed by grief, he might have realized how convenient that was.

The two of them were both silent for a minute.

Mark wondered what to say. The silence was unbearable, each second forcing him to think about what had happened tonight, and how it was his fault. He wanted to know they were still on for the dance tomorrow. He didn't want to think that she was so angry at him that she wasn't going to go.

"I'm sorry," Mark apologized again. He didn't know what else to say.

"Stop apologizing," Lauren said. "It wasn't your fault."

Mark stared at his shoes. He knew the truth. It was his fault. Yeah, the Atlantean criminals were the bad guys, but he was the one they were looking for. He was the one that united them towards a common goal. He wasn't entirely innocent in what happened.

"Mark." Lauren said sternly after a lengthy silence from the other end. "It is not your fault."

Mark nodded slightly. "Yeah," he managed weakly. "But I shouldn't have left you."

"No, you shouldn't have," she agreed. "But you were trying to help. I can't be too mad at you for that."

Mark smiled. He was trying to help, just not the way he had told her.

"So," Mark began carefully, "are we still on for tomorrow?"

"Yeah," Lauren answered, now sounding a lot less upset over the night's events.

"What time?" Mark asked, still trying to ease her into a normal conversation.

"Pick me up tomorrow at 5 o'clock and we'll meet with the group for dinner."

"Sounds good," Mark said.

"Alright, I'll see you tomorrow," Lauren concluded, now in a much better place than she had been at the start of the conversation.

"Lauren," Mark blurted out, wanting to say one last thing before she hung up.

"Yeah?"

"I'm glad you're safe. I was worried."

Lauren smiled on the other end of the line. "Yeah, I'm glad you are too. I'll see you tomorrow."

"Alright."

"Bye."

"Bye."

Mark grinned from ear to ear as Lauren hung up. He sat there, grinning like an idiot, for a moment before he realized he still needed to call his mom. But as rough as that realization was, it didn't totally dampen his spirit. He now knew Lauren cared about him.

Mark held his phone in his hand before calling his mom. He would've hesitated longer, but he knew that each second he didn't call only made things worse. Though he wondered if he'd already hit that ceiling.

The phone didn't even ring a full time before she picked up.

"Mark?" she asked, her voice full of worry and without a trace of anger.

"Yeah," Mark awkwardly mumbled as he picked himself back up into a standing position.

"I'm sorry, I lost my phone. And my keys." Mark hastily added. He realized that even without his phone, his mom would've expected him to come home. But if he didn't have his keys, there was nothing he could've done.

There was a pause on the other end.

"But you're okay?" she asked, again without any anger.

"Yeah," Mark replied, now making his way back to his car. "Did Sean get home okay?"

"Yeah, he got a ride home with some friends. Did you find your keys or do we need to pick you up?" she asked in an almost matter-of-fact tone, as if keeping the conversation business-like would keep her from breaking down in tears.

"I found them," Mark lied. "I'm walking to my car now; I'll be home in a few minutes."

"Okay. Drive safe. I love you," she said, her voice breaking as she was overtaken by emotion.

"I love you too," Mark answered. His heart felt like a stone in his chest after hearing that. He just wanted to get home.

He hung up and pulled his keys out from his pocket. His car was in sight. He could just go home and call this a night.

"Put your hands in the air," a voice from behind Mark commanded, calmly but firmly.

Mark kept the phone in his hand and placed them both above his head.

"I was just on the phone with my mom," Mark nervously explained.

"Place the phone on the ground, slowly," the voice ordered.

This was a cop, Mark realized. If it was a member of The Abyss, he'd probably be dead now. He slowly bent down and placed his phone and his bag on the ground and stood back up.

"Turn around."

Mark slowly turned around. He wondered for a moment if there was anything on his phone that might compromise his identity. He didn't have any pictures of himself in the suit, no incriminating notes or text messages, nothing he could think of. Otherwise, he would've simply smashed it beneath his foot. Accidentally, of course. But that was nothing compared to the bag with his suit inside. He tried not to think about it.

He was standing right in front of the officer he had seen during his first two battles. He recognized her instantly. But she didn't know Mark; she knew Solarflare. He tried to hide his expression from revealing that he knew her.

"Do you mind telling me what you're doing here?" she asked.

Mark gulped hard. He wasn't sure if he should say anything. If he was cooperative, she might just let him go with a warning.

But he was worried he might say something that justified her taking him in.

On the other hand, if he said nothing, she could get a warrant or court order or whatever she needed to figure out Mark was Solarflare.

"I was looking for my phone," Mark answered, the lie came naturally. It was lucky that he had already practiced it twice before.

"We evacuated this area," she explained, clearly not satisfied with Mark's answer.

"I'm sorry," Mark continued, "I really needed to find it." He hoped she'd just be cool and let him go. Did she really think the 17-year-old kid had anything do with a massive supervillain hostage situation? He did, but it must've seemed ridiculous to anyone else.

"That's no excuse," she answered after a pause. "I'm going to ask you to come with me for questioning."

Mark winced. This couldn't be happening. What were his rights, exactly? He didn't want this to get worse. He didn't want her to come back and ask him any questions later.

"I need to go home," Mark protested. "My parents are worried about me. They want me to come home."

"I just found you at the scene of an attempted terrorist attack," she began.

Mark wondered if supervillains counted as terrorists. It made sense, he realized, but it didn't feel exactly right. Supervillians were supervillians, terrorists were terrorists. They seemed so distinctly different in his mind. The word "terrorist" implied a ruthlessness that these guys didn't seem to have. Then again, they had nearly killed him, and they put Robbie in the ICU, so maybe it was fitting after all.

"Your presence here is probable cause enough for me to take you in for questioning. If you're telling me the truth, we can resolve this quickly at the station and you can be home soon enough. If you continue to fight me on this, it'll just make things worse for you."

Mark couldn't run or fly away from this. She had him.

"I'm going to need to look in your bag," she announced.

"I don't consent to that," Mark muttered in a panic.

She eyed him more suspiciously.

"You don't?" she asked.

She pulled out her radio and called into the station. She said something in codes and numbers that Mark didn't understand and someone on the other end said something equally indecipherable before she put it away.

"You have two options. You can let me look in the bag and answer some questions willingly or you can be arrested. I just checked. Those are your only two options right now."

"What're you, new?" Mark asked, annoyed at being backed into a corner.

The officer ignored his comment, luckily for Mark, and continued her explanation. "This isn't a traffic stop. A young man was nearly killed tonight, and hundreds of people were held hostage. You will cooperate or you will face criminal charges, do you understand?"

Mark bowed his head and tried to hide his anger and frustration. He nodded slightly.

"Do you understand?" she pressed, wanting a verbal confirmation from him.

"Yes." Mark answered tersely.

She bent down and picked up the bag. She carefully opened it and looked inside. Mark closed his eyes.

"Is this yours?" she asked, as calmly as she could when she saw the easily-recognizable colors of the Solarflare suit.

"I found it," Mark lied.

"You found it?" she asked, in disbelief.

"Yes." Mark repeated, but he knew it wasn't any good. He was going with her now, no question about that.

She allowed Mark to call home once again and tell his mom where he was going, but she made him hang up before their trip to the station. At the station, Mark handed over his phone and his bag with his Solarflare suit to another officer. He thought better of arguing against handing it over. He trusted he'd get it back soon enough. Or not.

She led Mark into the interrogation room.

"Please take a seat," she offered, in a way that made it seem like Mark had any sort of say in the matter.

Mark sat down on the cold, metal chair on one side of the cold, metal table. She sat down opposite him. He looked around. It was like what he'd seen in movies, he noticed. Single light, everything made of metal, mirror on one wall that probably had observers on the other side.

She pulled out a recording device and turned it on. "Ok, my name is Officer Petersen. Could you please state your name for the record?"

"Mark Michaels," Mark complied immediately.

"Full name, please."

"Mark Qingshan Michaels," he elaborated.

Officer Peterson nodded and marked it down as Mark spelled it out. Usually, people made a comment about how interesting his name was after they heard it. He knew they meant no offense by it, but it tended to get old. He was half-Chinese. Having a Chinese middle name wasn't that unusual.

"And Mark, what were you doing at the football field after it was evacuated?"

Mark was silent. He really didn't want to lie on record.

"I'd like a phone call," Mark said, again trying to remember exactly what rights he had in this situation. "I'd like a lawyer." He knew they had to let him have a lawyer present.

The officer glared at Mark.

"If you're telling me the truth, this will go a lot faster if it's just the two of us."

Mark matched her gaze. "I don't have anything else tonight."

Officer Petersen stood up and left the room, the heavy door slamming shut behind her.

She returned a few minutes later with a phone. She sat back down and slid it across the table to Mark. He picked it up.

"Do you have someone in mind, or do you need a list of public defenders?" Officer Petersen asked.

Mark thought carefully. He had just been stalling. If he called a real lawyer, that meant giving away the fact that he was Solarflare. He couldn't risk it. But the only people who knew he was Solarflare were the Currants.

That's it, Mark realized.

"I have someone in mind."

"Do you know their number?"

Mark nodded. He'd been calling Chuck's house for almost ten years. It was one of the few numbers that he actually had memorized in an era where everyone's contact information was just saved on their phones' contact lists.

"I'll leave you to it," Officer Petersen said as she stood up to leave the room again.

Mark nodded, grateful that she made the decision and didn't force him to ask for that. Mark dialed the number slowly, trying to keep his trembling finger from pressing the wrong numbers by accident.

The line rang. And rang. After the fourth ring, Mark began to worry that they might not be home. What if they didn't answer? What were his options then? The phone rang a final time. It went to their voicemail.

Mark hung up and hastily dialed again. He wasn't sure how many tries he would get at this phone call, so he had to take them as quickly as he could.

The phone only rang once this time before an answer.

"Hello?" answered the other end of the line.

Mark recognized Mr. Currant's voice. He breathed a sigh of relief.

"Hello?" Mr. Currant asked again.

"Hello, Mr. Currant. It's me, Mark," Mark frantically replied, worried that Mr. Currant was about to hang up. "I'm at the police station. I was picked up at school outside of the football stadium and I need your help."

Mark avoided mentioning why he was there. He didn't just think someone could be listening. He was confident someone was listening. He wasn't about to say anything about him being Solarflare. He just hoped Mr. Currant could get him out of this.

"I understand," Mr. Currant answered after a pause. "I'll be right there." And he hung up.

Mark sat in silence waiting for Mr. Currant to arrive. Officer Petersen didn't return. Maybe she wanted Mark to sit in silence and think about what he was prepared to say, or maybe she was frustrated and didn't feel like spending any more time dealing with a kid who wasn't going to cooperate. Either way, it felt like an eternity.

An hour, or one eternity by Mark's internal clock, later, Mr. Currant arrived at the police station. He walked with purpose through the station's doors in his finest suit.

"May I help you, sir?" an officer at the front desk asked him.

"Yes, you may," Mr. Currant replied in a tone that was polite yet firm. "I understand that you are holding a minor for questioning."

The officer turned to his computer and typed away, looking for who Mr. Currant was talking about.

"His name is Mark Michaels, he was picked up at North Delfield High School," Mr. Currant added, again in a tone that mixed helpful with stern.

"Yes," the officer said, pulling up Mark's info. "It says here that Officer Petersen found Mr. Michaels in the North Delfield High School parking lot at 2300 hours earlier tonight. His mother was notified en route, and he is being held for questioning."

"I see," Mr. Currant replied.

"And may I have your name?" the officer asked.

"My name is George Currant. I am a family friend, Mr. Michaels called me in as legal counsel."

"You're a lawyer?" Officer Petersen asked, stepping beside the other officer. She wanted to know who Mark had called.

"I don't practice, but I am familiar with the law." Mr. Currant answered casually. "And you are?" he added, in a voice that was just shy of outright condescension.

"I'm Officer Joan Petersen. I brought Mr. Michaels in for questioning."

"Ah, just the person I was hoping to speak with," Mr. Currant said, his tone now eager and slightly dangerous. "Would you mind telling me how you rationalized bringing in a minor for questioning on what is undoubtedly the most traumatic night of his life?"

"We collected statements from every individual present at North Delfield High School this evening. Mr. Michaels gave no statement and was found wandering school grounds after hours. I had every right to bring him in for questioning."

Mr. Currant exhaled and pressed his fingers against one another. He nodded slowly.

"And that's not even mentioning the fact that I found Mr. Michaels carrying an athletic bag with a suit identical to the one worn by the vigilante known as Solarflare."

This was news to the other officer.

Mr. Currant froze for just a second. Then he nodded again, his hesitation imperceptible to any outside observer.

"We have evidence that suggests that Mark Michaels is the vigilante known as Solarflare and that he may be connected to the string of elevated violence in the city. I will be questioning him tonight and you may be present, but I have already been cleared to do so by my superiors due to the nature of this matter."

"I see," Mr. Currant said. He inhaled deeply and removed his glasses. He folded them and placed them in the front pocket of his suit. His eyes glowed a deep, deep blue.

"Mark," Mr. Currant said as he opened the door to the interrogation room.

Mark lifted his head off of his folded arms on the table. He looked at the clock on the wall. It was past one in the morning. He had no idea how long Mr. Currant had been there or how long he had been speaking with the officers.

"You're free to go. I spoke with Officer Petersen and her superiors, and we cleared everything up."

Mark stood up carefully, worried about hearing a conflicting command from an officer. It was weird that Mr. Currant was the one bailing him out. But he was just grateful to be leaving.

Mark walked out of the room slowly and Mr. Currant handed him back his bag and his phone. Mark looked inside the bag. His suit was still there. He was sure that they would've kept the suit as evidence.

"Why aren't they —" Mark began to ask.

"Just walk," Mr. Currant ordered firmly in a hushed tone. "We do not want them to change their minds."

Mark nodded and walked on in silence.

They walked past the front desk, where Officer Petersen still stood. Mark made uneasy eye contact with her. She stared back at him and nodded slightly, as if to signal approval, yet her stare was vacant. Mark looked away immediately.

They left the station and walked to Mr. Currant's car. Even though they were out of the station, Mark remained silent. He stayed silent as Mr. Currant started the car and drove off. Mr. Currant did nothing to relieve Mark's uneasy feeling; he wasn't particularly happy at being dragged away from important work this evening to bail Mark out. He was content to let Mark sit in uncomfortable silence right now.

"Mark," Mr. Currant said when they reached Mark's house. Mr. Currant had sent Chuck to the school to get Mark's car and bring it home. Mark was grateful for one less hassle tomorrow.

"Yes?" Mark asked, afraid to look him in the eye.

"Do not tell anyone what happened tonight. Do not talk about it with any of your other friends, do not tell your parents. You told your mom you were going to answer questions, is this correct?"

"Yes," Mark answered, almost adding a 'sir' out of a fear that paralleled respect.

"That is all that happened. The police officer spoke with you. You answered all of her questions and they let you go. The issue is resolved completely. I gave you a ride home because I, as principal, was also called in to answer questions."

Mark nodded. Less was more in this case. They asked questions, he answered them, they let him go. Simple as that.

"I'm glad we are in agreement. You may go. Leave your suit, Charles will clean and mend it as necessary."

Mark stepped out of the car and walked through the door. His parents had both been up waiting for him. It was almost two in the morning by this point. His mom embraced him in a hug that seemed to never end, as his dad stared at him with a mixture of relief and anger over the emotional toll the night had taken. Mark didn't say anything until he eventually excused himself for bed. His parents let him go; the lectures could wait for tomorrow. He must be even more tired than either of them.

He kicked off his shoes before climbing into bed. He was too exhausted to brush his teeth or wash his face right now. The faintest streaks of remaining face-paint smeared his pillowcase.

Lying in bed, the full weight of the night finally settled in on Mark. The fight, the arrest, his conversation with Mr. Currant, everything. The conversation truly unsettled him. He sobbed silently for about ten minutes before exhaustion took him, and he slept until noon.

THIRTEEN
Before the Dance

Mark woke up the next day incredibly sore. Every muscle ached, and if it hadn't been the day of the Homecoming Dance, he probably would've just slept until Monday morning. He had slept plenty, though. He groaned loudly as he pulled himself out of bed and shuffled into the bathroom. He checked himself in the mirror. There were a lot of bruises from last night. His ribs and back and arms and stomach were covered. Pretty much everywhere above the belt and below the face. He was glad there wasn't anything noticeable on his face like a black eye. Explaining something like that to his parents wouldn't have been easy or fun.

It was almost another half hour before Mark came downstairs for breakfast. He had been in the shower for almost twenty minutes. Mainly because his torso was too sore to wash, but also because he kept dozing off.

"Someone's finally up," Mr. Michaels commented, glancing down at his watch as he saw his elder son dragging himself into the kitchen.

"I know," Mark muttered as he made himself breakfast. It was lunchtime, but since it was the first meal of the day, it was technically breakfast.

"You check your phone yet today?" Mr. Michaels asked, half sarcastically. Of course Mark had checked his phone, he thought; he's a teenager.

"I haven't, actually," Mark realized, a bit shocked himself. Last night was crazy. He just wanted to relax for a little bit this morning before thinking about any more Solarflare-related craziness. He was curious if there was any news about Robbie, though.

"So, I'm guessing you didn't see that the school board met this morning to talk about cancelling the dance tonight, in light of last night's events?"

Mark swallowed hard, sending half-chewed cereal violently down his throat. He coughed loudly. "They can't do that! I bought tickets."

"Well, lucky for you, the school district made an official announcement," Mr. Michaels said, "Homecoming will go on as planned. Just with a lot more security. But your mom and I need to have a talk with you beforehand."

Mark spent the rest of the day lying about the house. He didn't want to answer questions about last night. He knew they would come later in the evening, but that was a problem for later, he thought. He confirmed with Lauren that he would pick her up at five, they'd take a few photos, and then meet the rest of their group at Mt. Fuji's Grill around 5:45 for their group's 6 o'clock reservation. Sarah had stressed that they needed to be at the restaurant before 6 so that they'd make their reservation, Lauren relayed via text. Lauren then confessed to Mark that a small part of her wanted to be late and see just how insane Sarah went. She was a bit of a control freak, Lauren confided in Mark with an "lol," though he was already well aware of that. It felt good to be laughing with her after how things went last night.

Around 4 o'clock, Mark picked himself off his bed and readied himself for the dance. He shaved the peach fuzz off his face, styled his hair, and splashed some cologne on his wrists and neck. He believed he was using a reasonable amount, but it was way too much.

He put on the new suit his mom had bought him over the summer. It was a nice, dark navy suit, and when Mrs. Michaels purchased it in early August, it would've fit Mark perfectly. Unfortunately, after two months as Solarflare, Mark's physique had changed a good bit. He had since bulked up to the point that he could feel the jacket being stretched out against his shoulders. He hoped it wasn't noticeable.

He then tied his dark green necktie. Lauren had told him to get a dark green tie. She sent a text with a photo of the shade of green, but he wasn't completely sure that he'd be accurate from the photo alone. He entrusted his mom to figure that out.

When Mark got downstairs, he made eye contact with his mom. She noticed the poor fit of the new suit. She was not happy about it. She silently resolved to take Mark and the suit to a tailor soon. She didn't pay all that money for a suit Mark would wear once. Especially if it didn't fit.

She subtly signaled to Mark to unbutton the jacket. He did, and the jacket felt less constricting across his body. He grinned in relief, and she gently returned a smile.

Mr. Michaels gestured for his son to take a seat, and the mood suddenly became serious. Mark obeyed. Mrs. Michaels took the lead. She and her husband were good about sharing roles. Neither one was the sole disciplinarian.

"You know, after you got in last night, your father and I stayed up another hour talking about what we were going to do about what happened. We thought about not letting you go to the dance tonight."

"It wasn't my fau—" Mark began pathetically, knowing that she wouldn't listen. This time, of course, was especially pathetic because a part of him felt that it truly was his fault. Sure, he didn't invite The Abyss to come crash the game and ruin everyone's evening, but he was Solarflare and he let her worry about him all night. Truth be told, as he drifted off last night, he had a fleeting thought about never suiting up again.

"But we are letting you go. We decided that it wouldn't be fair to Lauren and that it really wasn't your fault. Your father is actually hoping to speak with Mr. Currant about that business with the police later." Her demeanor shifted, and she straightened Mark's tie. "Have a good time tonight, sweetie. Take lots of pictures."

Mark pulled up to Lauren's house five minutes before the agreed-upon arrival time. He looked at his watch, then his phone. They both said the same thing. He expected to have a harder time finding street parking close to her place. He contemplated his options. He could sit in the car for the next four minutes or so and arrive right on time, or he could go to the door now.

He opted for the second one. Sitting in front of her house waiting was way creepier than just going to the door a bit early.

Mark walked up to the front door, a corsage held tight in his hand. He adjusted his suit and knocked on the door. He waited. No response. He reached for the doorbell and paused before pressing it. Maybe they just didn't hear him; he didn't knock that hard. Or maybe someone was heading to the door and he was just being impatient.

As he was about to knock a second time, he heard footsteps behind the door. Lauren's father opened the door. Mr. Bay was an imposing man. Shorter than Mark by a few inches, but much more built. The hair on top of his head was receding slightly, but he compensated by growing out a well-trimmed beard. Even with the advantages of height and fire-powers, Mark didn't want to be on Mr. Bay's bad side.

"Mark!" Mr. Bay said with a grin. "Good to see you. How are your parents?"

"They're good," Mark said with a smile of his own. His parents and Lauren's parents had been good friends for years. No awkward pre-dance interactions with the date's parents, he thought.

"Hi Mark, Lauren's just finishing up. She'll be down in a minute," Mrs. Bay announced as she descended the staircase to the foyer, camera in hand. "I'm guessing your parents will want me to send them pictures?"

"That'd be great," Mark answered.

"So where are they tonight?" Mr. Bay asked.

"My mom wanted a few pictures of Sean's first Homecoming, so she drove him. And it just felt kind of weird for my dad to come here too when I can drive myself."

"Fair point," Mr. Bay offered with a laugh. "Well, tell them we'll have to catch up soon."

"I will," Mark agreed with a smile.

Mark made gentle small talk with Mr. and Mrs. Bay for a few minutes, diplomatically sidestepping any talk of the previous night, until they heard a young woman clear her throat from the top of the stairs.

"Lauren, are you ready?" Mrs. Bay asked.

"Yes," Lauren replied confidently, "I just want to be sure I have the attention of my audience."

The Bays and Mark gathered around the foot of the staircase for Lauren's grand entrance. She was not particularly vain, but she knew she looked good and felt that she should take full advantage of the moment.

And then Mark saw her.

She looked incredible. Her hair was done up and her make-up was flawless. She wore a stunning dark green dress. It matched Mark's tie perfectly. But Mark wasn't focused on coordinating colors; all he could think of was that she looked far more elegant than any attendee of North Delfield High School's Homecoming Dance had ever looked.

"You look incredible." Mark said. It was all he could say. And he knew he had not even come close to expressing his feelings on the matter.

Lauren muttered a sheepish response accepting the compliment. She knew she looked good, but Mark's compliment carried a greater weight.

Mr. and Mrs. Bay were kind enough to shift everyone's attention to picture-taking, sparing the teenagers from any further embarrassment. They took a multitude of photos from different angles, in different settings and lighting, until they felt they had immortalized the evening in every way a parent could ask for.

"Are you ready to go?" Mark asked once the last picture had been taken. He glanced discretely at his watch, which read that the two of them were running late at this point. Technically, he still could've arrived at the restaurant on time if they flew instead of drove, but that wasn't an option.

"Yes," Lauren replied with a bit of embarrassment. "Mom, Dad, we really need to be going."

Mr. Bay sheepishly lowered his camera with a grin, realizing that he had indeed kept the kids later than he expected.

"Have a nice time, kids," Mrs. Bay said with a smile. "Be safe."

Mark gave obligatory handshakes to Mr. and Mrs. Bay with a well-intentioned awkward smile and waited by the door. From there he watched as Lauren kissed her parents on the cheek and said goodbye before she placed a hand gently against a photo on the wall.

"Night Chris, love you," she said softly.

Mark said nothing. He already knew. Lauren's brother Chris had died in a car accident four years ago. Chris was ten. The community rallied to support the Bays, but there's only so much that can be done. Nothing anyone could do would erase that loss. Mr. and Mrs. Bay took on roles as volunteer EMTs whenever their schedules allowed, inspired by the efforts of EMTs at the scene that day.

So, Mark didn't say anything when Lauren paused. He made a mental note to be very careful driving tonight.

Mark opened Lauren's car door for her when they got outside. She playfully curtsied in thanks and got in. Mark drove the two of them to the restaurant as cautiously as he'd ever driven. He stopped at every yellow light, even though he normally hated to not make a yellow light before it turned red. They made good time, though. They reached Mt. Fuji's Grill at 5:46pm, just a single minute late. Sarah couldn't possibly be upset with them about one minute, Mark thought. Besides, he had something he needed to say.

"Before we go in," Mark began, before Lauren opened her door to get out, speaking slowly as he searched for the right words, "I want to apologize for last night. I'm sorry I left you."

"Mark, it's okay," Lauren answered, almost automatically.

"No, it's not," he insisted. "I shouldn't have made you worry like that."

Lauren nodded softly. The tone of the car had shifted considerably. Mark expected that much.

He clenched his teeth for a moment. The idea of telling her that he was Solarflare wasn't a new one. Maybe she'd feel better if she knew that he could — and did — handle himself in that type of situation. But the thought was quickly swept away, almost as quickly as it had appeared.

"I'm sorry," he said softly, just above a whisper. He struggled to keep himself composed. He had made a lot of people worry last night.

Lauren placed her hand on top of his, rubbing gently. Mark smiled. She smiled back.

"I forgive you," Lauren said. "I really do. Let's enjoy tonight and not think about it."

Mark grinned. "Sure."

He was wrong about Sarah not being mad, by the way. He and Lauren were the last two to arrive and Sarah's death-glare made them both instantly aware of it.

Mark pointed at Lauren in blame. "Lauren's parents would not stop taking pictures. It's like they're obsessed with me."

Most of the group chuckled. Sarah didn't.

Their group numbered eight. It was supposed to be ten, but Robbie was in no condition to go to Homecoming, and his date, Lexi, had opted to spend the evening with him and his family at the hospital. It was a nice gesture on her part. Sarah did an incredible bit of acting when she told Lexi that it was fine.

It was not fine. Sarah hated that she now had to change their reservation. She had called Nick in tears, convinced that the restaurant would be entirely inflexible. Nick made the phone call for her. He received a bit of pushback from the host at trying to change a reservation at the last minute, but then he explained that their missing party member was Robbie Perez, a local hero who literally saved Solarflare less than 24 hour ago. The reservation was adjusted.

Sarah and Nick were the first couple Mark recognized. She wore a chic, light blue dress and Nick wore a suit of the exact same shade with a bow tie to match.

Ben and Ana were also there. Ben was a few inches taller than Mark, with short-cropped brown hair and a sturdy frame. He was wearing a jet-black suit and dress shirt with a crisp white tie. Ana's dress was alternating white and black in a lovely pattern, set in a dress almost too sophisticated for a high school student. Ben was on the football team with Robbie. He was still a bit shaken from last night's events. But Mark still wasn't his biggest fan. It was hard to pin down exactly why, though.

Caroline was there with Ryan. The two of them had been together for a couple months at this point. As Mark had learned during last night's football game, the two of them had both applied to the same list of schools, and it was a safe bet that their decisions would be largely based on where they both got accepted. Not always the best idea, but no one was going to tell them otherwise.

And the last pair of their group was Mark and Lauren. Mark was obviously biased, but he believed he and Lauren were the best-looking pair out of all of them.

Sarah informed the hostess that the final members of their revised eight-person group had arrived for their reservation. The hostess nodded and led them to their table. The thing about Mt. Fuji's Grill was that it was a Japanese steakhouse where the food was prepared in front of customers on a large hibachi grill, surrounded by a long, thin wrap-around table, much like a bar. Had their full group arrived, they would have had a full grill to themselves. Each grill was surrounded by a ten-seat table, with two seats on the right side of the grill, two seats on the left side, and six seats in front. There were about a dozen grills throughout the restaurant. When Sarah made the reservation weeks prior, she had fully intended that their group have a full table to themselves. Now they might have two random people join their table. It was going to ruin their pictures, she thought, but she had the good sense to not voice this concern. After all, it's not like she could be mad at Robbie.

The group made their way to the table, passing other North Delfield Homecoming groups at their own tables. When they got to the table, Sarah *encouraged* everyone to take the seats she suggested. Everyone obliged, recognizing that Sarah was already tense over the last-minute adjustments and nearly losing the reservation.

Mark was seated at the edge of the table, on the right side of the grill, on the outside of the group. He tried to take in stride, recognizing that he wasn't too close with the group, but it'd be a lie to say he wasn't offended. Lauren sat next to him and the rest of the group sat in front of the grill. The waitress dropped off menus, said that their chef would arrive shortly, and went off. She returned a few minutes later with a middle-aged couple, presumably on their weekly date night, and sat them along the left side of the table. Mark could see Sarah's jaw clench in suppressed rage from across the table.

"So, what does everyone think they'll get?" Nick asked with a grin, doing his best efforts at damage control.

Ryan immediately jumped in to assist and soon the table was buzzing with excited discussion of their upcoming dinner. The middle-aged couple even jumped in once but recognized that less was more and largely kept to themselves for the rest of the evening.

"So, Mark," Nick began with full sincerity from almost the exact opposite side of the table. "Is Chuck going to Homecoming with a different group or is this just not his thing?"

Mark appreciated Nick's efforts to include him in the larger conversation, but he was a bit taken aback, having suddenly taken the conversational spotlight. "Uh, he's staying at home. It's just not really his thing."

"I mean, what exactly is his thing?" Ben asked sarcastically. He then added, dismissively, "It seems like all he cares about are grades and hanging out with you."

The members of their table chuckled meekly, Ben's joke ringing a bit too true.

"That's not true," Mark protested. "Lauren, you're on the cross-country team with him."

"Yeah," Lauren said. "But he never really talks to anyone."

"What, like, during practice?" Mark asked, genuinely surprised.

"Well, during practice, during races, before and after practice, before and after races. He treats it like an obligation," she said before pausing, as if she was looking for the words. She didn't want to say anything malicious about Chuck, but she wasn't about to lie. "He runs without complaints or enthusiasm. It's like it's his job. Only times I've really had a conversation with him is when the two of you are together."

"He's not that closed off," Mark countered. "He talks to people."

"When he's around you, maybe," Ben replied. "Lauren and I are in AP Physics with him this year. He answers questions when he's asked, but that's basically it."

"He never talked to anyone outside of group work in AP English last year," Caroline added. The rest of the group murmured agreement, even Ryan. He didn't even go to the same school, Mark thought, but it made sense he'd just automatically agree with Caroline. The rest of the group, however, had taken classes with Chuck. Apparently if Mark wasn't with him, he just didn't socialize. Mark found this hard to believe. Impossible, even.

Lauren sensed Mark's unease. "I mean, I'm sure he's just shy," Lauren interjected, addressing the group, trying to save Mark's best friend from the unending criticism she had accidentally started.

Mark smiled slightly. He was glad that Lauren was defending his friend, though this conversation was bringing a lot to light that he was uncomfortable with. Did Chuck really not talk to anyone when he was alone?

"Hello!" a friendly voice shouted, interrupting Mark's train of thought. It was the chef arriving at the table. He was a plump Japanese man somewhere in his late thirties, early forties. His smile was sincere and infectious. He surveyed the group and nodded. "You all look great. Where are you going? Funeral? Wedding?"

The group laughed. There were at least a dozen other Homecoming groups in the restaurant at that very moment. Mark wondered if they all said the same things to their tables.

"Homecoming!" Ben shouted, playing along.

"Homecoming," the chef repeated with a grim. "Special night. Well, let me say that I am grateful to be a part of your special night. My name is Ando."

The group greeted Ando in a murmur of polite welcome and he set to work prepping the grill. He rattled off some notes about specials, some well-rehearsed jokes, and left to give everyone a moment to decide on their meals.

"Mark, you should say something to Ando in Japanese when he gets back," Ben shouted from across the table.

"I'm not Japanese," Mark replied, with a slight incredulous glare. "I'm half-Chinese." He held his plastic menu in his hands and gripped it tighter, trying not to be overly sensitive.

"What's the difference?" Ben insisted.

Mark felt the menu start to get warm and fought off that familiar heat from building behind his eyes. Not worth it, he repeated in his mind. "There's a lot of differences, actually," he managed to eke out, in as congenial a tone as he could manage. He forced a laugh. "Not sure where I'd even start."

"So, Mark," Ana began, desperate to change the subject to one less confrontational. Ben was embarrassing himself and her. "How'd you ask Lauren to Homecoming?"

Ben kept going before Mark could answer. "There's a lot of differences, actually," he mocked. Had Mark been sitting closer, he might have noticed the smell of alcohol on Ben's breath. Not that it would've made Ben's behavior more excusable, but it would've made more sense. He'd told Ana it was to make tonight more fun, but the reality was that he was having trouble coping with what he saw the night before.

"What's your problem man?" Mark erupted.

Suddenly, a burst of flames erupted across the top of one of the grills back behind Mark on the opposite end of the restaurant. As the flames were sucked up by the ventilation hood, the chef and patrons were all staring dumbfounded at one another. No one was hurt, but the chef's eyebrows were a bit singed. He held a squirt bottle of oil in one hand and a stack of charred onions sat atop the grill, still smoking.

"I'm sorry, the volcano must've gotten away from me," the other chef could be heard meekly muttering to his table.

A mass of servers and other chefs and managers flooded the table, trying to assess the damage and, as a secondary measure, prevent any potential lawsuits.

Every eye at Mark's table was locked on the chaos across the restaurant. Mark knew immediately he'd been the cause. He kept his neck craned on the action. He needed to appear just as surprised as everyone else. He didn't feel his eyes change, but he worried that it might have happened for a split second. Did anyone see?

After a beat, he saw out of the side of his eye that Lauren had turned back around. He followed her lead.

"Well, that was weird." Nick declared. "Everyone okay?"

The group muttered in the affirmative, even the middle-aged couple. Sarah wasn't annoyed with them for answering this time. The table fell silent for a moment. Ben was shaken up enough by what had just happened that he remained silent.

"Mark," Lauren took the initiative. "Weren't you about to tell Ana how you asked me to Homecoming?"

"Yes." Mark eagerly replied. Anything to move past what had just happened. "Thanks. Yeah, I, uh, set up a series of signs between her place and school so that she'd see them during her walk to school."

"Weren't there flowers?" Ana asked helpfully, knowing full well the answer.

"Yeah, I'd left some flowers beneath the last sign, right by the school. Honestly, I didn't think about it until the next day, but I'm lucky no one else grabbed them." Mark concluded with a laugh. Wait. Did he leave flowers? He just did the signs. Did Chuck leave flowers and a note just in case? Had they talked about it?

"The flowers also had a card." Lauren added with a smile. "It said: in case you didn't see the other signs, want to go to Homecoming?"

"I just wanted to make sure." Mark said with a grin, pushing his uncertainty to the back of his mind. It had been a crazy couple of weeks, maybe he just forgot. He passed the question along. "Nick, what about you? How'd you ask?"

As Nick launched into a retelling of his own efforts to secure a date with his own girlfriend, Mark relaxed a bit. He'd just had another close call with his secret identity but, compared to last night, it was a pretty manageable one. The night was off to a solid start so far.

Mr. Currant arrived at Oracular well after normal visiting hours.

He sat in his car for a moment before sending a single text message. When he received a response, he made his way to the building.

Security did not ask him to sign in or for any identifying documents. He simply marched through the building and entered the executive elevator to the CEO's office. The CEO's office made up the entire top floor of the new facility.

When he arrived, Mr. Currant exited the elevator and stood there. Oracular's CEO stood up from her desk and stared at Mr. Currant. So, that answers the question posed earlier. The new CEO was a woman, and she detested any sort of public appearance.

She was tall and thin, dressed in exquisite business attire, with light grey eyes and her silver hair done up in a bun.

"What do you need?" she asked.

"Is that any way to speak to a superior, Sylvia?" Mr. Currant asked as he strolled into the office and took a seat.

She swung around the desk towards Mr. Currant in a single, fluid motion.

"How might Status Quo be of service to you, my king?" she asked with full sincerity in a sweeping bow.

"I need information regarding Edmund Price." Mr. Currant declared.

"Edmund Price?" she questioned, knowing exactly what had happened nearly a decade prior. "I thought he died years ago."

"Yes, I also thought that I had killed him back then," Mr. Currant replied, dropping all pretense. He remembered being on that boat and destroying it with Edmund aboard. He did not want to kill Edmund himself; he assumed that the sea would do the job for him. He now realized that was wrong. He had known that for weeks now. He should have killed him.

Sylvia reluctantly returned to her desk and pulled out a file from the overstuffed drawer.

"He has been doing his best to live off-the-grid," she prefaced as she offered this new information to Mr. Currant. "But he seems to have shown his hand recently."

"The apartment fire."

"Yes."

Mr. Currant flipped through the file, rapidly taking in the information. It indicated that Edmund Price survived the confrontation years prior and, since then, had been working as a hand on other fishing boats, offering a series of fake names the entire time.

Had he bothered to shave his hideous beard, he might have gotten away with it, Mr. Currant thought.

Mr. Currant paused as he came to the last fishing trip Edmund was believed to have joined. It had been over a month since then.

"Is he no longer fishing?" Mr. Currant asked dismissively. "Why did no one think to mention this to me?"

Sylvia retreated slightly before answering, "We don't believe he is a threat. He's just some fisherman that survived an encounter with you." She doubled-down. "He's not a threat."

"And what about those that you do consider threats?" Mr. Currant asked.

"Every threat brought in under your leadership has been extensively monitored per your orders. Had you instructed us to look out for Price, we would have, and this would be a nonissue."

Mr. Currant wordlessly walked over to the office's sleek, modern watercooler and poured himself a cup of water. He took a deep drink before refilling the paper cup. He paused for a moment before he took the water in the cup and whipped it at Sylvia. The water whip cut across her cheek before she could react. She didn't react to the pain at all.

"He knows exactly who he is, and what I am, and what I am after." Mr. Currant asserted, his voice firm but dispassionate. "He is absolutely a threat, and it is a failure on all of Status Quo that you did not let me know."

Sylvia held her still-bleeding cheek and tried to counter Mr. Currant's point, matching his firm but dispassionate tone. "Maybe we would have been more prepared had you not been so fixated on Mark Michaels."

Wordlessly, Mr. Currant flung another jet of water at Sylvia. This one stopped less than an inch away from her temple. He didn't want to hurt her this time, but he did want to show that he easily could.

"Mark Michaels is absolutely instrumental in my plan." Mr. Currant asserted calmly as the spike of water hung in the air, just shy of a fatal blow. "I will not hear any criticisms against his involvement."

Sylvia nodded gently and Mr. Currant allowed the water to fall to the ground.

"So does Edmund know how to command his inner-fire?" Mr. Currant asked, as if this was a simple round of questioning.

"Yes," Sylvia answered carefully. "We believe he does, but we believe he is somewhat of a novice in this regard. He did not have anyone from whom to learn."

Mr. Currant said nothing but stroked his chin pensively.

"We have taken care of more dangerous men than him easily," Sylvia declared, almost desperately.

"Are there any others that you believe may be making an effort for the ring?" Mr. Currant asked.

"No sir," Sylvia said in the most authoritative voice she could muster. It was the truth, but she needed to make sure that Mr. Currant believed her.

"Very well," Mr. Currant said. "I have other engagements."

He stood up from his seat and made his way back to the executive elevator that had brought him here. Sylvia said nothing.

Mr. Currant stepped back into the elevator and, before the doors closed, called back to Sylvia, "If anyone else comes for the ring, Ms. Wright, I will hold you personally responsible."

The doors closed before Sylvia could respond, but once Mr. Currant was gone, she collapsed upon her desk, desperate to catch her breath.

FOURTEEN
Homecoming Dance

Mark and Lauren arrived at the Homecoming Dance after their dinner. The rest of their group arrived around the same time, not too far staggered out. Mark was sure that Sarah had been fuming about the fact that they didn't think ahead and book a limo for the night. But it meant more time for just the two of them. Mark worried about his music choices during the drive over. He had known Lauren all these years but could not have guessed her preferred musical genres if his life depended on it. He hoped she liked alternative rock and pop punk. He felt that the combination worked, but that might have just been him. Luckily, Lauren didn't want to discuss the random grill fire during the drive. Because, as Mark knew, it was anything but random. Maybe Ben shouldn't have made that racist comment.

They held hands as they walked into the school's gym, now decked out for the most romantic evening high schoolers could imagine for late October. That basically amounted to streamers, glitter, and a disco ball. It looked nice, but it was far from the most romantic thing any of these students would see in their lives. The DJ seemed to be playing from the same setlist as Mark's car. Lauren nudged Mark playfully.

"He has good taste," Mark responded with a confident smirk. "Uh, would you like to dance?" he asked, not entirely sure how the current song was supposed to lend itself to dancing, but it felt like the right question.

Lauren arched an eyebrow. This was not the song to ask that question.

"Want to get punch?"

Lauren nodded. "Look at you, reading non-verbal cues," she said playfully.

The two made their way towards the refreshment table, exchanging glances and waves with friends already on the dance floor. Mark could hear a dozen overlapping conversations about last night. Supervillains attacked the game! Solarflare was there! Robbie saved Solarflare's life! Robbie was still in the hospital and barely hanging on! Mark winced. Robbie did get hurt and it was his fault. But Robbie wasn't about to die. He'd be fine, Mark told himself.

Lauren took the lead and grabbed Mark's hand, moving not aggressively, but with purpose. He suddenly became very concerned about the sweatiness of his hand.

"Is that Lauren Bay?!" an eager voice called out over the music. Both Mark and Lauren turned to find its source. An excited girl in a deep purple dress, her hair braided and done up in an elegant twist, was making a beeline for the two of them. Mark was impressed at how swiftly she was moving in that dress and how well she weaved through the crowd.

"Sheri!" Lauren shouted with a laugh as the two embraced. "What are you doing here?"

"I'm actually dating a guy on the football team. We went to my Homecoming last weekend. I forgot you went to North Delfield!" Sheri paused as she noticed the young man hanging off Lauren's arm. "Oh, sorry, I didn't see your friend. Hi, I'm Sheri."

"I'm Mark," he said. "Nice to meet you."

"Lauren and I went to the Katherine Johnson Black Girls' Leadership Retreat together two summers ago. It was between that or cheer camp, but cheer camp didn't have Mae Jemison as a guest speaker," Sheri responded before Mark even had a chance to ask the question she knew had to be coming. She spoke quickly and with great enthusiasm. Makes sense she's a cheerleader, Mark thought.

"That's cool —" Mark began. But it was too late, the conversation had moved past him.

"You know who else is here?" Sheri asked.

"Who?" Lauren asked.

"I'm going to go grab us a drink," Mark announced. Lauren answered with a quick glance and a gentle smile. Mark grinned, despite his best efforts to keep cool. Lauren was here with him and they had a good time at dinner, but he knew she was excited to see an old friend. Not being clingy was the right move, he told himself as he made his way through the crowd toward the refreshment table.

When Mark arrived at the table, he was underwhelmed. The dance was still in its first hour but the snack and drink offerings looked completely picked over. A number of water bottles drenched in condensation served as the only appealing thing on the table. He grabbed one in each hand and chuckled. It was fitting that a school run by a merman would have plenty of water to offer.

"Mark Michaels!" a voice exclaimed as Mark felt a powerful clap to his shoulder. Where did Mark know that voice from?

Mark turned to face him. It was Jason Sherman. Mark hadn't talked to him since the field trip back in May. After Mark came back to school, Jason was oddly quiet in AP Chem. Had it only been five months since the accident? It felt like a lifetime ago.

"Jason," Mark answered, his voice as friendly as he could make it, but he was a little confused by Jason's enthusiasm. It's not like they were particularly close. "Hey, how've you been?"

"I've been good. Yeah, I just came up from Albemarle yesterday."

"Albemarle? Like, in central Virginia?" Mark asked, "That's like a three-hour drive."

"Without traffic," Jason added.

"Right," Mark noted. "So, with traffic, probably closer to four?"

Jason grinned sheepishly and held up a hand with his fingers spread.

"Five?! Why?" Mark was incredulous.

"I've been dating Ashley for over a year," Jason explained with a chuckle, as if Mark should've known that. "Couldn't miss Homecoming."

"Oh, yeah," Mark nodded. He knew of Jason's girlfriend, Ashley Bishop, in the vaguest sense. He'd probably talked to her a grand total of three times. "Wait," Mark continued, pieces of the conversation falling into place. "You said you drove up here from Albemarle. You're at CVA?"

"I am." Jason said with faux humility. Mark then noticed Jason's tie. Yep, that was the logo for CVA.

"You got into the College of Virginia?" Mark wished he was better able to hide the surprise in his voice, but he was truly shocked. He never thought Jason was dumb, but the College of Virginia was the best school in the state.

"Yeah," Jason replied, trying his best to sound modest. It wasn't far off from sincere. "I had been put on the waitlist initially, but I got in. I'm going to try out for the baseball team when spring semester starts." Ah, that made more sense, Mark thought bitterly.

Dread crept into Mark's thoughts. He really needed to find a weekend and seriously focus on college applications, even if it meant Solarflare taking a backseat. His admissions essays were nothing more than rough outlines, his parents wanted him to take the SATs again, and, if he was being completely honest with himself, his evenings as Solarflare were taking a toll on his GPA. If he wanted to get into CVA, he needed to pull it together.

"Dude," Jason pulled Mark back. "You good? You spaced out for a minute."

Mark swallowed hard. "Yeah, I'm good. Thanks. Sorry, just a little stressed with college stuff. I've been putting it off lately."

"I totally understand." Mark believed him and he felt a twinge of relief. Chuck wasn't worried about college admissions. He was going to be valedictorian. So, it was nice for a normal guy like Jason to let Mark know he'd be fine.

"Thanks."

"No worries. Actually, I'm glad I caught you. I've been wanting to say something for a while," Jason's face became a lot more serious. He paused and took a deep breath, as if he was searching for the right words. "I wanted to thank you for what happened at Oracular."

"Yeah, that whole thing was crazy," Mark muttered awkwardly. The official version of events was that nothing happened. It just came very close to *something* happening.

"Nah, man," Jason said, he was making very intense eye contact at this point. In Mark's mind he desperately tamped down any thoughts about his powers, but it felt like Jason was trying to draw it out. Was he being paranoid? He could swear he saw hints of red in Jason's irises. Jason's hand was gripping Mark's shoulder. Why did it feel warm? "I know you likely saved my life. And I don't fully understand what happened, but I do know that. And I wanted to thank you."

"You're welcome," Mark replied, firmly. He tried to strip any emotion from his voice. Just accept it and let go of me, Mark thought.

Jason finally let go. His expression softened and his smirk returned. "Anyway, I'm currently rushing a fraternity down at school. You should check it out next year."

"Yeah, sure," Mark said, desperate to end this conversation and find Lauren. Still, he added, "If I get in."

"You'll get in," Jason said, as he slipped back into the crowd and made his way back to his date.

Mark looked down at the two bottles clenched in his hands. He realized his hands had been shaking. Maybe it was because Jason seemed to be yet another person to find out Mark's secret, if he didn't know it already. Seriously, how could he know? What happened at the lab, what *actually* happened, occurred too quickly for anyone to have seen. Still, after last night, a little paranoia about secret-identities was a good thing. It meant he was being careful.

Mark turned, prepared to seek out his date, when he bumped against a tower of a man.

"Mr. Michaels," Coach Kekoa said, his tone somehow both intimidating and friendly. Maybe the intimidation was unintentional; he was just naturally an intimidating man.

"Coach Kekoa, nice to see you," Mark answered, trying to keep as calm as possible. "Welp, I should get going." He quickly muttered as he tried to sidestep the large man.

"Just hang on a second," Coach Kekoa offered, in a tone that clearly expressed that this was not a suggestion Mark could just ignore.

"Sure sure sure, no problem." It was a problem, though he hoped his voice didn't give him away. He knew exactly where this conversation was going: the football game.

"So, I heard you were at the game last night." Yep, Mark knew it. "I was."

"And Ana mentioned that right before things got a little crazy, you left the stands."

His eyes bored into Mark, almost looking through him. Again, Mark felt himself suppressing some subconscious urge to let his eyes light red.

After a beat of unbearable silence, Mark realized that Coach Kekoa was waiting for a response. "Uh, yes sir," he meekly replied.

"And why is that, Mark?" Coach Kekoa questioned. Did he think Mark had something to do with The Abyss? Or did he suspect Mark was Solarflare? Or, most likely, did he just think Mark was a coward?

"I thought I saw something." Best to go with the excuse he'd used already. "I wanted to give someone a heads up without causing a scene. I was looking for an adult." That last sentence made him feel like a child. He was seventeen, he wasn't running for an adult, he was running to change into his supersuit and save people; people including Coach Kekoa.

Coach Kekoa nodded thoughtfully and smiled. "You're a good kid, Mark. That's what Ana thought you were up to as well." Mark grinned a bit. It was good to know Lauren's best friend didn't think he was a coward. "I just wanted to let you know you've got nothing to be ashamed of. Trying to find an adult was the right call." His voice softened. "I'll never forgive myself for letting Robbie get hurt the way he did."

"I heard he's doing a lot better today," Mark offered after a moment, trying to be helpful. Of course, Coach Kekoa knew already, but it couldn't hurt to remind him of that.

"You're right." He gave Mark a friendly slap on the shoulder as he made his way back to his chaperoning duties. "I'm glad we had the chance to talk, Mark. Now go have fun."

Mark nodded and muttered in the affirmative before he swept the sweat from his forehead and trudged back through the crowd to find Lauren. After all, she owed him a dance.

Mr. Currant took the stage as a song faded out and the students took a break from dancing. Mark was surprised to see him. Didn't he have to worry about tomorrow? Mark shrugged. It was going to be a big day for Mark too, and he was here. And Mr. Currant was the principal. It would look weird for him not to be here, even more so than Mark or Chuck.

"That's where Chuck is," Mark muttered as the pieces finally fell into place. Mr. Currant needed to be here to keep up appearances, but his son could be home doing prep work for tomorrow. Mark felt a quick twinge of guilt at Chuck missing out on a normal childhood over this. Homecoming was sort of a big deal when it came to the high school experience.

"What did you say?" Lauren asked from Mark's side, having heard his muttered realization. The rest of their group had joined the two of them by this point, though if anyone else had heard Mark, they didn't acknowledge it. They'd talked enough about

Chuck already, and it didn't surprise any of them that he was indeed sitting the evening out.

"Uh, I just realized why Chuck isn't here," Mark answered, too eager to answer to think of a lie.

"And why is that?" Lauren followed up. She was asking out of genuine curiosity, Mark realized. After all, she had defended Chuck during dinner when the rest of the group pointed out how antisocial he could be.

"A family tree project," Mark answered haltingly. The answer was not a lie in the grandest sense. At that moment, Chuck was pouring over countless genealogical records from the Outer Banks, North Carolina, and the mid-Atlantic in general. He saw the confused look on Lauren's face and continued. "It is a weirdly time-sensitive project. Also, he didn't really have anyone to go with."

"He should've moved a little quicker last year," Lauren whispered with a chuckle and a quick glance towards Ana. So, that confirmed it. Ana would've gone with Chuck last year if he'd asked sooner. Mark made a note to mention it to Chuck once Ana and Ben broke up. It seemed inevitable; Ben was a jerk.

Mark noticed as the music tapered off and glanced up at the stage. Mr. Currant caught his gaze and gave Mark an imperceptible nod.

"Students of North Delfield," Mr. Currant's voice boomed from speakers. At his voice, the entire student body took notice, with everyone turning towards the stage. Not one side-conversation continued. He knew how to command a room, Mark thought. Probably made him a good king back in Atlantis. "I am so glad to see all of you here tonight for this, our fair school's annual Homecoming dance. I would also be remiss if I did not welcome all guests joining us tonight. Now, I could dive into a rousing speech on the storied history of

Homecoming festivals, but I believe brevity is more fitting for this evening. After all, this a dance, not a lecture."

Gentle laughter swept the crowd. Mr. Currant paused to appreciate it.

"There are a few subjects that need to be covered in my speech before you all may get back to dancing. The first, yesterday evening's football game. I was, as I regularly am, proud of the support this student body showed for our North Delfield Eagles as they took the gridiron." There were scattered chuckles. Mr. Currant talking about football always sounded a bit off because of his accent, even though he was being completely sincere. He held up a hand in good-natured acknowledgement as his audience fell silent again.

"The second, I would like to recognize the extraordinary circumstances of yesterday's game, when we were threatened by unwelcome individuals," Mr. Currant's voice rang slightly harsh. He was offended that The Abyss had attacked last night. Mr. Currant wasn't just a high school principal whose students had been placed in harm's way, Mark realized. He was also a king who saw his former subjects attacking innocent people. Not a great legacy for Atlantis. "The members of this community acted with great aplomb. People maintained cool heads in the face of great danger and, most notably, our own North Delfield quarterback, Mr. Robbie Perez, leapt into action when the man known to us as Solarflare needed assistance."

The crowd erupted into wild applause.

Mr. Currant and Mark made the briefest eye contact as Mr. Currant waited to speak again. Got it, Mark thought. Need to work harder. Can't let people get hurt saving me.

"On the subject of Mr. Perez, there is good news. I spoke with his mother earlier tonight and she shared with me — and gave me permission to share with all of you — that Robbie is doing quite well. His condition is stable, and he is expected to make a full recovery, though it may be a number of days before he is ready to return to class. I am sure we all wish him a speedy recovery."

"Unfortunately, this does mean that our evening will be without our Homecoming King and Queen. I am proud to announce that Mr. Perez is this year's North Delfield Homecoming King and Ms. Alexis Brandon, who is spending the evening alongside Mr. Perez, is our Homecoming Queen." Mr. Currant paused for the cheers and applause to die down. "In the interest of full disclosure, all Homecoming ballots that were submitted for 'Solarflare' and 'the girl in green' were discarded, given that neither one is a student at North Delfield."

Mark suppressed a smirk. He was curious if he'd actually gotten more votes than Robbie. Robbie was obviously well-liked and a hero as of last night, but Mark was doubtful that he'd received more votes than the local superhero. He made a mental note to ask Mr. Currant about the true vote tally when things were a little less crazy.

"As relieved as I am to hear the good news regarding Mr. Perez, I must ask that members of this student body take every effort to keep their distance from Solarflare." Mark glared at Mr. Currant in disbelief, but Mr. Currant's eyes were elsewhere in the crowd. "We do not know this man and we do not know his motives, but we do know that he is dangerous. I do not wish to see another student harmed as a byproduct of Solarflare's presence. If you see him, I urge you to run to safety. Please."

Silence hung in the air. In just a few words Mr. Currant had turned Solarflare from a hero that urged excited conversation to a taboo, a pariah. Mark was so shocked from disbelief that his anger had barely registered consciously, but his eyes flickered crimson.

Mr. Currant scanned the crowd as they continued to absorb the weight of his words. Hushed murmurs had evolved from the silence as the students began to agree. He was right; Robbie did almost die last night. His eyes passed over Mark and an imperceptible smirk flashed across his face. Mark's eyes dimmed.

Maybe it makes sense, Mark thought. If people avoid Solarflare from now on, they'll be less likely to get hurt. The thought ached and he tried to push it away.

"Finally," Mr. Currant resumed, his air of solemnity casually shifting to a broad smile. "Enjoy yourselves!"

The crowd erupted into cheers and the music resumed full force.

As the rest of his Homecoming group started dancing, Mark was rooted to the floor, his eyes fixed on the stage. He needed to talk to Mr. Currant. His eyes tracked Mr. Currant stepping off the stage, heading towards the exit —

"Mark!" Lauren said forcefully, pulling Mark back to the dancefloor. "Everything good? Are we going to dance?"

He turned to answer. "Yeah, of course, I just need to talk to Mr. Currant for a sec."

He looked back at where Mr. Currant had been, where he had been heading. He was already gone.

Mark gritted his teeth. Fine, this would wait until tomorrow.

Until then, he would just have to do as Mr. Currant had said and enjoy the evening. It was a pretty good consolation, Mark thought as he and Lauren began to dance and the immediate concern of Solarflare's reputation slipped from his mind.

FIFTEEN
After the Dance

The gymnasium lights turned on as the music died away. Mark and Lauren stopped dancing as the music ended but didn't let go of each other right away. Something about the moment felt right.

Lauren's head rested on Mark's shoulder for a moment. Mark blushed, not sure exactly what to do at this point. Her hair smelled nice. Mark wasn't sure if it was weird that he noticed that. He didn't mention it. Mentioning it would definitely be weird.

Slowly, she lifted her head, also blushing slightly as she made eye contact with Mark.

Mark smiled. She smiled in return. They looked into one another's eyes.

"Thank you all for coming," the booming voice of Mr. Cranston called out over the speakers, ruining the moment. He droned on about leaving the gym and cleaning up on their way out or something, it didn't matter.

Mark and Lauren separated and turned towards their friends. Everyone else was still kissing their date, which was slightly uncomfortable for both of them. Mark wished he had kissed Lauren right when the music ended. Had it not been for the announcement, he would've. But the moment was gone, now they just stood there, watching their group continue to make out with their respective dates. It was a little awkward.

Mark looked at Lauren and made a face of mock-disgust towards the group. She laughed and grabbed his hand. Mark smiled and intertwined his fingers with hers as they waited it out.

"We're still not any closer to finding the heir," Chuck moaned. The underground training center was now a command center for the search. He was sitting on the floor with books and maps and charts sprawled out around him. He had bags under his eyes like he hadn't slept for days. He hadn't, so it was fitting. He didn't even sleep when his dad went to get Mark out of the police station because he was sent to deal with Mark's car and then wash and repair Mark's supersuit.

His father sat at their massive computer display, still in his suit, having just returned from the dance. He knew exactly who the heir was, but needed Chuck to ensure that Price didn't have any other relatives who might also know how to use their fire. He didn't trust Sylvia's work; she'd allowed Price to operate unmonitored for years. He would never forgive her failure. Six separate monitors, each focusing on a different subject, shone through the darkness of the cave. Chuck had never used all six at once. Most Solarflare issues only required two, three at the most. The football attack might have required four, had he been on duty when it happened.

If he had any time to think about it, he would've been shocked and upset over what happened and how he was unable to help his friend out. Chuck felt uneasy that his father got so directly involved in their work concerning Solarflare. It was just supposed to be him and Mark.

He lay down on his back and tried to rest for a second. He turned his head, his ear pressing against the cold, wet ground, and saw his father busy at work. He saw one monitor was opened to a genealogy map, one was calculating some sort of probability analysis, one was filled with text written in some language that wasn't English, one was flashing a series of faces in rapid succession, and the other two kept flashing from one thing to another too quickly for Chuck to keep up with. Maybe if he wasn't so sleep deprived, he'd be able to.

"Dad," Chuck called out, desperate for a chance to sleep, even if just for an hour.

No response.

"Dad." Chuck repeated, louder this time.

Still nothing. Mr. Currant was still wholly consumed with whatever data was currently displayed on the monitors. It cast an eerie glow upon Mr. Currant's face, which was already pulled tight with concentration. A Black man's face flashed upon one of the screens. His aged face was cruel and serious, with an aristocratic bearing that rivaled that of Mr. Currant. Mr. Currant's concentration wavered as a mixture of hatred and relief manifested in his mind.

"Dad!" Chuck shouted.

"Yes?" Mr. Currant answered, still not looking away from the computers. The face was gone, replaced by an Asian woman with an equally serious countenance.

"I need to sleep," Chuck declared.

"We need to work," Mr. Currant countered.

"I can't concentrate anymore. I don't even know what I'm looking for," Chuck whined, his exhaustion taking its toll.

"We do not have time to rest." Mr. Currant replied, not even considering Chuck's protest.

"Why not? Why can't I sleep for an hour? You know I'm not asking for a full night, but even we need to sleep."

"You know why we cannot rest. We do not have time. The eclipse comes tomorrow, whether we are prepared or not. All we know so far is that a descendant of Blackbeard will return for the Sapphire Ring when it happens. There may even be multiple claimants. I will not send Mark into such a dangerous situation unprepared." Mr. Currant concluded forcefully. It was a lie. Mr. Currant did know exactly who would come for the ring and where he would be going, but he needed to ensure that only that one would be coming.

Chuck nodded. He understood, but it didn't make him feel any less tired. They couldn't be seen. If Atlanteans were seen going after the ring, no matter who saw them, it might bring the war back in full force. Giving Mark all the information they could was all they could do.

"If we can find out who it is, or where exactly this person is going to retrieve the ring, we can take a break," Mr. Currant added, more gently this time. Again, this was a false promise. Mr. Currant knew exactly what he was asking his son to find.

Chuck opened a new book and went back to work.

"So, food?" Ben asked the group as school officials scooted them out the door and into the cold, damp night.

Enthusiastic murmurs signaled a general agreement with the plan.

Mark, wordlessly, took off his jacket and offered it to Lauren.

"Thanks," she said quietly, taking the jacket and resting it on her shoulders.

The group made their way to their cars and drove to a nearby 24-hour diner. Mark and Lauren were the last to arrive. He was driving carefully, but it did mean that they had to settle for street parking while the rest of their group managed to snag spaces in the actual parking lot. They were one of many post-Homecoming groups there, but they secured a table pretty quickly.

"It's a shame Robbie had to miss this," Ana declared once they had all sat down, everyone sitting next to their date.

The group murmured agreement. Mark thought he saw tears in Ben's eyes. He didn't call anyone's attention to it. He disliked Ben less in this moment.

The rest of their time in the diner was uneventful. Everyone had an opinion on the music played during the dance or a comment about other members of their class. And obviously, they all brought up the crazy fireball at the restaurant earlier. But Mark and Lauren had a good time with everyone, enjoying the company.

Rain was already falling again as the group left the diner. Tiny droplets fell from the sky, illuminated by the streetlights. It was a slow, peaceful rainfall, not a heavy one that required shelter. It accentuated the mood, rather than undermining it.

Mark and Lauren bid goodbye to the rest of their group as they walked towards Mark's car.

"Lauren," Mark said, his voice struggling not to break. His hands fiddled with his car keys as he stopped in his tracks.

"Yeah?" she replied, turning around and looking him in the eye across the hood of his car. She had gorgeous eyes, Mark noticed, even from a distance. The raindrops caught in her hair were highlighted by the nearby streetlamp. It added to the moment.

He fidgeted with his keys for a moment, trying to determine what to say. He wasn't sure if he should say anything.

"Mark?" Lauren asked, trying to bring him back to reality. "Can you unlock the car?"

"Uh, yeah," Mark stammered, his face turning crimson as he unlocked the car, "Sorry."

Lauren climbed into the car and began brushing the water out of her hair. Mark hesitated and grimaced in embarrassment. He regained his composure and hopped into the driver's seat, closing the door behind him with a loud thud that could only be attributed to his nerves.

Lauren didn't mention it.

Mark breathed a sigh of relief and started the car.

The drive to Lauren's house wouldn't be too long, only about five minutes. Mark simultaneously wished it would take longer and that it was already over.

His mind raced in the silence. He didn't want to turn on the radio; that felt like it would just diminish the moment.

The night had gone well. He had, as best he could tell, been a good Homecoming date. She had a good time. They laughed and danced and the only real low point of the night was at dinner, and that could hardly be considered his fault. Well, she couldn't know it was his fault.

The football game was his fault, though. Almost. Sort of.

"Hey, Lauren," Mark said carefully, keeping his eyes on the road.

"Yeah?"

"I want to apologize again for Friday," the first part came naturally, he was sorry. It was the rest of the apology that made him stumble over his words as he searched for them, making this feel like a rehash of things he had already said. "I'm sorry I abandoned you and didn't tell you what I was doing. I'm sorry I made you worry. I was worried something might happen to you if I didn't do something."

He blushed. That last part was true — truer than she would ever know, but he worried it made him sound self-important. He just wanted to let her know he wasn't just being a coward. Again, not that he could just say that.

Lauren played with her jewelry for a moment. Mark shifted nervously in his seat from the silence.

"I'm not going to say I'm not mad," Lauren began. "Trust me, I was mad. I'm still a little mad. But you saw something suspicious and did what you thought was the right call. I never thought you were just running off."

That last part was all Mark had wanted to hear. And now that he had heard it, he had never before been so relieved.

"Thanks," he muttered sheepishly, looking away from the road for a moment to make his point, "for saying that. And thanks for going to the dance with me."

"I had a good time, Mark," she said with a smile.

The two were silent for the rest of the drive home. It was a nice, pleasant silence in which the two of them considered separately what this night meant for them. The radio was still off and the only sounds they could hear came from the rain and the engine. The rain had grown harder over the course of the short drive. It was no longer a gentle drizzle, but a storm that sent rain down in sheets and left pools of grimy water all over the road.

Mark put the car in park.

"Do you have an umbrella?" Lauren asked.

"Yeah, I should have one back here," Mark said as he reached into the back seat and began fumbling around for his emergency umbrella. It was down there somewhere, amid all of the clutter. Mark had emptied his car of the messier contents earlier in the day, but some clutter seemed to be permanent.

His hand finally grasped the small, collapsible umbrella. He offered it to Lauren.

"Thanks," she said.

"I can just get it back from you on Monday," Mark offered.

"Or you could walk me to the door," Lauren countered, with complete sincerity.

Mark blushed. He was embarrassed he didn't think of that. "Sure."

Mark walked Lauren to the door of her home, covering the two of them with the tiny umbrella as best he could. As they reached the porch, rain had soaked the left side of his body jutting out from the umbrella's coverage. Mark grabbed Lauren's hand. The porchlight illuminated them, as well as the rainfall.

Wordlessly, Mark brushed her hair out of her face and over her ear. He leaned in and kissed her gently. She kissed him back, with great enthusiasm.

The two of them stood there for a moment, kissing one another. It wasn't an excessive amount, but it was significant.

Mark kept his eyes closed tight as he felt his eyes softly glow. He worried that she might see. But other than that, his mind was focused on nothing but how nice this moment was. The smell of Lauren's perfume filled his nostrils.

When the two finally pulled away from one another, they stood in silence. The rain continued falling, harder and louder now against the umbrella. They were both smiling.

Mark leaned in and kissed her once again, a single peck on the lips. He giggled slightly.

"Took you long enough," Lauren commented.

"I was building to it," Mark replied with a grin, now noticeably more confident. "Anyone can kiss at the end of a slow song during Homecoming. Kissing in the rain is a step up."

"Are you sure umbrellas count?" Lauren asked with a sly smile as she gestured to the thin canopy that was keeping the two of them dry.

"I mean, if you insist, I can close this right now," Mark answered. "But you have to admit, this is better than in the gym with a bunch of streamers, right?"

Lauren laughed. "But the rain is a nice touch. When you're right, you're right." This time, she kissed him.

"I should probably get going," he said, pulling away from her with some reluctance.

Lauren grabbed Mark's hand and squeezed gently.

"Thanks for going to Homecoming with me," Mark said after a moment, needing to say something to her after everything. Even if it was something he had said before. He couldn't just let the night end.

"Thank you for asking me," Lauren replied, with full sincerity.

They leaned in and kissed one last time before she opened the door and went inside. Mark stood on the porch for a moment, grinning ear-to-ear.

He looked at his watch. It was almost two in the morning. A bit later than he had told his parents he planned on staying out. He'd probably have to deal with that in the morning.

Mark got back into his car and quietly drove off from Lauren's house. He kept the radio off and drove home in total silence. It had been a good night, he thought with a smile.

Lauren smiled as she walked inside, thinking the same thing. Lauren walked into the living room of her family home and greeted her parents, who had waited up for her safe return.

"Did you have a good time, sweetheart?" Mrs. Bay asked with a warm smile.

Lauren was still beaming from the kiss.

"Yes, I had a good time. Mark was very sweet," she added. She knew her parents liked Mark already, but this input couldn't hurt.

"He's a good kid," Mr. Bay agreed with a yawn. "Well, this is late enough for me. I'm going to go to bed now. And I think that should go for all of us."

"We'll be up soon," Mrs. Bay called after her husband. Once Mr. Bay was upstairs and out of earshot, she turned to Lauren in a mischievous whisper, "So, do you want to call it a night or do you want to patrol?"

Lauren played with her bracelets for a brief moment and smiled, wordlessly giving the answer they both knew was coming.

"You should go get ready, then," Mrs. Bay said as she pulled out her laptop, from which she had real-time access to emergency situations across Delfield. "I'll see what we have to work with tonight."

Lauren swiftly ran up to her room and put on her new supersuit — the supersuit which she had no reason to suspect that she had been given by Mark.

She pulled the mask on and took a look in the mirror and admired the suit for minute. It was a lot more professional than her old green hoodie had been.

She grabbed her wooden staff and crept downstairs, careful to not alert her father. He had taken the plausible-deniability route with regards to his daughter's superheroism. He was impressed by what this new hero was doing, but if he ever had explicit proof that it was her, he knew he'd never be able to stop worrying. And so, he contented himself with the lie that Lauren and his wife were simply working some sort of support role for the hero. Lauren recognized this and allowed her father to believe whatever he wanted.

Mrs. Bay, however, was actually the original mastermind behind the girl in green, or "Ebony" as the two of them had recently decided she should call herself. Lauren wanted to run into Solarflare again and tell him about the new name so he could get the word out. How was it Solarflare seemed to be such a pro at all this? He had a high-quality suit, an official name, a website, seemingly everything a hero needed.

"I don't imagine there will be much going on tonight with the rain," Mrs. Bay quietly informed her daughter, a mix of relief and disappointment in her voice. Disappointment because she knew how much Lauren loved saving people, relief because she worried, too. But while Mr. Bay needed to distance himself to keep from being overwhelmed by worry, she needed to be involved. "But, if you want to head out there and post up on the rooftop of the Abble Building, next to Adams Park, that should keep you close in case I get word of anything. Does that work?"

Lauren nodded.

Mrs. Bay glanced at her watch. "Two hours. And try to stay somewhat dry, if possible. That fair?"

Lauren nodded again, noted the time limit in her phone before slipping it back into the suit's pocket, and made her way out the back door.

Lauren made her way over to the lone cypress tree in her backyard and, in an instant, scaled to the treetop. She paused for a moment to feel the rain against her suit and stare out at the world in the rain. She had complicated feelings about the rain. She loved the way this night looked as the now-gentle rainfall was illuminated by streetlights, but it brought up memories of losing her brother. She inhaled deeply and exhaled slowly to compose herself.

She leapt from the tree to a nearby rooftop, then another, making her way towards Adams Park and the Abble Building without ever setting foot on the ground.

Once she arrived at the Abble Building, Lauren found a space near the building's edge with a slight overhang that would shelter her from the rain. And there she placed herself, ready to help anyone if they needed it.

For about an hour she sat there, with nothing happening, as only a handful of cars passed on the street below. At this hour, in this weather, most people had the common sense to stay inside.

And then she felt it. Someone else was on this rooftop with her.

"I need to speak with you," the new rooftop occupant said.

Lauren grabbed her staff and stood up, wordlessly. She looked at this new person. He seemed to be a man. He was a bit taller than her, wearing a supersuit of his own. The suit was white, or close to it, she couldn't exactly tell in this light. It didn't seem to have any definitive markings, other than two bulky, metal bands on his wrists. His mask covered his entire face and had two large, circular lenses where his eyes would be. That was it, though.

Lauren thought about the members of The Abyss she'd seen Solarflare fighting these last few months. In their supersuits, all of them looked distorted and unnatural. Even from the stands of the football stadium on Friday night, she could see that there was something grotesque about them. The man in front of her didn't look like that. His suit looked more like hers; more like Solarflare's.

"Or I can do all the talking," the figure offered.

Lauren remained silent as she tried to make out his tone. It didn't seem overly hostile, but she didn't trust him.

"I know you're one of those mostly-silent heroes," he continued. "I mean, it's because of that that you still don't have an official name."

"I do. It's Ebony," Lauren said cautiously.

"I like it," the figure replied with full sincerity. "I've suspected your powers might be connected to wood and plant-based materials. I've seen videos of you with that staff. It's impressive. Don't worry, I'll take the necessary steps to make that your official name. You haven't been wearing the new suit for too long, so it should take easily."

Lauren's grip eased. The figure now actually seemed friendly.

"You work with Solarflare," she realized.

"You could say that. I prefer to be a bit more backstage than he does. And since he vouches for you, I'm willing to work with you as well and do what I can to help," the figure said.

"And you don't want anything in return?" Lauren asked.

"Well, yes and no," the figure began cautiously. "I don't want anything for myself, but I do want us to be doing this correctly. And that means there are rules."

"What kind of rules?" Lauren asked, her grip tightening even more on her staff.

"Rules like no significant others," the figure said knowingly, his voice now cold.

Lauren's heart dropped. Did he know about Mark? They'd just kissed less than two hours ago. Was this person just urging caution, or was it a threat?

Mark had thought about telling Lauren that he was Solarflare ever since she first agreed to go to Homecoming with him. The thought had been pounding in the back of his head all evening, especially since he didn't want Lauren to think he was a coward. But Mark didn't say anything. Chuck had told him not to. And so, because Mark kept his secret, Lauren had no idea that Mark and Solarflare were the same person. She had no idea that Mark could handle himself against any threat.

"It'd be a real shame if someone you cared about was hurt because of what we do, wouldn't it?"

Lauren swung her staff at the figure with her full strength. He dodged effortlessly.

"This isn't a threat," the figure replied casually. "People in our line of work get targeted. Or did you not see what happened last night at North Delfield High School's Homecoming football game?"

Lauren stood momentarily stupefied. How did he manage to dodge her attack so easily?

"Trust me," he continued, ignoring her reaction. "This is what's best, Lauren."

That confirmed it. He knows who I am, she thought. And he's threatening Mark.

Lauren once again attacked with her staff. She swung at his head, his feet, she jabbed at his chest. He dodged and deflected everything. He grabbed the staff in his hands and flung her to the other side of the roof.

"Lauren, listen to me. Please." the figure continued speaking, as if Lauren hadn't just attacked him with everything she had.

Lauren glared at the figure and studied the twin lenses where his eyes were. That must be how he's reacting so quickly; those lenses must give him some kind of edge. She quickly formulated a plan. She just needed to get his eyes off her for a moment.

She launched herself towards the figure, swinging at him again as she had before, and he dodged every attack as he had the last time. But this time, when she jabbed her staff, she went for his left eye, putting all her strength into the strike. He craned his head back and the staff shot right past him, hitting nothing but raindrops as they fell to the ground.

Before Lauren could react, the figure's lenses glowed a gentle blue and her staff was ripped from her hands and tossed out of reach.

She stared in her hands at bewilderment for a moment.

In Lauren's confusion, the figure struck. He swept her feet out from under her and she fell hard onto the rooftop.

"I don't want to fight you and I don't want to hurt Mark Michaels," the figure declared as she picked herself up. "But I need you to see how he's a vulnerability for you. You're not fighting smart right now."

Lauren stood up and said nothing. She glanced over at her staff. She could pull it towards her with her abilities, but he'd see that and be able to attack before it got back to her. He even noticed that she was considering this.

"Even with the staff, I don't think you can beat me," the figure asserted, further undermining her plan.

She was shocked. How did he know?

"I have had my powers since I was a boy, you've only had yours for a few years. I can train you to be better with your abilities, to be able to beat me. You have the raw strength for it, but you can't beat me tonight."

Lauren glared for a beat, before leaping towards him and launching into a barrage of punches and kicks. He dodged every single one, never once going on offense.

"Like I said, you can't beat me tonight," he said, as if her latest attack hadn't fazed him at all. "Especially tonight, with all this rain."

His lenses glowed that soft blue once again, and Lauren felt her suit being picked up and thrown. She landed hard on her side, the wind knocked out of her. So that was it, she realized. He controlled water, so he waited for a night with rain, when he'd have this extra advantage.

He didn't say anything else. He waited for Lauren to put the pieces together and realize that he had a point. She needed to be stronger if she was going to face whatever might be out there. And if she couldn't go up against everyone, how could she protect Mark?

No. She could beat this guy. She knew it.

She lifted her hand and called her staff back to her.

The figure sighed heavily. He wanted her to just admit that he had a point so he could call it a night, but somewhere inside, he respected her resolve.

The two leapt at one another and gave their attacks everything that they had. Lauren wielded her staff in her right hand and attacked with her empty left hand and both feet, landing a couple of good blows against the figure. But the figure was not about to be outdone. He went on offense. He punched and kicked and even used his command of water to blast a few jets of rainwater at Lauren in-between strikes.

His eyes glowed brighter than they had all evening, and water from the rooftop pooled up around Lauren and dragged her away from him.

"Afraid to fight me fair?" she shouted at him, now confident that she could hold her own. Her eyes flashed a deep emerald color.

The figure tossed his hands down towards his sides and the bands on his wrists released a series of mechanical tendrils that crawled across his fingers and extended onward. The thin chains of metal stretched down onto the rooftop and coiled ominously.

Lauren gripped her staff and flung herself at the figure.

In an instant, the tendrils from the figure's left hand had wrapped all around her and knocked the staff from her hands once again. She was held in midair, her arms pinned against her sides and her legs flailing for the ground. Her eyes glowed a fierce green as she struggled to muscle out of this hold.

"In what we do," the figure said softly, "you can't count on people fighting fair."

Lauren heard his words and the glow from her eyes faded. She stopped fighting. She accepted that he was right. She couldn't be Ebony and guarantee Mark's safety. Not now. Tears welled in her eyes. What had been such a wonderful night less than an hour ago was now ruined.

The figure placed her gently on the rooftop and released her. He took no joy in this.

"Solarflare and I will be in touch," he said softly as the mechanical tendrils retracted back into the bands. "We will do what we can to make you stronger. You're a good ally."

Lauren didn't hear him. She was still thinking of how, in a few short minutes, everything she hoped for with Mark was now gone.

"Hey," the figure declared. "I need you to tell me you understand why I did this."

Lauren looked up and glared at the figure. "You needed me to be stronger. Until I'm stronger, I can't protect everyone I care about," she said angrily.

The figure nodded.

"What about my family?" Lauren asked. "Are they in danger?"

"Yes," the figure responded thoughtfully after a moment. "Everyone you care about is in danger. But it's more manageable for Solarflare and me if you limit that number."

Lauren silently accepted this.

"I'm sorry, Lauren," the figure said, his voice choked with genuine sympathy.

Lauren said nothing, but gave a halfhearted nod, acknowledging he had a point.

The figure ran to the edge of the rooftop, leapt off and the tendrils erupted from his left hand, grabbing at the façade of another building and flinging him off into the distance.

Lauren stood on the roof of the Abble Building for a moment, processing what had happened. She pulled up her mask discretely and dried her eyes as best she could and made her way home. She thought about how much happier she would've been if she never went on patrol tonight in the first place.

She arrived home with well over an hour to spare before the agreed-upon time limit. Mrs. Bay began to ask how the evening went before seeing her daughter's face. She recognized that Lauren wasn't physically hurt, so she didn't ask.

Lauren made her way upstairs, took off her supersuit, and crawled into bed, hoping to wake up and realize that the night had ended right after Mark dropped her off.

Meanwhile, once the figure had swung across multiple rooftops and was sure he was well out of sight, he pulled off his own mask. It was Chuck.

Chuck pulled out his phone and called his father.

"I took care of it," he began when his father answered. "She does not think Mark is Solarflare, and she will keep her distance in order to keep him safe."

There was no response.

"Was this the right move?" Chuck asked. He did not like that he was hurting his best friend, nor did he like lying to Lauren. Lauren was nice and he understood why Mark liked her.

"We still have work to do," Mr. Currant replied through the phone.

"Yes sir," Chuck said, resigned to what he had just done.

SIXTEEN
Stormy Sailing

"Mark. Wake up."

Mark awoke with a start but remained silent.

Chuck was standing right over him. It was still dark outside and all the lights were off, but Mark could see his eyes glowing blue. Mark glared at his friend in the darkness.

"What're you doing here?" Mark hissed, keeping his voice as quiet as possible.

"We need to go," Chuck explained.

"Now?" Mark quietly asked as he reached over the side of the bed and pulled out his cell phone, without moving to an upright position. He wasn't about to sit up and wake up until he was sure he needed to. The light from the screen was nearly blinding in the dark room. It was 4 am. And his battery was almost dead because he forgot to plug it in. Not a great start to the day. "It's 4 a.m.," he mumbled.

"I know." Chuck replied, his voice calm yet urgent.

"It. Is. Four. In. The. Morning." Mark said, enunciating every word as he struggled to keep his eyes from glowing red-hot. He had only slept for about two hours. He was in no mood for Solarflare or Atlantis or anything but more sleep.

"I know." Chuck shot back. "But we have to go now."

"Why? Why now?" Mark asked, wondering what was so important that it needed to be addressed right now. There was nothing he could think of that would be worth it.

"We found it," Chuck whispered.

That was it. The one thing that was worth it. Mark's eyes flashed red.

"Are you serious?" Mark asked, now sitting fully upright and wide awake. His mind recalled Chuck's comment from months ago. He knew what Chuck was going to say before he said it.

"Yeah. We found the ring. We confirmed that it's in the Outer Banks, on Ocracoke Island. I'll explain more on the way, but we need to go."

The solar eclipse was today. They'd mentioned it months ago as a possibility. They told Mark that it might be their best opportunity to secure the ring. He wondered why it took so long for them to confirm. He still would've gone to Homecoming and he still would've been angry about waking up so early, but he would've known to expect it. .

"Fine," Mark answered as he stood up and gathered his things. "Just let me tell my parents I'm heading out."

Chuck was silent.

"What?" Mark shot at his friend.

"Do they know you came back last night?" Chuck asked carefully.

"What do you mean?"

"I mean, were they already asleep when you got home?"

"Yes," Mark answered cautiously, starting to sense where Chuck was going with this.

"What if they think you stayed out? Maybe you and I hung out and you stayed at my house overnight, and you'll be back home later today?"

Mark groaned. He hated outright lying to his parents. Usually with Solarflare stuff he could get away with half-truths.

"Fine." Mark finally answered.

"Thank you," Chuck said as he left the room. "I have your supersuit on the boat."

Mark climbed out of bed and threw on a t-shirt and a pair of jeans. He slipped his phone and keys into his pockets and made his way downstairs. Each step seemed to creak loud enough to wake up the whole neighborhood. Mark took the steps as slowly as he could, but it didn't seem to help. It felt like it took five minutes before he was at the bottom. He'd snuck out plenty of times since he started being Solarflare, but this time was different. There was a weight to it this time.

Mark carefully opened the door and the two of them stepped outside. The late October air was cold and damp, and the sky was completely dark from clouds. Chuck's car sat in the driveway, its engine still running. Mark closed the door behind him slowly and locked it. The sound of the lock echoed faintly through the house, and Mark could swear he heard it from the other side of the door. He exhaled heavily.

"Let's go."

Chuck nodded and the two of them walked over to his car. The doors slammed shut, and the car pulled out of the driveway and made its way down the street.

Mark dozed off again in the car. It was really early and he was still exhausted from the dance. When he woke up, he realized that the car was stopped. Mark was confused, there was no way that they were there yet. It was still pitch-black outside.

He looked over at the driver's seat. Chuck wasn't there. Mark stayed in his seat and peered through the windshield. He could make out two figures standing in front of the car, talking about something.

Mark wanted to just sit back and go back to sleep, but he figured there was some reason they stopped. It didn't seem to be a police officer; he couldn't see any flashing lights. And Mark had dealt with the police enough already this weekend. He watched for a few minutes before one of the figures noticed he was awake and gestured for him to join them.

Mark stepped out of the car and his nostrils were hit with the strong smell of fish. His eyes strained to see where they were. They were near the river; he could tell that much.

"Mark," Mr. Currant called out, extending his hand warmly. "I am glad you are here."

Mark nodded politely. He still appreciated Mr. Currant's help with the police, but he couldn't shake the uneasy feeling he now had around him. He had never felt as threatened as he had when Mr. Currant dropped him off that night and, considering how many fights he had been in lately, that was saying a lot.

Mr. Currant dropped his hand, sensing Mark's apprehension. He didn't allow himself to appear phased by it.

"So, where are we?" Mark asked. He couldn't have been asleep too long, they were most likely still near the Potomac River, but that didn't narrow it down a whole lot.

"We are at a private dock that I own," Mr. Currant explained as he started walking away from the car and, presumably, towards the water. "Driving would take far too long. I own a boat that will be much quicker."

"When will I get back?" Mark asked nervously as he followed. His parents would obviously get suspicious if he was gone all day, and he still had homework he had to do. It wasn't like he could just get Chuck's dad to excuse him from school tomorrow.

An uneasy smile flashed across Mr. Currant's face for a moment. He was unsure that Mark fully understood what he would be going up against. But it was a worthwhile concern if they weren't to make Mr. and Mrs. Michaels nervous or upset.

"This is a very fast boat," Mr. Currant explained. "We will be there in less than four hours, and we should return by the late afternoon. Before dinner, at the latest."

"Alright," Mark said with a heavy exhale. That wouldn't be too bad. He'd text his parents in a few hours and work on his homework on the way back. Except he didn't think to bring his backpack with him. Fine. He'd just do it tonight when he got home.

"Mark," Mr. Currant began again, interrupting Mark's homework-related train of thought, "this may very well be quite dangerous. I fear even more so than anything you have faced in these last few months, and that includes the events of Friday night. I hope you understand the seriousness of our undertaking."

Mark stopped. This tone was completely opposite the tone that he had heard in the car a little over twenty-four hours ago. It was full of genuine concern and not threatening at all. Suddenly, the man who had frightened Mark with how easily he dominated a tense situation was not in control, and it showed. Mark wondered if he ever should have agreed to do this. But it was too late for him to turn back, he could tell just how important it was.

Mark didn't say anything. He nodded once and kept walking towards the boat. In the dim light, Mark could see the name *Ranger* etched along its side in beautiful lettering. Chuck ran back to his car and turned off the engine. He hit the lock button on his keychain and his car beeped. The beep echoed through the silence.

Mark stood on the deck as Chuck and his father used their powers to silently pull the boat away from the dock and they started down the river. He was a little underwhelmed that this was the first thing he had ever seen Mr. Currant use his powers for, but thought it was cool how the two of them moved in unison.

"You may want to go inside and lie down," Mr. Currant suggested to Mark. "I imagine you would like to sleep for a while longer."

"Yeah," Mark responded, as he once again realized just how tired he was. He pulled out his phone to check the time. Nothing. The battery was completely dead. Great.

Mark made his way into the boat and looked around. He spied the door to a cabin and ventured inside without hesitation. He looked around. It was decorated in a manner similar to the Currants' house. It was obviously expensive and filled by someone with good taste, but there was something off about it. Something cold that made it feel like it was all for show, rather than actually lived in. It felt like their house.

But Mark didn't care right now. He pulled himself onto the large, overstuffed bed inside. He meant to ask Chuck if there was a charger on the boat but fell asleep almost immediately. Still wearing his shoes, and with his legs dangling over the side, Mark was out cold.

A few minutes out from their starting point, the boat reached the open water. Mr. Currant signaled to his son to head below, and he opened up the engines. The boat's engines roared and hurled the boat forward through the water. Somewhere deep in Mark's unconscious mind he felt the sudden increase in speed and it pushed him into a deeper sleep. Speed reminded him of flying around as Solarflare. He hadn't really flown much the last few days, so his mind put him in the sky, zipping around without anywhere to go or anything he needed to do.

Chuck sat down on a couch below deck, just outside of Mark's cabin. He leaned forward and rested his head in his hands. He was exhausted too. He was running on even less sleep than Mark. He could count on one hand the number of hours he'd slept in the last few days. Even if Atlanteans could run on less sleep than normal people, it still was far from ideal. He, too, was asleep within seconds.

Mr. Currant stood at the helm of his boat, guiding it through the water towards the Outer Banks. He was uneasy; he could travel faster through the water himself. A small part of him resented needing a boat to get there. But Mark was necessary. He was the only one who could find the Sapphire Ring and prevent any pyrates from getting it. He couldn't do anything further for his people, for his son, until the ring was out of the equation. He stood there, unmoving, as the sea spray stung his face for hours.

Below the deck, Chuck still slept. Even as increasingly rough waters flung the boat around, knocking him off the couch and onto the floor with a rough thud, he slept. His dreams were filled with memories from the previous days, when he and his father worked around the clock to determine who would go after the ring and where they would be. Chuck's unconscious mind still worked to sift through all that information, looking for anything extra that might make it easier for Mark to find the ring.

Mark, however, didn't dream about the past few days. As much as he would've enjoyed reliving the dance or his kiss with Lauren, his mind focused elsewhere.

He was no longer flying aimlessly through the clouds. He was going somewhere. His flight path became linear, he was on a mission heading straight for something.

In his dream, Mark stood on a dock, with waves crashing all around him and the sky dark with clouds, but there were no boats.

He looked around and was completely alone. Then he was on the beach. He followed something. Something was guiding him, but he didn't fully understand it. He found a set of footprints leading into a thick cluster of dune grass alongside the base of a steep hill. Then he was in a cave, still following the same footprints. The light from a small torch at the back of the cave was now greater than the light outside. Mark was following it. He made out a figure holding the torch. He was right behind them now. The torch-bearer turned around.

Mark awoke with a start, a considerable amount of sweat on his brow and his eyes glowing red. He rubbed his temple as his eyes cooled.

Mark was awake before Chuck. He opened the door and stepped out, nearly tripping on his friend, still asleep on the floor. His arms and legs were sprawled out awkwardly and it was pretty obvious that he didn't start out there. Mark was surprised he could sleep like that. If only he knew how desperate Chuck had been for sleep the last few days. Mark carefully stepped over his friend and made his way to the bathroom. Or, rather, the head; they were on a boat, after all.

After finishing his business, Mark took a look at himself in the mirror. His hair was messy with bedhead. He probably should've gotten it cut before the dance. Maybe if he hadn't slept in until noon and spent most of the day nursing his wounds, he would've. He tried to straighten it out with water from the tap.

He started thinking about the dream. He didn't recognize a single thing from it. But it seemed like that was what was about to happen, he thought. There was a dock and a beach and a tunnel. He racked his mind, trying to remember more details. There was someone there, he remembered. He couldn't remember if he saw the person's face.

He hung his head. This meant that someone else definitely was after the ring, and that they knew where it was. Or did it?

But it did mean that he would be able to find it, right? He reasoned with himself that having that dream meant that it was supposed to happen like that. He didn't normally remember his dreams so well, though he still only had pieces of this one.

Maybe he was putting too much stock into it. Maybe it was just a dream.

Mark splashed his face with water. Whatever was waiting for him, he hoped he'd be ready for it. He'd been through a lot in the last few days. He realized just how quickly everything had happened. In the span of 36 hours, he had fought all his enemies at once, been questioned by the police, and gone to Homecoming with Lauren. He smiled. Homecoming had been worth everything that happened to him on Friday.

Well, everything except Robbie getting hurt. His face fell as he remembered that. He was still upset over that. He resolved to visit Robbie once they got back, maybe even as Solarflare. Robbie would appreciate that, he hoped.

Mark finally pulled himself away from his thoughts for a moment and decided to check his bruises. He lifted his shirt and looked down, but there wasn't a single blemish, not even where Puffer had broken the skin. He was completely healed. Nothing at all ached, when less than 24 hours prior he was almost too sore to pull himself out of bed. Mark chuckled. Superhealing was one of the best powers he had.

Mark wasn't sure how long he'd been asleep and how long they'd been traveling. Not that he knew how long it took a boat to get down to the Outer Banks, anyway. He pulled out his phone and tried to check the time. No battery.

Mark looked out the window and saw that it was at least past sunrise. The sun wasn't too high up, though, so it was still early morning.

Mark stepped out of the bathroom, hoping that Chuck was now awake and might be able to help him find a charger. No such luck. Chuck remained in his awkward position on the floor, wedged up against the sofa. He must've really needed the sleep.

Mark decided against waking him and climbed onto the deck. As the wind whipped against his face and hair, he saw Mr. Currant standing at the helm.

Mr. Currant's face was set with determination. Nothing else could be read from it. He was going to get them there and see to it that Mark secured the ring. His eyes blazed a fierce cerulean as he pushed the boat through the water, his power acting in tandem with its engines. They would be down there in no time.

"Mark, you ought to rest more. Go back down." His statement was one of concern, but it lacked any emotion. It was if he was reading from a prompt.

"I'm good," Mark replied coolly as he stifled a yawn. Maybe he should go back down. But there was something he needed to bring up. Aside from the drive home from the police station, this was the only time it had ever been just the two of them.

"You said that I'm dangerous," Mark stated, his tone split between hurt and accusatory.

"Mark, you are dangerous." Mr. Currant's voice was harsh but his eyes stayed focused straight ahead. "You have done good things with your abilities, but you must understand that everyone would be better off if they allowed you a wide berth. Solarflare could have been responsible for the death of Robbie Perez."

"That wasn't my fault!" Mark shouted, tears welling in his eyes.

"It was, Mark. You know that." Mr. Currant said calmly. "Now go below deck and rest."

Wordlessly, Mark wiped his eyes and obeyed.

Chuck awoke with a loud, satisfied yawn after what felt like hours. At some point in the trip, he'd awakened and secured a more comfortable, and safer, spot on the couch.

"You have a charger?" Mark asked, holding his dead cell phone in his hand. Drawers and cabinets were open with their contents strewn about. He had really wanted to find it on his own. He didn't want to have to wake his friend up.

"Yeah," Chuck answered as he rubbed his eyes, trying wake up more fully. He hopped off the couch and walked over to an unopened nearby cabinet. He reached in and immediately pulled out a cell phone charger.

"Of course," Mark muttered.

"Look harder next time," Chuck said, tossing the charger to Mark.

Mark hastily plugged his phone in the charger and the charger into an outlet. The screen flashed for a moment. That was a good sign, but it would still take a minute before he could go ahead and use it. It was late morning now and he was sure his parents were up. He wasn't sure how long he could go without sending them something before they freaked out. The sooner, the better, he thought.

"So did you hear I fought seven Abyss members at once?" Mark asked, turning away from his phone. He and Chuck hadn't talked since before that all went down. It was weird to think that they still hadn't discussed something so big. It had been an interesting day and a half. He didn't want to discuss the police station pick-up, though.

"I did," Chuck answered excitedly as he plopped back down onto the couch. "I watched it instead of sleeping before I picked you up. You did good."

"How late were you up?" Mark asked.

"Very late. We had to figure out exactly where you needed to go."

"And you lecture me on procrastination," Mark pointed out.

"I was covering a lot of information. We were sifting through nearly three hundred years of Outer Banks history for clues. Anyway, that fight was great. I'm not even going to point out the mistakes you made."

"There were seven of them. And it was cold out. And, as I said earlier, there were seven of them," Mark said, annoyed at the comment about mistakes. "But seriously? How'd they all get together?"

"Well," Chuck guessed. "We do know they're all part of The Abyss, so it makes sense to think that they know each other. And Manta did get away when you fought against her. She probably broke them out."

"And there was a new guy, Seahorse. He was good at kicking," Mark pointed out. "I'd only fought the six of them before."

"Right," Chuck said hastily. "That's what I meant. I mean, he's obviously with them based on last night."

"Yeah," Mark said with a nod.

"So, what was his power again?"

"Kicking," Mark said.

"That's a pretty stupid power," Chuck said with a laugh.

Mark shrugged in agreement. It wasn't the best, but he did kick pretty hard. Mark had had easier fights.

"But why didn't either of us see that coming?"

"I don't know," Chuck sighed, shaking his head. "I shouldn't have missed something that big. I had alerts set up. I even have *special* access to police files. I didn't see anything about them breaking out of jail."

Mark was puzzled. He hadn't had time to give it much thought, but it was weird that the police didn't give the public a warning. Seven superpowered criminals loose at once should not have been a secret. Even if they didn't say exactly what it was, they should've said to be on alert, Mark thought.

"It was a prison break," Mark muttered before continuing louder, "That's not something that just goes unnoticed. There should have been a lot more talk about it."

"The police must not have wanted to cause a panic," Chuck guessed.

"No," Mark said, not willing to believe that. "When could they have gotten out without either of us knowing it? Why would the police just let me go if they thought I had anything to do with it?"

"They let you go because you're a minor and my dad told them that they had violated your rights," Chuck pressed, trying to reassure his friend.

"But I don't think they did," Mark continued. He wasn't a lawyer, but everything that had happened at the police station seemed perfectly reasonable.

"Well, it doesn't matter. You got out. And no one outside of this boat knows you're Solarflare," Chuck said.

"The officer who took me in saw the suit, though," Mark emphasized. "I have to be on a list or something."

Chuck exhaled deeply before responding. "If that's true, we'll deal with it after we deal with this. My father and I will do everything we can to keep your secret safe."

Mark nodded thoughtfully.

"Mark," Chuck continued. "I need you to be entirely focused on what's about to happen. We won't have a chance at a mulligan. Anything else you might be worried about needs to wait until after you have the ring. We cannot look past this."

"I know."

"I'm going topside to see if my dad needs anything."

"Alright," Mark replied. "Just let me send a quick text to my parents to let them know I'm with you and I'll be back later tonight."

"Sounds good."

"So, what exactly do I do when we get there?" Mark asked. They were getting closer. Chuck had taken over at the wheel.

"We will dock near the lighthouse. That's where you need to go. Charles and I uncovered documents that indicate that the current lighthouse is built above a deep underground cavern that leads towards the foundation of the original one," Mr. Currant explained. "Once we established that the ring did not leave the island, we were able to narrow down locations quite easily."

"Okay. But why would the ring be beneath the old lighthouse?" Mark asked.

"Construction on the original lighthouse began exactly eighty years after Blackbeard was killed," Mr. Currant offered. "It seemed a bit suspicious that the dates lined up, so I looked into the matter. A man named Thomas Bonnet was involved."

"Why does that name sound familiar?" Mark wondered aloud.

"Stede Bonnet was a pyrate who was acquainted with Blackbeard," Mr. Currant offered as a hint.

"Yes!" Mark exclaimed. Mark remembered hearing about him. Stede Bonnet was one of Blackbeard's allies and, for a short period, he went by the name Captain Thomas. All those summer road trips with his dad rattling off facts and stories about Blackbeard were paying off.

Mark sat in silence for a moment as he racked his brain for anything else he could remember about Stede Bonnet.

"Wait. But Stede died the same year as Blackbeard," Mark pointed out as he remembered.

"Exactly," Mr. Currant said. "But he did not die with Blackbeard. He was elsewhere. We have deduced that before his passing, he must have told his young son about Blackbeard's ring. The Bonnet family has most likely been protecting the ring for centuries. Rather, Stede's last known descendants have the surname Price."

"So, why wouldn't they keep it at their ancestral home or something?" Mark asked.

"They did," Mr. Currant explained. "The ancestral home was right next to the lighthouse."

"But it's not in the house?"

"The house no longer exists." Mr. Currant declared coldly. "It burned down decades ago."

"What happened? Did someone else come for the ring? I mean, any other pyrates aware of the legend would be looking for them."

Mr. Currant suppressed a smirk. "No one would have come for it before today. Touching the ring outside of an eclipse is a death sentence."

Mark stared at his shoes in silence. Months ago, he'd been given the slightest indication that he might need to be here today because of the eclipse. Now, Mr. Currant was making it sound like it had been a certainty all along. Mark felt used. He tried to brush it aside, given the importance of the day, and focus on the briefing.

"The members of the Price family learned that lesson the hard way," Mr. Currant continued. "By their folly, they ensured that the ring would remain unmolested until today." Mark nodded solemnly.

The inside of the boat was silent as Mark considered everything he had just been told. The mission seemed a lot more life-or-death now.

"So, it's in the foundation of the lighthouse," Mark realized. "How do we know it isn't just buried in the ground?"

"Good question, Mark." Mr. Currant answered. "I was able to secure excavation records from the county and state offices to confirm. Someone has undertaken a great deal of work in order to discreetly dig out the ring."

"And you're sure they didn't take it already?"

Mr. Currant was getting offended. "Mark," he began. His voice was stern, like it had been the night when he picked Mark up from the police station. "I would know if the ring was moved. You are here precisely because I know that it has not been moved. I do not want to hear another question on the matter."

Mark's face flushed with embarrassment, and a little anger. He was doing a favor for them; the least Mr. Currant could do was treat him with respect. He gritted his teeth and nodded gently.

Mr. Currant made his way back up to the deck. Mark called after him.

"How many?"

"What was that?" Mr. Currant asked. His voice was neutral now.

"How many other pyrates are going after the ring today?" Mark asked as calmly as he could. Something about the prospect of other pyrates frightened him, even more than The Abyss. Maybe because he had some experience with The Abyss.

"I don't know, Mark," Mr. Currant lied. He knew exactly who else was coming for the ring, but he needed Mark to expect the worst. He knew it would keep Mark focused, like he had been during the fight at the football game. "I hope that you are the only one who knows where to look, but I cannot assume this to be true. I simply do not have access to that kind of information." Again, this was a lie. Sylvia had told him the truth. She knew that Price was the only one in the world making a play for the ring today.

Mark nodded gravely.

"Mark." Mr. Currant said. "I need you to secure the ring."

"I know," Mark replied, a hint of annoyance in his voice. He knew they needed him to do this, but it seemed unfair that they would walk him into such a dangerous situation without taking on any of the risk themselves. It wasn't like they didn't have amazing powers of their own.

Mr. Currant sensed Mark's frustration. It was far more obvious than Mark realized. Maybe the child needed some proper motivation.

"I will say this," Mr. Currant added as he rose to his feet. "You may face a man named Edmund Price out there. He also goes by the *nom de guerre* Blackbeard. He was involved in the destruction of my home and the slaughter of my people. If he takes the ring, all is lost."

Mr. Currant walked back above deck and took the wheel from his son. Chuck came down and sat beside Mark. He didn't say anything. He knew now wasn't the time.

After about an hour, Chuck finally spoke. "You should probably go put your suit on."

Mark murmured in agreement and went back into the cabin to don his supersuit.

He held the mask in his hands and stared at it. Two months. He'd barely been doing this for two months and now they expected him to do this? Touching the ring is a death sentence. Those were Mr. Currant's words, he thought. Well, they were slightly paraphrased. But still. This wasn't fun or exciting anymore. He just wanted it to be done.

But here he was. The only way to go home was to come out of this on the other side. He took a deep breath, felt his eyes glow red, and threw on his mask. The mask helped. He felt confident that he could do this. Solarflare was getting that ring.

Mark climbed above deck in time to see Ocracoke Island appear on the horizon and steadily inch closer to their boat.

No one said anything else.

The water was exceptionally rough when they arrived. Waves crashed against the dock Mr. Currant was pulling towards. Mr. Currant's eyes glowed a deep blue and the water became calm in front of them. It seemed effortless. Mark leaned over the bow and looked. The sea still raged all around them, but this area immediately surrounding their boat was now perfectly calm.

Mr. Currant pulled into a slip and Chuck quickly tied up the boat.

"It's under the lighthouse. You've got this," Chuck said, with less confidence than Mark would've liked, before he embraced his friend.

Mark pulled away after a moment and turned to Mr. Currant. Mr. Currant gave an affirming nod, one appropriately selling the weight of what was to come while still expressing faith in Mark to do what needed to be done. Mark grinned nervously and turned towards the dock.

"My son," he heard Mr. Currant gently say behind him. "You really must get more rest. I will be here if Mark should need me."

SEVENTEEN
Blackbeard

Mark stepped onto the dock in his suit and pulled his mask down over his face. As he made his way towards land, he heard the boat pulling away behind him. He heard the boat's engine open up and speed off. He resisted the urge to look back, but he felt a deep unease at being left alone.

And he was alone, alright. There was no one else on the entire island. The island had been ordered evacuated. How Mr. Currant pulled that off, Mark had no idea. Maybe it was because of the approaching storm. But he wasn't thinking about it now. He had a job to do.

He saw the lighthouse. It was a small island and the lighthouse dwarfed everything around it. Not too far off, he thought, and flew over.

When Mark reached the lighthouse grounds, he opened the gate of the white picket fence surrounding it and walked over towards the lighthouse. He felt something familiar. It was similar to a chill running up his spine, but warm. He couldn't place where or when he had felt it, but he knew it from somewhere. And it made him even more uneasy.

The lighthouse grounds were covered in sand and patches of dune grass that swayed in the wind. Mounds of sand had piled up along the fence, leaving it half-buried in some places. A few feet away from the path, a sword stuck up from the ground, its hilt swaying with the dune grass.

He walked up to the sword and knelt down to examine it. It had a long, straight blade and a cap just above the hilt to protect the wielder's hand. It looked like a fairly typical pirate sword but with a jet-black blade. He easily made the connection. It belonged to a pyrate. Whoever owned the sword must have beaten him there.

Mark glanced up at the sky. No eclipse yet, which meant that they couldn't have the ring yet. He only needed to worry if he didn't have the ring when the eclipse ended; that was what Mr. Currant had told him.

Mark picked himself back up and made his way inside the lighthouse. The inside of the lighthouse was unremarkable, with nothing more than a winding staircase leading up to the top with a simple metal railing.

"Beneath the lighthouse," Mark muttered, searching for some way to get underground.

A small door, as if to a cupboard, was located beneath the staircase. The ground surrounding it was completely solid though. That must be it. He went over to it and opened it without resistance. On the inside, a simple lock was warped and broken. Yep, the person who got here first figured that out as well. The inside contained its own rough staircase, carved from the rock of the lighthouse's foundation.

Mark took a deep breath, steeling his resolve and descended down the staircase. His eyes flashed red and he braced for whatever might be waiting for him down there.

At the bottom of the staircase, the stairs became rougher and the ceiling opened up to reveal a deep cavern, darkness stretching out before him. The ceiling was not particularly high, but Mark wasn't at risk of hitting his head.

The time in Chuck's subbasement probably helped. It made being in a cave like this a lot less unnerving.

A dot of pale blue light illuminated the end of the subterranean tunnel. Mark made his way there; his pace measured, but not slow. As the light got larger and brighter, he could make out a silhouette between him and the light source. It was the other pyrate, the one who'd also come for the ring.

"You're the best they could find, huh?" the figure asked, not even turning to face Mark.

"Step away from the ring." Mark ordered in the most authoritative voice he could muster. It was not particularly impressive.

"Not happening, kid," the figure dismissed.

"I'm not a kid," Mark protested.

"It seems like you are," the figure continued in the same casual tone. "You're what, fifteen, sixteen years old?"

Mark opened his mouth to correct the man but thought it best not to tell this person that he was only seventeen.

"I'm guessing I was close, or you would've corrected me," he added.

The figure turned around to face Mark.

The man was slightly taller than Mark, but much more built. The lower half of his face was covered in a wild, thick black beard that extended down to his chest. His shoulder-length hair was dirty and matted and wild. He wore tattered clothes that he must've been wearing for weeks. In spite of his dirty appearance, he didn't carry himself that way. His frame was sturdy and muscular, far from that of a starving man. His attitude was casual and even condescending. It seemed as though he had chosen to allow himself to get that way, solely due to a mad devotion to getting the ring. He must have focused exclusively on building his strength so that the ring would be his, neglecting everything else, Mark thought.

Mark felt out of his depth. If this man was so focused on the ring, what chance did he have of getting it? He had barely thought of the ring at all in the last few months. A few hours ago, when he was with Lauren at Homecoming, the ring was the furthest thing from his mind.

"We've met before," the man explained, now that he had seen Mark.

Mark immediately got it.

"The fire," he said slowly. That was the uncomfortable warmth he had been feeling since he set foot on the lighthouse grounds.

"Yep."

"You started it."

"Sure did," he remarked casually before introducing himself. "The name's Blackbeard. Not the original Blackbeard, but you get it."

"There were people there. They could've been killed."

Mark didn't care what this guy called himself. He was too shocked at how little this man, this new Blackbeard, seemed to care about that fact. People almost died.

"Yeah, probably," Blackbeard coldly answered, without a moment of hesitation, before adding, "But, hey, they didn't. You got them out, didn't you?"

"Why did you do it?" Mark asked, wondering what could possibly be worth such a risk.

"I had to get you there somehow."

"Why?"

"You saw that apartment. You didn't think that was weird?" Blackbeard questioned.

Mark thought back to that day. He remembered the apartment that Blackbeard was talking about. The one where he found the hard drive. Yeah, it was weird. The place was eerily empty, save for the computer that looked at least twenty years more advanced than anything available today.

"Well?" Blackbeard pressed.

"Yeah. It was weird."

"And there are dozens more apartments just like it throughout the city. Each one belongs to a different member of The Abyss. That one belonged to the Pufferfish."

"What do you mean dozens?"

"I mean that there are a lot more than the ones you've been fighting. And they're all just patiently waiting for their signal to come after you. I set that fire, so you'd take that hard drive and get a look for yourself, away from your friend, the Atlantean prince."

"You couldn't have known that would work. You couldn't have known I'd take the hard drive," Mark protested, his eyes glowing red-hot. He couldn't believe that this Blackbeard nearly killed so many people just so Mark might find that computer.

"But I did. And you did," Blackbeard countered, his own eyes glowing red. Mark's eyes glowed deeper in response. "You're just like me. A creature of fire." Blackbeard continued with menace. "At some level, I knew you'd want to figure something out on your own, without being spoon-fed by some disgusting fish-man. I've been studying you since your first appearance. Can't figure out the flying though. How do you do it?"

Silence. He genuinely wanted Mark to explain. Mark thought better of it.

"Sorry, not sharing that."

"Can't blame me for trying. How did you know I'd be here?"

"The Atlantean King found you."

"Did he now? So why isn't he here?" Blackbeard questioned. His words grew frantic. He continued. "Why didn't he come here any time in the last decade when I was digging out this tunnel? Why didn't he finish me off then? Or did he not know I survived the last time he tried to kill me?"

Mark tried to sort through the information. The man had to be lying about Mr. Currant. He'd never do something like that. He focused on the one piece that actually seemed plausible. He glanced at the cavern beneath the lighthouse. "You dug this?"

"Yep." Blackbeard admitted proudly. "By hand. Only way I could get the ring."

"I was told that I have to do this. That I'm the only one who can get the ring."

"And why's that?"

"He told me it was because I'm descended from Blackbeard. The real one."

"And that makes you special?" the new Blackbeard sneered condescendingly.

"Are you?" Mark countered.

"Nah."

"Then I guess I am special. More than you at least," Mark said, trying to take control of the situation. He realized this guy was getting under his skin. He wanted to try and turn it on him.

The new Blackbeard just chuckled gently and shook his head. "Alright. You might just have a point there, kid. See, we got competing claims for this ring.

"You think because your great-great-whatever-grandfather was Edward Teach, the original owner of this here ring, that it should be yours. But do you know who your famous forefather left his ring to before he died? He left that ring," he gestured wildly with his whole body, revealing behind him a small, antique chest that housed the Sapphire Ring. "That all-powerful ring of blue flame, to my ancestor, Stede Bonnet, and told him to keep it safe. And he did. And his kids did. And their kids. All the way down to my father. And now it's my turn. And I'll be damned if I let anyone other than Edward Teach hisself take this ring from me. So, I suggest you cut your losses here and go home, kid." Blackbeard's voice dripped with menace. He was serious. Anyone that tried to come between him and the ring would regret it.

Mark said nothing. Part of him desperately wanted to just turn around and leave. He could tell Mr. Currant that he tried. But his feet remained glued to the floor.

Mr. Currant. Chuck. Mark wasn't just retrieving this so he could say he did it. This wasn't a test or a chance to show off. Mr. Currant had told him what this ring could be used for, how dangerous it was. He had been told exactly what this man had already done and had an idea of just how much more dangerous he would become with the ring.

No, leaving wasn't an option. He needed to stand firm on this. He needed that ring.

"You're coming with me. And you're going to answer for everyone that you killed when you attacked Atlantis," Mark declared, realizing that he wasn't going to get into Blackbeard's head easily.

"I never attacked Atlantis," Blackbeard replied coolly.

Mark glared at him.

"Don't lie to me," Mark demanded, trying to keep calm.

"I'm not lying," Blackbeard countered. "I've done plenty of bad things, but I never attacked Atlantis. I'm just trying to get the ring."

"Why didn't you move it sooner if you knew where it was?" Mark asked.

"I have to wait for the eclipse," Blackbeard explained, as if it was the most obvious thing in the world.

Mark stood there without a word. He didn't get it.

"They told you nothing about this, did they?"

Mark didn't answer. An angry stare was the only response he could offer that wouldn't betray his own ignorance.

"I have to wonder if it's because they thought you'd be easier to manipulate as a blank slate or if they're just as ignorant as you are," Blackbeard wondered aloud. "You're not special. You're expendable."

"Are you going to tell me or not?"

"You can't open it! I can't open it! No one can open it until the eclipse!" Blackbeard yelled, the mood suddenly shifting. The cruel, cold man Mark had perceived initially was now fully unhinged and wild.

"Why?" Mark asked.

Blackbeard chuckled. Then the laugh quickly grew manic and angry. Suddenly, Blackbeard screamed, and flames burst from his mouth. The flames swept the ground in front of him, filling the cave. Mark easily protected himself, though the flames were incredibly hot for so little effort.

"Edward Teach's power is still contained within that ring! The power of the greatest dragon in millennia!" Blackbeard explained when he finally regained his composure. "That ring and, by extension, the lock to the box it is in, cannot be touched. It burns so hot that it would kill either of us if we tried. You asked why I dug this cave," he held his arms out so Mark could take in the full magnitude of his efforts. "My father tried to open this chest over thirty years ago and he burned himself to death. He burned down our home and killed my mother in the process. I barely escaped. And when my grandfather learned what had happened, he had the rubble and my parents' remains buried beneath the earth where our home had once stood and he forbade me from ever discussing what I saw.

"But I saw it. And it stayed with me," Blackbeard continued. His words were less manic now, almost like he had rehearsed them as a monologue to be given on this day. He had rehearsed, in fact, often while digging out this passage. "And when the Atlantean King tried to drown me years ago, I knew I needed to come back here and dig up this ring so that, on the day of the eclipse, I could take the ring for myself and murder him with it. And I'll murder anyone else that stands between me and him. Understood?"

Mark looked at the chest behind Blackbeard. He could see heat radiating from it and the simple iron lock glowed a deep blue.

"I'm taking that ring," Mark said.

"Just try," Blackbeard chuckled angrily. His eyes burned. Waves of heat emanated from his clenched fists. He wasn't about to let some kid stand in his way. He had waited years for this. He would take the ring by any means necessary.

Mark stepped back into a fighting stance. He placed most of his weight of his back leg. If Blackbeard wanted a fight, he would get one. He opened his fists slightly and flames engulfed his hands.

Blackbeard raised an open hand in front of himself and unleashed a massive blast of flames at Mark. Mark released his own burst of fire to counter. The two met in the middle, and flames erupted, reaching all the walls of the cavern.

Blackbeard charged at Mark through the flames, tackling him to the ground. He pressed his forearm tight against Mark's throat.

"The ring is mine and I will do what I must to take it," Blackbeard whispered into Mark's ear, pressing harder against Mark's throat.

Mark struggled for air. He desperately clawed at the tattered rags Blackbeard was wearing, trying to clutch something well enough to pull the man off of him. He felt his eyes glowing dim. He knew he'd pass out soon. He needed to do something.

He racked his mind for his training. He spent all that time with Chuck, practicing his moves and style and weak points. Weak points. Thinking quickly, he took his right hand and held it right up against Blackbeard's eyes. He unleashed a blast of flames point-blank, and Blackbeard recoiled.

With the forearm no longer pressed against his throat, Mark popped back to his feet and retreated a few steps. He wondered what his best strategy was. He couldn't just charge in for the chest. Blackbeard said that touching the chest before the eclipse would kill him. And even if that wasn't true, Blackbeard was too strong for that. Mark could try to draw him away. That seemed like a better option, especially since Mark had the advantage of flight.

Blackbeard rubbed his eyes and blinked frantically, trying to restore his sight. Mark's attack had been painful, but ultimately no more than an annoyance.

"Hey!" Mark shouted.

Blackbeard squinted furiously, his eyebrows still singed and smoking.

"You wanted to learn about flying? Come see for yourself!"

Mark sprinted up the steps, hoping desperately that Blackbeard was not far behind. He exited the lighthouse, breathing in the dark, stormy air. The wind was picking up.

Mark took to the air and hovered around the lighthouse's perimeter. If Blackbeard wasn't following, he'd have to go back in.

The thought of his next likely course of action had barely entered his head before Mark got his answer.

Blackbeard erupted from the base of the lighthouse in a blast of fire and rock, shaking the entire structure. The door that was previously there a moment ago was now replaced with a massive crater.

Blackbeard landed at his sword and ripped it out from the ground with a ferocious yank. His eyes continued to glow and flames danced down the length of the blade. It would've looked beautiful if it wasn't so threatening, Mark thought. At least he was out of range of the blade.

He was wrong about that.

Blackbeard wildly swung his sword about, flinging flames through the air at Mark. Mark ducked and zipped through the air, narrowly avoiding the blasts, the heated air passing close enough to his boots to throw Mark off his balance and send him crashing to the ground.

Blackbeard pointed his sword at Mark and fired another blast at him. Mark rolled onto his front and popped himself back to his feet with a jet of flames from each hand, just before Blackbeard's attack landed. Way too close.

Mark readied himself in a stance again. He looked at Blackbeard. The chest wasn't with him. He'd left it behind in the cave. That was good. So maybe it was true, maybe the chest couldn't even be moved until the eclipse, he thought. Mark could just get him away from the lighthouse and circle back for the chest when the time was right. He figured he was faster than Blackbeard at least. But he would need to be careful about Blackbeard's flames messing with his boots.

"I'm giving you a chance. Just fly away, kid."

Welp, looks like he's not just going to chase me, Mark realized with a sigh. He gritted his teeth and planted his feet.

"I'm good, thanks," Mark replied, as casually as he could muster at this point. He yelled and whipped his fist around, launching his own fiery attack.

Blackbeard opened his palm and countered with a wide spray of flames of his own. Mark's flames crashed into it and the two attacks sent sand and dune grass flying, giving Mark an idea.

He took to the sky once again, trying to get high enough to give himself some more time to dodge any attacks. He unleashed a fury of jets of fire down at Blackbeard and the area immediately surrounding him. Blackbeard took a defensive position and the blasts crashed to the earth, flinging up even more sand and dirt than before.

A rocket of fire exploded from the dust cloud, aimed exactly for Mark's position.

And it would've made contact, if Mark hadn't taken the brief smokescreen as a chance to shoot down towards the earth and launch himself along the ground in an offensive sweep.

Mark's shoulder made contact with Blackbeard's gut, in a tackling form that Coach Kekoa would've been proud of. The contact was such a shock that Blackbeard dropped his sword. Mark had correctly assumed Blackbeard would've held it out to the side. The two of them tumbled across the base of the lighthouse, with Mark coming to a stop just a few yards away.

He felt good about getting that hit in but didn't have more than half a second to dwell on it. Get the sword or make some distance again?

He opted for the sword. The sword was too much of a threat and he doubted that tactic would work a second time.

Heat crept down to the soles of his feet and he launched towards the sword. He skimmed just inches from the ground, closer and closer to the sword. Almost there...

The sword was just out of Mark's reach when a devastating kick connected with Mark's ribcage, flinging him away from the sword.

Mark landed up against the lighthouse's picket fence with a thud. He groaned in pain. How did Blackbeard get back up so quick? He worried he might have broken a rib. That was a problem for later though.

Blackbeard was standing strong, sword back in his hand. He seemed to be almost unscathed by all of Mark's attacks, so far. Mark picked himself up, each breath more labored than he would've liked. He gritted his teeth and his eyes flashed red once again. His breathing became easier. Whether it was healing or adrenaline or something else, he didn't care. He needed to fight while he could, any instincts of self-preservation briefly dulled.

He sprinted into the fray, each step accentuated by the heat from his boots. Blackbeard braced for impact with a sinister grin. If he wanted this fight, he'd get it.

Blackbeard swung at Mark, aiming across his torso, the blade once again engulfed in fire.

Before he made any contact, Mark leapt into the air and flipped over his opponent, landing directly behind him. He levied a barrage of quick strikes into Blackbeard's backside, aiming for his kidneys.

Blackbeard turned, grabbed his sword tighter, and swung wildly at Mark. Mark pivoted and ducked, the blade missing him by mere inches. The black blade sliced through the air so fluidly,

Mark wasn't even thinking about dodging it. He was fighting purely on instinct. Those daily training sessions with Chuck were proving their worth.

Blackbeard swung downward with all his might. Mark turned and leaned back as the blade split open the ground at his feet. Mark stepped in and elbowed Blackbeard in the throat.

Blackbeard coughed violently and gnashed his teeth, as he released his sword which stood where it had cleaved the earth.

He threw his left arm around the back of Mark's neck and pulled him close. Before Mark could pull away, he laid a powerful uppercut into Mark's stomach. The pain made him want to vomit; his legs went weak for a moment.

As Mark was doubled over in pain, Blackbeard once again picked up his sword. He swung the blade upwards at Mark, the young hero too wounded to fully react in time.

Mark leaned away as best he could, but he could not fully avoid it.

Slash!

The blade sliced through Mark's goggles and he felt the warmth of blood on his face.

Mark, with a newfound desperation pushing his body into overdrive, blasted Blackbeard back with a jet of flames from both his hands and took to the sky, desperate to put distance between the two of them.

Blackbeard rolled backwards violently and came to a rest on his side, his sword knocked from his hands and his tattered clothes aflame. Mark landed several yards away from him, clutching at his right eye. He tried to look through his eye but couldn't see. He couldn't tell if it was his eye or the goggles. He yanked off his mask and blinked both eyes rapidly.

He could still see. The blade must've just missed his eye. He gingerly touched where he felt the sword slice him, just above and below his eye. He felt a sharp pain and realized just how deep the cut was.

Blackbeard picked himself up, laughing.

"So, you really are a kid," Blackbeard mused. He paused. "I don't want to kill you. But I'm not going to let you keep me from that ring, even if it means I have to take your life."

"Why do you need it so badly?" Mark asked. His voice was trembling. He was scared. He had never been scared like this before.

"I'm not going to let Atlantis wipe out our people. I'm going to defend myself. I'm going to find every one of the king's operatives and I'm going to end them. I'm going to burn them. And then," Blackbeard paused, trying — and failing — to compose himself, "I'm going after the king and his son. Atlantis will end by my hand."

"I won't let that happen." Mark declared, his voice far steadier now, even as blood flowed from his face.

"Kid, this fight hasn't exactly been going your way."

In an instant, Mark's boots propelled him toward Blackbeard as he delivered a powerful punch to the gut. Blackbeard made a loud, uncomfortable grunt and fell to the ground, dropping his sword.

"You were saying," Mark jeered.

"We're still playing it that way then?" Blackbeard asked between painful gasps, as he propped himself up on his elbows.

"Yeah, we are."

"Noted."

Blackbeard knocked Mark's ankles out from under him, sending Mark painfully towards the ground. Mark landed hard on his side.

Mark and Blackbeard both immediately released blasts of fire at one another as they both lay on the ground, mere inches apart. The force of the colliding flames propelled them both through the air, each landing several feet from where they started.

Blackbeard rocked himself onto his shoulders and popped back up, while Mark slowly rolled onto his knees. His breathing was heavy and his head spinning as the gash above and below his eye continued to bleed.

"You can't win this, kid," Blackbeard called out. "I've been doing this a lot longer. You and I both know you can't handle much more." Blackbeard began a slow, deliberate walk over to his sword as he continued speaking. "There aren't that many of us. Killing you would bring me no joy. You can leave and I'll just call us even. Consider that new scar of yours the price you pay for inconveniencing me."

Mark's eyes flashed red with a renewed intensity. He was no coward. He knew that the ring couldn't fall into the wrong hands and there was no way he'd allow this man to hurt his best friend. His hands balled into fists and heat began to emanate from his entire body.

He knew he couldn't win on strength alone. Blackbeard was right about one thing: he had been doing this longer. Mark had only had his powers for a few months; he hadn't built up a particularly impressive stamina yet.

But he did have one thing: speed.

Blackbeard was just a few steps away from his sword.

"So kid, what'll it be? Don't be an idiot."

Wordlessly, Mark pushed his energy to the soles of his feet, heating the boots and shooting him across the ground. Blackbeard dove for the sword, but he was too slow.

Mark placed a hand on the ground and swung the lower half of his body around, aiming the sole of his foot right against Blackbeard's chest. He pressed tight against the ground and sent even more power to the soles of his shoes. A concentrated burst of heat erupted from Mark's shoes and sent Blackbeard flying.

Blackbeard landed several yards away on the steps of the nearby dock. Mark grabbed the sword off the ground and looked at it. He had just taken away one of Blackbeard's biggest advantages. Without the sword, Blackbeard was a lot less lethal.

Thoughts raced through Mark's head. Break the sword. Fly up and throw it in the ocean. Hide it.

You could kill him.

Mark paused. That last thought didn't feel like his own. The voice was like the one that had told him to burn away the poison after Puffer had hit him. He barely remembered it before just now. Where did that voice come from?

Blackbeard noticed Mark's expression. Taking off the mask meant Blackbeard could read his emotions now. And he was distracted.

Blackbeard took a breakneck pace towards Mark, aiming to reclaim his sword in this momentary lapse. He pounced.

Mark realized his mistake. Fear washed over him in an instant. Was this it?

Without conscious thought, Mark stepped aside and Blackbeard's leap found nothing but air. Time slowed to a crawl. His enemy was vulnerable. The sword was in his hand.

Do it! Kill him!

No! That thought thundering in his head wasn't his own. He wasn't a murderer. He steadied his hand.

He couldn't keep this sword. He needed to get rid of it.

The ocean caught Mark's eye. He could fling the sword into the ocean. And, while Blackbeard pursued him trying to get it back, the lighthouse would be unguarded. The plan crystalized in an instant.

Blackbeard crashed to the ground. He struck at where Mark had been, but he was gone. Mark had taken to the sky and was flying towards the dock where he'd been dropped off.

That sword was an heirloom, made of razor-sharp obsidian and forged to be nearly unbreakable. It had been in the Price family for generations. Generations of men devoted to nothing more than keeping the Sapphire Ring secure, always at great personal cost. They guarded a treasure they could never hope to possess, a power they could never achieve. This was the irony of their collective obsession: it meant nothing. No actions could've brought them the ring any sooner than right now. Only on this day, could the ring be taken.

Blackbeard was raised to know this. The ring was paramount. The sword, which was named *Ichor* — inscribed upon the hilt and so named for the blood of the pantheon, blood which could be spilt by this unique blade — was the means by which it would be secured. But maybe it was rage at the kid who would not leave well enough alone, or sentiment for the only thing his father had left him aside from his name, but Blackbeard took off after Mark. He left the lighthouse unattended.

Mark stumbled to a landing on the dock, the day's injuries making extended flight unsustainable. He clutched at his side for a moment and began sprinting down its length. He knew Blackbeard would not be far behind. He needed to send the sword as far as he could, somewhere that Blackbeard couldn't just dive in and retrieve.

The water was even more violent than it had been when Mark was first dropped off. Mr. Currant's boat was nowhere in sight.

Mark had secretly hoped for backup. Whatever reason Mr. Currant had for needing Mark to get the ring alone didn't matter right now. He just wanted help.

He reached the edge of the dock and, without hesitation, heaved the saber into the water with all his might. Its black blade contrasted for a moment against the white peaks of the choppy surf before it broke the surface and plunged to the bottom.

"No!" shrieked a voice mixed with despair and rage from behind Mark.

Mark said nothing, only turned and glared at his foe. Blood still streamed down his face, though it had slowed to a trickle.

"I'm going to kill you." Blackbeard declared as he slowly paced towards Mark. "I have the time." He pointed up towards the sky.

Mark cautiously glanced upward. Still obscured by clouds, Mark could see the sun. The moon was still a ways off. The eclipse wasn't starting for a little while. Blackbeard did have plenty of time to kill him.

The ocean seemed to match Blackbeard's rage. The rough seas grew rougher still, with new waves crashing against the dock's support posts and the few boats still in harbor. Salt water sprayed them both constantly. It stung the gash along Mark's eye, but he could hardly think of that.

A desperate, bitter thought formed in the back of Mark's mind. He realized that somewhere out on that water was the boat that took him here. Mr. Currant and Chuck, two Atlantean royals with their incredible powers were on that boat, doing nothing. Mark was caught between a violent sea and a violent man, while the two people he had trusted abandoned him.

Blackbeard maintained his steady pace as flames poured from his hands and mouth. His attack was not cruel, but purposeful.

The wooden planks, soaked as they were and had been since they were first put in place, caught fire as he walked along. The flames rushed at Mark, who simply braced for impact as best he could, with just enough time to cover his face. The flames washed over him in painful waves of heat. How was he so outclassed now? His breathing became labored as he choked on the superheated air, starving for oxygen.

As quickly as the flames had surrounded him, they passed and dissipated over the rough seas. Mark fell to his knees, exhausted, the charred dock creaking underneath him. Every inch of his body hurt. His hair was still there, but he could smell that it had been singed. He couldn't take another attack like that.

"I didn't want to do this." Blackbeard had stopped his approach. His words were spoken harshly, but not without empathy. He added, in an attempt to assuage his own guilt, "The Atlanteans did this to you, not me."

Mark stared straight down into the planks of the dock, his mind working feverishly to save himself. The sea foamed violently just feet below, sending salt spray everywhere. Mark's eyes stung. Wounded and dazed as he was, he was still a smart kid.

The Atlanteans could still get the ring during the eclipse even if he couldn't. He could keep it out of Blackbeard's hands.

He placed his palms down upon the board beneath him, fingers spread out wide.

He pulled his head up and made eye contact with Blackbeard. The wound surrounding his right eye had ceased bleeding and now both eyes glowed an intense crimson. He summoned all his courage. This move would be dangerous, maybe even deadly.

"For the record, in a fair fight, you'd have won," Mark declared with a gentle smirk.

He yelled, and all his energy poured out from his hands, enveloping all the nearby planks and supports of the dock. Blackbeard sensed Mark's plan in an instant and made the choice to charge. Running back to the shore might have saved him from his fate, but anger clouded his judgement.

He was closing the gap between them. Just inches separated the two. But it was too late.

The dock's boards and support beams had been reduced largely to charcoal; it was no surprise when a large wave crashed into the dock and smashed away the last of its weakened supports, knocking Blackbeard and Mark violently into the sea.

EIGHTEEN
The Eclipse

Mark was tossed about wildly by the surf. He struggled to open his eyes beneath the waves. He was disoriented. Which way was up? The overcast sky was doing him no favors. He needed air.

He saw a glimpse of sunlight shining through the clouds above the surface. He frantically kicked towards the surface, his lungs aching for air. He didn't have any energy to put heat to his boots and jet out of there.

He broke the surface and inhaled deeply in large gasps. Water rushed into his mouth with each gasp and he sputtered, coughing the water up. His legs and arms did their best to tread in the chaotic water.

Blood had once again started flowing from above and below Mark's right eye. Mark was running on so much adrenaline at the moment that he didn't notice and didn't even feel the sting of saltwater and debris flooding the area.

He tried to orient himself and make his way towards land. His limbs felt like they were made of lead and the water seemed to be getting rougher by the second.

A devastating scream pierced the air over the sound of crashing waves.

Mark looked around for its source and saw him.

Blackbeard was being pulled further into the ocean, waves crashing over top of him, momentarily silencing his yells. He was kicking and flailing like a madman, trying to stay afloat. His hands were surrounded by flames, which he was using to attack the waves, but with no real success.

Mark's heart ached for a moment. He felt pity for the man who had just a moment ago tried to kill him.

They locked eyes for a moment, and Mark saw nothing but a man in need of help.

In spite of his instincts for self-preservation, he tried to make his way to Blackbeard.

The debris of the once-standing dock swirled violently between the two. Mark tried to dodge these obstacles and swim towards Blackbeard, as Blackbeard simply tried to stay alive. Mark's arms and legs strained to pull and kick towards the drowning man, but with each stroke the gulf between the two of them seemed to widen.

The waters around Blackbeard became even rougher and he was pulled under. He erupted above the surface with a desperate shout. He and Mark both knew that he would not resurface a second time.

He looked at Mark and shook his head sadly, as if to wave Mark off. Mark was frozen in place. He just couldn't get there in time.

Our hero watched helplessly as his foe was pulled beneath the waves a final time.

Mark had survived the one threat, but he had thrown himself in an even more dangerous one. The waves and broken boards continued to slam into him relentlessly. He swam towards the shore, struggling against the choppy sea. The current wasn't pulling him any further out to sea, but it wasn't exactly doing him any favors right now.

Each stroke and kick was made mechanically, with Mark's mind just telling him to take it one at a time. Just one more kick, one more stroke. Just throw his arm in front of him and pull himself closer to land. In this way, he inched closer to safety.

His movements slowed. His limbs were almost completely numb and he was breathing harder than he ever had in his life. The safe haven of the shore felt unreachable. He couldn't tell exactly how far away he was, but it felt insurmountable.

He kept moving, but his thoughts grew dark. He wasn't going to make it. This was Chuck and his father's fault. If the two of them hadn't been such cowards, they could've helped him. What was even the point of Mark doing their dirty work? They were already responsible for Blackbeard's death, and they'd be responsible for Mark's soon enough. They killed him. He hated them for a moment.

Unconsciously, his kicks and strokes became more determined through his anger. He was going to get out of this, he thought in the back of his mind. He was going to get the ring and keep it for himself. And once they got home, he had no intention to speak to either of them again.

Inch by inch, the shore grew closer.

His resolve grew. He began passing on his right side, what remained of the dock. Thoughts of helplessness were now replaced by bitter, justified anger. As he grew angrier, the sea grew calmer, as if the two were inverses of one another. He wanted to stand back on the deck of Mr. Currant's boat and declare that their relationship was dissolved. He never wanted to see either Chuck or Mr. Currant again. And in order to do that, he needed to survive.

He was close. His form was sloppy from exhaustion, and his body hung mostly in the water, nearly perpendicular with the surface.

He felt something with his foot.

It was the bottom.

Not quite shallow enough to stand, but he could feel it. He dipped beneath the surface and placed both feet on the sandy floor. But his left foot felt something other than sand. Something long and thin and hard.

It could've been anything, but Mark knew it wasn't. He knew exactly what it was.

He resurfaced for air but dove back down to get it.

He emerged once again with it in hand. It was Blackbeard's sword.

The sword that had just scarred him, nearly cost him an eye, nearly killed him, was now his. He gripped it tight, with a unique reverence. Maybe he thought he was honoring his fallen foe, that keeping it was a sign of respect. Or maybe it was because he considered it a trophy. Proof that he had bested his opponent, that Solarflare could not be defeated. Maybe a little bit of both.

He continued swimming, awkwardly pulling himself through the water with the sword in his right hand. Although the added weight and awkwardness of the sword should have made the work more tiring, Mark felt renewed. He had won the fight and now had a physical testament of that fact. He was a hero, and, regardless of his relationship with the Currants moving forward, he could keep being one.

The water became shallow and he could finally stand easily. He lifted his torso out of the water and began marching towards the beach. His arms ached and his legs felt like they were made of lead, but he continued. Small pieces of debris swirled about him, but the sea had quieted and was now no rougher than on a normal day. The clouds had largely parted and he could see the sun again, with the moon not far off.

He walked out of the surf and continued away from the water. He collapsed to his knees and paused. He placed the sword to his side, peeled off his gloves and gripped the sand. He had never before been so relieved.

He wanted to just roll over and sleep right there. He had definitely earned it. But he couldn't. He needed to get back to the lighthouse and get the ring for the eclipse.

He groaned and pulled himself back up to his feet. He bent over and grabbed the sword. He trudged back to the lighthouse.

He saw the massive crater that now stood where there had once been a door. He was almost nostalgic for the chaos of the fight before. He had never been challenged like that. Not even when he faced all of The Abyss during the football game.

"Whoa." he muttered, again realizing that the fight had been less than two full days ago. Even more, he had only been Solarflare since the beginning of September. He'd done so much within just two months. "Now this would be a killer college admissions essay," he mused aloud.

He stepped into the lighthouse and carefully descended into the cavern with the ring in its simple chest. Sunlight now more freely shone into the cavern, owing to Blackbeard's enthusiastic pursuit.

There it was. Sitting atop a simple podium in the middle of the cave was the chest with the ring. As Mark came closer, he could see the lock glowing a deep, ominous blue. Instinctually, he pulled his hands away. He knew not to touch it yet. Blackbeard said it would kill anyone who touched it. Somehow, after everything, Mark knew he was telling the truth.

Mark glanced up through the gaping opening in the lighthouse to see if it was time yet. Not quite. He continued to stare, waiting for the time to be right. He occasionally stole glances back at the chest, as if he was worried it would disappear from under his nose.

Then it started. The moon had crossed in front of the sun and the eclipse was total.

Mark looked back at the chest and saw the blue light dim and fade to nothing. A simple turning mechanism was all that kept the chest closed now.

Mark concentrated and tried to summon his own flames. Nothing. Mr. Currant had told him that that would happen during an eclipse.

He cautiously lifted it off the pedestal, sword still in hand, his breathing rapid as his mission was so nearly complete.

He had four minutes for the eclipse, Chuck had said. He wasn't sure what would happen to the chest once the eclipse was over.

He tucked the chest under his arm and marched back up the steps. The world was bathed in the eerie shadowy light that only comes from an eclipse.

He placed the sword and chest onto the ground and fumbled for the special pocket Chuck had made for him in the suit. He pulled out a pair of beaten up, soggy eclipse glasses. They had been in better shape before all of this.

He put them on and looked up. He marveled at what he was seeing. The sun was almost entirely blocked by the moon. A thin circle of light, the sun's corona, could still be seen. The world was dimmed by this great cosmic ballet. He felt insignificant, but in a way that oddly inspired him. He was here to see it. That had to mean something.

He could've spent the whole day staring up at it, but eclipses don't last that long. And he still had one thing left to do. He needed to get this ring.

He dropped to his knees and cautiously reached out to the chest's lock.

He took a deep breath and grabbed it suddenly. Nothing happened. He was okay.

He twisted the lock and felt it give. Mark opened the chest and saw a simple ring set with a large sapphire.

"Well, it's as advertised," Mark said to no one in particular, marveling at the simplicity of the object that had inspired such devotion from Blackbeard and Mr. Currant. This was what all the fuss had been about, this was why a man was now dead.

He turned it over in his hand and inspected it. No markings or inscriptions indicating the power of the ring. Just a large, flawless stone set in its center, not that Mark could tell it was flawless.

The eclipse was still going.

He slipped the ring onto his right ring finger. It was too big for him. It hung awkwardly. How could he possibly use this if it didn't fit? Would Mr. Currant get it sized for him?

He pulled it off and placed it back into the chest, leaving the lid open.

The eclipse ended and the sun shone all around once again. In the new light, Mark could see the destruction of his earlier fight.

He scanned the area. The lighthouse and its grounds were covered in scorch marks, with craters, holes and debris scattered everywhere. The meager white picket fence that surrounded the grounds largely remained in place, but some areas had been smashed to nothing. He felt bad about whoever might have to clean this up.

"Mark," a familiar voice called out after a few moments, pulling Mark from his thoughts.

Chuck stood just beyond the fence, holding something in his hand.

Mark smiled. As angry as he had been swimming back, and as much as that anger drove him to survive, he was just glad to see his friend right now.

"Whatcha got there?" Mark called out.

"Your mask," Chuck answered, with concern in his voice. He held it up and gently pointed at the cut that extended along the mask and cleaved the goggles. "Are you okay?"

"Uh," Mark began and assessed everything. "I got cut, but I'm fine. I can still see; it didn't get my eye. It would've been a nice heads up if I'd known the other guy would have a sword."

"That's good," Chuck said, audibly relieved. "What do you got there?" he asked in a parallel of Mark's earlier question.

"I got a sword and a ring," Mark replied proudly as he held up his spoils and made his way over to his friend.

"The sword's unexpected," Chuck said, as he put his arm around Mark and contained his surprise over the sight of an obsidian blade. "But I never had a doubt about your ability to get the ring. I'm proud of you."

"Thanks, buddy," Mark said with full sincerity. "But next time, get it yourself."

Chuck laughed.

"I'll consider it. Come on, I'll carry these, let's get you back to the boat."

Chuck took the sword and the chest from Mark and tossed the mask into the chest. The two of them walked to the boat, now docked elsewhere, since Mark had destroyed the original dock. Chuck led the way, walking at a slow pace for the clearly exhausted Mark.

Mr. Currant was waiting with a broad smile plastered across his face. He was usually so reserved; it was weird for Mark to see this much emotion. He pulled Mark aboard and embraced him in a hug.

"Mark," he began, still holding Mark tight, his normally posh and proper voice with a clear giddiness. "You have done something incredible today. By securing this ring, we can be sure that it won't be used for any wicked causes."

"Yeah," Mark muttered, somehow put off by this unusual display of emotion. He knew this meant a lot, but he felt uneasy. He was happy to see Chuck again, but that anger he felt during his swim was still there for Mr. Currant. "I should keep it," Mark said in a soft but determined voice.

"What?" Mr. Currant asked, pulling away from Mark. His face was now stern and his tone almost harsh.

"I got the ring. It is a pyrate ring. I think I should keep it, especially since I'm the only one here who can use it."

"Mark," Mr. Currant said tersely. "I can keep it safe better than you. Charles and I should take it." He searched for his words carefully, trying to avoid sounding condescending. But Mark could sense it anyway.

"I went through a lot for this," Mark protested. His entire body was drained and he wanted to just go below deck and take another nap, but he needed to make his point.

"Mark," Mr. Currant said in his most authoritative tone, one which shook Mark to the core. The tone instantly took Mark back to Friday night, back to when he was in Mr. Currant's car, following the police station. He placed a hand on Mark's shoulder. "I understand your feelings. There is no pyrate I trust more with this ring than you. But for safekeeping, it should go with Charles and me. Please, just go rest."

In the back of his mind, rightfully indignant protests erupted. He wanted to challenge Mr. Currant. But he didn't. "Yeah, okay," he mumbled weakly and went back below deck.

He climbed back into the bed he slept in on the trip down and glanced at his phone. There were multiple text messages and missed calls from his parents, his brother, and Lauren. He decided to just deal with these later. He sent a single text to his mom saying he'd be home in a few hours, tossed his phone aside, and fell into a deep sleep. He was still wearing the Solarflare suit and dried blood smeared against the pillow beneath him.

As he drifted out of conscious thought, he thought he heard a thudding beneath him, but put it out of his mind.

NINETEEN
New Allies

About halfway home, Mr. Currant handed the wheel off to his son and trekked below deck for a discussion with Mark. He knocked firmly against the cabin door. Loud, purposeful knocks that he knew Mark would hear.

Mark awoke and muttered a frustrated, "Yeah?"

"Mark, this is Mr. Currant. May I come in?"

Mark mumbled in the affirmative and Mr. Currant entered.

"Mark," he said. "I am sorry to wake you, but I believe I ought to examine that scar. In the moment, I was so overcome with emotion that I neglected to see if there was anything that might be done. Please, follow me."

Mark sighed an exasperated sigh and lifted himself from the bed, following Mr. Currant. He led him to the sink just outside of the room and pulled a stream of water and twisted it just above his fingers. Tired and frustrated, Mark still noticed the smooth, casual control Mr. Currant exercised over the water. He'd been training with Chuck for months now and seen what his friend could do, but he still hadn't seen much of Mr. Currant's own abilities.

"This may hurt." Mr. Currant said.

He placed his hand just above Mark's eye and the fresh scar, and the water flowed atop it. Before Mark had a chance to react, the water began to pulse and vibrate, reopening the wound.

"Are you serious?" Mark barked, now completely awake, as blood once again ran down his face.

"I'm cleaning the wound, Mark," Mr. Currant explained in a matter-of-fact tone.

Mark clenched his teeth and said nothing more. He knew Mr. Currant was right, but that didn't make it hurt less.

Mr. Currant tossed the used water, now full of salt and silt and blood, into the sink. He pulled another thread of water and rinsed the wound. He pulled this water back out and Mark felt the skin tighten back up.

"There," Mr. Currant announced. "I have done everything that I can."

Mark stood up and felt at where the scar was. The area was still tender and he pulled his hand away. There was no blood on his hand.

Wordlessly, Mr. Currant pointed Mark towards the closest mirror so that he could see for himself.

Mark avoided looking at it for a moment and prepared himself. He took a deep breath and looked. There it was, running above and below his right eye. He wasn't sure how bad it had looked before Mr. Currant treated it, but it was still very visible. He gently felt the scar and everything became real. The scar, the events of the day. He consciously pulled his hand away and shut his eyes.

Why didn't it heal like everything else? Mark wondered. He'd been through the grinder these last few weeks. This was the first scratch to stick. He didn't know it at the time, but that's just the danger of dealing with a blade made of volcanic obsidian.

He walked back to the bed. He tried to thank Mr. Currant for helping with the scar, but the words were caught in his throat. Mr. Currant seemed to sense this and nodded gently as Mark passed, allowing him to get back to sleep.

Mark lay down in bed, picked up his phone and began replying to the day's messages. His parents' messages had begun gently enough but turned stern rather quickly as he had failed to respond in time. He did his best to calm his parents, though it made a negligible difference at best. Lauren had texted him to thank him for a good time at the dance. Once Mark felt he had exhausted all efforts at calming his parents down, he texted Lauren and reciprocated her comment. He did have a great time with her. Honestly, it was the only enjoyable part of the weekend. He wanted nothing more than to see her at school again on Monday. Shocking. He wanted the weekend to be over and the school week to begin. But, as eager as Mark was to talk to Lauren, he soon fell back asleep and didn't wake until they returned home.

When Mark and the Currants returned home, there was no hero's welcome. No one else knew about what Mark had just done — the great risk he had undertaken to protect people.

Instead, he arrived at his house to a furious mother who only grew more enraged when she saw the new scar on Mark's face. It was one thing for Mark to spend the entire day with his friend, ignoring her calls and messages, and failing to tell either parent what he was up to. It was another, much worse thing, to do all of that and arrive home with a large, visible scar across his face.

He explained that he had received the cut at Chuck's house, as he had rehearsed. He tripped and caught the corner of a table. He did his best to sell the performance, but he strained against his personal annoyance that this was the best Mr. Currant could come up with, especially after what he had just done. He said Mr. Currant had treated it as best he could in the moment. That last part was true, but it was too deep for there to not be a visible scar.

It wasn't good enough for her. If Mark hadn't gone out, it wouldn't have happened. He wasn't supposed to be out anyway, given their discussion about everything that had happened in the last two days. He was lucky to have been allowed to go to Homecoming, she reminded him. He received no assistance from his father or brother, who both agreed that it could've been avoided if Mark had simply stayed in or at least come home sooner.

Mark excused himself to go to the bathroom and waited until he thought his mom's rage had subsided. He then waited another five minutes, just to be safe.

When he emerged, the scolding merely continued. She had an incomparable patience, Mark thought. He would've been impressed if he wasn't the subject of her ire. He sheepishly mumbled something about homework that still needed to get done and she let him return to his room. He shut his bedroom door and halfheartedly opened his laptop. He did have work to do before tomorrow, but he truly didn't want to do it. Even more so than usual. After a few hours of unenthusiastic typing and writing, he reached a natural conclusion and called it a night.

Tomorrow would be better, Mark thought. He'd handled his homework, he would see Lauren again, and, last in his mind, he'd saved the world.

Across town, Robbie awoke in his hospital bed with a start. He'd been in and out of consciousness since Friday night, but this was the first time he was fully awake and lucid. His breathing was labored, and he looked around, still perceiving danger all around him.

No one was anywhere near his room. He wasn't a particularly needy patient, so his room had been quiet. He was asleep but stable since he'd been admitted.

He sat upright and glanced around. A dozen wires were attached to him, monitoring his heartrate, breathing, and everything else necessary.

He struggled to remember why he was there.

What was the last thing he remembered?

He was at the Homecoming football game. And some men stormed the field. And then Solarflare showed up.

That was it. He was remembering. He rushed in to save Solarflare from Eel. He tackled him, and then he got hit.

He remembered the electricity surging through his body. Pain racing through every cell, and every nerve ending screaming.

His heartbeat raced, his breathing quickened, and an arc of electric energy flew between the fingertips of his opposite hands.

He stared intently, not believing what he had seen. He glared at his hands, just a foot apart from one another. Wisps of smoke emanated from them and the smell of burnt air hung faintly. He concentrated, once again thinking of the attack, the energy that had previously flooded his body, and the feeling that had accompanied it. As he remembered it again, it felt less like pain. He couldn't describe it, but it felt even more tangible now.

The electricity arced again between his hands.

He saw it clearly this time.

Having done it twice at this point, Robbie focused and reproduced the arc again and again. The action was near effortless. He was just bouncing energy between his own hands, nothing was leaving his body, except for a brief moment.

Well, that moment was all it took to throw off the monitors. After the sixth or seventh time creating the arc, a mob of doctors and nurses rushed into the room, demanding to see the cause. The little exercise had thrown Robbie's vital signs all over the place.

Robbie stared blankly at them before he sheepishly held up the series of wires connecting his vital functions to the monitors.

"Sorry," he muttered. "I guess I was playing with these. I'm sorry, I wasn't entirely sure what they all did." His lies were calm and fluid. As much as he was freaked out by what appeared to be new electrical powers, he was sure he did not want them anywhere near his medical record. Doctor-patient confidentiality could only go so far, he reasoned.

The medical staff all shuffled off, annoyed at this interruption in their standard medical duties. The kid was a hero, they reasoned, based on his actions at the football game, but it was still rude and inconvenient for him to play around with the equipment.

As the crowd faded away, Robbie called out with a question.

"Will I be able to go back to school on Monday?"

One doctor hung back with a sly smile.

"Well, Robbie," he began gently. "Tomorrow is Monday. We'd like to keep you here a little longer, for observation. But I will get you back to school as soon as I can."

Robbie searched the doctor's eyes. He seemed to be telling the truth.

"Okay," Robbie said before he drifted back to sleep. He'd spent most of the weekend unconscious involuntarily, but he was still exhausted. He fell into a gentle sleep. His last thought before unconsciousness consumed him was that he needed to find Solarflare soon. He needed to know if there was anything Solarflare could tell him about having superpowers; maybe he could even help Solarflare fight crime. He was determined to make the most of this.

That evening, following Mark's contentious departure, Mr. Currant marveled in his own success of the day. Chuck had gone off into the house to finish up his homework or something else trivial. Mr. Currant, however, had returned to the boat and retrieved the second most important prize of the day: Blackbeard.

The once-terrifying pyrate had not perished in the waves but had been saved by Mr. Currant. When the eclipse began, he ensured Blackbeard was still alive, though unconscious, beneath the waves.

That was the thing about eclipses, Mr. Currant mused. They provided for great change and great opportunities, if only one knew how to use them. A pyrate submerged in water at the end of an eclipse would find himself transformed into a merman, gills and all, assuming he didn't drown first.

Leading Blackbeard into an angry sea was the best possible outcome of Mark's encounter. If Mark had killed him, at least they'd still have the ring, which was acceptable. If Mark had been killed, the worst-case scenario, Mr. Currant was prepared to secure the ring during the eclipse, knowing Blackbeard would be sufficiently exhausted.

The end of the eclipse had shifted Blackbeard's nature from one of fire to one of water, granting him gills and a command of the water, just like the king and prince of Atlantis, but he had no idea how to actually wield these gifts. Instead, he spent the bulk of the past couple hours bound and gagged in a shallow cell beneath the hull of the boat.

Mr. Currant carried him behind him underwater, unconscious, before placing him in a bare cell made of metal bars beneath the water in the cavern below his house.

The cell slammed shut and Blackbeard awoke with a start.

He lunged desperately for the cell's bars and attempted to launch a volley of flames at his captor, to no effect. Only bubbles.

He glanced about his cell. His captor held a small source of light before him. Blackbeard saw his hair floating at the edges of his periphery and could barely make out what adorned the opposite wall: a human head.

Mr. Currant noticed his prisoner admiring the macabre décor. "Yes, Edmund, that is precisely what you think it is. That is the head of Edward Teach, the true Blackbeard. It was not easy to secure, I can assure you." Mr. Currant's voice was only slightly muddled by the water. He leaned in closer. "And here is something fascinating: until yesterday's eclipse, those eyes had burned with the blue fire for over three hundred years. Now they are snuffed out."

As the weight of seeing his namesake's lifeless head mounted opposite his cell, the man once known as Blackbeard fearfully resigned himself to captivity.

"So," Mr. Currant began, his voice tinged with a calculated malice. "How would you like to get revenge on the boy that did this to you?"

Edmund glared at his captor, the Atlantean King, for a moment. This was the man that had attacked him a decade ago, the man who took his grandfather's journal. He nodded sternly, still untrusting.

"His name is Mark Michaels. He is also known as Solarflare. And I will help you end him." Mr. Currant declared. "When the time is right, of course."

Edmund, captive of a lifelong enemy, could not resist allowing a broad, sinister grin to creep across his face. He'd lost the ring, he'd been beaten, but he was proven right. That kid should've listened when he said not to trust Atlanteans. He laughed at the irony, his laughter obscured and muffled by the water, but maniacal nonetheless. If he couldn't kill the kid the way he wanted, he'd do it this new way. The kid's challenges were just beginning.

Printed in the USA
CPSIA information can be obtained
at www.ICGtesting.com
CBHW032119130224
4332CB00002BA/10